Charlotte M. (Charlotte Mary) Yonge

The castle builders, or, The deferred confirmation

Charlotte M. (Charlotte Mary) Yonge

The castle builders, or, The deferred confirmation

ISBN/EAN: 9783741163517

Manufactured in Europe, USA, Canada, Australia, Japa

Cover: Foto ©Andreas Hilbeck / pixelio.de

Manufactured and distributed by brebook publishing software
(www.brebook.com)

Charlotte M. (Charlotte Mary) Yonge

The castle builders, or, The deferred confirmation

THE CASTLE BUILDERS;

OR,

The Deferred Confirmation.

THE CASTLE BUILDERS

OR,

The Deferred Confirmation.

BY THE AUTHOR OF

"THE HEIR OF REDCLYFFE."

I had a home, wherein the weariest feet
    Found sure repose ;
Aud hope led on laborious day to meet
    Delightful close.
A cottage with broad eaves, and a thick vine,
    A crystal stream,
Whose mountain language was the same as mine :
    It was a dream !

New Edition.

LONDON :

WALTER SMITH (Late Mozley),
34, KING STREET, COVENT GARDEN.
1885.

THE CASTLE BUILDERS.

CHAPTER I.

I would build a cloudy house
For my thoughts to live in,
When for earth too fancy loose,
And too low for Heaven.

Hush! I talk my dream alone:
I build it bright to see;
I build it on the moon-lit cloud,
To which I looked with thee.

E. B. Browning.

ABOUT two o'clock in the afternoon, the yellow foggy light of a spring or rather winter day in London came, for it could not be said to shine, through the two windows of a large apartment, which the long table and the numerous desks and books distinguished as a school-room. Large maps hung against the wall; there was a piano, a pair of globes, sundry drawing-desks and easels, in the midst of which were nearly a score of girls from twelve years old to seventeen, their gay chatter and bright looks proving how little power the restraints of school had to check their flow of spirits in this hour of relaxation. Yet there was an air of thoughtfulness on the countenances of two or three of the elder ones, who were seated at their desks, either turning over papers, or seeking earnestly in books which seemed of a graver cast than those in which their studies usually lay; blushes, too,

B

there were, and looks of nervousness and embarrassment, as if something unusual was impending. All started when the door opened and admitted two young ladies, evidently sisters, who came in, one with a downcast pensive eye, the other with her cheeks glowing, but looking relieved.

"Miss Enderby," said the second, "Mr. Walton is ready for you."

"Oh!" said Miss Enderby, slowly rising, "how I wish I had a sister or anybody to go with me! Must I go alone? I quite dread it! Does he say much, Kate?"

"Oh, he is very kind," was the answer. "You will find it much better than you expect."

"That I promise you, without even knowing what he is like. You see he has not quite eaten them up, so there are hopes for you!" cried Miss Allen, a lively young girl, as Miss Enderby left the room with a sigh and look of reluctance. "Oh, let me see," she added, arresting the hand of Katherine, who was going to put a small folded piece of paper into her desk. "Let me look, pray;" and two or three heads crowding together, their owners had the satisfaction of reading, "Katherine Eleanor Berners, aged 16, examined for Confirmation, and approved. J. Walton."

"And yours—let us see yours!" cried some others, fastening on the other ticket, which ran thus: "Emmeline Mary Berners, aged 17, examined for Confirmation, and approved. J. Walton."

"Did he ask you very hard questions?" proceeded Susan Allen.

"No," said Emmeline; "he only said a few words to us." And as if to put an end to the subject, she sat down to her desk, took up a book, and seemed to read; though a sigh now and then might prove that she was thinking.

Kate waited a little longer to answer the interrogations of her companions, until the return of Miss Enderby removed the general attention from her, and she was able to move close to her sister, and say, unheard by the others, "Emmie, dear, what do you think about it?"

"I liked what he said very much," was Emmeline's reply.

"Ah! but about *that!*"

"Oh! I am sure I could never go now," said Emmeline hastily. 'You know Miss Danby lets us do as we please about it."

"Constance used to go," said Kate.

"Yes, but Constance always was so different from us. If we had her still, or if we had Herbert to talk to us, it would do better; but here, among all the others, and thinking about all sorts of things, as we must do here, I am sure we could never be fit."

"He said if we were fit for Confirmation we were fit for the Sacrament," said Kate; "but I can't quite see how that can be. We promised all these things by our Godfathers and Godmothers, and are bound to do them now, so it does not seem so much to promise them for ourselves; but the other—it is a great deal too awful!"

"Oh yes!" said Emmeline, raising her eyes and sighing. "This is no place for preparation. When we have left school, and can manage as we please, it will be another thing. When Herbert and Constance come home, they will help us."

"If they were at home, I know what they would say," said Kate.

"Yes, and we should be fitter," sighed Emmeline. "I shall write and tell Constance all that I feel, and I think she will agree with me that we had better wait till we have more time for thought. Yet I am always afraid of teazing her by asking her deep questions in the midst of her journey, and when she wants to attend to Herbert. Oh, if he was better, and Mamma in England, how happy we should be!"

"Happy, indeed!" said Kate; "we all living with Mamma and Papa at Copseley, as you settled so long ago, that nice plan of yours."

"Yes, then I think we could be quite good," said Emmeline. "Think of walking into the little parsonage, and reading with Constance, as we used to do! And then how we would teach the children! I could soon learn Latin enough for Alfred, and

you should have Janet, and we could be so useful. Going to
the school, too! We would get Papa to build such a beauty,
all gable ends and chimneys, with roses twining over them; and
all the village children would be so fond of us, and bring us
nosegays!"

"Yes, and we would have one for our own little maid," said
Kate, "hear her read every day; and oh! what a garden
we would have!"

"Honeysuckle climbing up to our windows and perfuming
our room," said Emmeline; "and a green-house like the one at
Rowthorpe, where we might sit and read in the summer!"

"And plenty of ponies and donkeys to go out riding on!"
said Kate. "I do not think we have quite forgotten all Lord
Somerville's riding-lessons; and we shall have Alfred to go out
with us, and Herbert and Constance, too."

"Delightful!" said Emmeline. "Oh! but to have Mamma
and the children, that would be happiness enough anywhere! I
feel as if to nestle to her would be too much. If one could but
reach out with one's arms as one does with one's heart—dear
Mamma, dear Constance, how soon we would meet!"

At that moment a double knock re-echoed through the house,
and presently it was announced that Lady Frances Somerville
was come to call on the Miss Berners. These were pleasant
tidings, for Lady Frances was the elder sister of the already-
mentioned "Herbert," their brother-in-law, and with great
eagerness they descended to the drawing-room.

There they found a lady of about thirty, not pretty, but very
pleasing, with a sweet placidity of expression, and soft brown
eyes, which smiled more than her lips; she was tall and slender,
and her dress, plain, quiet, delicate in colour, and of handsome
materials, had that sort of wave and flow which might recall to
mind the forms which have occasioned the birch tree to be
called the "Lady of Trees." As soon as the girls had glanced
round to see that she was alone, and that they need not be
on their good behaviour, they flew up to her, and joyously
received and returned her affectionate embrace.

Yes, you ought to be glad to see me," said she, in a cheerful cordial tone, "for I have excellent news for you. Here is a letter from Somerville, with a capital account of dear Herbert."

"Oh, that is delightful!" cried Kate. "Thank you, thank you! Where are they? At Rome yet?"

"No, at Terni, hoping to get to Rome in two days' time. Herbert was much less tired than they expected, though they have been taking longer days' journeys than at first; he coughs very little, and has had no pain in the chest. He has really been able to enjoy the journey ever since they came into Italy. Then you had not heard from Constance?"

"No," said Emmeline, "not since they left Florence. It was very kind in you to come and tell us."

"The news was too good to keep to myself," said Lady Frances, smiling; "and it is such a treat to find some one to tell it to besides Papa. Oh, and I must tell you that Somerville says Constance is such a capital manager, and makes the rooms at the inns look so pleasant and comfortable directly, that he can do nothing but stand and admire, and think how different it was when he was there alone. Is that one of the arts you learn here?"

"It must have been inspiration that taught her," said Emmeline, laughing; "I never could make anything comfortable, not even a doll."

"You are looking white to-day, Emmie," said Lady Frances kindly.

"We have just had our last interview with Mr. Walton," said Kate, "and she is so nervous."

"Ah! I wanted to know when the Confirmation is to take place," said Lady Frances.

"On Monday, at eleven o'clock," said Emmeline.

"At St. George's, I suppose? I must try to be there; Constance will wish to hear about it."

"Oh, you are so kind!" cried Kate; while Emmeline looked down. "It will be a great comfort to know you are there, poor Emmie is so frightened."

"It is so awful," said Emmeline, blushing.

"Yes, indeed," said Lady Frances, "the vow would be too fearful but for the blessing, and that to which it admits us."

"There is what makes me uncomfortable," said Emmeline.

"About the Sacrament," added Kate.

"I cannot bear the responsibility of going or of staying away," said Emmeline. "Oh, I am so far from being good enough!"

"It is the means, not the reward, of goodness," said Lady Frances.

"O Lady Frances, I do think one talk with you would clear all up!" said Emmeline.

"I should like very much to try to help you," said Lady Frances. "Next time Papa dines out without me, I will send the carriage, and I dare say Miss Danby will let me have you. But I do not think one talk would do, especially with me, who am not the right person. Have not you been able to tell your clergyman your difficulties? Does not he see you in private?"

"Yes," said Emmeline, smiling, as she looked down and blushed; "but I do not know whether it was our fault or not, we never could say one word for ourselves when we were sitting up opposite to him, and he making a hesitating sort of lecture, wishing it was over, I am sure, quite as much as we did."

Lady Frances could not help smiling, though rather sadly, at the quiet grave humour of the manner in which Emmeline represented the mutual embarrassment of the young curate and his catechumens.

"It was all very well," added Kate, "when we were all together in a class, protected by numbers. It was not much worse to confront him than Signor Piccini; but in that room, all by ourselves, without so much as an exercise-book to look at! Oh, the awkwardness was beyond description!"

"If it had been but Herbert," said Emmeline.

"Yes, Herbert would be your right instructor," said Lady Frances; "and why should you not write to him?"

"I never could say what I mean in a letter," said Emmeline;

"I am sure I could not to him, nor even to Constance herself. Besides, it would worry him."

"No, that it would not," said Lady Frances; "it would give him more pleasure than anything to feel himself still of use. I do hope you will write to him, it is just what he would wish. By-the-by, where was Constance confirmed?"

"At Albury," said Kate, "just before we came here. She was only fourteen; but old Mr. Law, our clergyman there, was very anxious it should be done. He was very fond of her."

"Well," said Lady Frances, "when you come to me, I will show you some of the papers that were given me when I was confirmed."

The girls eagerly thanked her; and next she asked if they had heard lately from India.

"Not by the last mail," said Kate; "I cannot think why, for I am sorry to say the idea of coming home is given up again for the present. They think now of staying another year, and sending home little Alfred without them."

"Oh! that is a very great disappointment," said Lady Frances. "Where would the little boy go?"

"To Mr. Willoughby," said Emmeline, "the uncle Frank Willoughby spends his holidays with. We shall never see him at all. It is very vexatious after so many hopes of Mamma's return; but everything does go wrong now."

"No, no, Emmie; not Herbert's getting well," said Kate cheerfully.

Lady Frances looked sorrowful, and did not make any answer to this, only proceeding to tell them that the old elm at Rowthorpe had been blown down, and other news of the same kind; and soon after she wished them good-bye.

"Poor things!" murmured she, leaning back in the carriage, "I wish I could do more for them; I half promised Constance to do what I could towards supplying her place to them; and yet what can I do? I cannot inflict two school-girls again upon Papa, though he was very good-natured; and these are such nice girls, that I believe we all enjoyed their visit last year very much, even Somerville himself. Yes, we were very happy then; but then we were all in good spirits, and now—Oh, is it safe to let myself hope? Is it not foolish to catch at this first gleam, when I have suffered so much, and learnt how vain such hopes were, by seeing them fade away in Anne's case? No, this is ingratitude. Did not they come to cheer me, and support me through all that followed? and now why am not I more thankful that dear Herbert himself is relieved from present suffering, and his gentle little wife from anxiety? Yes, let me dwell on this, and then I shall be the better able to cheer Papa up, while I leave the future to Him who knows what is best for all of us. I wonder what is best to be done," continued Lady Frances, in her meditations, " to put these poor girls into the right way of thinking about their Confirmation. They have knowledge enough, but it is all a school-lesson, the clergyman a master; it all wants reality, and to be brought home to them—no wonder, I suppose—the only marvel is that it should be so different with Constance." Here Lady Frances's carriage stopped, and thus brought her meditations to a sudden conclusion.

Constance, Emmeline, and Katherine Berners, were the daughters of an officer who had married in India. They had been sent to England when Constance was six years old and Katherine four, and placed by their uncle, Mr. Berners, under the care of Mrs. Ellison, a clergyman's widow, with whom they had scarcely spent a few months before intelligence arrived that their father had died, after a few hours suffering, from one of the sudden short illnesses of India. Their mother, accustomed to an Indian life, with her father and mother and all her family there resident, was in no haste to return to England; and after about eighteen months, she married Sir Francis Willoughby, a General in the Company's service, and a widower with one son, who was of course in England for education.

When Constance was about fourteen, the three sisters were removed from Mrs. Ellison's, and placed at Miss Danby's establishment—a school which proved to have been better chosen than could have been expected from the careless habits of their uncle, who lived chiefly abroad, thought his little nieces a burden, and only tried to go as far as he could from the trouble of attending to them, or to his property. It was a superior style of school, well conducted, and where a good deal was taught; and if there was not the same careful affectionate motherly training as they had experienced from Mrs. Ellison, to whom they had been more like daughters than scholars, there was much well-judging successful care, both of their bodies and minds, though it might perhaps be that the care was more of their minds than of their souls.

The Miss Berners had no near relations in England, and were therefore obliged to spend their holidays at school, unless any of their companions persuaded their parents to take compassion on them. Constance was a person of many friends, and for her sake they were almost always in request, though Emmeline, more shy and less inclined to exert herself in behalf of acquaintance, clung to her elder and younger sisters, and though generally liked, did not form friendships. At seventeen Constance left school, and went to pay a round of visits to relations and acquaintances, before rejoining her mother in India. The first of these was to Miss Forester, a clergyman's daughter, who had long ago made Constance promise to come to the consecration of a new church just completed in her father's parish.

Lord Herbert Somerville had lately been ordained to the curacy of the new church, and was likewise staying at Mr. Forester's, waiting till his own abode at Copseley hamlet could be made habitable. Fresh from Oxford, with a high reputation for talent, and with goodness of which the Forester family were never weary of talking—with a fine intellectual countenance, set off by a pair of thoughtful yet lustrous eyes, Constance looked up to him as perfection in every respect, listened with delight to his conversations with Mr. Forester, and thought it marvellous condescension and good-nature in him to explain to her Church architecture, talk over books, wait kindly for her answer, as if it could be worth hearing, and listen to her singing.

Little did Constance guess at her own patent for popularity; to her an invitation for two days in the holidays seemed a great undeserved piece of kindness, for which she could never be sufficiently grateful; and she was the only person who was not sensible of the charm of her sweet modest countenance—her bright brisk helpfulness—her great refinement of tone and manner—her simplicity and earnestness—her full conviction of her own ignorance and insignificance, and her great desire for improvement of every kind. She was more surprised than anybody else when, at the end of her six weeks visit, she found this first of human beings actually asking her to marry him!

Her wonder was only equalled by that which she experienced at the tall grey-haired Marquis of Liddesdale, at whom, at the dinner on the Consecration day, she had looked from the other end of the table, on the principle that a cat may look at a king; when he, so far from setting his face against this attachment of his son's, came from Rowthorpe for the very purpose of seeing her again, and showed her all the kindness and affection she could have looked for in a father; when Lord Somerville was full of cordial good-nature, and when Lady Frances threw her arms around her, and whispered with tearful eyes that now she should have a sister again.

Nothing was waited for but the needful correspondence with Lady Willoughby; and in the summer the wedding took place, making Emmeline and Katherine, to say nothing of other people, supremely happy, and filling the heads of Miss Danby's young ladies to a greater extent than usual with visions of lordly lovers.

Never were Emmeline and Katherine more happy than during that summer. First, there was the wedding, which secured their sister to them, as they thought, instead of taking her away from them; then they spent three weeks at Lord Liddesdale's; after which Lord and Lady Herbert came, and at the end of another week took them, for the remainder of their holidays, back to their Copseley home, as they delighted in calling it. There they looked forward to spending Christmas; but a great disappointment was in store for them. Lord Herbert's health had never been strong, and in the autumn symptoms of complaint in the lungs began to show themselves; he was ordered without loss of time to a warmer climate, and in the early part of December he set off for Italy, with his wife and elder brother.

Instead of the joyous Christmas so eagerly expected, Emmeline and Kate had to spend a winter of anxiety and disappointment; the school more cheerless than usual in its deserted state, and their evenings only now and then enlivened by some treat devised by Miss Danby, or by an invitation from some compassionating London friend. Happily for them, they were a very fond pair of sisters, enjoying a very little together more than a great deal apart. Emmeline, though the most shy, retiring, and undemonstrative with strangers, was the leader in everything when alone with her sister, for Kate thought her unequalled save by Constance, and would scarcely have had such high buoyant spirits, if she had not been always at her side. Moreover, Emmeline was a most magnificent and unbounded dreamer, and Kate had implicit faith in her castles; so that as the two sisters sat over the fire, the comfortless present was forgotten in a future so clearly defined, that they might almost be said to live in it. They had built a mansion for Sir Francis and Lady Willoughby, where they could almost have counted the rooms—they had devised a plan of education for their little brothers and sisters, with abundance of ready-made moral stories for their benefit—they had restored Constance and her husband to Copseley, and had very nearly heard the bells ring for their return. Emmeline could have been almost sorry when the return of their companions put an end to these delightful romancings.

CHAPTER II.

We told o'er all that we had done;
　Our rambles by the swift brook's side,
Far as the willow-skirted pool,
　Where two fair swans together glide.
　　　　　　　　Wordsworth.

It was the day after Lady Frances Somerville's visit, and
Emmeline was almost lost to the cares of this world in the
absorbing task of finding English for one of those commence-
ments of German chapters, of which the author once said that
Heaven doubtless knew its meaning, but he did not. Katherine
was as earnestly and less hopelessly intent on the intricacies of
a circular temple in perspective ; and all the young ladies around
were as busily engaged, when the door opened, and Miss Danby
made her appearance, stately and formal as usual, but with a
certain affability of countenance which re-assured the lesser girls,
who had begun to tremble, lest she had captured certain stray
books and work-baskets.

"Miss Berners ! Miss Katherine Berners !" said this dignified
personage. Kate jumped up in hopes of an invitation from
Lady Frances. Emmeline was touched by her neighbour, and
rose, still mazed by the German mystification.

"I am glad to be the bearer of intelligence which will give
you much pleasure," said Miss Danby, measuring out her words
with precision, which ill suited the impatient Kate. "You
will be surprised to hear who your visitor is."

"Constance? Impossible !" thought Kate. "Oh, it must
be little Alfred. If she would but speak fast ! "

"Sir Francis Willoughby is in the drawing-room," came at
last. Emmeline and Kate looked at each other, one turned
white and the other red, and Katherine breathlessly asked,
"And Mamma ? "

"Lady Willoughby is in London," said Miss Danby ; then
seeing how Emmeline trembled with agitation, and her colour

varied fast, she added, "Compose yourself, my dear Miss Berners, pray do not be agitated. I am sure Sir Francis has a countenance full of indulgence and benignity."

Emeline drew two or three deep breaths, and trembling all over, would nevertheless have run at full speed to the drawing-room, but that she was obliged to follow the slow pacing steps of Miss Danby, which gave time for all her thousand hopes and fears about her mother and step-father to flit confusedly through her brain. Her cheek altered so fast from red to white, and the hand which clasped her sister's was so cold and shaking, that Kate's attention was almost entirely absorbed in watching her. At last they were at the top of the broad stairs, at the door. Miss Danby opened it, and waved them forward with her sweeping dignity. "Here are my pupils, Sir Francis.— This, my dear girls, is the moment you have so long desired."

" Ha ! my dears, how d'ye do ? Surprised to see me ? Come, you must let me have a kiss—your papa, you know ? Your mamma is all impatience to see you."

It was not the sort of voice for which Emmeline had prepared herself; and Kate, the first to look up, beheld something very unlike what they had expected—the General, of whom they were so proud, and who had actually distinguished himself, and earned his knighthood. They had intended him to be, not perhaps quite as aristocratic as Lord Liddesdale, but at any rate a fine old soldier, with a grand military air; whereas they saw a little man, with a face that looked as if it had been dried and baked to the colour and texture of a mummy's skin, thick eye-brows, and whiskers of a grey which did not agree with the black stiff curls of what Kate took to be his hair, and small sharp black eyes full of good-nature, which was probably what Miss Danby intended by benignity. Kate saw in a moment that there was nothing to be afraid of, and spoke out boldly, "Oh, we are so glad ! When did you arrive ?"

" We landed at Southampton yesterday, came up by railroad, drove to an hotel, and I set out directly after breakfast to take you to Mamma : she is thinking every minute an hour—"

"Is she quite well, and the children?" asked Kate.

"Quite well—oh yes, very, only rather fatigued with the bustle yesterday—custom-house—railway—new place—or she would have been here herself; and Janet is a little upset, too. Come, get your bonnets on, and a few things put together, and I will take you to her; but we must not lose time, for I have plenty of business on my hands."

The two girls hurried up-stairs, prepared almost without speaking, for Emmeline's heart was too full and throbbing for words, and were quickly down-stairs again. They found Sir Francis consulting Miss Danby about a governess for the children, saying he was in haste to find one, as their Hindostanee nurse was to return by the next ship, and they were quite too much for Lady Willoughby. Emmeline thought of her cherished plan of teaching them, but it was no time to put it forward; and Miss Danby was recommending little Miss Townsend, the small timid under-teacher, who, after being some years a boarder, had been placed in that situation to qualify herself for a governess. After settling that she should come to be inspected the next day, Sir Francis took his leave; the Miss Berners made their adieus in the most approved manner, and in a short space were seated in the carriage with him.

"Well, my dears," he began, taking hold of Emmeline's still trembling hand, "come, tell me what you think of Papa, now you have him at last?" Neither had the least idea what to answer, and he went on, "Quite surprised to see such a sun-dried old fellow?" and as he peeped under Kate's bonnet as she sat opposite to him, he laughed, and she was very glad to do so too, though in a nervous embarrassed manner. "Well, never mind," he continued, "we shall understand each other very well. I am sure I did not expect to see two such fine handsome young women. I do not wonder now at your sister's good luck. So you were quite taken by surprise, were you? I thought so; but you see—" and on he went with an explanation of the motives of their sudden return, and their adventures on the journey, till the sound of his voice blended confusedly

in Emmeline's ears with the rattling of the carriage-wheels,
whilst her whole soul was absorbed in the memory of days gone
by, in the vision of the soft caressing mother in white muslin—
in her fancy, the very impersonation of grace, sweetness, and
beauty—and in the still more shadowy remembrance of her
father. There were tears ready to spring in her eyes, and she
was glad to lean on Kate's arm, when they left the carriage,
and with considerable bustle were conducted up-stairs, and a
door was thrown open before them.

"Here they are—here are Emmeline and Kate!" said Sir
Francis; and Emmeline, for the first time speaking, cried,
"Mamma! Mamma!" and in perfect ecstasy, fell into the
outspread arms, and received the soft kisses just as of old.
Then it was Kate's turn; and then the mother and daughters
could gaze on each other, she sitting between them on the sofa,
holding a hand of each, and looking at them alternately, while
their eyes were fixed on her, half shyly, and half caressingly.
There was no disappointment in that gaze: Lady Willoughby
had all the grace and softness so well remembered; she was
indeed pale and faded, and her eyes at ordinary moments were
rather sleepy, but she was tall and graceful, with the remains
of considerable beauty, great gentleness of expression, and a
very soft, musical, though rather languid voice. With so many
attractions, it was no wonder that her daughters were delighted
beyond expression.

"My own darlings!" said she, drawing them closer to her,
and kissing them again; "and which is Emmie, and which
Kate?"

"Here—here is Emmie," said Sir Francis.

"No; I am Kate," was the answer.

"You do not mean it—you are Emmeline. Why, I am sure
the old lady—governess, mistress, what d'ye call her?—told me
as plainly as she could speak, you were Miss Berners, and you
Miss Katherine."

"I can't help it," said Kate, laughing; "I only know I
cannot profess to be anything but Miss Katherine."

"Never mind," said Lady Willoughby, "I shall learn you soon enough. You are my dearest girls, and that is enough for me."

"But," continued Sir Francis, "surely now, was not it Emmeline that talked so pleasantly in the carriage!"

The girls thought they might both safely have disclaimed the talking; but Emmeline said, "It was Kate that talked the most. You may always know her, because she is the tallest, and has the most colour—in general," added Emmeline, as she felt her cheeks burning.

"Ah! now," said Lady Willoughby, "I see my little Emmie's blue eyes, and Katie's own roguish smile. Ah! you were a sad little woman in those days, always too much for poor mamma. Take off your bonnets, sweet ones, and let me see if they are not the same dear little faces."

No one could be surprised at Sir Francis's mistake, for Katherine, though eleven months younger than her sister, was about an inch taller. Both were fair, slight, delicate-looking girls, with a beautifully fine and smooth texture of skin, pretty little features, blue eyes, and brown hair ; but Kate was always first remarked, from being rather more *prononcé* in every way. The light rose-bud tinge on Emmeline's cheek was almost a bloom on Kate's. Emmeline's eyes were so light, that they wanted all the length and darkness of her downcast sweeping eye-lashes to give them shade. Kate's were more widely opened, of the same clear blue colour, but of much deeper tint : her eye-brows were clearly-defined dark-brown lines, while Emmeline's were much lighter; and on comparison, it was the same with their hair, though, at first sight, it seemed of the same colour. If Emmeline was a little flushed, or Kate looked pale, the difference between them could hardly be perceived.

"And Constance, we only want her," said Lady Willoughby. "I am afraid she is not in London."

"Oh Mamma! have you not heard?" said Kate.

"No—what? We have not heard since she was just going to spend a day or two at Lord Liddesdale's place. Where is she?"

"In Italy, Mamma," said Emmeline sadly; "Herbert caught a very bad cold coming home from Rowthorpe one foggy evening; he has been very ill, and obliged to come to London for advice. Dr. —— ordered him abroad for the winter, so they went on the 12th of December, and Lord Somerville with them."

"Hum! ha! Decline, I suppose. That is a bad hearing," said Sir Francis. "Not in the family, I hope."

Kate looked down, and answered sorrowfully, "Lady Anne died of decline two years ago; but I do assure you, Mamma," and she raised her eyes, and spoke confidently, "the doctors all said that in Herbert's case he only wanted complete rest to his voice, and a warmer climate, to restore him completely, and he is much better already."

"Poor dear Constance!" said Lady Willoughby. "It is a great shock to hear this when we so little thought it. When did you see her last, poor dear?"

"A little before they sailed," said Emmeline, "when they were at Lord Liddesdale's house in London. We spent one whole day with them, and Herbert did not seem very ill; indeed, he was much better then; he was in the drawing-room, and I did not see but that he was just the same as usual, except that his cough seemed to hurt him; it made his colour come into his face, and sometimes was very bad indeed, but he was as cheerful as ever. And afterwards Constance came to Miss Danby's to wish us good-bye: she is quite well, and likes her journey very much; indeed, now Herbert is better, the tour will be quite a party of pleasure, only she will be so sorry to miss you."

"Poor dear!" said Lady Willoughby; and Kate went on the more eagerly, "But, Mamma, the accounts have been excellent of late. Yesterday Lady Frances came to tell us she had heard from Lord Somerville from Terni, with such a very good report of Herbert."

"Is Lady Frances in town, then?" said Sir Francis.

"Yes, she is very kind to us," said Kate warmly.

"Did she ask you for the holidays again?" said Lady Willoughby.

"Oh no," said Kate. "Constance told us she wished she could, only she is so devoted to Lord Liddesdale's comfort, and he is so anxious about Herbert, and altogether it would not do."

"And we did very well," said Emmeline ; "she had us twice to spend the evening when Lord Liddesdale was dining out, and she took us out driving with her several times, and once to a concert, and three days we spent with Miss Enderby, and—"

"Well," said Sir Francis, "you will have long holidays now. Good-bye to Mrs. Teach'em : Mamma will never part with you now she has once got you."

"No, indeed," said Lady Willoughby, softly pressing their hands.

"Dear Mamma!" said Emmeline.

Their eyes had been roaming all this time, and at last Kate broke forth—"The children!"

"The children? Oh yes, to be sure—here they are!" said Sir Francis, opening a door, crossing another room, and calling out, "Come here, come along, you young rogues; come and see your sisters."

A great noise came first, and Lady Willoughby shrank as if from an expected infliction, as in ran a fine tall fair boy of seven, followed by a girl a little younger, while a sound of crying remained behind.

"Where is brother Frank?" said the boy, standing staring; but there was no time for answering, for in came Sir Francis, carrying a little girl of two, whom he put into Kate's arms, saying, "There, look at your sister, Emmeline." The child, however, no sooner found herself in the possession of a stranger, than she began to scream ; upon which her father, much to Kate's relief, took her up again, and began to walk up and down the room with her, soothing her in Hindostanee, at present Miss Cecilia's only language. Then appeared a dark dignified lady, in white muslin and golden ear-rings, holding by the hand the four-years-old Edwin, who no sooner beheld the strangers than he wrenched away his hand, and ran back again roaring louder than ever. Sir Francis, on an imploring look from his wife, gave Cecilia to the Ayah, and sent her away, leaving only Alfred and Janet, who had the credit of being able, like Dandie Dinmont's two eldest, to behave themselves distinctly. This is to say, Alfred allowed himself to be kissed by his sisters, and then finding that brother Frank was not forthcoming, broke from them, and ran to gaze out at the window; while Janet, a white-faced, not very happy-looking child, stood staring with the full extent of her black eyes, and hiding her face if they tried to touch or speak to her.

In the lull that succeeded, Sir Francis announced his intention of immediately setting out again on his own affairs. Lady Willoughby plaintively entreated him to come back in time to go out with her; he promised to return to luncheon, and departed. Emmeline sat on the sofa by her mother, listening to her history of her journey, and its troubles and fatigues; while Kate joined Alfred at the window, and there, by telling him the names of the carriages, and pointing out all that could amuse him, made him sociable; and presently Janet, hearing him laugh, ran up to Kate, pulling her frock, and said, "Me too." For some time Kate kept them both happy and contented; but at last Alfred grew riotous, made Janet cry, and caused such a turmoil, that Lady Willoughby in despair rang the bell, and sent for the Ayah, who carried Janet off; but Alfred, being beyond the strength of any of the parties present, was allowed to remain, and Kate kept him quiet by drawing him a picture of a steamer, which seemed the most prominent object in his imagination. Lady Willoughby sighed, and wished the children were under a governess, they were so troublesome and boisterous, and Sir Francis spoilt them so much. Emmeline said encouragingly, that they would soon get into better order, and Miss Townsend was a very kind good little person; but after this specimen, her desire of volunteering the part of a governess herself had much abated. She did, however, say that she and Kate hoped to have the children with them a great deal, and to help to teach them.

"Oh, my dears," said Lady Willoughby, looking at Alfred, who was eyeing them all the time, and lowering her voice, "you do not know what you would undertake! Such wear and tear as trying to teach must be! Oh no, I would not have you undertake it on any account."

"Margaret Forester teaches her little brothers and sisters, and likes it very much," said Emmeline.

"Oh, some people are obliged; yes, some people are, I know; but there is no occasion for it here, my dear. And besides, you have no time; when we are settled, and a little at home, you must be introduced, you know: you are quite seventeen, are you not?"

"I was seventeen last week," said Emmeline; "but, Mamma, I had much rather not come out yet—not without Kate, at least."

"O Emmie! that is not fair," said Kate.

"Indeed it is," said Emmeline; "you know we have always been exactly on a level in everything, and I am too shy ever to enjoy myself where you are not. Oh, I should not like it at all without her!"

"I am sure it is a pleasure to see my dear girls so affectionate," said Lady Willoughby, smoothing Emmeline's hair. "We will see about it, my dears—it shall be as you please."

Kate was going to offer some further remonstrance, when they were interrupted by the return of Sir Francis; they had their luncheon, and went out for a drive. The sisters found themselves of some use, for their slight knowledge of London went a great way with people, one of whom had not been in England for twenty years, and the other for thirty-five. Lady Willoughby seemed quite helpless in any choice of the most trifling matters of dress for the children; and Sir Francis, as active and bustling as she was the contrary, asked numberless questions, and was a quarter of an hour at least in selecting each separate article.

Lady Willoughby was more alive than in any other part of her expedition when they went to a dress-maker's, the only one whose direction Emmeline and Kate knew, because she had made Constance's wedding dresses. They did not much like, however, to hear Sir Francis tell the lady of the shop that that lady was the mother of Lady Herbert Somerville, whom perhaps she recollected, and then to see their mother look pleased at what they thought vulgar praise of Constance's beauty and elegance. Perhaps Kate, at least, was a little mollified when Sir Francis made them each a present of a new bonnet and a mantle, though they would have liked to have had more exercise of their own taste allowed them in the choice.

It was late when they came back to the hotel, and they had only time to dress in haste, without exchanging many words. On re-entering the sitting-room, they found Sir Francis playing with the three eldest children, and allowing them to make noises to their hearts' content, till, on hearing the sweeping of a silk gown, he suddenly hushed them with, "Here comes Mamma!" There was very little more time before dinner was announced, when the children were kissed and dismissed to bed, Sir Francis carrying Edwin on his back.

Dinner seemed a very important business to Sir Francis, and occupied his conversation entirely till dessert was brought in, when, turning to Kate, whom he had at last learnt to call by her proper name, he asked her if she had seen his son Frank.

"Oh yes," said Kate; "he spent two days with us at Copseley, before he went back to school."

"Ah! yes, I knew Lord and Lady Herbert were so kind as to have him—very good-natured."

"He was there a week," said Emmeline; "but we were obliged to go back to Miss Danby's after he had been there only two days. He was to have come for part of the Christmas holidays, he would not for the whole of them."

"Well, and what did you think of him, eh? You know I have not seen him since he was little Edwin's age. Come, tell me how you like him."

"Oh, very much," said Emmeline and Kate, both a little disconcerted by the recollection that they had thought him very much in their way on the last day of their visit, rather awkward, and far from clever.

"He is very good-natured," added Emmeline; "and Constance wrote us word that he and Herbert got on famously together."

"I think Edwin is very like him, only fairer," said Kate, glad to find something further to say.

"Well, I hope we shall have him here to-morrow or next day," said Sir Francis. . "I have written to him, and to his master to ask for him."

"Yes, I wish much to see him, dear fellow," said Lady Willoughby, in her modulated voice.

"I shall get Kate to introduce me," said Sir Francis, shaking his head at her. "Here's a brown old shrivelled object of a father for you, Master Frank."

"Do not you think we learn better manners at Miss Danby's?" said Kate, who had found out by this time how Sir Francis liked to be answered.

"I am sure," said Lady Willoughby, "Miss Danby's establishment was most highly recommended."

"And I am sure," added Sir Francis gallantly, "she needs no better recommendation than her pupils. As I was telling them, I don't wonder at their sister's good fortune."

"Poor Constance!" said Lady Willoughby. "Which of you is most like her, my dears?"

"She is something between both," said Kate: "she is not so tall as I am, and she has lighter hair than either of us, and the same sort of pale colour as Emmeline."

"Her eyes and eye-brows are more like Kate's," said Emmeline; "but she and I were often taken for each other. Herbert was quite amused to see such a likeness."

"She must have looked lovely at her wedding, poor dear girl!" said Lady Willoughby.

"Yes, that she did, Mamma!" cried both girls eagerly, and

then simultaneously stopped, each ready to leave the field to each other.

"Come, now let us have the whole history," said Lady Willoughby ; "since I cannot see my poor Constance, let me hear all I can of her."

"Oh, if you could but have seen her ! " said Emmeline.

"She had that beautiful India muslin that you sent her, and a little lace bonnet, and a beautiful Honiton veil that Mrs. Forester gave her ; and you never saw anything look so beautiful or so like a white lily. The old clerk said they were the handsomest couple that he had ever seen married, and he believed as they were the best."

"Then Lord Herbert is handsome ? Indeed, I think you said so in your letters," said Lady Willoughby.

"When you see Lady Frances, Mamma, you will know just what he is like ; he is rather tall, and very slender ; and his face —oh ! I don't know how to describe it, it is so winning," said Kate.

"He has beautiful brown eyes, that seem to look through and through everything, and yet to be always bright with their own thoughts," said Emmeline.

"Hey-day ! " said Sir Francis, "the young ladies are quite poetical." Whereat Emmeline coloured excessively, and held her tongue ; while Lady Willoughby asked on, "And does he look delicate ? "

"He has a good deal of bright pink colour," said Kate, "and those beautiful transparent-looking teeth that Mrs. Forester says are very apt to belong to people with delicate health. He never was very strong, but they say that a winter abroad is likely to do him a great deal of good."

"It was from Mr. Forester's that they were married, I think?" said Sir Francis.

"Yes," said Kate, "the Foresters would have it so, because the whole affair had taken place there."

"And they made quite a small party of it?" said her mother.

"Yes, quite small, it was so much more pleasant and comfortable," said Kate; "there were only ourselves, and Uncle Berners, and Lord Liddesdale, and his son and daughter, and Mr. Grey, the other Curate. There was very little of a breakfast, for Constance and Herbert would not hear of their making a great fuss. I am sure it did excellently. Mrs. Forester said she had never known a wedding-day go off so well; she said they were generally such long dismal days; but I am sure we only wondered when we found how late it was, and Lord Liddesdale's carriage came to take them to the train—Herbert and Constance, I mean."

"Lord Liddesdale's carriage!" exclaimed Lady Willoughby. "Did they not go in a carriage of their own?"

"No; they only had a little pony-phaeton till they were obliged to have a travelling-carriage for their journey abroad."

"What could poor Constance do?" said Lady Willoughby.

"Oh, she walks—she is a capital walker. She and Herbert walk all over the parish together, and go to all the cottages."

"And when they go out to dinner?" said Sir Francis.

"They don't," said Kate, "because church-time is at seven in the evening."

"Church-time—of course, as a clergyman, he would not dine out on Sunday."

"This is every day," said Emmeline; "we used to have such delicious evening walks to and from church, through the pretty wooded common, after the heat of the day was over."

"Oh ho!" said Sir Francis; "daily service, evening air—no wonder poor Lord Herbert's lungs are out of order. That is the way young clergymen kill themselves now-a-days."

"Poor Constance!" again said Lady Willoughby.

Emmeline and Kate, having nothing to say to this, became silent, and Lady Willoughby returned to the matter of the carriage, which seemed to distress her more than anything else. "People are so strange," she said; "but it must look very odd to see a person of Lady Herbert Somerville's rank without her own carriage. And everything about his fortune was so satisfactory too."

"Yes, Lord Liddesdale behaved in the handsomest manner, and Lord Herbert too, about settlement," said Sir Francis.

"I am sure I do not understand these things," said Lady Willoughby; "but surely you told me, Sir Francis, that his fortune was very good."

"Oh yes," said Emmeline, "I know they are well off, for Margaret Forester told me they were so glad the curate of Copseley should be a rich man, because the place is so poor."

"It wants schools, and all sorts of things," said Kate.

"Poor Constance!" repeated Lady Willoughby.

"And how does Lord Liddesdale like all these notions?" said Sir Francis.

"Very much," said Kate; "he gave a great deal to Copseley Church, and he is a great friend of Mr. Forester's. Indeed, it is all managed just like his own parish at Rowthorpe. Oh, Mamma! you cannot think how we enjoyed our visit there."

"Ah! I should like to hear about it," said Lady Willoughby.

Nothing loath, Kate began. "You know we were to go home with them after the wedding, and you can't think how we dreaded it—especially poor Emmie; we thought it would all be so awful and so grand; and Miss Danby gave us such a lecture as to how we were to behave, that she made it ten times worse. We did not care so much about Lady Frances, for we had seen her once or twice when Constance was in London, and we got on famously with her at Margaret Forester's great school-feast on the wedding-day. But as to Lord Liddesdale and Lord Somerville, how we dreaded their speaking to us, and how poor Emmie coloured with fright if they did but look at her! And what do you think the end of it was? Why, that I am sure I felt a great deal less on my good behaviour than ever I did with Miss Danby!"

"Does Lord Somerville live with his father?" said Lady Willoughby.

"Yes; he was at home all the time we were there," said Emmeline, "and he was very good-natured. It is such a comfort that he is gone with Herbert and Constance, for he promised us so kindly that he would take care of her."

At this period of the conversation, Lady Willoughby rose, and the girls followed her to the drawing-room, where she lay down on the sofa; and with one of them at her feet, and the other on a footstool close to her, she said, "Go on, my dears; 1 like to hear you talk. Where were you? Oh, at Rowthorpe."

"Oh, how happy we were there!" said Emmeline.

"And is Lord Somerville as handsome as his poor brother?" said Lady Willoughby.

"He is a fine-looking man," said Emmeline: "but he can't be as handsome as Herbert—he is so old."

"How old, my dear?" said Lady Willoughby, surprised.

"Older than Lady Frances," said Emmeline; "and he has been in Parliament ever so long. He cannot be much under thirty-five."

"Ah! Emmie," said Kate, "what a tremendous scrape you did get into with thinking people so very old. I must tell how it was, if you don't mind it."

"Oh, not a bit," said Emmeline: "Mamma is not Miss Danby."

"No, indeed, thank Heaven, my dear; but I hope you were not rude—impossible!"

"Quite the contrary, Mamma," said Kate: "it was all her great politeness. Lady Frances found we knew very little of Shakspeare, so she began to read some of it with us, and Emmie was reading 'As You Like It' aloud, when the two gentlemen came in from the dining-room. She was going to leave off, but Lord Liddesdale begged her to go on, and they sat down and listened. Presently, Lord Liddesdale said, 'Why, have I forgotten the order of the play, or what has become of the Seven Ages of Man?' Poor Emmie, her face lighted up like a red-hot coal, and she hung down her head as if she would never look up again."

"I am sure I never thought he would have missed it," said Emmeline. "Oh, it was dreadful!"

"Lady Frances said it must be there, and came to look over to see if anything was the matter with the book; and there it was, sure enough. So poor Emmie was obliged to confess why she had missed it, and she whispered it into Lady Frances's ear, 'she thought Lord Liddesdale would not like it.' Well, Lady Frances tried to stop herself from laughing, but she could not, and at last she was obliged to tell, for they looked and wondered."

"I cannot think how she could do it so little disagreeably," said Emmeline, "considering that it was rather absurd of me. 'Papa,' she said, 'you ought to be very much obliged to her: it was out of her great consideration for your feelings!' 'For my old age and infirmity,' said Lord Liddesdale, and then he did laugh, I thought he would never have stopped; but the great beauty of it was, that they could make so much fun of it without annoying us in the least. Lord Liddesdale wanted to know whether I thought him the lean and slippered pantaloon, or if he had arrived at second childishness and mere oblivion."

"Yes; and then Emmie roused herself up to answer. 'Certainly not mere oblivion, when he knew so exactly where the Seven Ages ought to be,'" said Kate; "and then he bowed in the most magnificent way, and said that he had never heard a more prettily turned compliment, and Emmie blushed up to her ears again!"

"It was lucky it was so very absurd!" said Emmeline, smiling, "so that one could laugh heartily at it; for to see that tall splendid old man, such a picture of a real nobleman, and to hear him talk of the lean and slippered pantaloon—I could not help laughing at myself for having been so silly as to think it possible the passage could hurt his feelings. How we did laugh! We were quite tired when we went up to bed at night, and in the middle of the night Kate waked me with laughing again in her sleep. Oh, there was no end to the merriment we had there!"

"Our delightful long scrambling walks," said Kate.

"And better than all, the going to the ruin," said Emmeline. "Oh, that was of all things delightful!"

" What, a pic-nic party ? " asked the mother.

" Not exactly ; but some little way from Rowthorpe there is a beautiful bit of an old castle, which was pulled down in the Wars of the Roses. It belonged to Earl Warwick, the King-maker, and Edward IV. once slept there. So Lady Frances made a scheme to go and see it ; it was to be one day when Lord Liddesdale was obliged to go to a county meeting, because he said no slipperd pantaloon ever dined on damp grass, and that Emmeline would think the owls and bats so affecting to his spirits, that her sympathy would not allow her to enjoy herself. Besides, how did we know that he had not been at Edward IV.'s levee there ? So the party was only Lady Frances and Lord Somerville and ourselves ; we went down the river in a boat. Lord Somerville and one of the gardeners rowed us."

" How very nice that was ! " said Emmeline. " Do you remember how the birds sang, and the weeping-willows that hung so gracefully into the dark pools, and the kingfisher that darted out of the bank ? "

" And how Lord Somerville laughed at us for being senti-mental about the lime-kiln, which he managed to make us think was the castle itself ! "

" And Lady Frances sitting by, smiling in her quiet way at our grand fit of enthusiasm," said Emmeline. " Oh, but I can never forget what they ended by saying, about being enthusiastic for the wrong thing instead of the right ! "

" That strong enthusiasm is a noble feeling when it is right, only it is spoilt and worn out by being thrown away—on lime-kilns instead of castles, as Lord Somerville finished," said Kate.

" And when we came there," said Emmeline, " oh ! what a pretty picture it was—the bit of arch with the feathery birch growing out on its side, and the little country children playing with their dog on the slope. We tried to sketch it, but Lady Frances was the only one who could draw the children at all ; and, tiresome little things, they all left off play, and stood staring at us. Lord Somerville pretended to call out to them,

'Sixpence apiece if you'll be natural!' and his sister told him he was encouraging the worst sort of affectation."

"Oh, and the fun of all," said Kate, "the riding, Emmie, though I doubt if it was much fun to you at the time. We ladies were to ride home on a donkey and two ponies, but neither of us had ever been on the back of anything before, and I do not know where Emmie would be now, if Lord Somerville had not led her donkey almost all the way. Oh, how merry we were!"

"I was much happier when they let me walk," said Emmeline. "Do you remember the round red August moon, rising like a globe of fire in the east, and the darkness sinking on the harvest-field full of sheaves? And that cottage with the deep eaves, and the porch and windows glistening white in the moonlight, and the long shadows of the trees across the smooth turf in the glades of the park?"

"And the luxury of feeling tired and fresh both at once, as we drank our tea round the open window in the drawing-room?" said Kate. "Oh, that was a day to be remembered!"

"Then there was the school-feast," said Emmeline.

"And the little children's strawberry-feast," said Kate.

"And the mornings when we worked, and drew, and read," said Emmeline; "and the sitting among the geraniums on the hot afternoons."

"And the grand expedition all together, after Herbert and Constance came, when Herbert said he must go and show his wife to his old nurse, and we took the pony and donkey, and you rode so much better—I think that was the merriest of all our walks. The old woman was so pleased; she told Herbert he had brought home as bonnie a bride as had ever been seen in those parts, and she would pray night and day that she might be as good as she was bonnie. Constance blushed, and thanked her with all her heart; and the old nurse said, 'Ay, and you are, I can see. You are not of the kind I feared, that would only be sorted up with finding yourself my Lady. You know what Lord Herbert is for his own sake; and I can tell you'

—and then she looked at Herbert over her spectacles, and laughed—"you might search far enough, and never find a better bargain than you have of him, and I should know him as well as most folks.' "

"Oh! and the best of all was her lecturing Lord Somerville about bringing home a wife too."

As Kate was finishing her sentence, Sir Francis came in from the dining-room, and behind him came the waiter with the candles. The light revealed what the sisters had little suspected, that their mother was very comfortably asleep. However, she awoke at the sound of the opening of the door, and told her husband that the girls had been entertaining her so pleasantly with an account of their pic-nic party from Lord Liddesdale's.

She was not very wide-awake all the rest of the evening, but to make up for it Sir Francis talked much, and told them a great deal about the children, chiefly about Alfred and Cecilia.

And now the day was over, and the two sisters shut into their own room, Emmeline threw her arms round Kate, and exclaimed, "Well, and it is come! O Kate I can you fully believe it, that we have had our mother's kiss and good-night at last, after all our weary wishes? If Constance did but know how happy we are!"

"Mamma is so exactly what we always fancied," said Kate; "only we should not have talked so long when she was tired."

"So like her letters, and so like Constance," said Emmeline. "Oh, what joy it is! I could sit and look at her for hours, and feel that I really have a mother. I wonder if people are as happy who have never known what it is to be without."

"It does seem very odd," said Kate; "that we, poor isolated things as we were, should suddenly have jumped into a ready-made family—mamma and papa, and children and all."

growing at a noble fellow Alfred is!" said Emmeline; "and with the quite a beauty. And sweet little Janet, how fond Frances we of her! only I am afraid Miss Townsend will get and, tiresome."

staring at us her a bore," said Kate; "we shall have to be so civil to her. I did not want her at all; we could have taught the children so nicely, and they are to have a nurse when this Ayah is gone."

"O Kate, did not her dark face and her mixture of Hindostanee and English bring back strange memories? Our bungalow and the palm trees, and the tree with the pink flowers, and the bottle-nested sparrows—I almost thought I could hear the sound of the gong, and see the broad sunshiny river. And papa—our own dear father, I mean—I saw him in my memory dearer than ever before; while I was looking at mamma, his bright hair and pale face, and his dress all white, as he used to sit under the verandah and hold out his arms to us. Ah! you cannot remember, you were so little. How I wish Constance could have seen that Ayah!"

"We must write to Constance the first thing to-morrow," said Kate; "and how she will wish herself at home! But do you really think, Emmie, it could be the daily service that did Herbert harm?"

"I don't know," said Emmeline, "it never seemed to tire him; and you know Mr. Forester and Mr. Grey often came to help him. Oh, no! it was that foggy evening drive from Rowthorpe; you remember that Mr. Forester was alarmed at the cold he caught then from the first, and hardly allowed him to do anything after it began!"

"Perhaps Mamma will be more hopeful when she has seen Lady Frances," said Kate. "How good-natured Sir Francis is! I will never be afraid of anyone again beforehand."

"And how fond of his children!" said Emmeline. "He is not at all what we expected, and yet I am very glad of it; it is a great relief to have no one to be afraid of."

"Yes, this time that we have looked forward to so long, is as delightful as possible!" said Kate.

"All I am afraid of now," said Emmeline, "is Frank; to have a great tall clumsy school-boy like that, all the holidays, will be very tiresome!"

CHAPTER III.

"Now, thought he. I see the danger that Mistrust and Timorous were
driven back by. The lions were chained, but he saw not the chains."
Pilgrim's Progress.

THE girls were very busy the next morning writing letters, one
to Lady Frances and the other to Constance, when they were
interrupted by the announcement of "Mr. Frank Willoughby!"
and in walked a youth of seventeen, rather short for that age,
with hair of unnecessary length and shagginess, and a round
rosy face, so like little Edwin's, that it would have suited better
at the top of his white frock and broad sash, than surmounting a
tail-coat.   He looked rather disappointed, and a little doubtful
whether he had come to the right place, when he only saw two
young ladies; but Kate, rising, and holding out her hand, said
cordially, "How d'ye do, Frank?"

"Oh," said he, as if suddenly recollecting her, "how d'ye do?"
shook hands with her and Emmeline, and abruptly asked,
"Where's my father?"

"Gone into the City," said Kate; "he will be back again by
half-past one."

"I will go and call Mamma," said Emmeline.

She found Lady Willoughby sitting by the fire in her own
room, wrapped up in a great shawl, and with writing materials
on the table before her.

"Here is Frank, Mamma," said she.

Lady Willoughby's face did not express much alacrity or
satisfaction.   "Dear me! Is he, indeed? I had no idea he
could come so soon."

"Railroads bring people very fast," said Emmeline.

"And I was in the midst of a letter to your aunt in India;
and I wanted to have my dresses taken out, for I am sure I have
nothing fit to be seen.   What can have brought him so early?
What shall we do with him, my dear? And Sir Francis will

not be at home until one o'clock. I wish he would not go away.
And what is this boy like, dear Emmie ? "

" A nice, good-natured fellow," said Emmeline, "honest and
downright, not very polished, perhaps, but Herbert and Constance
liked him very much."

" A great rough school-boy! Oh! dear me!" sighed Lady
Willoughby; " I wish his father was at home."

" He is very good-natured," said Emmeline, almost as if she
was persuading her to confront some strange dog. "Won't you
come down, Mamma ? "

" I suppose I must, presently. Think what we can do with
him, my dear, until Sir Francis comes home."

" Perhaps he has not breakfasted," said Emmeline ; " he must
have come away early."

" Ah ! yes, order some breakfast, and say I will come presently ;
but you know I am not at all strong, my dear, and it always hurts
me to be hurried; but tell him I will come presently, and take
good care of him ; I will be there before Sir Francis comes in."

" Very well, Mamma," said Emmeline, thinking this scarcely
a requital of the kindness Sir Francis had shown them.

" What a comfort it is to have a daughter!" said Lady
Willoughby, kissing her with fondness that drove away the
uncomfortable sensation.

Conversation had not gone on fast in her absence : Kate
wanted to be civil and sisterly, but did not know exactly how
to begin. "Did you set off early ? " said she, after a moment or
two of uneasy silence.

" At half-past six," was the answer. " I have only got leave
out for the day."

" Sir Francis will be very sorry not to be at home," said Kate.
And then there was a pause, while Frank looked anxiously at
the door. He rose eagerly when the lock turned, but the blank
expression returned when Emmeline entered alone.

"Mamma will come down in a few minutes," said she;
"but she has been rather tired with all her journeyings, and
cannot well be hurried. Have you breakfasted ? "

D

" No."

Glad to be doing something, though shy of giving orders, Emmeline rang the bell, and hastened to clear the table. Breakfast was sent for, and then came another silence. The girls guessed how Frank must be wishing to hear about his ready-made family, and yet it was quite impossible to begin about the heads.

" Should you like to see the children?" said Emmeline.

" Oh yes."

" Then I will call Alfred and Janet; the two little ones are so shy, that I don't think we could get them into the room without their papa; but Alfred will be delighted—he could hardly speak to us, he was so disappointed that we were not brother Frank."

Emmeline went to fetch them; and so great was the curiosity and eagerness excited by the news of brother Frank's arrival, that even Edwin ventured down under the protection of his new sister.

Frank kissed them, but still seemed rather shy of them, and let Alfred stand by him for some moments without speaking, while Edwin sat on Emmeline's lap and stared, and Janet took refuge with Kate. However, when the girls began to play with Alfred, Frank joined them, and had become tolerable friends with them before it was time to send Edwin away for his siesta.

Then Frank asked abruptly, " How is Lord Herbert?" listened with much interest to the answer: and looking at the writing-case on the table, said, " I suppose you are writing to them."

" Yes."

" Then I wish you would say, I thank them for their letter. *She* wrote me a very nice letter about their not being able to have me at Christmas, and he put in a note at the end."

" Here is room, if you like to write a note yourself."

" No, thank you," said Frank. " I have got nothing to say, only thanks, and I am glad he is better."

" Very well, I will certainly tell them," said Kate. " It

would have been very nice to be there all together last winter."

"Yes. What became of you?"

"We stayed at school most of the time."

Frank fairly started with horror. "Why, that is awful! What could you do? Be like the Domum boy, I should think."

"That we could hardly be," said Kate, laughing, "considering that we have scarcely acquired a Dulce Domum."

"Well, I never heard of such a thing. Stay at school all the holidays!"

"You see we have survived it," said Emmeline, "so you need not bestow so very much pity on us. Where did you go?"

"Home, to be sure!" said Frank, surprised at the question.

"To Mr. Willoughby's?" said Kate.

"Yes, to Dumblethwayte. That has been my home ever since I came from India."

"How long ago was that?" asked Kate.

"Thirteen years." Frank was growing quite confidential. "I don't remember my father the least in the world," and he looked inquiringly at Kate. She would have told him how Sir Francis had told her to introduce him, but she thought it would not do before the children.

"Is Lady Willoughby ill?" asked Frank presently.

"Mamma always stays in her room in the morning, and goes to sleep, just like the little ones," said Alfred. And then he went on, "I love Papa best, because Mamma won't let us make a noise."

"As if anybody could like such a noise as you can make!" said Frank; but Alfred, finding no one else willing to give his brother the desired information, took it upon himself, whispering and looking shyly at his sisters, as if he suspected he was doing something wrong. "I'll tell you what, Mamma is much the prettiest; Papa is almost as ugly as the old man in the steamer, but Papa is much the most good-natured."

"I'll tell you what," said Frank, overpowering these awkward communications with his strong voice, "you are an undutiful young dog, Master Alfred, and if you say another word, I will —I will—I will put you up the chimney."

A great struggling, laughing, and screaming succeeded, much to the relief of the girls. It was past one o'clock, and in the midst of the uproar they did not hear the approach of Lady Willoughby, who opened the door while the noise was at its full height. For a moment all stood silent and surprised; then Lady Willoughby, advancing with all her grace and prepossessing manner, said, "My dear Frank, what pleasure this is!" then kissing him, she looked at him, saying, "You see, my dear boy, I knew I need not make a stranger of you, and so I did not hurry myself, though I was anxious to see you; but I had so much on my hands, and I am such an invalid. Besides, I know young people always get on better by themselves, and you have made acquaintance with Alfred and Janet already."

"Yes, and Edwin has been here, Mamma!" said Kate triumphantly.

"Well, Alfred," said his mother, "you are a happy boy at last, now you have got your brother Frank."

Nothing could be more gentle and caressing than Lady Willoughby's manner, yet Frank was stiff and awkward, and in a great cloud of bashfulness, giving short embarrassed answers to her soft questions about his journey, and the time he had set off; and heartily did Emmeline wish that her mother had come sooner, or that Alfred had held his tongue. Yet when she looked at Frank's chubby childish face, she could not think that he had any acuteness of feeling or perception, and was willing to attribute his embarrassment to dulness and stolidity, as Lady Willoughby went on perseveringly asking questions, and being affectionate, without effect; and Kate escaped from the awkward group, under plea of finishing her letter to her sister.

Many a time had Frank started up hopefully, before Sir Francis actually entered the room.

"See," said his wife, rising, and taking Frank's hand as if to lead him forward, "see who has been waiting for you all this time."

"Ha! eh? Who? Why, it is Frank himself, I believe! How d'ye do, my dear boy? Well, I am glad to see you, Frank; I should have known you anywhere! How long have you been here?"

"About two hours, Sir," said Frank.

"Two hours! well, that is unlucky, you must have come just as I went out. But never mind, you have been making acquaintance with all the others here."

"Yes, he is on excellent terms with Alfred already," said Lady Willoughby. "You little thought what was in store for you."

"Not I, or I should have been at home long ago. Why, Frank, you are the very picture of what you were when I saw you last—I should have known you among a hundred in the street; but I suppose you hardly remember me?"

"Not in the least, Sir," said Frank, in an open way that made the words seem far more cordial than his replies to Lady Willoughby.

Sir Francis laughed, shook hands with him again, and then asked, "Well, and how is your uncle?"

"Oh, very well, thank you, Sir," said Frank.

"Grown a thorough country parson, I suppose; but that he always was. And how does he wear? Pretty well, I suppose; he has got an easy life of it there."

"He has a great deal to do," said Frank; "but he is very well and very active."

"I wonder whether Dumblethwayte looks as it did six-and-thirty years ago—yes, six-and-thirty years ago, when I was a young shaver with a round face just like yours, Frank, and went there to wish my brother good-bye, just before I went out to India. Pretty banishment I thought it then; and how I envied George, set down there in his pretty parsonage, with nothing to do but to enjoy himself."

"I should not think it had altered much," said Frank.

"Not quite as much as your uncle and I, no doubt. I wonder if George and I should know each other again; I dare say he is the youngest-looking of the two now."

"Perhaps he is, Sir."

"Ah, well!" said Sir Francis, laughing, "one meets with it everywhere; there was Kate yesterday, now, could not recover from her surprise at meeting such a sun-dried old object in a wig. Well, and so you have got your Aunt Willoughby for a neighbour?"

"Yes; they live about two miles off, just on the other side of the hill."

"I must make acquaintance with her, I suppose. I think of going to see Dumblethwayte as soon as I can get things a little settled. There is only one daughter unmarried now, is there?"

"Only Juliet."

All through luncheon-time such inquiries as these went on; and afterwards Sir Francis and his son went out walking together, and the girls with their mother had a drive in the park. The arrangement did not please Lady Willoughby, and as they drove from the door she did not conceal her annoyance from the girls, saying that Sir Francis had promised to go somewhere with her, but she supposed everything was to give way to this boy. However, the park revived her spirits by the novelty of the scene, and she entertained her daughters with a description of the course by the river, the evening airing of the gay world of Calcutta, and of her own grand equipage there. As they were returning, Kate, who was sitting forward, exclaimed, as she eagerly acknowledged a bow, and her face lighted up with a delightful smile of recognition—"Lord Liddesdale and Lady Frances! How surprised she looked! I wonder if she guesses. O Mamma, look at her pretty horse Fairy, the bright bay; I had one little ride on it."

This encounter put Lady Willoughby into great good humour; she talked with more animation than she had yet shown, and on coming in, told Sir Francis she had enjoyed herself very much. The dinner was earlier than usual, because Frank's time was short; and as soon as it was over, he wished them good-bye, and departed, looking very happy. Sir Francis seemed quite as happy, and talked in praise of Frank half the evening, in which his wife joined so heartily as to surprise her daughters, who had not fancied her very favourably impressed with the young gentleman. However, they thought Sir Francis was easily pleased, when he showed them, with great satisfaction, a letter from the head-master of Frank's school, speaking strongly of his application and good conduct, but saying that his abilities were not of the highest order.

"I am heartily glad of it," said his father. "Your first-rate men never get on in the world; they always have some absurd quirk or crotchet of their own, that nobody else can understand."

"They never can be contented," said Lady Willoughby.

"They never know what is to their own advantage or other people's," continued Sir Francis; "they won't do this, and they can't bear that, and they have some notion or some pursuit of their own, and do everything except their own business. I declare I should have been quite vexed if I had had a letter to say that Frank was up to the ears in Latin and Greek, and carrying all before him. Now, I dare say," turning suddenly on Emmeline, "your brother-in-law, Lord Herbert, is one of your first-rate high-flying men."

"One of mine, at least," said Emmeline drily.

"He distinguished himself at school and college," said Kate; "and would have done much more, but for his health."

"Yes, of course; and with his connections he might have been anything. And what does he do with all these abilities? Why, he settles down into a country curacy which is a dead loss to him, and wears out his lungs with daily service, or some rubbish or other. No, no, give me good practical sense, such as knows how to take care of itself; and that is what you will find in Frank." Emmeline looked at Kate, and felt contemptuous; but their attention was required to a story of a clever young man who had made a great sensation in India by his eccentric conduct.

As soon as the two sisters were alone in their room, Emmeline burst into indignation: "First-rate talents to be disdained, as if nothing was precious but money! Better be a Californian gold-digger, then, than Milton or Goethe."

"As if mind and its powers were not a thousand times more precious than all that gold can purchase!" cried Kate.

"Get on in the world, indeed!" proceeded Emmeline. "That is all our mind was given us for, then. Money hunting and consequence hunting, and the more you have the more you must strive for. Slavery indeed! What do such people know of the purposes of being?"

What did Emmeline herself know of them?

The next day was Sunday, and Lady Willoughby not feeling equal to going to the morning service, Emmeline and Kate went with Sir Francis. At Church they were, for the first time, reminded of the Confirmation, which had slipped entirely out of their heads with the other interests and occupations of their school life; and they went home, each intending to speak to the other about it. After luncheon, sundry old Indian acquaintance of Sir Francis and Lady Willoughby came to call, and the two sisters were obliged to sit up demure and formal, without the power of escaping to the afternoon service; and the evening service was at the very hour of dinner. They felt that this was not a right state of things, and as they went to bed they speculated on the possibility of finding their way to Church by themselves another time.

"And, Emmie, the Confirmation is to-morrow."

"Yes," said Emmeline doubtfully; "but I don't see how we can go. Mamma would never go out so early, and our tickets are in our desks at Miss Danby's."

"Yes, I suppose it could hardly be managed," said Kate.

"To be sure," said Emmeline, "we could get Sir Francis to set us down at Miss Danby's, and we could go with the others there. But yet I don't know; it is not the sort of thing to ask him about."

"If we could see Lady Frances, and go with her."

"If—yes, if—I wonder if she will be really there, looking out for us."

"She said she would go, but perhaps she will change her mind now she knows where we are," said Kate.

"I don't know what to do," said Emmeline. "I am very much inclined to let it alone until a quieter time. All that I learnt seems gone entirely out of my head, and all our books and papers are at Miss Danby's."

"I am sure I am too sleepy to think it all up again now," said Kate.

"It is so great and awful a vow, that I am sure it ought not to be taken lightly and without due preparation," said Emmeline.

"We never seemed half good enough for it before," said Kate.

"And all the little preparation we had seems driven quite out of our heads," said Emmeline. "No, it would be awkward, and a hurry, and a bustle, and a fuss, to have it now, and that such a sacred thing should never be, so we will let it wait for a quieter time."

"Then we shall not have that other great responsibility," said Kate, sighing, as if her sister's decision relieved her from a weight.

"But we will take care we do not miss church next Sunday," said Emmeline, as if to atone for the rest by this one good resolution.

"And we will get our books from Miss Danby's, and read our Christian Year every Sunday, as we promised Constance," said Kate. "I like to do that, because it puts us in mind of those shady Sunday evenings at Copseley."

"And I see beautiful poetry in those hymns, here and there," said Emmeline; "I wish I could enter into them as Constance does."

They put the thought of Confirmation out of their heads, and went to sleep. On Tuesday, on returning from their afternoon drive, they found the cards of Lady Frances and her father, accompanied by a little note from her to Emmeline, congratulating them on their mother's arrival, and ending thus: "Was it the fault of my eyes that I did not see you at St. George's? I watched in vain, for one white dress and white cap was so like another, that I could not make you out. However, I was very

glad to be there, it brought so many pleasant thoughts; and I
am sure you must be rejoiced at being thus able to begin this
fresh start in life; indeed, it seems as if the Confirmation had
been timed on purpose for you."

"Lady Frances does not know," said Emmeline, as she folded
up the note; not, however, without some feeling of self-reproach,
though not exactly directed the right way. She was sorry that
she had not been able to wind up her feelings to the point
which she considered fit for receiving the sacred ordinance.
She did not perceive how the grace therein received might
have strengthened her on her entrance into the new sphere of
trial and duty in which she had been placed. Emmeline and
Kate did indeed know that life is a time of trial, but they did
not so feel it; they were drifting quietly on the stream, without
much thought of the course; and though they acknowledged
the necessity of attending to Church ordinances, these were to
them duties in themselves, which stood alone, unconnected
with practical life, and without influence over it. So, as Confirmation was to come but once in their lives, why not at one
time as well as at another? And the thought of the Holy
Communion made them still more inclined to defer it, since
they would be afraid to stay away and yet dreaded to go without due preparation. They did not feel with their hearts,
though in some degree they knew with their understandings,
that prayers, Church services, Confirmation, Communions, were
all steps to lead them on in the track of daily life, the way-
marks set about their path; nay, further, the wings which
might bear onwards their steps.

They had not much time for thought at present, for there
was much to occupy them. They had to go and finish packing
up their goods at Miss Danby's, to take leave of their school-
fellows, and to receive the adieus of the great lady herself.

They were not without feelings of gratitude and kindliness
towards Miss Danby. They had not been unhappy at school;
indeed, from their homelessness, they had more affection for it
than is usual; and although their complete reliance in and

devotedness to each other had prevented· them from forming close friendships with other girls, they were people universally to like and to be liked. Their standing and importance in the school had caused them to be missed; and on their re-appearance they were greeted with such eagerness and affection, as gave them very pleasant impressions to carry away. It was odd to find how all was going on just as usual, and how short the week had seemed to their companions, which to them had been so very long.

"Though we have not been without our event," said Susan Allen. "By-the-by, you were not at the Confirmation."

"No," said Kate; "we thought it best to put it off to a quieter time."

"What! when you are leaving school and all, and Emmeline will be coming out, too?" said Susan. "Who would think of coming out without being confirmed?"

"She is not coming out," said Kate: "she means to wait for me."

"What edifying devotion!" cried Miss Allen. "Really you two do deserve to be proposed as models of sisterly affection, as much as Jane and Susan Woodbine in my old spelling-book. And so you won't be women after all—neither confirmed nor come out!"

"Must they go together?" said Emmeline, smiling.

"I know I wish they did in my case," said Susan, yawning. "You are lucky girls, you two: I wish you could give me a bit of your good fortune. I should not mind giving you all the additional womanliness derived from my Confirmation, for the liberty you have got at home."

Kate shook her head at the rattling Susan; Emmeline looked at Anne Forester, her chief friend at school, and who had, like Susan, been recently confirmed. Anne looked grave, and as if she did not like this light way of talking, but she said nothing: it was not her way. Emmeline watched her face and movements, and wondered if Confirmation had made any difference in her; but there was a certain peevish tone in which

Anne used to talk of lessons and restraints, which recurred again during this visit, and did not suit with the idea of a person fresh from the solemn rite, and feeling this solemnity as deeply as Emmeline knew she did.

It was time to go, and after many kisses, promises of correspondence, and hopes of future meetings, the Miss Berners went down to the drawing-room to Miss Danby and all her assistants. The knowledge that Miss Danby had sent a very high character of them to Lady Willoughby, and the remembrance of her many condescending attempts for their amusement during their solitary holidays, made them feel a sort of affection for her; and perhaps not one of her scholars had listened with a better grace to her parting discourse, or heard less impatiently her benignant conclusion, instructing them to remember that the most important part of education had yet to be completed. Now her last farewell had been spoken, and their school-life was among the things that had been!

CHAPTER IV.

I will have a lover,
Riding on a steed of steeds ;
  He shall love me without guile ;
And to him I will discover
The swan's nest among the reeds.
                              E. Barrett Browning.

THE Ayah was sent back to India, and her place supplied by a stately English nurse and a pretty young nursery-maid, of both of whom little Cecilia testified strong disapproval, spent a considerable part of her time in squalling, and for three nights refused to go to sleep till she had victimized her father by making him walk up and down the room for an hour and a half.

One day intervened between the departure of the Ayah and

the arrival of the nursery-governess, Miss Townsend ; and by
the end of it, Emmeline and Kate were by no means disposed
to lament her coming. Alfred, now familiar, was riotous and
overpowering, Edwin almost as bad, Janet fretful and exacting—
none of them had any principle of obedience, or any power of
finding amusement for themselves, nor had the sisters much
notion of managing them ; they had no experience of children,
and no command. They knew it was only for one day, and
as three children could not be spoilt in that space, they hardly
contested anything, but allowed themselves to be nearly pulled
to pieces, permitted the destruction of numerous toys of the
children and knick-knacks of their own, and never were more
tired than when at last they had wished Alfred good-night,
and set down to tea as peaceably as they could, while Cecilia's
screams were still heard in the distance.

Miss Townsend came early, by especial desire, and was very
kindly greeted. She was about twenty—one of the smallest
and most timid of womankind, and with a voice that it was not
easy to hear. She had been popular among the younger girls at
Miss Danby's, but always looked almost frightened out of her
senses if addressed by the elder ones. The Miss Berners had
for the last twelve months been at the head of the school, and
their sister's marriage had given them a sort of *éclat*, which
occasioned the poor little woman to look at them as still more
awfully remote than the rest, though not perhaps personally as
formidable as the lively and satirical Miss Allen.

All that was further known of her was, that she was the
eldest of a very large family, and that her father was " in reduced circumstances." Persons who are themselves bashful,
suffer the most from the shyness of others ; and Emmeline felt
it a dreadful infliction to have to introduce the children to her,
and take her to her room, and hear her " Yes—yes, Miss Berners
—thank you—very kind "—so often repeated under her breath.

" Poor thing," said she, when she had left her alone with the
children, " I feel as if I was committing a cruelty, shutting a
dove up with two or three young eagles."

About an hour after, Kate said, "I shall go and see if there is anything left of her."

Presently Kate came back in surprise; "Well, Emmie, it is really marvellous. There they are, all three, as happy and as good as possible. She is mending that unhappy cart that the boys broke yesterday, and they sit watching as if their lives depended on it, and Alfred asking scientific questions about wheels and steam-engines."

"Some people have the art of managing children," said Emmeline; "and at any rate, they are off our hands. If they had been reasonable well-trained children, like the little Foresters, it would be a different thing; but these are only fresh-caught! Well, I hope her power will last, and that she will work wonders; but how she is to get on when it comes to lessons, I cannot think."

"With that great Alfred, and sturdy Edwin," said Kate, "who look enough to demolish her in a moment; and worst of all, Janet to whine the life out of her."

"I could bear with the rest," said Emmeline; "but Janet's whining is dreadful!"

Miss Townsend's power did last; the children were contented with her, and if she had any difficulties with them, these did not transpire. Indeed, but for the quietness, no one would have discovered her presence, for she kept out of the way as much as she could, spoke as little and as low as possible, and never said more than "Yes, Sir," in reply to Sir Francis's harangues. Emmeline and Kate pitied her very much, and meant to be very kind to her.

The next great event was dining at Lord Liddesdale's.

On the morning of the day on which they were to go, Emmeline received a letter from Lady Herbert Somerville, full of kind Confirmation wishes, and speaking of that ordinance as the great step in life from which all the rest may take its colour. Constance had reckoned that her letter would reach her sisters on the day after their first Communion; and her husband had written at the end a few words of affectionate exhortation, warning them not to think that present warm feelings would last for ever, and reminding them that steady prayer and consistent practice were more than ever required of them, now they had taken their place as grown-up members of the Church— admitted to its full privileges, and permitted to approach and offer themselves "a reasonable, holy, and lively sacrifice." What holiness did not such a privilege require of them!

The sisters looked at each other, in doubt whether they should consider themselves to have missed a great blessing, or to be as yet free from a great peril.

"We will keep the letter till we are confirmed," said Emmeline.

"Herbert will be at home by that time, and able to speak to us himself," replied Kate; "but keep the letter by all means. How glad I am to have such a good account to take this evening!"

So they laid aside the subject, and settled into an impression, that their conduct was not of so much importance, while they were still unconfirmed.

It was a very pleasant evening for the girls; their friends were as kind to them as ever, and both Sir Francis and Lady Willoughby seemed exceedingly pleased. The former kept Lady Francis half dinner-time listening to a story which Kate had already heard twice before, and perceived she might probably hear many times again; and Lady Willoughby looked unusually animated whilst Lord Liddesdale was talking to her about Constance.

The only disappointment was, that their mother took up Lady Frances's attention all the evening, so that though they had quite their share in the general conversation, they could have none with her in particular, and could not convince her that they had acted for the best in delaying their Confirmation.

Could it have been because they had been seeing as they thought Lady Frances would see, that there were no such expressions of strong admiration of their mother that evening, when they were together, as one or other of them had hitherto been always uttering; and that Kate actually complained of Sir

Francis's continual prosing and fidgeting? The first rose-coloured
light in which they had viewed everything, was wearing off; and
in fact, there were many difficulties in their situation. A family
grown up together has become so accustomed to the different
peculiarities of its members, as scarcely either to feel them or to
view them in a strong light; whereas Emmeline and Kate came
into the midst of their home as strangers, with no old recollections, with eyes that could scarcely avoid seeing foibles, and
without being, as it were, unconsciously moulded to fit into the
ins and outs of their family. Strong principles of duty and
forbearance were doubly needed in their case; but of this they
were not aware, and no friend was near to warn them. Their
sister was at a distance, and was too much of a girl herself to
have thought of the possibility of these difficulties; and indeed,
she was happy in the full belief that all was right with them,
that they were under the best guidance, and that there was now
no reason to regret her absence.

From the strength, support, and aid, that was offered to them
by the Spirit of Counsel and Might, they had, in their ignorance
and faint-heartedness, turned aside; and now they stood in their
weakness, exposed to temptations of which they had not even
thought.

Sir Francis's brother, the uncle with whom Frank had hitherto
spent his holidays, came to London for a few days, to see the
brother whom he had not met for five-and-thirty years. He was
by several years the elder, and it was curious to see how much
the two brothers had grown apart during their separation.

Mr. Willoughby was a small old man, though not quite as
brown and shrivelled as his brother, and with thin iron-grey hair
instead of wig, with the same activity of manner, and quickness
of speech—perhaps a little inclined to prosiness, especially about
his nephew Frank; but in addition to this, Mr. Willoughby was
the very model of an old-fashioned clergyman, in look, dress,
and manner; and there was a beaming kindliness, almost a sun-
niness about him, that did everyone's heart good, down from
Lady Willoughby, who always called him "Poor, dear, good old

gentleman," to little Cecilia, who, instead of her usual screams, stretched out her arms to go to him on his very first introduction.

His parish was far away in the north, and it was half a life-time since he had left it. One day he begged, as an especial favour, that the young ladies would come out with him, and help him with their advice in the presents he must take home. They were much amused by the expedition, which was a whole long day's work. First, there was a gown for Grace, his old housekeeper, which was not to be too gay nor too dingy, neither common-looking nor smart, neither too dark nor too light; and then came an infinity of other articles, needle-books, pin-cushions, bodkin-cases, of all varieties, for the old women or little girls, of each of whom he spoke by name as a particular friend, and with reference to her tastes or wants held grave counsel as to what she would like best, thanking the girls earnestly for any suggestion.

They smiled to each other at his simplicity, and were almost ready to think him lost in trifles, till, entering a book-shop, he met with a great black-looking dusty quarto, on which he seized in transport, and was soon so deep in its contents, as to quite forget where he was. Kate, growing weary, peeped over, saw it was Greek, and drew back in awful respect; and they waited long, till, suddenly recollecting himself, Mr. Willoughby closed the book, and asked the price. It was thirty shillings. "Ah, I feared so," said he, sighing, looking lovingly at the title-page, and laying it down in despair, though his gifts had already cost twice the sum, and he was proceeding to spend as much more. Then turning to the sisters, he apologized so earnestly and humbly for having forgotten them, and kept them waiting, that they hardly knew which way to look.

Almost every mention of his parishioners was connected with his nephew. Frank had done this for one person, had given that to another, had reformed one naughty boy, had won the hearts of the whole parish. He was his right hand, almost his curate; he mended his clock, and made his man keep the garden in order—nay, the walking-stick in his hand was Frank's cutting

E

and curing for him: there was nothing which Frank had not
done, and to which he was not *apropos ;* and little Edwin was
soon brought to think that it would be the summit of human
felicity to go to Dumblethwayte with brother Frank and Uncle
Willoughby.

Everyone was sorry when Uncle Willoughby bade them good-
bye on Saturday morning; and the girls wished very much that
Lord Herbert could have known him, they would have liked
each other so much. And that a person would be *very much*
liked by Herbert, was the highest praise they could give him.

When the amusement of his visit was over, Emmeline and
Kate began to grow very tired of London, their few books, their
daily drive, and their mother's evening nap. They sometimes
talked of commencing some regular employment for the morning,
when their time was apt to hang on hand; but while they were
expecting a change, it did not seem worth while, nor had they
been long enough released from school to cease from feeling
loitering a luxury. So they idled, read a little, worked a little,
played with Cecilia, the beauty, and the most engaging of the
family, and looked in now and then on the school-room, when
they could do so without too much alarming Miss Townsend.

Alfred and Edwin were fast becoming civilized, and the
former could amuse himself so well and quietly, that it was no
penance to have him in the same room with his mamma; but
poor little Janet was whiter than ever, and whenever she was
taken from under Miss Townsend's wing, something was sure to
happen, which caused her to cry and to be banished. She was
by no means a popular child, and her sisters troubled themselves
very little about her.

They were obliged to entertain themselves extensively with
day-dreams; and in addition to the cottage, all chimneys, gable-
ends, and roses, and to the grand plans of charity and usefulness
in which Emmeline delighted to indulge, she had another which
no one but Kate should have heard for worlds, about a perfect
hero, " just like Herbert," as Kate said at first.

" Oh no, not like Herbert," said Emmeline; " at least, not

accustomed to England, and she could not find any absolute reason to prevent Sir Francis from taking a holiday.

He talked only of staying one week, but he was absent for three, during which he went to see Frank, made a visit to his brother, and looked at several houses, ending by taking by the year what called itself Bellevue, a marine villa on the outskirts of Herringsby, a small new watering-place on the coast of Lancashire.

He came home in high spirits, and nothing remained to be done but to pack up their property and set off. It seemed so tremendous an affair to Lady Willoughby, that her daughters wondered how she had ever been carried away from India; but at last, by very little personal interference on her part, and a great deal on her husband's, it was effected, and off they set.

Perhaps the impressions of the heroines of this story will be best conveyed by a letter to Lady Herbert Somerville, written about a week after their arrival.

MY DEAREST CONSTANCE,

Here we are settled at last: and here is a full account for you, which, as I venture to hope, will convey more ideas than Emmie's half-asleep letter the first day. Our house, which rejoices in the elegant name of Bellevue, does very well deserve it, for it stands high, and we have a very pretty irregular sort of lawn, from the top of which we can look over certain trees, houses, and hedges, and obtain a very respectable peep of the blue sea, most delicious to look upon ; while in the other direction we can see the grey cloudy heads of some of the Cumberland mountains, neighbours which we regard with awful reverence. In sight of mountains and sea, it makes us feel quite grand, and I expect Emmie will soon begin to write verses in such an atmosphere. Moreover, we have a species of modern Gothic battlemented tower, regarded by Janet with the utmost dread, as the abode of some giant who consumes naughty children, but whence the adventurous climbers may behold a beautiful view of the coast, with capes running far out into the sea, one stretching behind the other, and little white-sailed boats gliding over the waves. We are at about a quarter of a mile distant from the beach, which is a very satisfactory one, with nice smooth sand, where we can stand and lose ourselves in wonder at the mysterious tide, coming in with all its curling breaking waves ; and there are fine, bold, dark rocks, standing far out into the sea, and making promontories for the waves to dash and foam against ; little narrow coves and bays, too, shut in by rocks, where one may get away quite alone, and read or sketch. The children are down there half their time, dabbling after seaweed and shells, and building sand castles ; and they are all looking much more blooming already.

As to the garden, that is not much : there is a greenhouse, but very little in it, and we do not think we shall have time to take to it much. There is plenty of room in the house : two drawing-rooms, and a library, besides the school-room, and a great many bed-rooms. Ours is a very pleasant one, with a view of the mountains, and also a little bit of the old church spire, rising up among the slated roofs of the town.

The town is a mixture of new and old ; there is a High Street, with alternate shabby little old houses and great plate-glass shop windows ; and there are terraces and crescents and marine villas without end, all staring at the sea ; and the great smooth Marine Promenade, as they call it, where Mamma goes and drives up and down.

The churches are two, a new and an old one. Our pew is in the old one, which is not very pretty, though a great deal has been done of late with very good effect to embellish the east end. The vicar is a Mr. Brent, a middle-aged sort of man, with two curates, whose names I have not learnt yet ; he has choristers to chant the hymns, which we like very much, because of pleasant old Copesley recollections ; but our elders are not at all inclined to like him. He has called, but he does not go out in the evening, so I suppose we shall not see much of him. He has schools, &c., but he is said never to allow ladies to have anything to do with them ; very strange, is it not ? Indeed, he has done other very odd things, which I have not room to tell you.

There are some schools connected with the other church, however, where they will be very glad of our help ; there are two dear, funny, old, good little sisters, the Miss Shaws, who have undertaken to get us a time fixed for going to teach in the week, and a district appointed for us to visit. They are connections, in some roundabout way, of Frank's mother, and so we are obliged to be very civil to them, though I do not think Sir Francis was very much gratified by the discovery of the relationship.

There are great numbers of such houses as ours all through the neighbourhood ; quantities of people have called, and are still calling, and there are two invitations to dinner arrived already. Miss Berners was included in one, but she keeps resolutely to her vow of not coming out before me, which is so very kind of her, that I ought to be marvellously entertaining during the evenings we shall spend together.

Perhaps Mamma is telling you all that I have been writing, but never mind : I dare say you will not mind reading it twice over. We took great delight in your description of the Bay of Naples ; and one pleasure in it is, that your enjoying it so much was an excellent proof of Herbert's being better. We are longing for the account of Pompeii you have promised us : it will make us know ten times more about it than all the grand book descriptions. How I wish Mount Vesuvius would be so kind as to make an eruption while you are so near him ; but I am come to the end of my paper, and have only room for Emmie's message—that she thanks you for your letter, and hopes soon to write.

Your most affectionate Sister,

K. E. BERNERS.

Such were the intentions with which Emmeline and Kate began their residence at Herringsby. They seemed likely to have a good deal of leisure to themselves, as Lady Willoughby always spent the time between breakfast and luncheon in her own room, writing letters, or looking over dresses; and when Sir Francis was ready, as was usually the case, to drive out with her in the afternoon, there was no room for either of the girls, who were thus left quite at liberty to pursue what occupations they pleased.

The example of their sister and of Lady Frances made them think school-teaching the most dignified and delightful of tasks; and into it, therefore, they rushed with all possible speed and eagerness.

The first of their visitors whom they could consult were Miss Shaw and her sister, Miss Penelope, two good, bustling, active old ladies, both talking very fast, and seeming very much in earnest. Mr. Brent, the vicar, would not allow any interference with his schools, they said, but kept them entirely under the management of himself and his curates; and though they did not like, they said, to speak against anybody, they knew that he had been very uncivil to several excellent persons who had attempted visiting and instructing the poor in his district. Indeed, some tracts which they had themselves given, had been returned to them by Mr. Brent.

"It was with a very civil note, I must say," said Miss Shaw.

"Yes, that we must allow, civil to us personally; but nothing could excuse the thing itself. Ah! to see to what lengths party-spirit will go!" said Miss Penelope.

"And then," added Miss Shaw, "he positively turned good Mr. Denham out of poor John Andrews's house; he had been reading to him, and talking to him, and had brought him to the most desirable state of mind, when Mr. Brent interfered, caused a scene, which I am told was actually violent, in the poor man's own house, and finally induced the wife to prevent his ever gaining access to him again."

"Oh, my dears, pray have nothing to do with it," said Lady Willoughby; "I would not have you expose yourselves to anything unpleasant on any account."

"Very strange, indeed," said Emmeline; "I wish we were not in his district."

"Then we really shall not be able to do anything," said Kate, with a deep sigh.

"Oh, I assure you," cried Miss Penelope, "we cannot afford to lose you, my dear Miss Katherine : your assistance will be most valuable to us in our district. How delighted Mr. Hunter will be to see what excellent recruits we have brought to his work!"

"Delighted indeed," said Miss Shaw: "there is something so charming in this energetic spirit!"

This looks very like flattery, when written down; but it was all perfectly genuine, and came from the hearts of the good old ladies, as every feature of their little aquiline faces testified; there were dimples fixed into lines of a perpetual smile on the permanently red and rather yellow cheeks, and their heads seemed used to no occupation so much as nodding in acquiescence with each other.

"We will be just like them, when we are two cosy old maids," said Emmeline to her sister, as they were setting off to the Miss Shaws' house, by appointment, thence to be conducted to the school. They felt very good, and very useful, as they walked along, in the cheerful early summer sunshine, quite sure of their own good intentions, and without one doubt either of their own fitness for teaching, or whether they were setting about the work in the right way.

Mr. Brent met, bowed to them, and passed on.

"I do not like his looks," said Kate; "I am sure he cannot have a good temper."

"I should be sorry to think a man ill-tempered who preached a sermon like that one last Sunday," said Emmeline; "but perhaps people are not always conscious of their own defects."

"Well," said Kate, "I think I should preach most of all against a fault I was conscious of, in hopes to frighten it out of myself. But did you call that such a *very* good sermon, Emmie? It did not seem to me a very remarkable one, and it put Mamma to sleep."

"I will say, it is a remarkable sermon that keeps her awake," said Emmeline drily. Kate laughed, and there was a little silence, after which Emmeline went on : "I have remembered something out of each sermon of Mr. Brent's that I have heard, and that is not usual with me; but I agree with you, Kate, that he has nothing prepossessing about him."

"People ought either to have Herbert's high-bred courtesy, or else good old Mr. Willoughby's sunny, open-hearted benevolence," said Kate; "there is no medium. And I am sure, by all accounts, Mr. Brent has been neither courteous, gentleman-like, nor kind-hearted in his dealings."

"Yet they all talk of his excellence," said Emmeline; "but I must say, I cannot understand how it is possible for a man who pretends to charity, to be a stickler for etiquettes of boundaries of parishes and districts."

"His charity must have a very narrow boundary indeed," said Kate, "and must decidedly begin at home."

Considering the inexperience of the sisters, and the information they had received, this impression was more to be lamented than wondered at; but if they had talked less about it, its effects would have been less mischievous.

It was about three-quarters of a mile to Miss Shaw's house, and the walk led them partly through pleasant path-fields and partly through the town, on the broad flags in front of the new houses, the fresh sea-breeze blowing upon them, and the wide expanse of waves sparkling far away in the distance ; and Emmeline, with her head full of the good and great things she was going to do, had never felt more joyous or more fully satisfied. It was the very moment when "Virtue is its own reward."

Soon the ladies were pouring their affectionate greetings into their ears, and shaking them by both hands.

It would be in vain to repeat how much they said of kindness and pleasure, and the advantage to the children, and of Mr. and Mrs. Hunter's satisfaction, and Mr. Denham's, and Mrs. Anderson's. Emmeline and Kate felt themselves conferring

a great favour, and were proportionably happy. They looked
round the room, and admired. It was like a penny-club office;
there were business-like-looking large parchment books, and
small red-leather ones; there was a great lending-library book-
case, with the top shelf covered with bundles of little tracts,
in covers of all the colours of the rainbow; there were long
lists of names and numbers upon cards; the corner was filled
up with bundles of poor people's clothes and rolls of list; the
chimney-piece ornamented with missionary boxes and cards for
shilling and penny subscriptions; and each good lady had a
great basket full of poor-work.

" You seem to have an immense quantity of occupation,"
said Emmeline.

" Why, yes, my dear," said Miss Shaw: " you see we have
nothing else to do, and we are very glad of it."

" And how very useful it must be!" added Kate.

" Why, my dear," said Miss Penelope, with her usual laugh
and nod at her sister, " everyone must give what they can, and
as we have got no money and plenty of time—you see we give
what we have."

" And to give time is much more and better than money,"
said Emmeline.

" Quite true, my dear Miss Emmeline, quite right," said both
the sisters together, as pleased with "the sweet girl's" views, as
if her truism had proceeded from the profoundest wisdom.

" Ah! we shall never be like you," said Kate, " but—"

There came a confused chorus of sincere disclaimers of any
real merit in what they did, of which " Oh, don't say so!" was
the most prominent expression.

Then Kate returned to beg to hear what she and Emmeline
could do.

" We have very little money," said she, hesitatingly; "but
Emmeline and I can give a sovereign a year between us, to
anything you would tell us of. We don't like to promise
more," she added, smiling and colouring; "for though Sir
Francis is very kind, and makes us quantities of presents, we

have not much of an allowance of our own, because we are to be rather poor, I believe."

It had been agreed upon beforehand that Kate, as the boldest, should make this speech; but they need not have questioned how it was to be done, for the Miss Shaws were delighted both with their generosity and candour. The pound was divided into various small subscriptions; and the girls received a bundle of children's clothes to be made up, and some little books to give away; after which they all set out together for the school.

It was a very large room, airy and fresh, with a great number of children ranged in squares, and at present at work. Emmeline and Kate were to come, if they could, every Tuesday and Thursday afternoon, and each take a class; but it was now too late to do anything but look round, inspect the work a little, and observe which of the children had pretty faces. What were they to teach the children, was Kate's question, and certainly an expedient one. They were to hear them repeat their texts or hymns, give them others to learn, or let them read a chapter in the Bible, and explain it.

"In fact," said Miss Penelope, as they left the school, "we allow great latitude to our kind afternoon assistants. So many have been lost by too rigidly insisting on rules, and everyone is not so willing to be guided as you and your sister, my dear Miss Katherine.

"I do assure you," said Kate, "that you must not think we know much about it. All that we have ever had to do with school-keeping, was in that short visit to my sister at Copseley."

"Ah! but that was everything! Everything, I am sure. Besides, it is the desire, the will, more than anything else. Dear me! I often think what a happiness it is, that it is the wish and the heart—or what should we be good for?"

"What, indeed!" responded Miss Shaw, smiling and nodding her head in unison with a little laugh of humility.

The next thing was to show them "their district," a countrified street, comparatively clean, and without the fishy smell of

the lower part of the town.   They went to one house, where
the girls, who had heard of such things as reading and praying
with the poor, and were afraid it was incumbent upon them,
were very glad to find that all the Miss Shaws did, was to hold
a good-natured gossiping colloquy with the woman about her
husband's work, and other matters of the same description.

They then wished the little ladies good-bye, and returned
home in high spirits, as well they might at discovering such an
excellent receipt for obtaining a good opinion of themselves.

CHAPTER VI.

Go, the rich chariot instantly prepare,
The Queen, my Muse, will take the air.
Cowley.

"I THINK, my dears," said Lady Willoughby, as she finished
dressing to go out to dinner, "I think it would be a good thing
if you were to ask Miss Townsend to come and sit in the drawing-room with you this evening.   It would be a pleasant thing
for you, and she would like it, poor thing: I am sure she
must be moped with spending all her time in the school-room."

"Yes, Mamma, we will," answered Emmeline, recollecting,
with a little compunction, her intentions of taking great pains
to be kind to Miss Townsend, whereas all that she had done
was to speak civilly to her whenever she came in her way, and,
once or twice, to carry her the newspaper or some flowers.

"We certainly will," added Kate.   "As you say, Mamma,
she must be getting moped.   Did you not see how she cried
almost all last Sunday?"

"What could be the matter?   Poor thing!" said Lady
Willoughby.

"I had a great mind to ask her," said Emmeline; "but we
knew she would only say it was nothing, and shrink away.   But
did you not see, Mamma, all through afternoon service?"

"Dear me!" said Lady Willoughby, "I hope she is not going to get low-spirited, hysterical, or anything of that sort, for she is a real treasure, and manages the children to perfection!"

"Oh, I dare say it is only being so lonely here by herself, poor thing!" said Emmeline. "I am sure I could often have cried when I was at school, and what must it be to be away from everyone, without even a sister?"

"It will never do!" continued Lady Willoughby. "Sir Francis would be much vexed. So bad for the children to have a low-spirited person about them."

"No, no, don't be uneasy, Mamma," said Kate; "she is always cheerful with them, I assure you she is: and we will cheer her up, and do all we can to brighten her. I will go this minute and ask her to come down."

Kate ran quickly to the school-room, where Miss Townsend, with a book in her hand, was watching the three children building a tall lantern-tower with wooden bricks. Alfred, as the steadiest hand, was raising the edifice, which began to reach a giddy height, Janet supplying him with materials, and looking at his progress with breathless interest, and little Edwin sitting by, also holding out bricks, but when Alfred did not take them quickly enough, secretly making threatening thrusts with them at the walls, with a droll sly face of mischievous glee, as if trying how near he could go without being found out.

Suddenly, just as Kate was saying, "Well done, Alfred, that is a beauty indeed!" Edwin's hand glided along on a slippery brick, his weapon penetrated the frail wall, and down came the tower almost covering him with the ruins.

There was a start of consternation; then Alfred angrily exclaimed, "Edwin did it!" and Janet put out her lip, and drew up her face for a cry. Kate had designs of retreating from the quarrel and scolding that she saw impending, but she was curious to see how it would turn out.

"You did it on purpose, you naughty child!" cried Alfred.

"'Twas very cross of you!" sobbed Janet.

"I didn't!" cried Edwin fiercely.

"Hush! hush! my dears," said Miss Townsend, coming forward, and taking Edwin by the hand. "Edwin, you must come away if you spoil the others' play. I hope you are not an ill-natured little boy, and that you did not mean to do it."

"No," said Edwin, "my hand slipped."

"Well, then, kiss Alfred, and tell him you are sorry. Alfred, you recollect what you told me this morning?"

Alfred stood as if he was trying to gulp something down, then suddenly turning round, he readily received and returned Edwin's kiss, himself kicked away the foundations of his tower, and said cheerfully, "Never mind, Janet, don't cry, we will build it up again in no time. Come, Edwin, you be mason's man."

"It will never be so tall again!" whined Janet, deplorably.

"Yes, it shall," said Alfred. "Why, don't be silly, Janet— crying will never build it up."

Still Janet cried, or rather fretted, for it was not absolutely crying.

"Come, Janet," said Miss Townsend, cheerfully. "I thought you were going to be a brave little woman. There is your sister Kate, you must not treat her to a crying fit now she is come to visit you."

"We have never made it so high before!" Janet went on.

"Yes, it was a great pity," said Miss Townsend; "but you know we must try and be brave when we are sorry—try and have self-command."

"Have I self-command now?" said Janet, trying to bring her crying face out of its puckers, in such a droll way that Kate could hardly help laughing; but she wondered, as she said to herself, "Are these the same children that teased us two months ago? What fine fellows the boys are, and how beautifully they made it up!" Wherewith she sat down on the ground among them, and gave her counsel and active assistance in the re-construction of the tower, talking merrily to the children, and making her visit a regular treat. She asked Miss Townsend's leave to take Alfred down to drink tea with her and Emmeline, to reward him for his good behaviour; and then said, in her bright courteous way, " We hope you will always come to sit with us, in our solitude, when they are gone out."

Miss Townsend looked up with something of pleasure and something of surprise. "Thank you," said she; " if you are so kind, I shall be very glad."

"Then we shall see you this evening," said Kate. " Come, Alfred."

" Thank you," again said Miss Townsend. " As soon as the children are gone to bed."

" Provoking woman!" said Kate to herself, as she left the room; "why will she not let us put her on an equality? it would be much more convenient!"

Little Janet stood amongst her bricks, looking after her sister, in her eyes one of the most beautiful, happy, and privileged creatures in the world, one who never cried, who had no lessons to learn, dined down-stairs with Papa and Mamma, who might go where she pleased, who could talk about that great bright mystery to Janet's imagination, sister Constance, and whose notice was itself a sort of happiness. Poor little Janet, there was a sore undefined sense of injustice, when she saw Alfred praised and led off in triumph, while she, conscious of a grand struggle and victory, was scarcely even spoken to. She turned her large dark eyes upon her governess with a sort of piteous appealing look, and in another moment would have found something to fret about, had not Miss Townsend come cheerfully forward, and diverted the course of her thoughts by calling on her and Edwin to put away their bricks, and promising them a story afterwards. " Who could shovel up the most bricks in one handful?" " Oh, Edwin, those fat hands are over-loaded! Down they go!" " That is right, careful Janet, slow and sure! Your basket will be full first, after all!" " Take care, Edwin, don't be rude." " Did you ever hear of the Hare and the Tortoise?"

"Oh, no, tell me that story," said Edwin.

"When you have finished putting the bricks away. Don't

leave Janet to do them all alone. There, well done. Drag the
basket away between you. That's right."

And soon there were the children leaning against her on each
side, looking up in her face, while in the most circumstantial
way she told the story of the celebrated race, dwelling very
nearly on every step of the tortoise's progress, so that the
children seemed to have their whole hearts engrossed in the
story. Janet clapped her hands when the tortoise at last reached
the goal; but Edwin held that if he had been the hare, he
would have gone to sleep with one eye open, and have yet
overtaken the tortoise. Miss Townsend did not attempt to
reason with the varlet, whose opinion, as she saw, was taken up
for the sake of argument; she was contented with the story
having occupied and encouraged Janet.

Miss Townsend felt brightened that evening ; there was something in the Miss Berners' notice almost as pleasant to her as
it was to Janet, and though a little afraid of them, it was a
treat to spend an evening elsewhere than in that one room, and
with other companions than her own thoughts. There was also
a prospect of more pleasant hours to be spent with them, to
invigorate her for the spirit-wearing work of the day ; and might
not this lead to more intimacy ? sufficient to overcome her own
foolish shyness, and encourage her to talk about the children to
them, so as to convince them that poor little Janet would well
repay a little more notice, and that they did harm by always
preferring her brothers.

And above all, did not this invitation open a way to her to
make a request which would relieve her of a heavy burthen !
There was weekly Communion at Mr. Brent's church, and Miss
Townsend had been used to know the benefits of that great
privilege ; she looked to it as the means of strength and of grace,
and dreaded to turn away and neglect the call. She had had no
opportunity since she entered upon her present situation, until
they came to Herringsby ; but there she had the charge of the
two elder children at church in the morning, and knew not how
to dispose of them. The servants sat in a distant part of the

church, and besides, were not inclined to be very courteous to
the poor little governess ; and though Sir Francis never remained
on ordinary Sundays, and she knew the Miss Berners were
unconfirmed, her invincible timidity added to her natural
reluctance to enter on the subject with them. It was this that
had been the occasion of her tears on Sunday, feeling herself
debarred from the great blessing of which she longed to partake,
blaming herself for not acting a bolder part, and conscious, more
than she had ever before been, of loneliness and friendlessness.
But now she had hopes of being able to venture to beg the Miss
Berners to take the little ones home, or even, what would be too
delightful almost to be hoped for, they might make the offer
unasked.

Miss Townsend's spirits rose with the hope, which began to
increase when Alfred came to bed in high glee at the various
delights he had enjoyed with his sisters ; and when she had
heard him repeat his evening prayer, and bidden him good night,
she looked out her company-work, her little bit of crochet, and
prepared to descend, without even sighing as she looked at her
bag, the parting gift of a sickly sister.

In the mean time, as soon as Alfred had wished them good
night, the sisters had taken out their bundles of garments, and
their needles. Perhaps it was from not having been used to it
at school, that they had rather an affection for plain work, and
liked the bright polished needle, the long white thread, and neat
stitches, so that the small pink and blue frocks with which Miss
Shaw had provided them, were more attractive to them than
their purse-netting and Berlin work.

Just then came in the late post, and a long letter from
Constance was given to Kate. Much did it say of the sights of
Naples, which all the travellers, including Lord Herbert, were
enjoying greatly ; and Constance spoke much of the pleasure of
hearing them talked over by her fellow-travellers. At the end
came an answer to what Kate had said of her present designs.

" It is very good of you to send us so many particulars about
Heringsby ; I should like to be able to fancy the room where you

F

are all sitting, and what you are doing every hour of the day; but I must just tell you what Herbert said to the latter part of your letter. When I read to him about your plans for district visiting, &c., he said, ' Ah! that will not *do*,' and he thinks it would be safer, at your age especially, not to engage in such matters without the full sanction of the clergyman of the parish. Another thing that he says, is that he hopes you are not listening to all the stories that are sure to float about a place like Herringsby, respecting the clergyman; and he thinks that if he were in Mr. Brent's place, he might probably do things which you would consider quite as odd, even perhaps not allowing his school-children to be taught by chance visitors, whom he could not very well examine, to see if their doctrine was safe."

This was rather a chill to the girls for a moment, but Emmeline quickly recovered it, saying, " Oh, you know we have Mr. Hunter's sanction, and he is the clergyman of the parish in which we visit; I must tell Constance so, and that must be what Herbert means."

" Of course," said Kate, " no reasonable person could mean otherwise."

" Oh yes," said Emmeline, " the full particulars must satisfy him completely, and I will write and give them. Ah! and as to doing things as odd as Mr. Brent, Herbert little knows what his ways are. He would not have done anything so discourteous as sending back the tracts to the good old Miss Shaws."

" And just fancy Herbert turning the kind gentleman out of the poor man's house !" said Kate; " or refusing that whole starving family the least assistance because the woman went in the evening sometimes to a prayer-meeting."

" Or turning out that poor boy from his choir because he did not turn to the East one day," said Emmeline.

" Yes," said Kate, " we must tell Herbert all this, and then he would think us justified."

" I tell you what he would think," said Emmeline, " that we have been listening to more stories. The truth is, Kate, that it is quite impossible for anyone to judge without being on the spot and knowing all the circumstances. Just fancy letting that sweet-looking little girl, that Alice, grow up in ignorance, and half clothed, only because Mr. Brent chooses to set his face against anyone but himself doing anything."

"Certainly, that child has one of the loveliest faces I ever saw," said Kate, "and the north-country dialect sounded so very pretty in her mouth."

And her simplicity was so nice when she said she used to go to school, but she could not now, because father had had words with Mr. Brent," said Emmeline.

"Ah, that was no vague floating story," said Kate, "when we had it from the very child's own mouth. How delightful the teaching her will be!"

"We will have her once a week for two or three years," said Emmeline, "and that will raise and refine her; she has a great deal of natural refinement already, don't you observe it, Kate, in her manner of addressing one? We will bring her on, and see her mind grow, and then we will get Mamma to let us have her for our own little maid, and she will be almost a friend. And then, O Kate, when we settle and build our beautiful Elizabethan school, she shall be the mistress, and she shall—"

As Emmeline was in the full swing of her animated description, a slow timid step crossed the outer drawing-room, and Miss Townsend stood at the door. The eager voices were instantly stilled, and there was a sort of momentary blank, of which no one was so painfully conscious as the poor little author of the interruption.

There was no want of civility on the part of the girls, however; Emmeline hastened to set a chair near the table, and Kate asked if she liked having the window open.

"Oh yes—yes—thank you—oh, thank you," said the low frightened voice; and then followed a dead calm.

"How hot it has been all day!" presently said Emmeline, in the formal tone with which she used to address visitors in the presence of Miss Danby.

" Yes, very."

" I suppose you did not walk far to-day," said Kate.

" Only on the beach, it is always cool there."

" And the children enjoy it so much," said Kate.

" Yes, very much, indeed."

Then came another silence ; Emmeline began to grow restless under it, walked to the window, leant out, wondered if it was much warmer at Naples, drew in her head again, and returned to her work.

Kate, glad of the mention of Naples, spoke of her letter; Miss Townsend hoped Lord Herbert was better, and Lady Herbert quite well ; and Kate, having begun on the subject, read aloud what she called " the traveller's wonder" part of her letter. Miss Townsend was interested, and very much pleased, but she took it for granted that the Miss Berners knew so much more about Pompeii than herself, that they grew ashamed of seeming to lay down the law about antiquities, and let the conversation drop once more.

Kate tried to revive it again, after a little interval, by saying how very well Alfred and Edwin had behaved about their little quarrel. Miss Townsend, anxious to say a good word for poor little Janet, ventured to observe that she had made a great effort to be good.

" Poor child, I dare say she did," said Kate ; " but she will not be presentable till her efforts are rather less apparent."

This was cold water, indeed, upon Miss Townsend, who stifled a sigh of disappointmemt, hooked away with her crochet-needle, and wished she could dare to say a word to controvert the speech, which, given as it was with a gay jesting air by the light-hearted Kate, had something in it which to her seemed hard and almost unfeeling.

Emmeline did not mend the matter by saying, in a tone of commiseration, that she wished Janet were more engaging, but she began to think, with the old school-mistress at Copseley, that boys had always better tempers than girls.

Now they had arrived at Copseley, there was plenty to say

between the two sisters, and on they talked about Margaret
Forester, and her house, and her school, and Lord Herbert's
arrangements in his curacy, and their regret that he had been
obliged to give it up. They talked, and Miss Townsend listened
—a plan which suited both parties very well ; and the wheels of
time did not move quite so heavily between nine and ten, as
they had between half-past eight and nine. Nevertheless,
Emmeline and Kate agreed, that if all their evenings at home
were to be like this one, the sooner they came out the better ;
and as Miss Townsend returned to her own room, there was at
least as much disappointment as gratification in her feelings.

She knew that the two sisters were very happy alone, and
though grateful to them for wishing to be kind to her, she
could not bear to come down and be an encumbrance to them,
so she resolved not to join them again in the evening without
another invitation. Kate thought she had asked once for all ;
and the next evening that Sir Francis and Lady Willoughby
dined out, the two sisters began doubly to enjoy the time
which they looked upon as their own, expecting it to be very
short. They fetched their work, and Emmeline placed a paper
before her, on which was a half-composed poem about a "fisherman's child," a ballad in numerous stanzas, which were now just
ready for Kate's advice and admiration. Kate was a most
delightful critic, for she never failed to see what Emmeline
meant—admired with her whole heart—was a capital finder of
rhymes, and remodeller of lines, and could even, on occasion,
insert a whole stanza, which no one would have known from
Emmeline's own.

No less than four times had " the blue-eyed fisherman's
daughter" been made to look forth upon the stormy water ; and
as many times had the sea-fowl's cry, so loud and dreary, replied
to her fainting call and weary, when the clock struck nine, and
Kate, looking up, wondered at the lateness, and supposed Miss
Townsend would not come down that night.

" You gave her a general invitation," said Emmeline.

"Oh yes, that I did ; I wonder she does not come."

" I suppose she finds it as great a penance as we did," said Emmeline.

" I suppose so," said Kate. " Well—

'And o'er the raging water's swell.' "

The raging waters had by no means been satisfactorily lulled, when the clock struck ten, unregarded; and the "broken bark and dripping crew" had not yet reached their home in safety, when Sir Francis and Lady Willoughby reached theirs, and wondered at finding their daughters up so late.

The teaching at the school was to begin on the next Thursday, and Emmeline and Kate set off together, refusing an invitation of their mamma's to take a drive with her. Soon they were at the school, the mistress receiving them very politely, and the monitors setting chairs for them.

Emmeline, eagerly as she had undertaken the work, began to wish herself anywhere else, when she found herself sitting up in the midst of a square of girls, who seemed all eyes, staring at her, and that not in the shy unsophisticated way in which village children gaze at the unusual apparition of a stranger, but with the bold searching looks of town children, used to a variety of teachers, and with no awful reverence for the name of lady. And what in the world could she, or should she, say to them? She recollected how at Copseley, Lord Herbert had put the book into her hand, shown her the portion she was to hear, and told the children that he hoped she would be able to tell him they had been very attentive. That was teaching under authority, and what was this? · Though she did not quite ask herself this question, she could not but be sensible of the difference.

All she could do was to reverse the usual order of things, and asked the head girl what they had to say to her.

" Our texts, teacher," was the answer, in a pert ready tone; and out came a card containing a number of texts, each framed in a scolloped border, which the girls proceeded to repeat, one after the other, very fast, and dwelling on the references to chapter and verse—Corinthians, Ephesians, twenty-third chapter, sixth verse, &c.—as if these were by far the most important and remarkable parts of the lesson, while the most sacred names were slurred over without any of those outward tokens of reverence which Emmeline had learnt to think their necessary adjunct; nay, she even thought there was an inclination on the part of the girls to look at one another, and smile, when she herself bowed her head.

The repetition was over, and she wondered what was to come next, or whether the texts were chosen with reference to any particular subject, for they seemed to her to be all gathered by chance, and to have little or no connexion. Seeing her at a loss, the head girl looked at the others, some of whom seemed ready to titter, and said, "Teacher expounds."

Teacher had not the least idea how to expound, but being obliged to do something, she looked at the first text, which was, "Let me die the death of the righteous, and let my last end be like his," and asked if they knew who said it?

"Numbers, twenty-third chapter, tenth verse," was the first answer she received.

Here was something to begin upon, and she proceeded to ask whether they thought Numbers was a man. The upper ones laughed, and said no, it was a book; some of them knew who wrote the book, and what it was about. And then she came to the history of Balaam, with which it was possible to get on very well, and it occupied her very tolerably till she saw Kate standing up in the midst of her class, looking ready for her to make a move to come away. Kate had had some hymns to hear, and these had taken up so much time, that she had no leisure to feel as awkward as her sister had done, and was pleased, on the whole, with her day's work. Emmeline was, however, resolved to go next time with some plan in her head, and not to be left to the mercy of the class, or to be called upon to discourse on texts at a moment's warning, a work which, she was quite sure, Lord Herbert would never have set her to do.

She resolved, but not very fully, for, after talking over half a dozen plans with Kate, she went to school the next Tuesday without having settled upon any, and the texts were again brought out. The first was, this time, from one of the Epistles, and there was, therefore, none of that history belonging to it which had served her so well on the former occasion ; so she decided, in haste, on the first of her plans that came into her head, and asked if they had said the Catechism that day?

"No." And the girls stared.

Emmeline took out her Prayer-Book, meaning to go straight through, and then question them upon it ; but she found that these, though the head girls, were very far from having anything like a proper knowledge of it ; they made numerous mistakes, and when she seemed surprised, the foremost girl said that they only repeated it once a week, and not always the whole of it then.

Emmeline was quite glad to find a line she could take, and something positive to be done ; she told the girls she should hear them again next time, and hoped they would be more perfect, and then to stimulate them more, told them what little children she had seen at Copseley saying it without missing a word. They smiled, and seemed to like to hear her, for the great gentleness and refinement of Emmeline's manners were exactly calculated to win the attention of even these girls, who had been used to little like them.

"Yes," said Emmeline to Kate, as they went home, "it is just the thing for us to do, since no one else takes any pains about the Catechism."

"I wonder how they can teach without it," said Kate ; "it is not at all like Copseley."

"No ; I suppose it is from their having so many teachers and allowing them such great latitude, as Miss Penelope calls it ; everyone teaches what she pleases, and we will take the Catechism on our hands. I have got a little book about it somewhere, I am sure, which we used to learn when we were at Mrs. Ellison's."

"And we may learn plenty of questions to ask them, by listening to Mr. Brent's catechizing in the afternoon service," said Kate.

"Yes, that he certainly does well," said Emmeline. "I am sure I can see nothing to object to in his ways in church, whatever other people may say. But come, shall we go to any of our poor people, or is it too late?"

The sisters liked to say "our poor people," and they really did like one old man, one woman, and three children, in their district. The old man was half blind, very thankful to them for reading to him, and more fond of telling them how the place had altered within his recollection; the woman was a cheerful, thankful, contented body, who liked a chat with anyone, gentle or simple. And of the children, one was the Alice whom they designed for a heroine; another was a fat, laughing baby; and the third, a poor little gentle blind child.

These they went often to visit, but the others they did not like: there was a woman who smoked a pipe; there was a discourteous woman, who always seemed to wish them out of her house; there was an untidy woman, out of whose house they always wished themselves; there was a woman who, as Mr. Hunter had warned them, did not tell the truth; there was a whining woman, who tried to extract shillings from them by deplorable stories; there was a woman who always fancied her children were ill-used at school; and there was a scolding woman of whom they were positively afraid, she used so to rail against everyone concerned in any of the charities of the place, who, according to her, were always combined to do her injustice.

CHAPTER VII.

No, cast by fortune on a frowning coast,
Which neither groves nor happy valleys boast,
Where other cares than those the muse relates,
And other Shepherds dwell with other mates,
By such examples taught, I paint the cot
As truth will paint it, and as bards will not.
                                        Crabbe.

IN the mean time the family had settled down into the way of
life which seemed likely to be usual with it. Breakfast-time
was called nine, but the meal was seldom over till past ten ; for
though Sir Francis was always punctual, would have the urn in
exactly at the right moment, and always himself began breakfast
with the girls, Lady Willoughby was seldom down-stairs till
considerably later, and as she was very delicate in her proceedings, it lasted an unbearable time.

Emmeline and Kate could not bear it, and used to make their
escape, tea-maker though the former was, and though they knew
that their absence was not liked.

Their stroll generally lasted till they had reason to think Sir
Francis would soon be coming out to look at a certain ornamental
fence which he was having made, and which he would be sure
to ask them to come and visit ; and then there was no end to
what they would have to hear about wood, paint, railings, and
patterns.

From the fence, he walked into the town to choose the fish
for dinner, and looked at the newspapers at the reading-room.
Lady Willoughby was in her own room, and the girls were free
to draw, read, or practise their music, as they pleased.

When Sir Francis came home, but before luncheon, he was
sure to be "*put out*" if there were more books or papers about
the room than he approved ; and it was a time, too, when he
used to see ways of improving the arrangement of the furniture,
so that the little quiet, comfortable nooks of the sisters were

continually liable to be demolished, and they used to congratulate themselves when the piano was allowed to remain in the same place for a week together.

Luncheon was another long affair, and it was a " white day " when there was no fault found with the cookery. Kate and Emmeline very seldom saw the end of it, for they had a horror of being caught and kept in by a succession of visitors, and hastened out of doors as fast as they could, to their school, their poor people, to take their work to the Miss Shaws, or to enjoy a little idleness by the sea-shore.

The children were always in the drawing-room before dinner, and Alfred and Janet came in at dessert. When they went to bed, Lady Willoughby liked to be read to, out of some circulating library book, and this was very pleasant in itself, only that there was so little time in the evening, that they proceeded very slowly, and Emmeline and Kate generally knew the whole story to the end before she had heard half through the first volume.

Then came tea, and Sir Francis. Emmeline and Kate tried to make reading compatible with hearing him talk, but were generally obliged to give it up in despair. Now and then he told something entertaining, but more often he went prosing on interminably about what he had read in the newspaper, or his plans of buying an estate, or his fence, till sometimes even Kate, the most enduring, could bear it no longer, and used, at the first pause, to ask her mamma if she would not like some music.

Emmeline could not help feeling, with a soreness of heart, that she and her sister were as much alone together, and as entirely dependent on each other, as they had been at school. There was no real companionship from anyone else ; and though they were very happy and sufficient for one another, it was disappointing to recollect her hope. Without her sister, Kate would have been more generally obliging, and less fault-finding ; but then, on the other hand, she would have grown entirely into the tone of the people with whom she lived, and never have known any of those aspirations for the true, the good, the great, the beautiful, which she shared with Emmeline, and which, though fitful, failing, and often misdirected, were nevertheless a straining after the course which alone could lift them above the things of this present life.

The middle of the summer came, and brought with it Frank Willoughby's holidays. He arrived on a Saturday afternoon, looking very bluff, rosy, and good-natured, with his child's face on his great boy's person, and seemed very happy and joyous, and ready to treat them all as if he had known them all his life. Everyone, excepting Lady Willoughby; but though he was always remarkably polite and attentive to her, the more softly and affectionately she addressed him, the more shy and embarrassed he grew.

On Sunday morning, on the way to church, Frank was walking with Emmeline and Alfred.

"Who is that behind with Janet?" said Frank.

"Miss Townsend," said Emmeline.

"I thought so, only you seemed to have sent her to Coventry."

"She is so shy, poor thing, it only is a pain to her to be spoken to."

"I suppose I must put her to that pain some time or other. Shall I now? The sooner the better. Come, introduce me, Emmeline; do it genteelly."

"I assure you, Frank, there is no occasion for it; it would make her think we were laughing at her."

"Why, I thought you went to school to 'larn manners,' or were they an extra?"

Emmeline laughed. "I tell you we never do introduce people to her, it would only distress her."

"I don't want you to introduce people; I want you only to introduce me. So you don't know how! Well, I should have thought you would have done your fine school more credit! I must take myself in my hand and introduce myself."

Emmeline was really alarmed lest he might intend to make game of the poor little governess, and began anxiously, "But, Frank, I beg you won't do anything to annoy her. You don't know what a frightened creature it is."

Frank shrugged his shoulders as if in disregard, and Emmeline began to think what dreadful things school-boys were, so reckless of anyone's feelings, when, as they stood still, Miss Townsend and Janet came up.

All Frank did was, however, to hold out his hand, and say, "Good morning!" Miss Townsend certainly did look very much surprised, and answered in her breathless way; and with this Frank seemed satisfied, let Janet take his hand, and went on with her and Alfred, while Emmeline found herself obliged to walk a little way by Miss Townsend, and observe upon the fineness of the day, &c. She was obliged to perceive that Frank had acted from a sense of the courtesy due to Miss Townsend, and very much surprised she was; but she was to find more subjects of surprise in her step-brother before she in any degree guessed at his real character.

They missed him when they had all left the church, and returned home, the walking party having supposed he was with the carriage, and Lady Willoughby and Emmeline, who had driven back together, being surprised that he did not appear with the walkers. Sir Francis fidgeted about him, fancied he had found some acquaintance, or else had missed them, and lost his way; but at last, just as luncheon was half over, in walked Frank, looking as brisk and happy as possible.

"Where have you been?" was Sir Francis's instant inquiry.

"At church, Sir," answered Frank.

"Oh—what—staying?" said Sir Francis. "Ah, Frank, your uncle has made you his own nephew."

To which Frank made no answer.

It was a pleasanter Sunday evening than usual. The children were down-stairs, and Frank helped Edwin and Cecilia to set up their Noah's Ark, making absurd speeches about the birds and beasts; and when they were gone to bed, Lady Willoughby to sleep, and Sir Francis into the "Times," the girls went out to stroll in the garden, whither Frank soon followed them, and began asking questions about the two churches, the name of the Vicar, &c.

It was not to be supposed that such an opportunity of telling the stories against Mr. Brent could be missed, and they were fast poured out; but there must have been a strong spirit of contradiction in Frank, for all he said to the turning out of Mr. Denham, which was always the head and front of his offences, was, "Served him right."

"O Frank! when he was reading so kindly to the poor sick man."

"Poor sick man, indeed! why, I am sure I should be obliged to anyone for keeping Mr. I don't know who from marching up into my bed-room at all manner of times, and reading me to death."

"But this was a poor man," said Kate.

"Well, and do you think poor men have not their feelings as well as rich men?"

Kate found that she was not getting the best of it in this argument, so she shifted her ground, and proceeded to the tract story.

"I dare say the people were glad to be saved the trouble of reading them," said unreasonable Frank.

"It is of no use to talk to him, Kate," said Emmeline; "he is bent on defending Mr. Brent through thick and thin."

"Of course," said Frank. "What else should I do?"

"If you knew anything about it," said Kate.

"How much do you know?" said Frank, turning his round blue eyes upon her with a roguish look.

"There is no answer to that," said Emmeline, for 'everyone' is an authority which, of course, it is not worth while to quote."

"Can one get to the top of that tower?" exclaimed Frank, suddenly quitting the subject.

"Yes, to be sure," said Kate; "the door is open, and there are the stairs, only it is very dusty work."

Frank ran towards it, and in another minute was hailing them from the top of the tower. Making a fantastic bow, he cut a caper in the middle, gazed all round, then disappeared again, and presently, with a great effort, compelled the rusty hinges of a small pointed-arched window to open, called out, "Here is such a famous lot of bats!"

"I should think so!" said Emmeline.

"It is a very nice room," said Frank. "Why don't you have it cleaned up, and sit in it?"

"I do think it would be a capital plan!" cried Kate.

"So it would," said Emmeline; adding, in a half-whisper to her sister, "we should be out of the way of company, and Sir Francis too."

Frank presently came forth again, with something under his handkerchief, which proved to be a bat—a creature of which the sisters had never before had so near a view—and they were delighted to look at its velvet ears, sharp eyes, clever-looking face, and strange wings. Emmeline said it put her in mind of some unearthly monster, and she thought nothing could be more appropriate to ruins and twilight hours, than this weird-like thing; and then lines began to float through her mind of some wild "song of the bat," when the awkward recollection occurred to her that bats are not in the habit of singing.

"What are you going to do with it?" said Kate, in some dread of school-boy cruelties.

"Do you want any more of it?" said Frank. "Then there!" and he threw the bat up high in the air, where they could see its dark form flitting about with its rapid and silent flight, now visible against the still bright blue sky, now lost against the darker trees.

They were sorry when Sir Francis put his head out of the window and ordered them all to come in out of the dew.

Frank attended his father's inspection of the fence the next morning, but as soon as he was released from it, he was off to the tower. Emmeline and Kate could not help leaving their avocations to come and see what he was about. He was in all the glory of an immense rummaging, poking out rubbish of all sorts, of which the unfortunate place had been made the depository—broken bottles, dilapidated brooms, old garden tools, and scraps of carpet—nearly choked with dust, and yet declaring,

and they concurred with him, that nothing could be more
" nice " than the place was.

Miss Townsend had a real holiday that afternoon, while her
three charges were in the extreme of happiness, helping their
brother and sisters at the tower, carrying off the rubbish, the
more charming because it was so very dusty, wheeling it off,
and discovering strange treasures in it. There were Emmeline
and Kate pulling out the hoards of dirty rubbish with their
dainty little hands ; and there was Frank, busiest of all, con-
triving schemes for the renewal of the apartment. Never were
people happier than those six, more especially when Kate was sent
on an embassy to the housemaid, to borrow a broom, and all in
turn essayed sweeping. Nor was the sport less the next day,
when Frank set himself to repair the deficiencies in the wood-
work ; and the tower was the great delight of all the holidays,
for there never failed to be something to contrive there, or
something to admire.

The girls sometimes wondered what Frank would have done
without it, for he was not much of a reader, seldom opened
even the books which they accounted most entertaining, and did
not seem to have many pursuits of his own. They were surprised that he was so pleasant a companion ; and perhaps they
would have been still more surprised to find that, often as they
thought him very odd and very unreasonable, there was no one
whose opinion they held in such esteem.

The next Sunday, Frank asked Kate if she had not been
confirmed. She explained. He gave a whistle of disapproval,
and then said, " Why don't you take the children off the hands
of those who have been ? "

" Miss Townsend ? " said Kate. " Oh, do you mean so that
she might stay to the Sacrament ? Well, so we might, but
surely she might have asked us."

" Surely you might have asked her," said Frank.

" Why, so we would, if it had been Easter or Christmas, or
any other time like those ; but I never thought of a person's
wishing to stay every Sunday."

To this Frank made no answer; and Kate went on, "It was monthly at Copseley, and I thought it was only every week here, because this is such a populous place. But do you really think it necessary to stay always?"

Frank suddenly called to Alfred to look at a white-winged sea-gull.

Kate did not think much without Emmeline to help her, but she could not help perceiving that Frank had much higher ideas of the privileges he enjoyed than she had of those which she had as yet missed. The offer was made that same evening to Miss Townsend, of taking charge of the children whenever she wished them to leave church without her.

"Oh, thank you, thank you," she answered earnestly. "And since you are so kind, I may as well say it at once: would you think it too much if it was as often—as often as once a fortnight?"

"Every Sunday, if you like," said Kate.

"Oh, thank you, thank you," exclaimed Miss Townsend; "you do not know how happy you have made me."

Kate was struck by the great joy and gratitude expressed in her countenance.

"I am very glad you mentioned it," said she to Frank the next evening, when the three were sitting at tea together, their elders being gone to a dinner party, "the poor little woman could not have been more grateful if I had relieved her of governesship for life."

Frank put on one of his odd faces, and said, "I should think so!"

"I would not be a governess!" said Emmeline.

"You may earn a good livelihood at papering," said Frank, looking towards the tower, where they had all day been papering the walls with Punch and the Pictorial Times.

"Well, when you sit up to be builder and upholsterer, we will come to you for work," said Kate.

"Bargaining that you don't upset the paste over me again," said Emmeline. "But, by the bye, Frank, what are you really to be?"

G

"Oh, a clergyman," said Frank.

"I should think you were just made for it," said Emmeline. "You must be Herbert's curate."

"No; I am to be Uncle Willoughby's," said Frank.

"I suppose you will like that very much?"

"To be sure," said Frank. "He has almost more than he can well do now, and I should be very glad to help him."

"How very fond of him you must be! You cannot think how we enjoyed his visit to us in London, and the day we went shopping with him."

"I wonder if you will ever go to Dumblethwayte!" said Frank. "I should like you to see it! Emmie would soon be for making her fine descriptions."

"Oh, do tell us about it! Is it such a beautiful country?"

"Oh, very well for that. There is such a walnut tree in the garden as you never did see, and the kidney potatoes are the best in all the country round."

"Well, but are there mountains, and water, and scenery?"

"There is a famous great horse-pond just as you come into the village."

"Horse-pond!" cried Emmeline in horror, at which Frank delighted to laugh.

"A very good thing too," said Frank.

"How foolish of me to think you knew what scenery meant, you wretch!" said Emmeline.

"I know what it means," answered Frank, his eyes fixed on a framed water-colour drawing; "it means a black crooked tree, with dirt-coloured cabbages growing all over it, and two or three powdered wigs up in the air, and a blue thing like a snake running up-hill, and a red sack with a cat's face and a pair of horns in front. I am afraid, Emmie, there is no scenery at Dumblethwayte!"

"That is for you, Kate; you must answer," said Emmeline.

"Oh dear! is it Kate's doing?" said Frank, putting up his hands before his face, and pretending to shrink away with shame, in the most ludicrous manner. "What shall I do! I ask pardon with all my heart!"

"Just as if you did not do it on purpose," said Kate, laughing. "Well, when I do a picture for you, there shall be a horse-pond in the middle, 'a round pond and a pretty pond too,' a walnut tree on one side, and our tower on the other."

"And all the leaves on the trees shall be as green as grass," said Emmeline.

"Well, so you shall," said Frank; "I hold you to your bargain, Katie; and mind you make plenty of walnuts on the tree. I'll tell you what is fun; to pelt the children with the walnuts when they come out of school, and see them scramble for them! Well, I wonder when I shall go there again. It is just getting to harvest time now, and old Jem Churcher rings the harvest service bell at half-past five, and all the people come to church before they go out to the fields! That would be what you would call like a picture, Emmie, seeing them all come out from under the church gateway with their reap-hooks, and their little wooden kegs of beer. Yes, and just this very time—'tis eight, is not it?—he will be ringing the curfew; and nobody stops a bit in the field after that, but in they come—almost all of them, at least—to church; and you can't think how pretty it is coming out, to see the porch and the church-yard all heaped up with their sheaves of gleaning. My uncle always likes to look at them so much, and it is a famous time to hear what they think of the weather, and how the crops are."

"How beautiful!" said Emmeline; and Frank looked much pleased.

"But," said Kate, "is the having service your uncle's doing, or was it always so?"

"Oh, always!" said Frank. "The Dumblethwayte people would as soon think of a year without harvest, as of a harvest without Church. Oh! and then the best of all is the harvest supper. We have only one farmer, Mr. Dorey, and as soon as the last load is carried, he always gives a supper to nearly all the parish, men and women and all."

"And so you go to see it!" said Kate.

"See! we do more than see, I can assure you," said Frank "Uncle Willoughby has got to say grace for them all, and then we have to eat! I can assure you that Mrs. Dorey's cold beef, and her cheese, and home-brewed, are not to be despised. And then they drink the Queen's health, and Uncle Willoughby's, and the farmer's; and then comes the singing."

He entertained them with imitations of some of the harvest songs, which made them almost weary with laughing, and Emmeline suggested that Miss Townsend would wonder.

"Ah!" said Frank, "that poor little Suburb. By the bye, does she never appear, or is she imprisoned up-stairs?"

"We have asked her to come down when we are alone in the evening, but she has only done it once," said Kate.

"And I suppose you only asked her once," said Frank.

"He means to make us ask her again," said Emmeline.

"Bring her down, Kate, there is a good girl," said Frank. "I want to see if I can see her without a magnifying glass when she is in the same room. I took her for a tom-tit the other day in the garden, and very nearly walked over her, expecting she would have flown away."

"She is not pert enough for a tom-tit," said Kate.

"But she is just the colour of one," said Emmeline. "All pale grey, and black, and straw-colour."

"Come! half-a-crown to fetch her down!" said Frank.

"Will you really give me one if I do?" said Kate.

"That I will," said Frank, "provided you fetch her down diligently every time they dine out, to the end of the holidays. Ah! and I have not done yet—provided the half-crown does not go in tracts from my long-nosed cousins, the Miss Shaws; and that it does not go to that humbugging child that tells you long stories about Mr. Brent being the hard-heartedest of men; and that it does not go to Mr. Hunter's school, where they let you teach—what did you call it—great latitude?"

"Then I think it is not worth having on those conditions," said Kate.

"See, here 'tis," said Frank, balancing it on his finger. "Look, Kate, 'tis not to be despised; a bran new shining Victoria half-crown, just as bright as when it came out of the mint, save that her Majesty has got a little dent, or dulness, or something, under her ear. I'll let you off one minute in consideration of that dent, Kate. There, 'tis a fair offer, and such as you won't get many more like it, I assure you."

"Half-crowns?" said Kate. "I could get plenty just like it any day."

"Any day that you happened to have a sovereign in your purse," said Frank; "but no, Kate, no, you forget the dent. That is unrivalled, unequalled, unsurpassed, modelled from an original beauty-spot on her Majesty's own face! Think what you throw away, Kate, by rejecting the original dent! a thing for which you might search three hundred half-crowns without finding the like, three-sixteenths of an inch from the tip of the nose. Consider it well, Kate, three-sixteenths of an inch from the tip of the nose!" he concluded, impressively.

"You very absurd boy!" said Kate. "Well, I must try and earn it, if only for the sake of laughing at you, so here I go in search of the Suburb."

It was not long before Kate ushered Miss Townsend into the room, whereupon the former was greeted by Frank with a patronizing nod, and the glancing of a little rim· of silver above his waistcoat pocket.

After settling Miss Townsend comfortably, Emmeline and Frank pursued the subject they had been talking of when the others entered.

"They are coming to stay with us, you know," said Emmeline.

"Who are?" said Kate.

"Mrs. and Miss Willoughby, Frank's cousins," said Emmeline.

"Are they?" said Frank. "Is Juliet Willoughby coming? Dear me, Emmeline and Kate, I hope you can talk Hebrew?"

"Why? Is she so very learned?"

"I tell you, Emmeline, if learning can set the Thames on fire, Juliet Willoughby is the woman to do it. She talks

Hebrew and Arabic with Eastern professors—half her books begin at the wrong end, and are all in squares, and dashes, and ridiculous-looking letters. I expect every day to hear she is off to Nineveh to help them to read Nimrod's private account-book and diary!"

"Come, now, are you talking sense or nonsense?"

"Never was anything in this world more true! Ask Uncle Willoughby, if you won't believe me, if he did not give her his Hebrew Bible. And as to Greek, she could hold a conversation with old Homer himself, it is my belief, and set him right if he spoke bad grammar."

"Oh dear!" cried Emmeline, "what a formidable person! What shall we do with her? Only I hope it is only one of Frank's figments."

"Ah! you will see," said Frank. "I suppose you know at least a little German, or some Latin."

"German, yes; though we have not touched it since we left school."

"Ah, well! then perhaps she may notice you a little. But really, Emmie, have you never seen any of Juliet's things, books, writings—"

"Has she really published anything?" cried both girls in awe.

"Oh yes; she would as soon publish as you would sew up a seam! Why, there was a German story she translated, that they gave her ever so much money for, and she has put no end of verses and stories in magazines. Ah! you may well look at each other; Juliet is not a sight to be seen every day."

"I should like very much to see her," said Emmeline, in a tone of consternation; "just to see her as a sight, but to have to entertain her! What shall we do, Kate?"

"Oh, she will make allowances," said Frank.

"But do tell me," continued Emmeline, "where are all these things that she has written, and why did we never hear of them before?"

Frank named the magazines, and one or two of the stories;

and the sisters found, to their delight and surprise, that they already knew and liked them.

"She is very mysterious about them," said he; "she signs them with only a J, for fear any one should guess them to be hers; so you must not tell any living creature; I only gave you a friendly hint, that you might not expose yourselves."

On they talked, much after this fashion; and Miss Townsend, meanwhile, sat by, and often smiled at the jokes. She did not wish to be addressed, and was happier thus looking on. The change and refreshment enabled her to resume her work next morning far more cheerfully.

CHAPTER VIII.

Thus dost thou hear the Nemean lion roar
'Gainst thee, poor lamb, that standest as his prey.
Love's Labour Lost.

FRANK was tolerably civil to the Miss Shaws, and they admired him vastly, but he always got out of their way as far as he could, and used to make great fun of their complimentary speeches as soon as he was alone with the girls. Emmeline used to grow angry, and contend that they were perfectly sincere in their flattery.

"So much the worse for you," said Frank.

"Why?"

"Of course you are not so stupid but that you would find them out if they did not really mean it, let them do it ever so naturally; but as they think it all true, you can't help believing it."

"I am sure, whoever flatters, Frank does not," said Kate, laughing. "He might walk into the palace of truth any day, and never be different for one moment."

"No," said Emmeline, "I almost think he would begin to pay compliments."

Frank turned an odd face upon Emmeline, as if she had detected him.

About this time, Frank, while going down among the fishermen to try to get some shells, sea-eggs, &c., for the decoration of the tower, met with a sad cas ⟩ of distress—a sick man, and a number of wretched-looking small children, without a mother.

The girls' feelings were excited, and they were eager to apply immediately to all the various funds managed by the Miss Shaws, for the garments which they had to make up were not theirs to give; moreover they had none finished, not having worked with nearly as much alacrity as at first.

But as soon as Frank found that the house stood in Mr. Brent's district, he announced his intention of speaking to him about it.

"Speaking to him! Why, you don't know him," said Emmeline.

" Yes, I do; my father introduced me one day when we met him in the street, and I have had a few words with him several times since."

"How can that be? I have never seen you meet him, and you are not out often alone."

"He has spoken to me two or three times," said Frank.

"But I assure you it will be of no use," said Kate. "Miss Penelope—now don't laugh, Frank—Miss Penelope says all the good they can do in this district is by stealth."

"We shall only be prevented from doing anything," said Emmeline.

"Yes, Frank, now don't," said Kate. "The committee will never give them anything if they find we have been in communication with Mr. Brent about them."

"And then Miss Penelope says what a sad thing party spirit is," said Frank.

"Hush, now," said Kate; "here comes Sir Francis."

Emmeline, however, took Frank in hand, and really thought she had persuaded him that an application to Mr. Brent would be followed by a rebuke for having dared to look into a cottage.

Next morning, however, when she came down to breakfast, she found Frank in the dining-room before her, looking triumphant.

"Well, Emmie, Mr. Brent is writing an order for the man to be taken to the hospital, and a cart will come for him in an hour's time."

"Mr. Brent!" Emmeline stood aghast. "When could you have seen him?"

"This morning," said Frank. "I waited for him when he came out of church."

"Have you been to church this morning? Surely not. It is at seven o'clock!"

"To be sure," said Frank. "Why should not I? What is the good of lying in bed on such fine summer mornings as these?"

"You don't mean to say that you generally go!"

"Of course I do. If I have to go at half-past six at school, I think I may go at seven at home."

"But about the poor man?" said Kate. "And what did you say to move Mr. Brent?"

"I told him the state in which I found him, and it seems that he knew all about him before. He had tried to make the man send the children to school in vain, for he is a hardened heathenish sort of fellow; but the illness came on suddenly, and the poor children are too young to know who to apply to."

"What did he do?"

"He walked with me to the place, and saw the state of things; he settled it all in a minute; the man is to go to the hospital, and he knows of a good old woman who will take care of the children. Then I told him"—Frank looked archly at the girls, as if he doubted how they would approve—"that I had two sisters with a great deal of energy running to waste, who would be very glad to make little coats and things for the children, and he said it would be doing a great kindness, and he should be very much obliged to you."

"You did not really give that account of us !"

"Is not it true?" said Frank ; and they were obliged to take this reply for want of a better answer.

In the space of a week they completed sundry garments, the interest which Frank took in their progress keeping them steadily to it, though their ardour for the poor was on the wane. It had been a fancy and not a principle, and as the disagreeables made themselves more felt, it ceased to engross Emmeline's mind, and her old weariness began to ensue.

Still they went to the school, where they had for some time been making a point of the Church Catechism. By rewards and praises, Emmeline had obtained of her class its perfect repetition, and now, with the help of questions caught from Mr. Brent's catechizings in church, and with recollections of the teachings of her own earlier days, she was endeavouring to instruct the children in its meaning. It brought out various thoughts with regard to her Confirmation ; she began to learn that the life of a child is its preparation for that solemn vow and blessing, and while she taught her scholars to look forward to it, she more than once felt sincere regret for her own neglect.

A good many people used to walk in and out of the school ; all the committee were privileged ; and there were many teachers on the same terms as our heroines, besides visitors, and people who came to speak to the school-mistress about work. They generally went to the mistress's throne of office, or else to some unemployed class, and Emmeline had learnt not to heed them, and to have no eyes for anything beyond her own square of girls.

One day, however, when she was in the midst of questioning on the Catechism, she was startled by a short dry cough of disapprobation close behind her, and looking up, saw a tall thin gentleman in black, with rather grey curling hair, a long narrow face, and a solemn expression, standing near her chair.

Annoyed and confused, she found it impossible to go on. She waited a moment, expecting the stranger to apologize and depart, but as he did no such thing, she shut up her book, and;

with Kate, left the school very indignant, though they did not divulge the adventure, for fear Frank should triumph over them.

A day or two after, the Miss Shaws called upon them, and Miss Penelope, in rather a mysterious manner, asked Emmeline to take a walk in the garden with her.

"My dear Miss Berners, you will forgive me," said she. "You know how grateful we are for your assistance in the school, but you must allow me just to make one little suggestion. I am sure you mean it all most rightly, but people talk about it. Could you not dwell rather less on the Church Catechism?"

Emmeline started. "I thought," said she, "that it was one of the chief things to be taught."

"My dear, I say nothing against the Catechism itself, it is a most admirable compilation, but you know it has been made so much a badge of party, and people talk—"

"But what do they say?" asked Emmeline, in a maze of surprise, perplexity, and displeasure.

"O my dear Miss Emmeline, people will say things; they remark on your dwelling so much on that and nothing else; and some of the children's parents are Dissenters, and have scruples about their learning it. Indeed, I think you had better adopt some other line."

Gentle as Emmeline was, she never felt less persuadable, perhaps from a secret conviction that this must be the result of the spying of last Thursday's visitor. "What can people have to remark?" said she. "We taught the Catechism because no one else seemed to do so, and you told us we might teach what we pleased."

"Yes, yes, my dear; I am sure it is a good thing; only it has become a badge of party, and—and—there is your connection with Lord Herbert Somerville, whose views are so well known. I hope you will not be vexed with me, my dear, but I thought it would be as well just to give you a hint; I do so dread anything of party spirit."

"If you would but tell me what Lord Herbert Somerville can possibly have to do with it," said Emmeline, growing very angry, and very formal.

"Ah! my dear girl, how I envy your sweet innocence of party! I would not say a word against Lord Herbert for the world, only everybody knows what a High Church intolerant part his family have always taken."

"I know where the intolerance is now," thought Emmeline to herself; but she let Miss Penelope go on as far as "Mr. Denham—" before her schooled manners gave way, and she interrupted her by saying, "Was that Mr. Denham that came and listened to me last Thursday?"

"My dear, you must not be annoyed—I am sure you have too much good sense—"

"I disliked it very much indeed," said Emmeline. "I cannot think how he could do such a thing."

"Ah! your retiring nature, which would shrink from observation, my dear; I can quite sympathize with you; but you must consider what an interest good Mr. Denham takes in the school."

Emmeline's cheeks were tingling all over, and the more smoothly Miss Penelope spoke, the more agitated and irritated she grew. Yet her former life had been a good discipline in exterior politeness, and she spoke with more calmness and civility towards Miss Penelope than many other girls would have done, whose self-command was more the effect of principle and less of habit. Her voice scarcely altered from its usual rather constrained company tones, as she said, "I am afraid I cannot look upon it as you do. It was exceedingly unpleasant to me to find myself overlooked the other day: and I cannot think it is treating me properly to spy me out and then complain of me. If Mr. Denham was the clergyman of the parish, he would have some right to inquire into my teaching, and I should not complain; but I do not consider that he has any authority."

"You forget he is on the committee," said Miss Penelope, hastily interposing.

This was Emmeline's weak point; she had sought sanction from the committee instead of from the Church, and, sensibly as she had spoken, her argument failed; but in the heat of the moment she did not feel it, and took up another point. "Surely he has not been complaining of me to the committee."

"Oh no, no," said Miss Penelope; "you do not know how much consideration good Mr. Denham has. Indeed, you do not do him justice."

"Certainly," said Emmeline, "I should like to know what he could complain of! I don't know how long he thought proper to listen to me, but I am quite certain he heard nothing that was not the right teaching, in which I have always been brought up. But it is of no use to talk over it any longer; I shall never be able to teach at all, unless I may do so freely, and without being listened to and remarked upon; and I cannot believe but that the Church Catechism ought to be taught and explained."

"Oh dear! oh dear! how badly I have managed!" exclaimed poor good little Miss Penelope; "how I do wish Maria had been here to help me! Now I have vexed you, and made you angry with poor Mr. Denham, when I meant to have set it all straight! Oh dear! how silly of me to try to do anything alone! If Maria had but been here, it would have been all right!"

It was impossible to be angry with Miss Penelope, at any rate; and Emmeline could not help smiling, as she said cordially, "I am sure you meant everything kind, and I am very much obliged to you, indeed I am."

"Are you sure, quite sure?" said the good lady. "Yes, I see that sweet face quite forgives my silly mismanagement; I was sure your good sense would see it so. And you will not take it amiss of poor Mr. Denham; he would be quite grieved, I am sure, to know that you felt annoyed; it would hurt him very much. And you will not dwell so much on the Catechism? It does you harm with several people; I do assure you it does, my dear, though you might not imagine it."

Emmeline had been much softened at first, but she could not forgive Mr. Denham, and grew harder at the mention of his name. She heartily wished the conversation at an end; and happily she had only time to say, "I cannot think Mr. Denham has used me well," before Sir Francis and his eldest son appeared at the other end of the walk. The Miss Shaws soon after took their leave, Miss Penelope saying, as she shook hands with Emmeline, "I have more to say to you, my dear; I am sure I shall bring you round." Then, nodding at her at the door, she disappeared.

Then out it all came. Emmeline was much too excited and angry not to impart her indignation, and Sir Francis and Lady Willoughby fully shared it, to say nothing of Kate, her other self. As to Frank, he sat by in a state of the most provokingly mischievous delight and triumph, making indications of clapping his hands at the relation of each affront that Emmeline had received; and whenever she told of any particularly silly speech of Miss Penelope, exclaiming, in a low voice, "Bravo!"

"I am sure," said Lady Willoughby, "I can't guess what they can mean. I am sure, when I was last in England, I used to hear of nothing but teaching poor children the Catechism. I was quite sick of it."

"It is that Denham—a low, Methodistical sort of a fellow," said Sir Francis; "only too glad to be impertinent to a lady when he has the opportunity; 'tis he that is at the bottom of it. I should only be glad to kick him down-stairs this minute."

"Poor dear Mr. Denham!" softly murmured Frank; "how ill Mr. Brent used him!"

"You won't go to school again after this, my dears," said Lady Willoughby.

"No, surely; not if they give you no more thanks than this," said Sir Francis.

"Why, Mamma," said Emmeline, "I should not much like to fly off upon an affront, as if we were angry with everyone."

"Oh no, certainly not," added Kate; "we must show we are

not displeased with the Shaws, or Mr. Hunter, or any of the others."

"Besides, as I told Miss Penelope," said Emmeline, "I don't see what right Mr. Denham has to interfere! I should like to go on teaching the Catechism in spite of him."

"Well done, Emmie; there spoke a girl of spirit!" said Sir Francis. "But I must say, I would have no more to do with them; let them settle their affairs their own way; you have plenty of better things to do; and it is my maxim, never to do what there is nothing to be gained by, not even thanks."

"But the poor children!" said Kate; "no one will teach it to them at all if we do not."

"Oh, they will learn it somehow," said Lady Willoughby. "Indeed, my dear, it will only be exposing yourself to more of this man's impertinence, and I can't bear you should shut yourself up all the afternoon in the hot room with those dirty children. Emmie looks quite pale after it."

"The room is not at all hot, Mamma," exclaimed both girls; and the more they were persuaded to give up their attendance at school, the more resolute they grew in pleading for its continuance.

"Give it up! No, never!" said Emmeline, with a sort of would-be-martyr look, as soon as she had Kate to herself.

"Never!" echoed Kate; "it would be giving up our principles."

"Yes; and think of the influence it must have upon all the school, to see how important we think it, and how steadily we keep to it."

"It is not like some trumpery question-book, to be taken up one week, and thrown aside the next," said Kate; "it is something to hold fast and value."

"Yes; and we will show them our value for it," said Emmeline. "Committee, and children, and all, shall see that we think the Catechism no badge of party, but the watch-word of the English Church. I dare say this controversy about it will make the children value it all the more."

"The children are so fond of you, they will love it for your sake," said Kate; "that little Mary Parsons, her mother told Miss Shaw the other day, she would do anything for her dear teacher, Miss Emma Line."

"Sweet child!" said Emmeline, smiling. "Yes, Kate, our names shall go on in their imaginations coupled with the Catechism; and how do we know? perhaps it may bring back some of these Dissenters to the Church, if they really do love us."

"Frank would laugh at us if we gave it up," said Kate.

"Frank laughs at whatever we do," said Emmeline. "Though, certainly, after this it is impossible not to allow that Mr. Brent was justified in turning Mr. Denham out. Kate, the enmity of such a man is an honour!"

And Emmeline's happiness was extreme all that evening, and the next morning, in the belief that she was persecuted; and she treated Frank's raillery about Mr. Brent, and poor dear Mr. Denham, with a magnificent superiority that was quite edifying.

In the middle of the day she received a note, four sheets of small, closely written note-paper, from Miss Penelope Shaw.

The first page was taken up in lamentations on the little lady's part that she had not managed matters better in their interview; then followed a warm panegyric on Mr. Denham, declaring that no one could have been further from any thought of annoying her; next came her dissertation on party spirit and the Catechism, so mixed together in a double parenthesis, that it would have required numerous commentaries before it could be guessed what was the meaning; and after they had both read it separately, besides going over it together, the sisters really could not tell whether Miss Penelope would have them continue the Catechism or not. The sting was, however, in the tail; and that was an assurance, that rather than be supposed to have any thought of annoying Miss Berners, Miss Penelope would induce Mr. Denham to tell her so in person, and make the fullest apology. Indeed, she had not a doubt that he would of his own accord take the earliest opportunity of so doing.

The scream of dismay with which Emmeline beheld the sentence betrayed her to Frank, who had been watching her face; and he immediately proceeded to act both Mr. Denham's apology and her manner of receiving it, so absurdly, that, vexed as she was, it was beyond her powers not to laugh. He was urgent to be allowed to see the note, but she would not have it laughed at, and carried it up-stairs to meditate upon the answer, and try to make out the meaning—a task at least as difficult as the translation of the German sentence, and possibly for the same reason.

To face Mr. Denham and endure his apology, was, above all, not to be thought of, and therefore she must express her forgiveness; but still there was no certainty that he might not choose to apologize after all, and, as Emmeline and Kate agreed, nothing could put them in a more unpleasant predicament. It was wonderful, now that the opposition seemed to have died away, how their vehement desire for going to school was fading. Mr. Denham's apology frightened them a hundred times more than his "enmity," and all Emmeline felt was a desire to find an excuse for keeping out of both his and Miss Penelope's way till it was all forgotten.

Fortune favoured her, for before many hours had passed, a letter arrived fixing next Wednesday for Mrs. and Miss Willoughby's visit; and as they were expected to stay a fortnight, this was exactly the break which Emmeline wanted, and she almost forgot to tremble at Miss Willoughby's acquirements, in the relief at the opportuneness of her coming.

It was much easier now to write her note, which Kate thought an excellent piece of diplomacy, as it ignored the Catechism altogether, and only expressed great thanks to Miss Penelope, hopes that attendance at school would only be interrupted for a very short time, and a very strong and repeated entreaty that not a word might be said to Mr. Denham that would lead him to think an apology would be otherwise than very unpleasant. And so she sent school affairs entirely out of her mind for the present; and, whenever she was not amused by Frank, was a prey to her old yawning dissatisfied fits.

H

CHAPTER IX.

Hast thou seen that lordly castle—
That castle by the sea?
Golden and red above it,
The clouds float gorgeously.
Uhland. (Longfellow.)

REPORTS of Juliet Willoughby's learning and cleverness preceded her, alarming Lady Willoughby even more than her daughters.

She summoned her "dear boy," Frank, and asked a description of these much-feared powers. He was much more sober in his delineations than when with the young ladies; and it only appeared that Juliet was very clever, understood more modern and ancient tongues than most young ladies, dabbled in one or two more, and had made and published sundry translations, as well as original verses, and stories.

This was so far satisfactory, that the girls were sure they knew the worst. Lady Willoughby thanked Heaven that she had daughters to take the brunt of entertaining the stranger; and Sir Francis laughed, and said he had no doubt but that his little Katie would be a match for anyone: whereupon Kate felt much and sincerely distressed that he would always take her for the clever one.

By way of further preparations, the magazines containing Juliet's contributions were brought out. Sir Francis looked at their names, while Lady Willoughby desired to have them read to her, and she had slept through three-quarters of the first, before the day which was to bring the visitors. Then came a difference of opinion; she was for letting the said magazines lie on the table to receive their author, while Emmeline could not bear that they should have the air of being set out on purpose; and Kate at last proposed that all should be put away except the last number, which would look just as if they were only taking it in regularly.

At length the young lady and her mother arrived, neither of

them looking in the least distinguished or remarkable. And the eyes of the sisters only beheld a quiet-looking person, well-featured, but of a muddy complexion, and with eyes and lips which had a good deal of expression in them, though surface observers did not readily find it out. She was just above twenty, but looked younger, for her figure was girlish, and she had the air of depending on her mother for protection.

She and Frank seemed very glad to meet, and he was the only person who looked perfectly at his ease as they all sat round in the formal circle of the newly arrived; and though he did not say much, he now and then rubbed his hands together with a certain mischievous glance of triumphant fun. At last Lady Willoughby proceeded to conduct Mrs. Willoughby to her room; Juliet's was up another flight of stairs, and therefore she was consigned to the care of Emmeline and Kate.

Up they went, Emmeline first, very well behaved, very polite, and very nervous; she ushered Miss Willoughby into the room, but the next moment company-manners were suddenly disconcerted, as all three with one voice exclaimed, "What is that?"

On the state pincushion upon the toilet table waved a huge piece of orange-coloured paper, of the form and tint of a hand-bill, covered with enormous letters, setting forth, in all the varieties of type, ridiculously thick and ridiculously thin, that on the fourth instant, at 8 p.m., a Lecture would be given at the Town Hall, Herringsby, on the Sanscrit, illustrated by the Ramjonnybunveda, by the celebrated professor, Miss Juliet Willoughby, F.S.B.S.

It would be hard to say which predominated with the two sisters, diversion or consternation. Emmeline could not speak at all; Kate made various exclamations; Juliet's colour rose, but she laughed heartily, crying out, "Oh! that wretch Frank!"

"Indeed, we had not an idea what he was doing," said Kate.

"Indeed, we are very sorry," said Emmeline, feeling very guilty.

"I don't know what you have to be sorry for," said Juliet. "I know Mr. Frank of old, and don't mind his tricks. What a boy he is, to be sure!" added she, examining the elaborate lettering.

"Now I know what he borrowed the Indian ink for," said Emmeline. "I could not think what he was doing in his own room the last two days!"

"I saw some mischief was in his head," said Juliet. "Certainly it is lucky that all his jokes are good-natured, for there is no end of them."

"Does he often practise them on you?" said Kate, with an intonation of respect, and at the same time of great surprise, for Frank had somehow made them fancy that he was as much afraid of Juliet as they were.

"Play me tricks? yes, the rogue, that he does, for ever," said Juliet. "Does he not with you?"

"Oh yes," said Emmeline, smiling at the recollection, and perceiving that Miss Willoughby would think it rather a dishonour that Frank should not think her worth playing tricks on. "But come, Kate, we are hindering Miss Willoughby's dressing."

So, after due politeness, the sisters withdrew. Juliet and her mother were full early in coming down, and only Sir Francis and Frank were in the drawing-room.

"O Frank! I have such a scolding for you!" said Juliet, fastening on him, and drawing him, nothing loth, into a window, out of hearing.

"What, did not I make the letters big enough?" said Frank.

"But what absurd accounts have you been giving of me? Oh! Frank, I see you have been saying all sorts of monstrous things!"

"Never mind, Juliet, your presence will undeceive everybody."

"Yes, especially when you take delight in making me look foolish. And now, Frank, do be obliging, and tell me a little about them—your—I mean those girls, the Miss Berners."

"My opinion goes for nothing when you have made up your own already," said Frank.

"Have I—how do you know I have?"

" By the way you said ' those girls.' "

" Well, I will tell you what I think, and you shall say if I am right. They are school-girls."

" Did you know that before, or find it out now?"

" I saw it from the way in which they carry their elbows. Favourable specimens, though, are not they? but drilled, like Russian soldiers, out of all individuality of mind and manner. Eh, Frank?"

" That's very grand," said Frank.

" Don't pretend not to understand; 'tis an answer I want; I want to know what to talk to them about; must I stop short at —Do you ride? and do you draw? or may I go on to books?"

" Ask them how they like the Knight of the Silver Crescent," said Frank.

" Now, Frank, you have not told them about that, I hope!" exclaimed Juliet, colouring, in very decided unfeigned annoyance; then relieved, " Oh no, I see you have not, you only tried to frighten me."

Emmeline and Kate at this moment came in, dressed alike, their hair sitting exactly in the same manner, and their arms held in precisely the same position. Emmeline, thinking the mother the least formidable, placed herself where she might be talked to by her. Kate went towards Miss Willoughby and Frank, and with more manner than Juliet possessed, began to make talk about the pretty country.

Juliet answered readily, and they began to get on well together; in fact, before they went in to dinner, Juliet had made up her mind that Kate had some information and some originality. But after dinner it so chanced that Emmeline fell to Juliet's share, and in the course of the talk, she made three or four of the very same remarks that had previously been made by Kate; and Juliet went to bed wondering whether Emmeline borrowed from Kate, or Kate from Emmeline.

The girls, on their side, began to find their fear of Miss Willoughby wearing off. She appeared so much less habituated to society than they were, that it seemed to diminish the distance between them. It was not awkwardness, nor was it any deficiency in good breeding; but there was a bashfulness about her, and a reliance on her mother for taking the lead, that made her seem to be younger than her real age, and struck them as very strange in a person of such undeniable cleverness; a little abruptness, too, when she did speak, which was so unlike the demeanour to which they had been trained at Miss Danby's, or had seen in the manners of Lady Frances Somerville, that it surprised and almost confused them.

The demure good behaviour of all parties continued for the space of breakfast-time next morning, after which Emmeline rather timidly proposed a stroll in the garden. They were parading together, when Frank suddenly burst upon them in this manner: " Upon my word, I am delighted to see a meeting of—what is it—what is the word? help me, Emmie, or you, Mrs. Romeo—a meeting of kindred spirits. I believe it is—"

"Frank, Frank, how can you?" said Emmeline, colouring scarlet with shame, and fear that Miss Willoughby might dislike having ignorance itself likened to her knowledge. Kate did not mind it in the least, so sure was she that it was not meant for her.

"Where have you been learning such elegant sentiments, Frank?" said Miss Willoughby.

"Where—why, where should I, but in such good company as I keep? Did not I tell you they were kindred spirits?"

"I wish you would not say such things, Frank," said Emmeline.

"What, not when it is quite true? Deny it if you can, that I found a whole foolscap sheet full of verses, all about a river gliding and gliding on for ever."

Here Emmeline's desperate attempt to stop his mouth succeeded for a moment, she looking very piteous and imploring; Kate, half proud that Miss Willoughby should hear all, half vexed at her sister's annoyance, but scolding Frank all the time; Juliet, partly curious, partly sympathizing, and sorry for Emmeline.

" Never mind," said Juliet good-naturedly ; " Frank is a great rogue ; but as we can't keep him in order, we must submit to his bad behaviour."

" Now, if ever I heard ! " cried Frank. " When this cousin of mine, this Mrs. Romeo, was coming to me last evening to ask me for a hint how to talk to you—and I not only gave her a hint, but a full broad explanation—nay, and set you down to talk German and poetry from morning till night ; here are all the thanks I get ! "

" Did you, really ? " said Kate innocently.

" Of course," said Juliet, laughing ; " what else should I do but ask what two stranger young ladies were like ? Would not you have done the same ? And so this is the way Mr. Frank chooses to answer me. A broad hint, indeed, it may be called."

" Indeed, I am very much ashamed," said Emmeline. " As to my being compared with you, Miss Willoughby, you know Frank's nonsense too well to mind that ; and indeed, indeed—"

" Indeed what ? " said Juliet, rather maliciously.

" Yes," said Kate, coming to her sister's aid in her quandary, though not quite as Emmeline had intended, " Emmie does know a great deal—nothing compared with you, to be sure— but more than anybody at Miss Danby's. And as to the verses, she does write a great many, only no one ever saw any but Constance and me, except some that I got leave to give Lady Frances. So, though a great deal is Frank's nonsense, some of it is true."

In the meantime Frank had disappeared.

" Indeed," said Miss Willoughby, turning to the blushing Emmeline, " I do feel for you very much, it is very disagreeable ; but I suppose Frank did it on the principle that we should get much better acquainted if he broke the ice for us."

" He has broken it with a good hard plunge," said Emmeline.

" So he has ; but now we have all tumbled in, and all scrambled out together, we must be the better friends from our companionship in disaster. Don't be afraid, I won't ask to see

one line of your verses till you feel that you know me well
enough to like to show them to me."

"Thank you," said Emmeline, sincerely, feeling it possible
that the time might not be distant.

"And don't be afraid of dear good Frank," said Juliet,
earnestly; "you have not known him as long as I have; and
he does teaze sometimes, but you may trust him with all your
heart, he will never do anything that is really and fairly disagreeable, and he will never betray you to any but safe people.
Oh, I do hope you all understand Frank."

"Understand him? that we hardly do," said Emmeline; "but
we do like him very much; I should not have thought that so
short a time could have made us so like brother and sisters."

"Yes, yes, I am glad to hear it," said Juliet eagerly. "You
see Frank has been used to be so happy at Dumblethwayte, he
and Uncle Willoughby fit so well together, and he is so fond of
the place, and garden, and poor people, and so useful there, that
I was afraid he would be out of his element almost anywhere
else. And then Frank has such quick perceptions in some
things, and such strong feelings, too, in spite of that round
merry face of his, that I was very much afraid he might not be
happy."

"I am sure I hope he is," said Kate; while Emmeline recollected what had always dwelt on her mind with regard to him
and her mother, and she did full justice in secret to his quick
perception.

"Yes, I think he is," said Juliet; "by his ways with you, I
can see that he is. And Frank is so good, I know nobody like
him. But what does he find to do here?"

This question led to an introduction to the tower, but they
found the door fastened against them; and it presently appeared
that Frank and Alfred were there, putting things to rights to
receive Juliet.

Then into the tower she went, looked, laughed, admired, and
finally aided, hand, heart, and soul, in the half-finished papering,
and before the luncheon bell rang, had won the heart of Alfred,

and caused Edwin to run incessantly after her, calling her his
dear Mrs. Romeo.

For the rest, Emmeline ahd Kate were perfectly at ease with
her ; and as her shyness also wore off, and she talked as she
thought, without repressing quotations or illustrations for fear of
display, her talent began more and more to impress and almost
enchant Emmeline.

She did not either play or draw herself, but she took intense
delight in good music, and had much scientific knowledge of the
merit of drawings or prints, as well as delight in fine scenery.
Two or three excursions were made to the beauties around ; Sir
Francis managed them all in as formal and inconvenient a guide-
book way as man could well do, but he could not spoil the
mountains, the lakes, or the rivers ; and besides, he had to do
the honours to Mrs. Willoughby, so the four young people had
a good deal of liberty to be happy together. If it had been for
nothing else, the long drives would have been a great delight to
Emmeline, for she generally sat alone with Juliet, and such talks
as they had about abstruse German I about historical personages,
and metaphysical questions, as Frank declared, enough to frighten
the horses.   It gave Emmeline a much better opinion of herself,
and made Kate very proud of her, that she should find herself
on anything like equal terms with Juliet Willoughby ; and the
occupation, the engrossing of her mind, was most delightful to her.

All the German in the world would she read—Spanish, Latin,
Greek, would she learn—be as clever as Juliet ; that, perhaps,
was impossible, but at any rate she must reach towards her
knowledge, she must taste of the wells which Juliet found so
delightful.

Book after book did Juliet promise to lend, and she promise
to read ; and her letters, instead of simple records of facts and
of feelings, were grand in descriptions and criticism of books ;
and Kate's were just the same, for Kate's head had gone into
literature as far and as deep as her sister's, though she thought
it was all on her own account.

Emmeline, before the close of the fortnight, had heard the

plot of Juliet's next story, and read two or three manuscript poems; and it can scarcely be doubted, that in return her own verses were shown.

They were smooth and regular for the most part, much in earnest, and sometimes with a good deal of quiet pathos; for Emmeline, like most young things, liked best to dwell on sadness. Juliet admired them, but she showed her sense, and disappointed Kate, who wanted her very much to propose to put them in the magazine.

"I see what you wish, Kate," said she, in her usual abrupt way, "but I do not advise it."

"Oh, I am glad you don't," said Emmeline.

"It would be poor praise to say that I have seen worse published; and as to the nonsense about literary ladies, that is all stuff; but Emmeline is so young, and I dare say will do so much better, that she would look down upon these and get ashamed of them, and of having begun the world with what was not her best. And then another thing, Emmeline, one's first fresh young ideas are the best of all; they spring and grow with one, but the manner of them is apt to be imitated from something, and they want the judgment that one gets in growing older, either to modify or strengthen them, and so they are wasted by being put forth too soon, like early buds. I dare say Waverley was much the better for being put away and forgotten all that long time. I do think it is a very bad thing to get so easily into print as one may do now."

Emmeline fully agreed to this, for her notion was to let authorship be a very grand future vision; and she saw the faults in her verses, the weaknesses rather, sufficiently to know they would look worse some time or other. There was enough to engross her for the present in the desire of study.

Juliet's visit was a very bright spot. She was in the midst of all their sports, laughed at by Frank, and laughing with him, playing with the children, and going deep into the confidence of the sisters, who told her a good deal about Constance, and more than was advisable about Sir Francis; which, besides being wrong, was unnecessary, as she found it all out for herself.

The crowning delight was the last evening of her stay, when Frank and Kate, by a great exertion of influence, obtained permission from the elders for all the "old young ones," as Alfred called them, to secede from the dinner-table, and have a great inauguration tea-drinking in the tower—children, Miss Townsend, and all.

Janet, with considerable aid from Miss Townsend, made a flag for the top of the tower; Emmeline composed a mock heroic ode, which Juliet, rather against her will, was obliged by Frank to translate into all the languages she knew, and more too; Frank mended the table and chairs; Kate, unassisted except by Edwin, who brought the sticks, made and lighted the fire to boil the kettle; and all, down to little Cecilia, assembled round the table in the highest spirits.

How they did eat bread and butter and drink tea! how they talked and laughed! and what slight jokes or little blunders sufficed to set all, wise and foolish alike, into perfect paroxysms of mirth.

When Frank proposed having toasts, only that they were to be eaten instead of drunk, what a laugh ensued; and forthwith Kate and Juliet went down on their knees before the fire to toast sundry pieces of bread. Then began the healths: Frank proposed "Romeo, and all the Montagues." Juliet in her turn proposed, "The Fair Emmeline, and might all her castles, modern Gothic ones especially, prove as substantial and produce as much happiness as the tower." But it would take too long to tell all the speeches made on the occasion, bad, good, and indifferent; they all alike answered their purpose, and that was enough. Frank treated them to one of the harvest songs of Dumblethwayte; and then, as the children had by this time grown tired, Miss Townsend carried them off, while the others took a turn in the garden, and talked of Uncle Willoughby and Dumblethwayte, every stick and stone of which seemed to have an interest for Frank and Juliet. It seemed so simple and homely; so happy and so good, that to Emmeline it was like a sort of vision, and she did not wonder at Frank's intense affection for it.

"Yes," said Juliet, "it is remote enough to have missed a great deal of modern corruption; and then forty years of such a '*kindlich*' man as Uncle Willoughby has not been lost upon it."

"What's that about my uncle?" said Frank; "something you are ashamed to put in plain English to meet my ears, Mrs. Romeo. Come, out with it."

"I meant it as high praise, you suspicious mortal!" said Juliet. "I don't think you would understand me if I said in English—such an old child as Uncle Willoughby; and yet it is just what he is."

"I suppose you would have me think that is metaphysics or some such tomfoolery," said Frank; "but it sounds to me very like impertinence."

"Moreover," continued Juliet, "you will be just such another, and that is my delight in thinking of Dumblethwayte."

"Nonsense!" said Frank; not, however, looking absolutely displeased.

"Let me see, you are seventeen and a half, Frank, are not you? In six years time, then! How choice a thing it will be to see you settled for good in the parsonage with my uncle; and old Lawrence with the actual presence, instead of only the fear, of Master Frank before his eyes, to make him cut the lettuces before they run to seed. And then, Frank, when you are really there for good, we won't trouble you more than once a week to walk over the hill and see us. And you will invite us to all the school tea-drinkings, won't you?"

"To be sure I will," said Frank. "Don't you know, if I had been at home—there, I mean—these holidays, I meant to have made you such an arbour in the laurel-hedge as you never saw, to sit in between the services on Sunday. I meant you to have taught that great Peggy Graves and those other girls there."

"So I will, Frank, I promise you; I will offer Uncle Willoughby as soon as ever I get home, and tell him I have got leave to be his curate's curate.—Emmeline and Kate, won't you come and stay with me, just to see Frank's house?"

"They must come when I am at home," said Frank, "or you won't show them about half well enough. Besides, Kate has promised to do me the picture of the walnut tree and the pond, for my rooms at Oxford, and she can't do it properly without my looking over her."

Sir Francis here tapped the drawing-room window: "Come in, come in, you giddy young things; we have spared you quite long enough, and now you are catching colds and will have no voices at all this evening."

"So our holiday is over," sighed Emmeline, as they entered the house.

Mrs. and Miss Willoughby were to depart the next day, and at breakfast in the morning much was said of future meetings; Sir Francis opined that he should remain at Bellevue some little time longer, as he wished to have time to look about for the estate he intended to purchase. But he said he should go to London in the course of the winter, for he wanted to make inquiries about some person who prepared young men for the army; he thought it would be a good thing for Frank to leave his present school some little time before going into the Guards.

It was like an electric shock, to at least three of the company. Juliet, Emmeline, and Kate, cast glances of dismay at each other, and then looked at Frank; his red cheeks might be a shade redder than usual; but he proceeded with his breakfast in a business-like way, and neither raised his eyes nor spoke. Mrs. Willoughby, being a prudent woman, simply talked on about hopes that they would make it convenient to come and stay with her, &c., and so the breakfast concluded.

Emmeline and Kate went up with Juliet to help her to put on her things; and as soon as she was in her own room, she exclaimed, "Well! I am sorry! Poor Frank, what will he do?"

"I never heard anything that surprised me more," said Kate.

"Oh, I don't wonder, Sir Francis wants to make an eldest

son of him—but Frank to be uprooted from Dumblethwayte—
Frank in the Guards—Oh! how can it be? and how disappointed
Uncle Willoughby will be? Frank is the very light of his
eyes!"

"Surely Sir Francis will not persist if Frank dislikes it,"
said Emmeline.

"Depend upon it, Sir Francis will not be thwarted." said
Juliet. "Frank will be victimized among you, he will get
among a set of people who will laugh at him, he will have
nothing to do, nothing to care for, he will be utterly thrown
away!"

"I should think Frank had a great spring within him
wherever he was," said Emmeline.

"Yes, that is right, Emmeline," said Juliet eagerly. "Frank
is too good ever to be really thrown away; but his whole being
and life are so at Dumblethwayte, and he is so made for it!
Oh, it will be a cruel thing if Sir Francis should! Well, I
can't bear to think of it; and besides, there is our carriage, I
must run down. Write to me, Emmeline, and tell me how it
goes on. I will send you the books as soon as ever I can, and
tell me what you think of those verses of Chamisso's. I hope
you will come to us, though—oh dear! poor Frank spoils it
all—"

Alfred came running up with a message to ask if she was
ready, and she ran down-stairs. They were all standing in the
hall wishing good-bye. Juliet looked inquiringly in Frank's
face as she shook hands; but the features expressed absolutely
nothing. She asked if he had any message for their uncle.
No, he would write; and they went, with a parting injunction
from Juliet to Emmeline to write soon.

Lady Willoughby went to her room, Sir Francis to his fence,
and Frank followed him; the girls after talking over his prospects, and Juliet's perfections, sat down to some German.
Kate wanted to ask Frank what he thought of his father's
designs, but Emmeline deemed it better not. He was just like
himself; and, when called on to teach the Greek alphabet, put

on his most teasing manner, and would only make nonsense and fun, much to the annoyance of Emmeline, who was quite in earnest.

Sir Francis was evidently out of sorts. He found fault with the weather and the dinner, was displeased with the girls for leaving their books about, and was even testy with the children.

CHAPTER X.

If in pure aims, and deeds, and prayers,
His path mount high, and far from theirs.
Lyra Innocentium.

THERE was a silence and constraint over all the party at breakfast the next morning; and Emmeline was sure that her mother had been desired to do something which she thought very troublesome, but did not know how to resist, for she sighed two or three times, and sent her cup for more coffee with a sort of plaintive air of importance, which Emmeline had learnt to understand full well.

Nothing transpired till Sir Francis finished his last cup of tea, and rose from his chair, saying, "Well, then I leave him to you, Lady Willoughby—or, stay, here's Emmie too, and my little Kate, sensible girls both. They have plenty of influence with him, I'll be bound, and will bring him to hear reason. Look here, then, look at that boy: you heard the offer I made him yesterday, to get him a commission in the Guards, make him heir to a landed estate, and now what do you think he goes and tells me? Why, that he has set his mind on going into the Church—sitting down as a country curate, where no one will ever hear of him. I declare it is enough to provoke a saint, when there are youths enough in the world who would give their ears for such an offer."

There was a pause: Emmeline had been watching Frank;

she thought she saw his forehead once contract a little, but it passed off, and he sat with his face as unmoved as ever, and his eyes fixed on his plate, where he was making some ungainly movements with his knife.

"But there!" said Sir Francis, "I have set all the advantages before him, talked to him till I am sick of it, and not an inch does he move."

"I told you, Sir," said Frank, looking up, "that I must do as you chose, only my wishes were the other way."

"As I chose; what care I for that, if it is all against the grain? No, it shall not be *must*—I am no tyrant, as you would make me out—I must have you willing, or not at all."

Frank was silent again.

"Oh, he will be persuaded," said Lady Willoughby; "he must see the advantages, and not grieve us all by opposing all our wishes—so amiable a youth as he is, too, and when we only wish his own good."

"Well, I am tired of talking of it. I wash my hands of it, and leave it to you," said Sir Francis. "Talk him out of his folly, there is a good little Kate, now."

Away went Sir Francis: and poor Frank remained with a look upon his face which, interested as she was, made Emmeline think, for a moment, that now she knew what was meant when a man was said to look as if he was going to be hanged.

Lady Willoughby began by looking very soft and gentle as she took Frank's reluctant hand, and said, "My dear boy, I feel sure that you consider me as a mother, and will have full confidence in my earnest wishes for your welfare."

"Thank you," said Frank, when she paused, finding he must say something, and speaking in a subdued voice.

"Ah, I am sure of it, and I am sure you will listen to me when I beg you to oblige your dear father, and give pleasure to all of us, sincere pleasure, by consenting to what is so much to your own advantage."

"I have told my father that of course he must dispose of me as he likes," said Frank.

"Yes, but that is not all; Sir Francis is so kind, so indulgent, that the last thing he would wish would be to force your inclinations."

"Then I can't help it," said Frank; "I can't help what I wish."

"But I can't understand it at all, my dear. What is this great charm in the Church as a profession?"

She waited for an answer, but none was forthcoming, and she went on triumphantly, "I know you are very much attached to your uncle, poor dear good old man, and to his parish, what is its name? A sweet place, and so romantic, as Mrs. Willoughby said; of course you must be attached to it, and it does you great credit; but then, you will know, when you have seen a little more of the world, how different it is; a country curate is a mere nobody, and unless you have connexions in that line, there is no rising, and in such a remote place, no bringing yourself into notice. Your uncle, dear good man—"

"I don't want notice, Ma'am," said Frank, who had been looking even more resigned and uneasy under this speech than before.

"Ah! this is the way people talk when they are young and romantic; I can quite sympathize with you, my dear; but then, you know—" Here she could not get on, but she began on another tack: "Have you thought of the advantages, my dear? just remember, an officer in the Guards is in the very best, the very highest, circles of society, without anything to fatigue you, a London life, introductions everywhere. And then the estate that Sir Francis is going to buy—some fine place, no doubt. Dear me, think of such a position—eldest son, and heir to a fine property, and an officer in the Guards, with a handsome allowance, such as dear liberal Sir Francis would be sure to make to his eldest son!"

"Then I wish he would make an eldest son of Alfred!" said Frank despondingly.

Lady Willoughby looked bright for a moment, but then shook her head: "Ah! that is so generous—"

I

"Not at all," said Frank, with a little more hope.

"Oh, but it is, my dear boy, it is very noble, and you shall not say otherwise; and if anything could add to my affection for you—but you see it would never do, it is quite impossible, your father would never consent, and I am the last person in the world who could make such a proposal—you must see that. No, you must yield to all our wishes, make us all happy. Let me have the pleasure of telling your father that I have prevailed."

Frank returned rather doggedly to his old formulary. "My father must do as he pleases, but I cannot speak the truth, if I am required to say I like it."

"Ah! well, you will come round in time, I know you will! you are only taken by surprise, just now; but you will yield, you will see what is so much to your benefit. And now I shall leave you to talk it over with your sisters."

She sailed away, and they all felt it a relief to go out into the garden. Kate was the first to speak.

"O Frank, is not it horrid?"

"When you have never thought of anything but going into the Church all your life!" said Emmeline.

"I am in the Church," said Frank bluntly.

"Oh yes, of course, in that sense," said Emmeline; "but you know what I mean. And you and Uncle Willoughby suit so beautifully, as Juliet says. Oh, I do hope you will persuade Sir Francis."

"A very honest person you are, Miss Berners," said Frank, suddenly turning round on her. "Prettily you are doing the work you were set to do!"

"But Frank, Frank, you surely did not think we should be unkind enough to tease you about these foolish Guards," said Emmeline.

"Then you had better say nothing about it," said Frank. He tried to speak in his bantering way, but not succeeding, he next put on his churlishness. "I can manage my affairs with my father my own way; then again he failed, and there was a suppressed sob in his voice as he finished. "Thank you, let me alone; you will either be double-faced or get into a scrape if you meddle, so have nothing to do with it. I can write to my uncle." So saying, he resolutely walked away from them.

They looked at each other. "Is he angry? is he sullen?" said Kate.

'Oh no, no!" said Emmeline, whose eyes were full of tears; "it is all his goodness, poor fellow; but I wish he would not be so cautious for us; I should like of all things to get into a scrape for his sake. Come, Kate, we will try if it is possible to get some comprehension of the state of things into Mamma's head."

They accordingly did the very unusual thing of making an inroad upon Lady Willoughby in her own room, and they were thus received: "Well, my dear Emmie, are you come to pity me? I suppose I need not ask whether you could do anything with him; but I am sure you can bear me witness that I said everything to him that could be said."

"Yes, Mamma," began Emmeline.

"Sir Francis would have me try what I could do," continued Lady Willoughby, "though I was quite certain it would be of no use; the boy knew no more what I was saying than a block. You saw how it was, did not you?"

"I assure you, Mamma, I think there is a great deal more in Frank than you suppose."

"My dear Emmie, how can you say so? you see with Miss Willoughby's partial eyes, I suppose; but I assure you I never saw a more clumsy, dull, heavy youth in my life. I know you won't repeat this, of course. But though I heartily wish it was settled—because, till it is, his father will let us have no peace—it is really vexatious to think what advantages will be thrown away upon him. Make them over to your little Alfred, to be sure! the boy could not have said a wiser thing, only it is quite impossible; all the world would be thinking it was my doing."

"I wish it could be so settled," said Emmeline; "for I know

very well Frank will never be so useful or so happy anywhere as at Dumblethwayte; he has grown up all his life with the hope of being his uncle's curate, and it is what he is just fit for. Indeed, Mamma, he is neither dull nor without feeling, and this project is giving him more pain, I am sure, than you or Sir Francis can guess; so if you can do anything for him to put Sir Francis off the scheme—"

"Impossible, impossible, my dear. You don't know how his mind is set on it. For my own part, as I say, the boy should be welcome to do as he pleases, but it would never do to say so to Sir Francis; and don't you by any means either, my dears. If he thought you were backing up his son against him, I really can't tell what would be the consequence; we should never have any peace again."

"I am very sorry for Frank," said Emmeline, with a very sincere long sigh; and they were both leaving the room, when Lady Willoughby said, "Oh, my dears, are you going? I wanted you to help me look over these collars and things, to see which to have made up again."

"Yes, Mamma," said Kate, and stayed; but Emmeline could not bear it, and went to the drawing-room. She leant out of the window, and saw Frank with his arms folded, pacing slowly up and down the walks, and much did she long to go and comfort him, and tell him that he had two sisters who loved and felt with him; and then, when she thought of his rejection of their sympathy, for their sake, not for his own, she saw a nobleness in it, which for a moment made her heart swell as if he had been a hero of romance. "Double-faced, he said," thought she; "I know who is double-faced! Oh, it makes my heart sick. Oh, that I could still think of her as I did before her return; but it is rather as if I had lost than found my mother! she putting everything before Frank, indeed! as if Frank's was a mind to be satisfied with finery, and society, and London life, and the world; what have they to do with happiness?"

What have they indeed? but Emmeline was not right in the highest sense. She viewed them only as contrasted with the

quiet pleasant life at Dumblethwayte Parsonage, and she thought
she sympathized with Frank; but deeper, far deeper, was the
tide of feeling that filled his heart. Words, or formed thoughts,
he had not; but his temper was that of the young brother of
St. Bernard, who, finding himself left heir of his father's estate,
when his brethren entered the convent, exclaimed, "What!
earth for me, and Heaven for you! that is not fair." When or
how the idea that he was to be a clergyman had first risen in
his mind, Frank knew not, for he could not remember when
he had been without it; it had grown up with him; and to be
worthy of the sacred calling had ever been his fondest thought
and care. His temper and taste were in themselves such as to
render his father's plans far less inviting than they would have
been to most other boys of his age, and coming in contrast as
they did with such hopes as he had hitherto entertained, there
was something more painful in them. Then, too, came the
unreasonable requirement to take pleasure in the project: to
submit might have been possible, but of professing to like it he
was incapable, and at the same time there were doubts respecting what was his duty, and a dread of a certain dogged sullenness of temper under contradiction, which Frank well knew to
be his besetting sin, though it had long been so well subdued,
that, heavy as his heart was, and irritating as Lady Willoughby's
persuasions were, not one of the party could ever have made it
an accusation against him.

Lady Willoughby, however, in her desire for her own peace,
did him an important service; for when her husband was beginning on the subject again in the evening, she looked very winning, and said she had a proposal to make, namely, that since
at any rate Frank would remain till Christmas at his present
school, no more should be said about it till that time, when
Frank would have had full opportunity to think about it, and
make up his mind.

It was a truce which everyone was willing to accept, for all
were tired of the question; so the next day began just as usual.
Frank got up his spirits again, and in gratitude to the girls for

their willingness to sympathize with him, did actually teach
them the Greek alphabet, laughed at them more than ever, but
forbore to tease them any more about the Miss Shaws.

CHAPTER XI.

The day is cold and dark and dreary,
It rains, and the wind is never weary ;
The vine stillclings to the mouldering wall,
But at every gust the dead leaves fall,
And the day is dark and dreary.

Longfellow.

EMMELINE and Kate were as sorry as their mother was glad when
the holidays came to a conclusion ; and Frank, after giving
considerable praise to Kate for her good behaviour to Miss
Townsend, bestowed on her the half-crown, and conducted her
into the town to spend it on the poor children whom he patronized. Moreover, he left his love for Mr. Denham, finished the
last touches to the tower, and put it under their charge, and left
them a legacy of an old Greek Testament, which, by the help of
an English one, Emmeline could make out very well.

Thereupon Emmeline and Kate went without much interruption into their strong fit of learning. It was particularly
convenient just at this time, for there were things which they
could wish to have driven out of their heads. There had been
less favourable accounts of Lord Herbert of late—not so much
that he was worse, as that he was not better; and though
Constance's letters were still cheerful, Lady Frances, who had
her elder brother's report, wrote of the climate of Italy not
having had the hoped-for effect. The shadow of a coming grief
seemed to be darkening upon them from that quarter ; and nearer
at hand were poor Frank's perplexities, which Sir Francis would
not let them forget; and the unsatisfactory light in which they
had seen their mother, made Emmeline more than ever willing

to throw herself out of present things, and to make a world for herself.

Her world of poor people had passed away ; Miss Willoughby's visit had made an interruption, and the sisters were unwilling to begin again, just as everyone is reluctant to resume a piece of work put away with a mistake in it.

The Miss Shaws, Mr. Denham, the battle of the Catechism, had passed out of Emmeline's thoughts, and did not recur to them pleasantly ; the opposition had not been strong enough to make her feel herself heroic and persecuted ; and Frank had left an impression on her mind that it would have been wiser not to have meddled with Mr. Hunter's parish at all. Therefore they both managed to forget or miss their visiting days ; they avoided the Miss Shaws, did not go to school, did no poor work, and in fact, neglected all they had undertaken.

Very poor and tame did the ideas of teaching idle children, and reading to blind old men, appear beside those with which Emmeline had at present filled her own head and her sister's. First came their Greek, good hard satisfying work ; next their German, wherein they bewildered themselves in the metaphysics more than ever. They translated verses, and sent them to Juliet, and delighted in Fouqué's beautiful romances ; thirdly, there was poetry, Tennyson's especially, to which they had been introduced by Miss Willoughby ; and as to the "Princess," it so embodied an ancient vision of their own, that it perfectly enchanted them. They might be said to rave about it for at least a fortnight, and Kate wrote such a letter of rapture to Constance, that in return she received a good-natured message from Lord Somerville, to ask if she had got into a lime-kiln !

But, above all, there was Emmeline's romance, which she communicated to Kate in full order, as far as it was composed, one evening, when their elders were dining out. Kate, indeed, knew each idea as it had occurred, but she had yet to hear them altogether, and judge of their effect.

It was to be a romance of the League ; the hero, Olivier de Montmorency, was to be fighting in the cause of Henri Quatre ;

and the battle of Ivry, and the white plume, were to be in some way connected with the *dénouement*—but how, was not at present very clear. All that was as yet settled was, that a certain lovely Rosalie, a great friend and a maid-of-honour of Henri's sister, Catherine of Navarre, was to be in the hands of the Duke of Guise, imprisoned in a castle, and in great danger of being married to some bloody-minded individual of the House of Guise. The Princess Catherine, in despair about her, entreated in vain the adventurous gallants of her brother's army to attempt her rescue, but no one could be persuaded till Olivier de Montmorency rose, and promised that if the Princess would send the Lady Rosalie a token by his hands that he might be trusted, he would undertake to bring her in safety.

Thereupon Olivier set off, disguised as a minstrel, sung a song under the Lady Rosalie's window, unfolding his purpose, gave her the token, in return for the guerdon which she bestowed on him, and, in a few words, appointed the place whence he undertook to carry her off. In the middle of the night, Olivier was at the postern-gate with two horses; Rosalie kept her appointment, and safely mounted; but just as they emerged from the shade of the walls, and rode across a broad strip of moonlight, several shots were fired from the battlements. Olivier hastened the lady forward; they rode through the wood, rode all night, the knight cheering the lady, and expressing his devotion to her all the time. At last they arrived, just as the morning meal was commencing in all solemnity in the hall; Rosalie was aided to dismount; Olivier gave her his hand—she wondered it was his left—to lead her into the hall; he led her to the Princess's feet, and there sunk down and fainted, his right arm having been broken by the shot from the battlements.

It was at that moment that Miss Townsend walked in, having been taught to do so fearlessly, whilst Frank was at home. The sisters looked blank; she could see that she was not wanted; she thought it very amiable in the Miss Berners to be so perfectly happy alone together, and resolved to disturb them no more.

They did not even miss her, or know that it was past her

hour for coming down, the next evening, when Emmeline made the first attempt at writing out the beginning of her romance— a thing she found much more easily said than done. Her fine beginnings with " It was," would get into a tangle ; her sentences were so interminable that even Kate could not find breath to get through them ; and her thoughts went so much faster than her pen, that she had not even arrived at the commencement of the conversation in which the Princess was to propose the adventure.

The Greek, the German, the poetry, the romance, altogether absorbed Emmeline and Kate.

They used to sit in the tower all the morning, and often all the afternoon too, reading, writing, romancing, impatient of interruption, and unwilling to give a minute's thought or time to the despised world of life.

Their mother might reasonably speak in her plaintive notes, when she said they were always so engaged that she could never get them for a moment ; Sir Francis grumbled in vain, and said that he never had any music, or that he did not wish to see them learned ladies ; and as to the children, who had always been used to a ready welcome and plenty of amusement in the tower, they were told to run away, for their sisters were busy. How it fared with the Miss Shaws, and with the poor, has already been shown ; and it was a deeper, graver, sadder question, how it fared with Emmeline's and Kate's own souls.

The Confirmation, with its attendant fears and hopes, had slipped out of their minds ; and had they interrogated themselves, they would have thought they were just the same as they were last year, at school ; but that could scarcely be, for an opportunity had been neglected, and duties were being left undone every day. Last summer they were in a state of more humility and obedience ; and though many of their present errors were owing to the want of guidance in their own family, yet they were so far their own fault, as they had neglected the means of grace, which might have been a safe-guard.

This seems like harsh treatment of slight faults ; but the

question is, not whether the faults are slight in themselves, but whether they are not the greatest that can be committed under the circumstances. Emmeline and Kate could hardly have done anything very bad, but they did the worst they could.

For instance, Emmeline would come down to breakfast in a brown study, and pay no attention to Sir Francis's particular likings as to the mixture of green and black in his tea; Lady Willoughby would appear towards the end of the breakfast, thinking herself nervous and unwell, and wanting to be petted and made much of; but Emmeline, being sure it was only a fancy, would rise and look restless till Kate joined her; Miss Townsend might have a head-ache, or a distressing letter from home, and sit in her room exerting every faculty for the children, not relieved from them for one quarter of an hour, not refreshed by one word of sympathizing inquiry. They knew it not, but whose fault was that? Or she was harassed by some injudicious petty regulation or interference from Sir Francis, which a hint might have turned aside. Alfred might look in vain for the sisters who once used to tell him stories, Janet pined in secret for love and notice, Edwin was boisterous, and Cecilia was an interruption. Then, again, Lady Willoughby was left to take her drive in solitude, while her daughters were roaming on the sands, arranging the adventures of Olivier's midnight ride; they had no ears, when she came home, to hear whom she had met, and who had bowed to her; they had settled that it was of no use to read to a person who only went to sleep; and as to conversation, when Sir Francis came in, he found one with a book, and the other with a dictionary, and if he said, "Now, let us be sociable," he was met by "Do let us finish this."

All these neglects would not, perhaps, happen in one day; it was sometimes their own pleasure to be attentive to conversation; sometimes it was agreeable to play with the little boys; and in their demeanour towards their parents, gentle dispositions and good breeding concealed want of respect; but none who regards this long list of omissions, and recollects the pride of intellect, and disdain of aught but her own romantic dreams, which

Emmeline was fostering, can think her otherwise than in a perilous state of mind. It could not go on long, and the first check was from the inconvenience of having a fire in the tower when the mornings became cold. The housemaid was cross, the chimney was crosser; the damp was said to be brought out by the fire; and what in the days of Frank and Juliet was an excellent joke, was now unbearable. Emmeline and Kate were smoked out of the tower, and Sir Olivier de Montmorency and the Lady Rosalie were smoked out of existence. To do them in the morning, with the chance of Sir Francis coming in, was impossible. They gradually occupied less of Emmeline's imagination; she ceased her researches into French history, and there was once more a void in her mind.

. One Autumn day when the withered leaves were whirling in the eddying gusts of wind, Kate came into the room where Emmeline was standing, pensively watching them, with a book hanging from her hand.

"Have you been waiting for me, Emmie dear?" said she. "I was kept by Sir Francis. He is in a fuss about the rattling of the stair-case window, and he would keep me to grumble to about it, till I called the housemaid to stop it."

"It is not worth while," said Emmeline; "it will do just as well to worry about as anything else! Oh dear!"

"I really am afraid I have kept you too long waiting," said Kate.

"Oh no! it is not that; I don't know whether watching the sere and withered leaf does not suit me better than reading. I am tired of German, Kate; I don't see the use of it; I can't care for it as Juliet does."

"It is a disagreeable dreary day, when one does not care for anything," said Kate, coming to the window, and throwing her arm round Emmeline's waist.

"I've been thinking of all sorts of things!" said Emmeline. "People might say I am too young for such thoughts as those brown leaves bring about dreariness, and loneliness, and fading; but it seems to me that we go floating and ebbing about on all sorts of blasts, just like those poor leaves."

"Together at least!" said Kate; "like those," as the wind brought a twig bearing twin leaves, which dashed against the glass and then were whirled off again.

"Together—oh yes, together!" said Emmeline, kissing her. "Yes, I must not speak of loneliness, while I am so rich in my own Katie. But oh! Kate, it is well for us that we have sisters' love to support us, for how forlorn all would be to us but for each other!"

"Forlorn indeed!" said Kate. "Oh yes, Emmie, we are all in all to each other, and these disappointments—" she sank her voice, and looked timidly round—"do but make us more precious to each other!"

Emmeline returned the caress, and was silent, while Kate's head rested fondly on her shoulder. Just then she felt, as Kate did, that she wanted no more, but it was a passing feeling; deeply as she loved her sister, there was a craving in her heart for something more, something satisfying. So, when she was in good spirits, she dwelt upon her original vision of that love which she thought would satisfy her; and the hero suspected of a great crime received some very important embellishments.

Next came an unsatisfactory account of Lord Herbert; a return of cough, and of oppression on the breath, which, though Constance accounted for it as "a fresh cold," could not but be considered as very alarming. The party were to spend the winter at Malta, and Emmeline's weary wishings took the form of longing to be with them, so as to be a comfort to Constance, and to see her brother-in-law's kind face and bright eyes once again.

She and Kate settled that Lord Liddesdale and Lady Frances would certainly go to see Herbert, and would offer to take them, and they would get there just as he was recovering, and enjoy themselves. But as they heard of Lord Liddesdale being laid up at Rowthorpe with a fit of the gout, this charming scheme soon passed away.

The next vision was suggested by reading Miss Kavanagh's beautiful history of "Madeline." Home cares, home annoyances, should all fleet away, and Emmeline and Kate should be the foundresses of such an institution as Madeline's; they would receive the sick and poor, and devote themselves with their whole hearts and souls. Constance, too—it was finding such a home, such an occupation for her, as would be a sort of happiness, if their fears for her husband were accomplished—they would make her a sort of Lady Abbess, and cling to her as they used to do in old days. It somehow satisfied them for their neglect of the poor of Herringsby, to lodge the most deserving of them, in imagination, in their hospital; and it should be upon a mountain, in the free breezy air, in a beautiful style of architecture, with a little chapel close to it, a school for their orphans, and no Mr. Denham. It became so real, that Emmeline and Kate counted the years that had to elapse before they should both be of age, and able to devote their fortunes to the purpose; but all the time they were very comfortably pleasing themselves, while they were talking and dreaming of self-devotion.

It was pleasant to receive Frank from school; and the fortnight before Christmas passed away without a return of the dreaded subject. Sir Francis chose to give a grand children's party, though his lady, in secret, disliked and dreaded it so much, that she would have made Lord Herbert's illness an excuse for getting rid of it, but for an invitation to a dinner-party the next day.

It would probably have been as great a nuisance to the sisters as to her, had not Frank warmly taken up the preparation, worked very hard, and made helping agreeable to them. He managed that the Miss Shaws, who never went to regular parties, should be asked to this one, and took the two girls and little Alfred with him to give the invitation. The good ladies were highly pleased, and as kind as ever; but not a word was said about the school.

The party went off well; and there was a certain serenity about the Christmas-tide, of which Emmeline was conscious when it was over. Frank made her and Kate, and sometimes Alfred, go with him to the Saint's-day services, at eleven o'clock; and afterwards they had some delightful frosty walks. He could not help talking, more than once, of the Christmas delights of Dumblethwayte, where his heart evidently was, as much as ever; and but for his always changing the subject if ever the girls tried to learn his plans, it would have seemed that the question of the last holidays were entirely forgotten.

It was not, however, long to remain so. One morning Frank came into the drawing-room, and as Kate made some observation, replied with a churlish grunt, which caused Emmeline to look up and observe a cloud on his face. He threw himself down in an arm-chair, and held up the newspaper before him, but only continued in this manner for a couple of moments, then springing up, said, "Don't you want me for some of your Greek nonsense?"

They were too glad of the opportunity, and he had never been a pleasanter master than on that day. Homer proceeded more prosperously than he had ever yet done, and they were all laughing together when Sir Francis came in, and in the very sound of his shutting the door, Emmeline perceived that he was in a fume.

"Very merry you all seem here!" said he, with an angry look at his son; and certainly the merriment did not continue. Frank bit his lips, his forehead contracted for an instant, and then expanded, and he went on looking out a word in the lexicon.

"So you are resolved to go poring on with your learning!" said Sir Francis to Kate, in a tone that was meant to be civil, but which was full of annoyance; "nothing but books all day long for any of you. Why, the room is full of books," said he, glancing at the sofa, where grammars and dictionaries were lying heaped together.

Frank, saying in a low voice to Emmeline, "Do you want any more of these?" began to gather them up.

"I don't want to be treated like a tyrant, Sir," said his father. "I want none of this submission, as if I was not to be spoken to—I don't want to interfere with your sisters' pursuits —it is submission I want.—Where is your mother, Emmeline?"

"In her room," answered Emmeline, who thought he might have known this without coming to disturb them ; and away he went.

For her life, Kate could not have helped saying, "O Frank, has he begun about it again ? "

"Yes," said or rather sighed Frank ; and a silence ensued.

"You said the same as before ? " asked Kate at last.

"I don't know what else to say," said Frank, with a deep sigh. "I can't say what is not true, and I can't help it."

"I wish I knew what was to be done ! " said Emmeline sorrowfully.

"But do you dislike it so very much, Frank ? " said Kate.

"I—what should I do—stuck up in London like an ape in a scarlet coat, with nothing to do but to be a fine gentleman ? But, however, that's not the point," said Frank, recalling himself ; "if that was all, I suppose I could bring my mind to find something tolerable in it—at any rate, I should be quit of an awful lot of Latin and Greek—but 'tis the being obliged to say one likes it better than the other. But it is of no use to talk about it. I shall go and see if Alfred has done his lessons, and take him out for a walk."

From this time, if the argument itself was not perpetually going on, the effect on Sir Francis's temper was. Frank could say or do nothing but what was displeasing ; cheerfulness provoked him, silence was supposed to be sullenness, obligingness was hypocrisy. He was called perverse, obstinate, ungrateful ; and worse than all, Sir Francis took to calling himself a fool for having allowed him to spend his holidays at Dumblethwayte, and in unmeasured terms found fault with those views which he believed to be at the bottom of Frank's opposition.

Emmeline and Kate used to grow very angry, and long to say something—for all this was almost as much against Lord Herbert as against Mr. Willoughby—but they never dared ; they could only watch Frank anxiously, and sympathize with him in their hearts, though he would not let them do so outwardly.

How he bore it was to them a perfect marvel, worried as he

was about whatever he did, and whatever he did not do; and they did not guess at half of the pain which this occasioned him—how much more his deeper sense of reverence suffered from these sayings of his father—how much more strong his feeling was for the blame cast upon his uncle—how grievous were the doubts whether he was failing in duty, or which was the superior duty. Besides, Frank had not naturally the sweet buoyant temper, that can throw off vexation, and scarce feel it except at the moment, and had he given way to his impulse, he would hardly have done anything but sit brooding over his provocations, or repaying unkindness with sullen silence; but so carefully did he guard against his disposition, that it never appeared, except in a sort of constraint in his voice, when forced to speak in answer to some soft persuasion of Lady Willoughby, or to some annoying reproach of his father.

He was always ready to interest himself in their pursuits; he played with the children, told Alfred what he would have to do at school, kept Kate up to her good behaviour to Miss Townsend, and though he did not make fun on his own account as usual, he was always ready with some quaint answer.

It was one Sunday afternoon, towards the beginning of February, than an almost forgotten subject was recalled to Emmeline and Kate, by hearing Mr. Brent give notice of a Confirmation, to be held soon after Easter, desiring the Candidates to come to him in the intermediate time for preparation.

"Well, I am glad of that," said Frank, as he walked home with Emmeline. "I was getting ashamed of you two."

"Should you be more ashamed if I told you I was rather sorry?" said Emmeline.

"I am ashamed that you don't know any better," said Frank.

"I don't think it is so much knowing as feeling," said Emmeline sadly.

"Feeling goes for nothing," said Frank.

"So people say," answered Emmeline; "but all I can feel is that I am very much afraid, more so now than last year."

"And so you will go on getting more afraid every year of

your life, the longer you put it off. But luckily you can't do that."

"No, because no one else does; but that makes it worse. I can't bear the thoughts of doing such a thing only because it is the fashion."

"If it does other people good, why should it not do it to you?"

"It is a foolish question, perhaps a wrong one," said Emmeline, "but I should really like to hear someone say they knew it had done them good individually."

"One must believe it, not only feel," said Frank.

"Take it on trust? I don't like that always."

"You ought, then," said Frank; and there was a silence, as if he had done with the subject. But presently, while Emmeline was feeling discontented, and wondering if he thought very ill of her, he said, in an odd blunt way, "I want to make you see it and wish it, Emmie, and I don't know how. Will it do you any good, I wonder, to tell you what I think of it myself?"

"Oh, pray do!" said Emmeline.

"Well then, I don't know or remember how much I felt or cared about my Confirmation at the time—a great deal too little, considering all the pains that were taken with me; but this I do know, that I should be a dozen times worse than I am now without it; and as to getting through all this—this fuss, this affair—I—I am quite sure I could not do it at all."

"Only being confirmed!" said Emmeline.

"No; you know what more I mean. You can't get on without *that*—in or out of trouble—so I only hope you won't dawdle out of Confirmation again. If you are afraid now, you will be ashamed another time."

"But, Frank, is not that—I beg your pardon, for I am sure you are right—but is not that putting one's trust in forms and ordinances?"

"Stuff! Emmie, you learnt that of the Miss Shaws, I suppose, No more than it is for the beggar to ring the bell at the gate. I should not have expected that of a person who stands up for

K

the Catechism.   It is not all, but it can't be without it: it is
the means, as the Catechism says, and that's it."

Emmeline thought, and the confused words penetrated her
understanding. She was silent for some time, and then said,
" It certainly will be a great pity if you are not a clergyman."

" Never mind," said Frank.

She told Kate what had passed, adding that Frank seemed so
much in earnest, that she thought his blundering way would go
further than many more clear and lucid statements; but they
agreed in a great dread of going to Mr. Brent, and hoped that
he would allow their old Confirmation tickets to serve without
a second examination.

On Monday morning the girls were surprised by the entrance
of Sir Francis, looking more amiable than for a long time past.

" Well, my dears," said he, " you must give me joy—you
must give the young guardsman joy—he has come to his senses
at last—given up his nonsense, and now all is right ! "

Emmeline opened her eyes wide in consternation ; she was
very sorry that Frank should have yielded to persecution. Kate's
first idea was, on the contrary, that the torment was over, and
her " Indeed " was therefore a pleased one.

" Yes! he has yielded, and with a good grace at last," said Sir
Francis.   " I was sure, when he had seen a little more of the
world, and knew what my proposal was, he never could stick to
that boyish fancy ; all very well for a boy who had never looked
beyond the hills of Dumblethwayte, but we know better what
is worth having now, don't we, Katie ? "

Lady Willoughby here came down, and she kissed Frank as
she told him that she was so rejoiced, but that she had been sure
from the first that his affectionate nature would yield to their
united wishes.

To which Frank answered, " Thank you, Ma'am ; " and then
Sir Francis proceeded to orate on the steps he was going
to take.

Emmeline was decidedly vexed, and as soon as she left the
breakfast-room, throwing herself down on the sofa in the drawing-

room, began to exclaim to herself that constancy was not in man.

Kate came in about ten minutes after, and with her came Frank. Had the conversation depended on Frank or Emmeline, not one word would have been said; but Kate, more curious and venturesome in her sympathy, was the first to say, "O Frank!" and there stopped.

"O Frank!" said Emmeline, and she too stopped.

"Well," said Frank, as if he would fain have smiled.

"You have given it up!" said Kate.

"Yes, I suppose—" he leant against the window, and spoke low—"I suppose I was not good enough."

"But what did you say?" continued Kate.

"I said I would try to like it, and I had no doubt I should in time."

Emmeline watched him intently, but as his face was against the window, she could see nothing but part of a very red cheek and ear.

"We shall be comfortable now," said Kate.

"That was not your reason, though," cried Emmeline, springing up, "was it, Frank? You would never have yielded to persecution."

"Nonsense about persecution," said Frank gruffly.

"But you yielded because you thought it right."

"I've no business to hold out against my father," said he, and walked off.

CHAPTER XII.

At sultry evening's fall,
The gorgeous lines be duly shown,
That weave Heaven's wondrous pall;
Calm be his sleep whose eyelids close
Upon so fair a sight.

Lyra Innocentium.

FOR the first few days after Frank had come to his decision, there was universal satisfaction, and even Emmeline could not help being sensible of the great relief from Sir Francis's ill-humour.

There was a great deal of occupation, too, of another kind; Alfred was going to school, and preparations made them all very busy.

His father took him to school, and afterwards went on with Frank to London, to make his proposed arrangements; and it was not till then, that Emmeline had leisure for a great fit of weariness and craving—she rather believed at present that it was for Constance. There was good reason for thinking much of Constance, for the accounts of Lord Herbert were unfavourable, and there seemed to be so much present suffering, that willing as the sisters were to close their eyes to the danger, they could not but be much grieved.

The gloom did not disperse when Sir Francis and his son returned; Frank was graver and more at a loss for occupation, as if the interest of his life had been taken away. He wrote often to his uncle; but Emmeline and Kate soon found that he could not speak of Dumblethwayte, and though he walked with them as good-naturedly as ever, he would sometimes go three parts of the way in absolute silence, or sit with the newspaper before him half the morning without speaking; and as on these occasions he seemed best pleased when the girls were practising their music, they played much more than they had done for some time.

He, however, was doing his best to give his mind to his destined profession; he listened and answered cheerfully when his father discoursed about it, and of his own accord asked Kate if she should dislike the trouble of teaching him French. She was delighted to consent, and a very slow scholar she found him; and the marvellous attempts he made to pronounce the French words, which he began by reading just like Latin, were the cause of laughter, which did them all good. Also he brought out his mathematics, of which Emmeline and Kate, whose school had taught everything, just understood so much, that they, being clever girls, could soon surpass a boy who was far from clever. And as they took it up keenly, all three launched into Euclid together with great satisfaction, Emmeline rushing on from proposition to proposition, fancying she understood all, but often "brought up," as Frank called it, when obliged to make things clear to him. Those were by no means unpleasant hours that they spent together over triangles, circles, and parallel lines, though they generally ended in extensive yawns.

All might have done very well, and Frank's own energetic spirit would surely have soon made him happy, but it soon appeared that even his sacrifice had not contented his father. It has already been said that Sir Francis fancied those religious views which he found so much more prevalent in England than previously, had been the cause of his son's reluctance to fufil his wishes; and instead of being indifferent to them, or treating them with a sort of dignified superiority, as before in the case of Lord Herbert, he began to rail against them as exemplified in the masters of Frank's school, and in Mr. Brent. Very painful things did he both say and do, and to hear him approach the subject was dreaded by all the three young people; Mr. Brent's manner of conducting the service, his daily prayers, and weekly Communions, were all matters of reprobation, especially when Lent began and the services were more frequent.

Worse than all, he began to regard Frank's constant attendance on these ordinances as a perverse clinging to his former intentions;

and Emmeline saw, Sunday after Sunday, with a sort of terror, how his face darkened when Frank and Miss Townsend were left in Church. The daily morning service was so early, as to remove Frank's attendance from his notice; but on several occasions when it was later, he had shown considerable annoyance. Once he said to him, "Remember, you are not a parson now, Frank!" another time, "Sticking to the old shop still!" or, "Always at it!"

Emmeline was sure a storm was gathering, and wondered whether Frank, whom she considered as having once given way, would still be firm. One fine bright Wednesday towards the latter end of March, Kate and Frank were gone to Church, when Sir Francis came into the drawing-room hastily asking for Frank.

"He is gone out with Kate," she said.

"You need not try to mince matters," said Sir Francis; "to Church, I suppose?"

Then followed what sounded to Emmeline so like what school-children call a bad word, that she felt her colour flush and go away again in horror.

"It shall not go on! it shall not!" proceeded Sir Francis, as he hastily opened the drawers of the table, and shut them up again with a violent noise. "I'll make him know that I am to be obeyed, heart and soul, as well as outwardly. Did you ever see anything more perverse, more ungrateful, than that boy, after all I have done for him, after pretending to give up this absurd notion, after I have talked to him till I am sick of it, to be going after that Church—that Church for ever—and that Brent, with his new-fangled fancies—when he knows my opinion? I tell you, Emmeline, it is perverseness, pure perverseness; and that is the reason I have no patience with it! Just tell me, did you ever hear of the boy in your life that would go to Church when he could help it? No, no; 'tis nothing on earth but obstinacy, and he shall see if I will suffer it. I am sure, the plague, the disappointment, that young fellow has been to me—"

Emmeline, though not venturing to say a word, was rejoiced to be the receiver of his wrath, since she knew that it was often exhausted in this manner before the actual subject came in his way—nor was she on this occasion mistaken ; a visitor luckily came, and stayed to luncheon, and his displeasure had passed away before the family were alone together.

This was, however, only the first clap of thunder; the next followed on Lady-day, when, the service being longer than they had expected, they did not return till the luncheon bell had actually rung.

The girls ran up in haste, threw off their bonnets, and came down again, but before they reached the foot of the stairs they heard Sir Francis's voice. Emmeline would almost have turned back, but Kate pressed on, and they entered the dining-room: Frank stood by the fire, his elbow on the mantel-piece, and resting his forehead in his hand, while his father, leaning back in his chair, and almost stammering with passion, was pouring out a whole torrent of reproaches against his brother, Mr. Brent and his whole system, as well as against Frank.

Frank stood the whole time in the same attitude, till his father, having stormed on for a considerable time, at last began to find fault with his silence, and called on him to answer.

Then he looked up, and said, " I don't know how."

" Don't pretend not to know what I expect," said his father. " Obedience is what I require."

" Then, Sir, I am sorry to say I cannot obey you in this."

" Frank, my dear boy ! " said Lady Willoughby ; " now Sir Francis, I do beg you will let us have a little conversation together."

" Not a bit of use," said Sir Francis ; " he is as obstinate as a mule ; feels no more what I have done for him than—"

" I am sure," said Lady Willoughby, actually taking the trouble to rise, approach Frank, and take his hand, " I am sure he is actuated by the best of motives, and that on reflection, a little over-scrupulousness must give way to your wishes. These scenes are so very trying to one's feelings ! " added she, with tears in her eyes, " and we know already how dear Frank can sacrifice his own wishes to ours."

Frank drew his hand from hers, and raised his head. "I
gave up my wishes then," said he, "because they were only
wishes. I cannot give up my duty."

"Your duty!" exclaimed Sir Francis; "and do you pretend
to stand there, and tell me I am no judge of your duty? I
should think your uncle at least might have taught you to obey
your father; but I suppose that is not a part of your new-
fashioned doctrine!"

All Kate's fears could not keep her from exclaiming, "O Sir
Francis, recollect what he has given up!"

"Given up! As if a curacy of sixty pounds a year was a
sacrifice to be thrown in my face in the place of what I would
do for him! I hate such hypocrisy and ingratitude! Hanker-
ing after it all the time, as if it was on purpose to provoke me!"

"I have done my best, as you know, to do as you wish," said
Frank; "and honestly, I am much obliged to you, and can look
forward to the plan with some pleasure now."

"You hear him! There are all the thanks he gives me for
what any other youth would have gone down on his knees to
his father to do for him! It makes me sick to hear it!"

"I am very sorry, Sir," said Frank, "that you—"

"Sorry! well then, show it. Deeds, not words!"

"Then, Sir, I must say again, and once for all," said Frank,
speaking more readily than Emmeline thought he could have
done, "that you do not know what you are doing in requiring
me to give these things up. I have been brought up to know
that if I yielded this to you, I should be doing wrong, and soon
should do worse. If I have said what was wrong, if I have
given you reason to think me ungrateful or obstinate, I beg your
pardon; I do not mean to be so, and I am very sorry for any
sullenness I may have shown; but this I cannot give up."

There was a silence when Frank had ceased speaking; even
Sir Francis did not reply for some moments, and Frank was
emboldened to step nearer to him, and holding out his hand, to
say, "Then you forgive me?"

"Foolery, Sir!" said Sir Francis, pushing away his hand

indignantly. "You think to stop my mouth with sermons and hypocrisy, do you? but I'll have none of it. I wash my hands of you. You may go off to your uncle, and have done with it, if you have no better submission than this."

Angrily shoving his chair back from the table, Sir Francis left the room by one door; Frank turned, and with equal precipitation departed by the other; Lady Willoughby sat and cried, and said these scenes were so distressing to her feelings, and she wished Sir Francis and his son would settle their disputes by themselves. There never would be any peace while Frank was in the house, and her nerves would never recover it. Emmeline, who knew it was useless to attempt to talk reason to her, soothed her as well as she could. Kate consoled her for the coldness of the untasted luncheon, and after persuading her to eat and drink as usual, saw her go to dress for her drive, and promised to send the nurse, with little Cecilia, to go out with her.

"And now, what shall we do?" asked Kate of her sister.

"Oh, I don't know; I don't feel much in tune for anything. I wonder what poor Frank has done with himself."

"Miss Townsend asked me," said Kate, "whether we should dislike taking Edwin out with us this afternoon. She said Janet was so uncomfortable with her cold—which means fretful, I suppose—that she did not like to leave her."

"Yes, very well," said Emmeline; "it will be rather a comfort, for there is no pleasure in talking or thinking of anything."

Accordingly Edwin was called, and delighted by hearing that he was to go down to the beach with his sisters. Just as they were setting off, he saw Frank, with his arms folded, pacing up and down the garden walks.

"May not Frank come too?" asked the little fellow.

"Oh yes, if he likes," said Emmeline; "only take care, Edwin dear; perhaps he had rather not be interrupted."

But though Edwin had long since learnt that sister Emmie did not like interruption, it was a lesson which he had never been taught by brother Frank; so he bounded across the green to him, pulled down his hand, and told him, "Sisters and I are going down to the sea, and you must come too."

"Must I ?" said Frank, letting himself be pulled on. "Why, Eddy, you go at me like a wild horse."

Edwin took up the idea, and instantly became an imaginary wild horse, with great tossings of the head and kickings of the heels.

Frank joined them, without one word on his troubles; and by general consent, they all gave themselves up to amuse little Edwin. They raced, they skipped, they ran on for Edwin to catch them; they were his horses, his hounds, his elephants, or his camels.

None of them, and Frank least of all, had quite left childhood behind them; and the glory of the sunny spring day shed itself over them, as it did over their little companion, or over the birds and flowers, in free, careless, unthinking glee. There was the blue sky overhead, the sun shining as if it would set everything in enamel; the broad white sands spread out; the blue capes, clearer than ever they had seen them before, stretching far away in the distance; the glorious sea, with its tracts of different-tinted lights, the little rippling waves each tipped with gold, the white line of breaking waves on the coast;—how could any-one be sad in such a scene? Edwin stretched out both his arms and fairly laughed aloud; and either at him, or from the same feeling, the others laughed too—Frank and Kate first, and then Emmeline, though she wondered more at them and at herself, and while she gave herself up like them to the *abandon* of complete enjoyment, it was with the feeling, "I will be a silly child for once in my life!" They found a cove some way on, quite shut in with rocks, and which they had all to themselves, and there they looked for shells; they found sea-anemones in the pools under the rocks, and made them shut and expand. They played each other tricks with long pieces of wet sea-weed, they ran after the waves, and finally united their efforts to raise a grand castle of sand, as earnestly as if it was the one great purpose of their lives.

Too happy were they to take any note of time, till just as a tall flag was planted on the summit of the castle, and Edwin was clapping his hands in delight, Emmeline looked up, and exclaimed, "How fast the tide is coming in!"

"We shall have a race with it," said Frank. "Come, Edwin, that must do."

The waves were, in fact, advancing very fast, and there was but a narrow space left between them and the projecting promontory of rock which formed the boundary of the little bay.

"O Frank," said the little boy, "just let me see that great wave knock down the tower."

"No, no, Eddy," said Emmeline, beginning to get into a fright, "we sha'n't get home to-night, if we stop now. Come along."

"Here, give me your hand," said Frank; "let Katie and Frank swing you along fast—there!"

They drew him on fast—faster; Emmeline could scarcely keep up with them, for her breath grew tight under a sensation of terror, at the thought that this was but the first of a series of such coves, which must be passed ere they could reach the place where the path led upwards from the beach. The space which had appeared so short when they had trodden it just before, now spread itself out into an interminable length; and there were the waves rolling nearer and nearer, and spreading out a whole field of water in front, as if in eagerness to take possession of the fast lessening sand. They reached the rocks; the sand before them had already been once covered, and they were obliged to run fast, while the wave was retreating. Kate gasped with fear and want of breath; Edwin said he was tired, and Frank took him in his arms, whilst the sisters in silence locked their hands fast together.

On they went without a word—the rocks which they were next to pass did not project equally far; but before they could reach them, the sea had won the race, and a wave had already broken against the farthest advanced.

Now there was an interval, while the third, the most resolute wave, was gathering its force. Frank looked at the girls: "There is time," he said; "don't hurry too much." And he hastened on through the shallow water steadily—they followed closely, feeling the danger a reality indeed as the waters rose above their shoes.

They were on dry sand again, within another such little bay; but here Frank first stood still, then faced about, and looked at them, and they perceived, with a thrill such as they could never forget, that it was bounded on the other side by a very far projecting wall of rock, against the outer end of which the waves were already dashing and rebounding in white spray.

"O Frank, Frank!" exclaimed Kate.

"Hush!" said Frank. "Perhaps there is some way of climbing up."

And setting his little brother down, he was running to what appeared the most practicable part, when Edwin screamed out, "O Frank, don't go away!"

Frank stepped back: "No, Edwin, I won't; I want to try if we can get home over that great rock," said he, in the same quiet good-natured tone he always used with the children; and Edwin seemed satisfied to remain, holding Kate's hand. They breathlessly watched, as Frank, raising himself, clambering, twisting, and seeming sometimes to hang upon but one hand, mounted the slippery rock. It did not last long; he soon swung himself down again, and tried another place, and another, but with equally ill success; and at last he came back to them, shaking his head, and looking at his watch. They had been obliged, while watching him, to retreat some space from the waves, giving ground almost unconsciously; and now that they looked back, it was fearful to see how much smaller was the space of sand behind them, than when they had first entered their ever-narrowing prison.

"Where is high-water mark?" said Emmeline, speaking for the first time.

They looked round, but there was no portion of the sand

that did not appear to have been recently covered, and there was a fringe of sea-weeds at the very foot of the rocks.

"I am sure I have seen this cove full of water!" said Kate.

There came a silence upon them all. Emmeline looked, as if fascinated, at the curling waves, which rolled over and dashed into foam with a monotonous sound, advancing steadily and surely. Kate was even obliged to draw her out of the way, when the sand on which she had been standing was overflowed.

"I want to go home," said Edwin, breaking the silence.

"I am afraid we cannot just yet," said Frank. "We must wait till the water will let us go."

"Are you frightened?" said Edwin, looking up at Kate's face. "I am not;" and then he suddenly threw his arm round her waist, and hid his face in her dress.

Kate put her arm round his neck, and embraced him fast; Emmeline then spoke—"When will it be full tide?"

"Not for two hours—it has to rise a great deal higher yet," said Frank.

"Can nothing be done?" said Emmeline. "Will nobody hear us?"

"I had not thought of that," said Frank; and he shouted as loud as he could several times; but no sound was heard in answer, except the dull dash of the ruthless sea.

"Could not we climb a little way at least?" said Emmeline; "we might be out of—" Her voice failed, and she could not say of "the waves."

"A little way!" said Frank; "there is nothing else to be done."

They looked round for the best spot. At the innermost part of the bay, the rocks rose not only in a perfect wall, but slightly inclining forward, so that that side was perfectly hopeless; but where Frank had made his previous attempts on the projecting boundary of the cove, the rocks were more broken, and here they resolved to make the attempt. It was high time, for the water was already at their feet; but such was the steepness of the rocks, that the girls would have thought it at any other time perfectly impossible to mount them. Frank first showed Kate how to raise herself, and pushed her up, till she found herself on the top of the first rock; next he lifted Edwin up, she received him in her arms and placed him securely; and then Emmeline, lifted by Frank, and dragged by Kate, was lodged by her side on the narrow slippery ledge, where she could hardly stand. Lastly, Frank mounted, and by grappling with his hands, and dragging himself up with his knees, managed to gain another elevation, up which he again succeeded in pulling them, and then by another giddy feat of climbing, and by writhing round a sharp projecting rock, they gained the summit of a tolerably large flat stone, where there was standing room for all. It was hardly five yards above the beach, and a sheer precipice rose straight above them, which even a fowler could scarce dream of scaling. The hue of the rock, and the little pools that remained in the crevices, showed that they were not yet out of reach of their enemy.

"Here we come to a stand-still," said Frank.

"Is there no more to be done?" said Emmeline.

He shook his head in silence, then raised his voice and shouted again; but the cry of the sea-gull was the only reply.

"We must sit down here and wait," said he calmly.

Emmeline was not sorry to sit down, chilly as it was, for her breath was gone, her heart throbbing, and her limbs trembling. She and Kate crouched down, half sitting, half reclining, leaning against each other, with their arms interlaced, and they drew Edwin to rest between them and the rock, in what was almost a comfortable corner. Frank was further out, nearer the edge of the precipice beneath them.

Not a word had passed between them as to the danger, yet they felt what was in each other's mind, and no one broke the silence till little Edwin spoke: "Miss Townsend and Janet don't think where I am."

It made Emmeline shiver, so unconsciously did it echo her feeling how little their danger was suspected at home, how their mother was probably returning from her drive, and Sir Francis reading the paper, without guessing that their children were watching death slowly advancing on them, without a hand stretched out to help them.

Kate bent down and kissed the little fellow's forehead, and wondered how far he understood his situation; then a thought like his came across her, and she murmured, "O Mamma! O poor Constance!"

Frank had all this time been looking out intently on the sea; but on hearing this exclamation, he turned and looked at his sisters, and marking their trembling lips and frightened eyes, he said, "Shall I read something?" He took his little Prayer-book from his waistcoat pocket, and uncovering his head, read in a low solemn tone, strangely accompanied by the surging rush of the waves, the prayer to be used at sea, beginning with, "O most glorious and gracious God—"

The girls clasped their hands more tightly together. In their lives never had they so followed any prayer.

When it was over, Emmeline repeated, "The living—the living—oh! if I did but live—" and there she stopped.

"You will not put off the Confirmation any longer," said Frank eagerly.

"Oh no, no," said Emmeline, "if—if—"

"Call again, Frank," said Kate.

Frank hallooed again, but all in vain.

"But, Frank," said little Edwin, leaning forward to look at him, "tell me, Frank, are we going to be drowned?"

A silence of horror came over the sisters at that word.; but Frank's answer was not long in coming.

"I cannot tell, Edwin; it is as God pleases."

"I saw a little dog drowned," said Edwin, with a sort of composure that nearly set Kate off in a hysterical laugh; "its hair was all wet, and out long—I don't want to be like that."

Emmeline was not wrong in thinking that Frank did actually smile as he said, "Edwin, you are not like the little dog."

"I've got a soul!" said Edwin.

"Yes, and only think what your soul will go and see. Don't you remember?"

Edwin tumbled and scrambled across his sisters at the imminent danger of upsetting them, and said, "Tell me about it!" And Frank, in a low half-whispering voice, scarcely audible, gave partly in his own words, partly in those of Scripture, some of the glorious descriptions in the Book of Revelation, whilst little Edwin listened intently.

Suddenly he broke upon Frank's speech with the exclamation, "Look, there is a path of glory!" and Emmeline, raising her eyes, saw the declining sun reflected in the water, in a long line of dazzling light.

Frank saw it too, and the sunlight seemed to have bathed his countenance and hair, as he sat with his face turned westward, looking intently, as he had done all along, as if he saw something far beyond the horizon-line of pale glimmering light. His answer was to begin the ninety-third Psalm : "The Lord is King, and hath put on glorious apparel!"

"But I don't like to go," said Edwin, when the Psalm was finished, "without Alfred, or Janet, or Papa, or Miss Townsend."

Frank put his arm round him, and whispered something that Emmeline could not hear ; then Edwin knelt, with his little hands clasped, while Frank rested his cheek on his shoulder, so as to whisper in his ear.

Thus they remained for some little time, the sisters holding each other fast, and still silent, a sort of torpor over their minds, their teeth chattering from the cold wind, that almost numbed their senses, unable to keep themselves from watching how rock disappeared after rock, and yet scarcely awake to what was about to befall them. At intervals Frank still shouted for help, but still in vain. The church bell began to ring. It was bitterly cold. The waves came rippling closer, the pointed rock up which they had scrambled began to reject the water in spray. Frank called once, twice, again. Oh, joy! there was an answer—another shout—the answer came nearer—Emmeline and Kate pressed each other fast, and listened breathlessly. There was a distinct sound of a word, "Where?"

"Here!" cried Frank; "on a rock. We want a boat—a boat—in haste!"

" A boat—in haste—as fast as possible!" repeated the voice above, and it was gone.

The girls kissed Edwin and each other, shook hands with Frank, and exclaimed in ecstasy. But the foam tossed higher, and presently Kate said, "Oh! if it should not be in time!"

" It will not, if you don't sit still," said Frank, for they were moving about in a violent agitated manner in their reviving hopes.

"Oh, don't! don't say so, Frank! Oh! what shall we do? Oh! it is coming nearer! Oh! to be drowned now with help so near!" cried Kate, while Emmeline burst into tears, and grasped at Frank's arm.

" Be still," said Frank, sternly; " be still, as you wish to be saved—don't cling to me—I am the least safe of all here.— There, Edwin, go between your sisters and the rock, as you were before."

Emmeline trembled, gasped, and sobbed: "Oh! if he would but come—he never will come in time! oh! Frank, Frank!"

Frank laid his hand on her: "Hush! hear what I have to say. If you are saved and I not—"

" O Frank, don't—we must all be together—"

"Emmie—Kate—you have been very kind to me always; be kind now, and listen, for there is but little time. Give them all my love; don't let my poor father distress himself about what passed to-day; tell my uncle that I am sure it is best as it is, I had rather it was so; and my love to your mother, and the little ones, and Juliet; and my uncle will give it to old Grace, and all at Dumblethwayte. Emmie, Emmie, don't cry so—I tell you I had rather—it is much brighter out there! There's an end of trouble and temptation. And, Emmie and Kate, you promise me—the Confirmation and Communion—"

"Oh, we promise!" said Kate.

L

" Look in my room, and you will see two volumes of sermons. I would have given them to you to read, only I thought my father—but that is all over now. Oh, I hope—I pray it may turn out best for all."

A wave dashed high and completely drenched them with spray, which struck like sharp blows ; Kate screamed, and grasped with her hands on each side; Edwin cried out too, "O Frank, Frank!"

" Lift him up higher—let me lift him up on that rock !" cried Frank, raising himself on his insecure and slippery seat on the rock. Emmeline did what she was told, she hardly knew how, and Edwin was placed on a narrow ledge on a level with their heads. " Hold fast, Eddy dear, you will soon be safe," said Frank. " Now then, Kate, Emmie, remember what I have said—kiss me—for you have been my own kind sisters, and—"

As they silently and tremblingly kissed him, the dash of another wave beat over them, blinding and deafening them. In the pause that followed, Emmeline and Kate heard a voice, "Into Thy hands I commend—" Then came a shout from another quarter—" The boat, the boat !" screamed Edwin from above. Kate caught a glimpse of it rounding the opposite point, but she saw it only for an instant. The waves would not be disappointed of their prey, another was rolling upwards, and the next moment she was conscious of nothing, save that Emmeline and she were clutching each other in a convulsive grasp, and the support of the rock was no longer beneath them, the rushing waters were in her ears—sight, sound, sense, failed in one agony, as if her head were crushing and bursting.

CHAPTER XIII.

What would we give to our beloved?

He giveth to His beloved sleep.

E. B. Browning.

WHEN Kate next awoke to consciousness, it was by candle-light, and she was lying wrapped in warm blankets before the nursery fire at home, and something burning was being poured into her mouth. She heard a confused sound of voices around her, and with some effort opened her eyes. The children's nurse and one of the maids were busy over her, and she heard them saying that she was coming to herself.

She struggled to speak. "Emmie, Emmie," said she, "where's Emmie?"

"Oh! Miss Katherine, I'm glad to hear you speak again!" cried the nurse. "Do you feel better now?"

"Where's Emmie?" again said Kate, and this time in a stronger voice, as she raised herself on her hand and tried to look round.

"Miss Berners is in her own room," said Nurse. "Well, I am so glad to see you doing so nicely.—Run, Anne, and let my Lady know that Miss Katherine is so much better."

"What is the matter?" said Kate, laying down her head again, for she felt very dizzy and confused. "Why am I not with Emmie?"

"You shall go to her when you are better, Miss," said the nurse soothingly, and giving her some more hot drink. A few minutes more repose, and it all came upon her in one flash, she was on the rock again, the waves dashing round her, and Emmeline strained in her embrace. But no—Emmeline was not near, and she was in the warm nursery, and footsteps were coming near. She looked up and saw Miss Townsend.

"My dear," said Miss Townsend, and her voice was tender

and trembling, "I am glad you are better—here is Mr. Edwards come to see you."

"But the rock—the water—Emmie—Frank—Edwin—I thought we were out there—where are they?" asked Kate.

"Edwin is in his mamma's dressing-room, fast getting better; and the others are in their own rooms," said Miss Townsend; and Kate was satisfied for a minute, and allowed the doctor, who had followed Miss Townsend, to feel her pulse. He said she must be kept warm and quiet, and that she was doing well; and then came that very grand person, her mamma's maid, with " My Lady's love to her, and she was very glad she was better." The next minute someone was calling at the door; Mr. Edwards went, it seemed to be a message to him, and Miss Townsend sat down close to Kate. After lying still a little while, her confused thoughts began to arrange themselves; she saw how it was now, she had been almost drowned, and that was what was the matter with her, but then—the others—her own Emmie—the doubt became agony.

"Miss Townsend," said she, "you are quite sure the others are safe?"

"They are both in their rooms, my dear; Mr. Brent brought them home at the same time."

"But Emmie—why is she not here—why did you take me from her?" Miss Townsend remembered how Mr. Brent, in the few hurried words that passed as he came in, carrying Kate in his arms, had said that the sisters had been linked so fast in a death-like embrace, that it was with great difficulty they were parted. She could hardly keep back her tears as she said, "My dear, we thought we could attend to you better apart."

"Is Emmie ill? Has she come to herself? Oh! she must want me," said Kate, sitting upright, and looking round for her clothes. "I must go to her directly."

"I think you had better lie quiet a little longer, my dear," said Miss Townsend. " You shall be sent for if your sister asks for you, but in the mean time you had better try to go to sleep."

"Oh no, I can't sleep without Emmie. I am sure she cannot

sleep without me. No, let me go to her directly, I am quite well now, and perhaps she may want me and not send for me if I don't go now. Dear Miss Townsend, do be so kind as to get me my dressing-gown, or something, and let me go!"

Miss Townsend paused a little, then said, "Wait quietly, my dear, and I will go and see about it."

She went, and presently returned softly, looking a little . perplexed. Kate, who was still sitting up, was disappointed to see no garments.

"Well!" said she impatiently.

"My dear," said Miss Townsend, "you could be of no use to your sister now, she would not know you, and you had far better—"

Miss Townsend was checked by Kate's face of misery.

"Oh yes, yes!" cried she; "I must go; Emmie will know me if she knows no one else. Miss Townsend, dear Miss Townsend, do not keep me—I cannot, cannot bear it!"

There was an energy in her manner of insisting, to which it was impossible not to yield, as she sat up with her hands clasped together imploringly, her eyes lifted up, her face pale, and her damp hair hanging about her shoulders. Be it as it might, Miss Townsend saw that it would be actual cruelty to keep her apart from her sister.

Miss Townsend perhaps tried a little to delay, but Kate's impatience was not to be baffled; hastily and with trembling hands she dressed herself, folded her hair round her head, and though her knees still shook so much that she could hardly stand, it was at a running pace that she hurried to her sister. Emmeline lay on the bed, white, her eyes closed, without sense, without motion; some of the maids were busy in applying means of restoration. Kate pushed between them, and in a low earnest voice cried, "Emmie, dear Emmie!" Then, when there was no answer, she looked about to see what the others were doing, and taking one of the powerless hands, began to rub it vigorously. Happily for her, the thought that this might be death never once crossed her.

Mr. Edwards came in presently; Miss Townsend looked at him inquiringly without speaking, and he shook his head mournfully—but this Kate did not see, so entirely was she absorbed in her sister. He was much surprised to see his late patient not only on her feet, but one of the most active and ready in following up the measures he recommended. She knew where everything was, and flew backwards and forwards between the fire and the bed, she would hardly let any one but herself touch her sister; the only thing in which she failed, was that when a feather was held before Emmeline's nostrils to see if there was breath in them, her fingers shook so helplessly, that she was forced to give it up.

Again Mr. Edwards was called away, but still they persevered; and at last there came a slight, a very slight, heaving of the chest—it moved. Kate hung over her, and again called her by name. A gasp, a sort of moan, answered. Miss Townsend sent for Mr. Edwards; and by the time he came, the feeble spark of life had revived so far, that, with a sort of instinct, Emmeline's hand had clasped upon Kate's, though she had not yet opened her eyes, while Kate was hanging over her and covering her with kisses.

Perhaps Miss Townsend had never known a brighter moment than when she saw that that sweet two-fold cord of sister's love had not been severed. Still there was much cause for anxiety, for Emmeline's revival was by no means as rapid or as complete as her sister's had been. Mr. Edwards said that she wanted air, and would not let Kate put her face so close to hers, though Emmeline retained her hold of her hand, and at last, in reply to her repeated calls, raised her eyelids, saw her, and stretched out her other hand to cling fast to her.

Very gradually and cautiously stimulants were administered, until Emmeline was able to gaze feebly round, turn her head on the pillow, look affectionately at her sister, and murmur something indistinct, then closed her eyes again, and fell asleep.

Watching her all the time, Kate, who had grown thirsty with anxiety, accepted a cup of hot tea; and while she was drinking it, there was a rustling of silk in the passage, and Lady Willoughby came in, looking frightened and partly eager. She held out her arms to Kate, embraced her tenderly, and wept over her, but in almost complete silence, from regard to Emmeline's slumbers.

" Oh, my dearest—Oh, what have I gone through!" whispered she in broken sentences ; " Oh, the horrors ! Poor little Edwin, he was so fearfully chilled and frightened ! And then I was so nervous, I knew I could be of no use here, and Miss Townsend was so much better a nurse than I ; and I was obliged to soothe Edwin ; I was half afraid it would bring on a fever. He was perfectly stiff with cold. My sweet Emmie, how soundly she sleeps ! but you, Katie dear, you should be in bed ; you will be quite ill, darling. You must tell me all to-morrow, my dear girl. I will not stay, for fear of waking dear Emmie. I must go to poor little Edwin, or he will wake again, and scream about the waves. Oh, horrible ! I know I may safely trust you to Miss Townsend's care. Good-night, Katie ; you will go to bed now, promise me."

" Yes, Mamma, if Emmie does not want me. Only just tell me how Frank is."

" I have not heard just lately, my dear," said her mother ; "his father and Mr. Edwards are with him, and I believe there is no fear but that he will do very well."

" Oh, I am glad of it !" cried Kate, as if words would not express her thought. " Mamma, we should none of us have been saved without Frank."

" Oh, my love, you must not begin the whole frightful history now ! Sleep and forget it all till morning, and then I must hear it all. Good-night, sweet Katie. Oh, what a day it has been ! "

Kissing her again, Lady Willoughby departed ; and Kate, whose mind was now comparatively at rest, began to be conscious of so much lassitude, that she offered little or no opposition to Miss Townsend's entreaty that she would go to bed directly, and was quite satisfied when the governess said she would remain for the present to see whether Emmeline wanted anything. Kate's senses were not awake enough to perceive that this was really an announcement of an intention to sit up all night, and consented to sleep on a mattress on the floor. Though for a little while the dashing of the waves was in her ears, and when she shut her eyes the sea seemed to be closing in on her; these fancies soon gave way, and she was soundly asleep.

Her first waking was caused by some restless movements of her sister's. She started up in an instant, and found Miss Townsend already at Emmeline's side. Emmeline seemed but half awake, and scarcely conscious ; she knew her sister, and that was all ; she said she was thirsty, and complained of pains in her limbs ; and then, when something had been given her to drink, she turned round and went off into another doze. Kate, who was quite stiff with sleepiness, lay down as Miss Townsend desired, and was soon fast asleep again, more soundly than ever ; and when in early twilight of the morning she was waked by Miss Townsend's holding a parley with someone outside the door, she felt so fresh, and so much as usual, that it was with some difficulty that she recalled what was the reason of the uncommon condition of the room, and why it was her first impulse to spring to Emmeline's bed-side and look at her so anxiously, as she lay there asleep, with her face slightly flushed. Her powers of thought, feeling, and recollection, had all come back ; she remembered all at once how it had been ; she felt curious to know how they had come home, and above all, she had awakened again to anxiety for her brothers, wondering that she had not thought more of them, and then scarcely surprised at having forgotten, when she recollected the state in which she had seen Emmeline.

Uneasy at the length of Miss Townsend's conference, she threw on her dressing-gown, and ran to the door. Miss Townsend was returning, and they stood face to face. Miss Townsend looked pale and unhappy ; but Kate did not stop to mark her countenance, she only said in an eager hurried whisper, "How are Frank and Edwin ?"

"Nurse has just been giving me an excellent account of dear

little Edwin," said Miss Townsend; "he does not seem in the least the worse for it. And you are better?"

"Oh, I am quite well," said Kate; "but Frank—why don't you tell me about him?"

Miss Townsend glanced at Emmeline, who still lay asleep, and breathing heavily; then taking Kate by the hand, she led her into the spare room, which stood open, and there, still holding her hand, stood looking at her, and trying to speak.

Kate stood silent too, for some moments, afraid to ask, afraid even to think; at last she said, "Did not Mamma say he war doing well?"

"We—we hoped he might at first," said Miss Townsend; and then there was another pause.

"But is he ill?" exclaimed Kate.

"Remember your sister, my dear!" said Miss Townsend, as she saw Kate's agitation increasing; then, while the tears started from her eyes, her voice came in a low choking whisper, "It must be a very great grief to you both. Don't let her be waked and hear it suddenly. It might be extremely dangerous."

Kate stood, seeing nothing, hearing nothing, knowing nothing. Frank—Frank dead—that was the one idea which, indistinct, incredible itself, seemed to swallow up all else! But at that moment they heard Emmeline move, and say, "Kate!" and both, with the feeling of having been off their post, hurried back to her; Miss Townsend dashing away her tears, and Kate passing her hand over her face, as if to drive away any traces of emotion.

They need scarcely have feared, for poor Emmeline was too unwell to observe them. She was suffering from high fever and acute pains in her limbs, and the attempt to relieve her occupied them entirely; Kate could only feel a general sort of impression of a heavy grief, without being able to enter into what it actually was. She had never seen illness, and was excessively frightened, more so indeed than she had appeared even during Emmeline's unconsciousness. Miss Townsend, whose timidity seemed to have quite gone away, assumed the direction of affairs, quietly

and naturally told her what to do, quieted her alarm, and not
making the least bustle, nor putting herself forward, was in
reality everything to them both.

Mr. Edwards was sent for again, and pronounced it to be a
rheumatic fever; at which Kate could not wonder, when she
remembered the dreadful cold from which they had suffered the
night before. Miss Townsend assured her that she might quite
believe what he said about its not being dangerous, though it
might be a long as well as a painful illness.

There had been several messages from Lady Willoughby
during this time, and at about nine o'clock she came up-stairs
herself. She spoke to Emmeline, who was moving uneasily,
and only gave a moaning uncomfortable sort of answer; and
then, after a few kind words to Miss Townsend, she seemed to
think her duty was done, and asked Kate to come down with
her to breakfast in her dressing-room.

Kate was obliged to say, "Yes, Mamma, thank you," and to
follow, though she felt a great dread of meeting Sir Francis;
and as she followed her, the sight of the blinds drawn down,
together with the silence of the house, weighed heavily on her
spirits.

The dressing-room, however, looked bright and cheerful, with
the fire burning clearly, and the breakfast-table set out with all
its luxurious appliances. No sooner were they there, than Lady
Willoughby sank on the sofa, exclaiming, "Oh, my dear Kate!
was there ever anything so dreadful, so distressing, as this?
Oh, I am sure I shall never get over it—I suppose you have
heard it?"

Kate leant her head against her mother, and burst into a
flood of tears.

"Yes, my dear, you were very fond of him, and so were we
sure we can do ourselves the justice to say he was
one of ourselves, poor dear fellow; but, oh dear!
thought it—so frightful! poor fellow, I little

"Nurse has just cried heartily, sincerely thinking that she

had been everything to Frank that his own mother could have been; and honest-hearted Kate thought so too, and was much comforted by crying with her.

"He sent his love to you, Mamma," sobbed she.

"Did he—did he—dear boy!" exclaimed Lady Willoughby. "Ah! he knew—yes, no one can say that I did not do all that could be expected of me—and it is such a comfort now!"

"And he made us kiss him, and told us we had—always been —been kind sisters," said Kate. "Oh, I thought, as Emmie said, we must all be saved together! O Frank, Frank!"

Lady Willoughby let Kate cry in peace, as long as she felt inclined to cry herself; then she began to say, "But, my dear, you must control yourself; you will be quite nervous and exhausted if you begin the day with crying so much—after all you have gone through too—come, look up, my dear; he was a very good youth, I am sure, and he is gone to a better place."

"Oh yes, yes!" and Kate cried the more uncontrollably.

"And after all, my dear, he was not your brother."

"Oh! don't say that—O Mamma!"

"It is a very amiable feeling, my dear," said Lady Willoughby, "but, but—I do declare it is very distressing—" (this word was spoken much as if it had been "provoking,") "there is poor Sir Francis in such a state now!"

"How, Mamma?" said Kate, looking up, and feeling rather ashamed of not having inquired before.

"Oh, he is almost distracted—that unlucky conversation yesterday, you know—I am so. glad I tried to make peace between them; it makes it so much worse."

"But he ought to know," said Kate, springing up, "that dear Frank begged he would not distress himself about that. Where is he?"

"Oh, my dear, you can't go to him; don't think of it! he is in the study down-stairs; he has been walking up and down his dressing-room all night, ever since Mr. Edwards gave up poor Frank. I could not sleep all night, I assure you, Kate, for hearing him walk up and down—yes, and groan out quite loud, and call Frank, and talk to himself. And now he won't see anyone. He will not hear of my coming to him, and I am so nervous, that Mr. Edwards thinks it would be quite unadvisable. My agitation would only grieve him more. I am sure I do not know what to do."

" I wish—I wish Uncle Willoughby was here!" said Kate.

" Ah, yes, I must write to him. Well thought of, my dear; a clergyman, and everything."

" But he cannot come till to-morrow," said Kate, " and surely something ought to be done! I cannot bear to leave poor Sir Francis in this way. Would it not do good perhaps if—" and Kate spoke with an effort, for she did not much like the notion —"if I was to take Edwin to him?"

" Oh, my—dear poor little Eddy, after all he has gone through, I could not think of it, poor dear little fellow. And after such a shock, I am sure the utmost care must be necessary for both of you. Oh no, on no account."

Kate, afraid of the sight of violent grief, was easily diverted from the design, and thought herself presumptuous in proposing it. Edwin, who had slept late, and had since been sent to the nursery to be dressed, and to have his breakfast, here came in, and his sister threw her arms round him in a transport of affection. He did not look as if anything was the matter with him; and having probably been told in the nursery not to mention Frank, he said not one word of him, but applied himself with great good will to eat all the good things which his mamma gave him. Kate, though feeling as if it was impossible, tried to eat, at her mother's desire; and weak and exhausted as she had been before, after her long fast and all her agitation, she found that breakfast did her a great deal of good. She wanted to go back to Emmeline; but she and her mother had first to exchange histories of the dreadful evening. It was Mr. Brent who had at length heard their cries as he was going to evening service: he had hastened to the nearest cottages to call the fishermen to put out their boats, and had himself gone with them. Just as they turned the opposite corner of the little bay, and he could recognize those who were in danger, he had seen the wave dash over Frank and the two sisters, and wash them from the rock; and it had not been without considerable danger and difficulty that they had been dragged into the boat, the sisters first, and Frank not till some minutes after. It was thought that he had been stunned by being dashed against a rock, for he had made no attempt to keep afloat, and there was a bruise on his temple. Life must have been extinct before he was taken out of the water. Little Edwin was taken safely from his nest on the rock, and, worn out with fear, cold, and fatigue, was fast asleep before they reached the landing. place. Kate had shown signs of life as she was lifted out of the boat, and Mr. Brent had therefore himself carried her to the house, brought her in at the back entrance, and consigning her to the maids, had come to prepare the parents for what they had to hear. They had already become anxious at the lateness of the hour, and therefore he had the less to tell. All the rest Kate knew.

At this moment a message was brought that Mr. Brent had called to inquire; Kate, in the full flow of her gratitude, would have flown down to see and thank him, but Lady Willoughby said it would be improper—it would be impossible to see any one; she was sure they were exceedingly obliged to Mr. Brent, and she would tell him so in a few days, but now—oh no, it would not do.

"But, Mamma, the man who saved us? Only think if he had not come! Oh do, Mamma! if you are not equal to it, let me!"

"Well, my dear, but won't it be odd? My dear Katie—"

But Kate, the energy of gratitude overcoming all other considerations, caught hold of Edwin's hand, and ran down with him to the drawing-room. How different did his usually uninteresting face and dry manner now appear, as she went up to him, held out her hand, and said, "Mamma does not feel equal to coming down, but—but—" and there her voice faltered, and with an eloquent look, she put Edwin forward.

Mr. Brent was a good deal touched with Kate's sweet look

and action of gratitude, but he was one of those people, who the more they are affected the more stiff and cold they outwardly become, so he only kissed Edwin, said he was very glad to see him and Kate herself so far recovered, and inquired for their sister. It drove back Kate's overflowings of feeling, and she made a mannerly matter-of-fact answer. So also she did about Sir Francis and her mother, and then came a pause. Mr. Brent rather awkwardly said, " I hope you will tell me if I can be of any use?" and Kate hurriedly answered, " No, we are very much obliged to you, very much: but I do not know. No, we need not trouble you, Mr. Willoughby will be here to-morrow. Indeed, we are very much obliged."

" Well, I hope you will be sure to let me do anything in my power," said Mr. Brent. " I will call to inquire every day, and pray send to me if—"

" Oh, thank you, thank you. Oh, you are very kind," said Kate hastily; and behold there was Mr. Brent shaking hands with her; and now he was gone. Should she not have proposed his seeing Sir Francis? Would that she had! And what had become of all her thanks? Oh, why could she not thank him? ".Very much obliged!" all that she could say to him who had saved her own Emmie! She was greatly annoyed with herself as she went up again; and leaving Edwin with his mamma, who had devoted herself to petting him, she was on her way to Emmeline, when she found Janet sitting on a step at the top of the stairs, with her finger on her lip.

" Janet dear, I have not seen you before," said Kate in her universal benevolence; but at that moment the voice of Clements, the ladies' maid, exclaimed, " Miss Willoughby is naughty, Miss Katherine!"

" Oh," said Kate, " I am very sorry to hear it; I hope you will soon be good, Janet dear. Won't you try?"

Janet sat down again with a dogged look, and put her finger up as before.

" Oh, that is very sad," said Kate. " I can't stop to talk to sulky little girls; I must go on to Emmeline."

Janet still sat as if she cared not a straw for any of them, so Kate proceeded to her sister's room. Emmeline was much the same; and as the nurse was now ready to come and help in her room, Kate begged Miss Townsend to go and take a little rest. Miss Townsend thanked her, and went; but there was another word to that matter. Clements, the ladies' maid, did not at all like having the charge at once of Janet and Cecilia, and Miss Townsend had scarcely come to the end of the passage before she was met with the renewed accusation of "Miss Willoughby being a very naughty child;" and there stood Janet leaning against the wall, the very impersonation, apparently, of sulkiness. "Yes, there she stands," proceeded Clements; "not a word I can say will she mind. She does not care for all the trouble in the house, not a bit; I do believe it is all jealousy of her poor little brother that has been almost drowned."

"Come with me, Janet," said Miss Townsend; and Janet followed her to the school-room without looking up. "What is this, Janet?" asked she. "Have you been disobedient?"

Janet raised her face, and murmured, "I did not mean it."

The child did not understand her own feelings. She had learnt that Frank was dead through the gossiping converse of the maids, and her natural reserve prevented her from asking, or saying one word to such unsympathizing people. There was a dead, aching, sorrowful, wondering feeling, heavy at her childish heart, and she tried to shake it off by playing with Cecilia. Then the maids scolded her for having no feeling for her dear brother, and that doubly wounded and hardened the poor child. Next came the hero, Edwin, too triumphant in the pride of the petting of his mamma and all the maids, to care much for Janet's kisses. She hung back, and the dark thought that all were loved save herself, overshadowed her again; the maids told her she was jealous; the name fitted the latent feeling of which she was conscious: Janet put her finger up to her lip, and there was an end of aught but hardening, and bitterness, and self-pity. Kate was like the rest of them, and poor Janet was dull, dry, hard.

The first thing that broke on the heavy dream was when, as she stood before her governess, Miss Townsend looked into her face, and said, "My dear, have you thanked God for His love in saving your dear brother Edwin and your sister?"

"Let me," said Janet, not warmly, for nothing chills a child more than to be accused of being cold; but Miss Townsend would not notice this, and the little girl knelt down by her while she dictated a few simple words of thanksgiving. It was a softened face that Janet raised up from her clasped hands, but all she said was a question whether she was to do any lessons to-day?

"I am afraid, my dear," said Miss Townsend, "that I can hardly hear you to-day. Your sister Emmeline is so ill, that I have been up all night with her; and now I am afraid that if I do not rest, I shall be too tired to be of any use to her by-and-by."

"Are you so tired?" said Janet.

"Yes, rather, my dear, and so I should like to make you my useful little woman."

"Oh, how?" and Janet's face lighted up, and lost its heavy discontented look.

"First, I should like to lie down on the sofa, if you will fetch my plaid shawl to cover me up." Said and done in a moment, and very pretty it was to see the carefulness with which the little girl spread out the shawl and turned down the folds.

"Are you comfortable now?" she asked.

"Yes, very; this is very nice, my dear little nurse. And now I think I might go to sleep if you would read to me. Get one of your little books, and read to me nicely. And then, another thing, Janet dear; you must keep the door open, and listen, and wake me as soon as ever you hear your sister Kate or anyone coming out of Miss Berners' room. Thank you."

Janet moved about on tip-toe, grave, subdued, but feeling herself important, and though sadness hung on her, with a gentle and loving spirit stifling the jealousy and sense of injustice that ached within her. She did not read so that it was much pleasure to hear her; and without her Miss Townsend could have rested much more quietly and comfortably; but when after a half-waking, weary, dreamy sleep of two hours, the governess awoke, and saw that the little slight figure had not moved and the brown eyes were watching her intently, her own lonely heart thrilled with fondness, and she sighed to think of the depths of love unstirred by those who ought to have made them sunshine instead of gloom.

The day passed quietly and wearily. Emmeline was restless and suffering, and Kate could do little but watch her, do her best for her comfort, with little success, and grow frightened at her moans and complaints, and at the burning skin and flushing face; so frightened that she would not even trust the assurances of Miss Townsend and Mr. Edwards. She hung over the patient with quivering lips and tearful eyes, as if she felt, every pain that her sister was enduring, unwilling to let anyone touch her or do anything for her but herself, and unable to bear the least attempt at consolation.

Towards night things grew better; the violence of the rheumatic pains lessened, the fever abated, and Emmeline, quite exhausted, fell asleep. Kate was persuaded to go down to tea with her mother, who, she found, had kept Edwin as her charge all day, and had still not been near Sir Francis, who, report said, went continually backwards and forwards between his sitting-room and the chamber of his son, like a man distracted. Kate would have been very sorry for him, but Emmeline's suffering and, as she thought, danger, was her only care now.

'As she was leaving the room to return to Emmeline, a letter was given to her. It was from Malta, and the sight of Constance's hand-writing was a refreshment. It was directed to Miss Berners, but Constance's letters were always to both, so Kate had no scruples about opening it, and as she found Emmeline still asleep, she sat down to read it.

Lord Herbert was not better, the cough was more frequent and painful, the oppression on his chest had increased, his strength was failing; it was the worst account that they had ever received, and what marked it especially was, that Constance

M

expressed no hopes of amendment, and did not try to account
for the bad symptoms by some casual circumstance, as she had
always done hitherto.   Kate read on hastily, in hopes of some
such cheering expression before the close of the letter, but there
was none; she found, indeed, that Herbert was very cheerful,
and sent them his love, but he was not able to speak much, and
there Constance ended her letter; but there were a few more lines,
dated the next day. " I could not bear to say so yesterday, but it
is right that you and dear Mamma should be prepared for what
the next letter may tell you.   This last month has opened my
eyes to see that I have been deceiving myself with hope all this
time, and that it is time to look at the reality.   It cannot last
much longer now, and it is but rebellion and unkindness to wish
that it should.   Though, thank Heaven, his cheerfulness never
fails, the sight of his worn face, and the sound of his painful
breath, reproaches me with not being willing that he should enter
into his rest; but he thinks for me, and tells me that the feeling
will come; and so, dear sisters and dear Mamma, try to think of
it as he would have me do, and do not be afraid for us.   I am
very well, and nothing can be kinder than our brother."

Kate hid her face in her hands.   O Constance, dear, dear
Constance! and was it come to this?   Had that bright happy
home fleeted away like one of Emmeline's visions?   What
might not Constance be doing now?   Kate saw her bending
over her dying husband even as she herself was hanging over
Emmeline; she pictured her quiet gentle face, and the little
nervous movements by which her mental agitation used to relieve
itself.   And, oh! what a meeting might be in store for them!

CHAPTER XIV.

The sea is past, the desert near,
  Where thou shalt walk with manna fed ;
Scarce trodden yet the path of fear,
  Not yet for thee the feast is spread.
                                        C. F. A.

ANOTHER morning had risen, and found Bellevue still in the same condition. Kate was heavy-hearted and lonely, weighed down with grief, without the comfort of sharing it, like all her former troubles, with her sister, and not knowing where to turn. She knew that there was such a thing as praying, and casting her care on her Father above, and she thought she tried it ; but it did not seem to comfort her ; it could not bring back her dear, kind, bright-faced Frank ; she could not realize that it was doing good to Herbert or to Constance ; and now, since Emmeline was rather better, and Mr. Edwards did not think badly of her, Kate had the fancy that it was treating her like one in danger to pray for her. Kate's fears for her had gone away, and now she was chiefly sorry for her present suffering, and that she could not tell her these tidings, which, while she knew them not, were a double burthen to Kate.

Emmeline was much more able to take notice to-day ; she thanked her nurses for each attention, liked what they gave her to eat, and asked a few questions ; but Kate, who was in fear and dread lest she might inquire for Frank, was much relieved by her not saying one word of him or of the adventure which had occasioned her illness. Miss Townsend thought that she had guessed how it was, and Kate hoped so, for she felt sure she could never make the evasive answer her mother advised.

Kate was with her mother when the tidings came that Mr. Willoughby was arrived. Lady Willoughby desired her to go down directly, promising to follow in a few minutes.

Kate trembled at the prospect of meeting the uncle who had

loved Frank as his own son, and lost his all in him; but she could not do otherwise than hasten down, though willing to conceal the tears that would rush to her eyes.

Thick, dazzling, blinding, did they rise, and at the door, though she wiped them away, more followed. She hung her head as she gave her hand to Mr. Willoughby's, and felt it pressed tight in both his.

"Yes—yes," said he, in a broken voice, "yes, he was very fond of you."

Kate's tears came faster and faster, and she struggled in vain with them, for she wanted much to speak. Still Mr. Willoughby held her hand, and she knew he was looking at her kindly, and that his tears were flowing too.

"This is not right, my dear," said he presently, but rather as if he was rebuking himself than her; "this is not what he would have us do."

"Oh no," said Kate, recovering her voice, "he desired me to tell you that—that it is best as it is."

"It is—yes, I am sure it is," said Mr. Willoughby; "but now tell me, are you quite well? and your sister?"

"Much better to-day."

"I am very glad of it," said he with earnestness. "And my poor brother—ah! that is the worst of it."

"Yes," said Kate sadly.

"How does he bear it?" said Mr. Willoughby anxiously.

"Oh, it is very dreadful," said Kate. "I have not seen him —he will not see anyone—he is quite overwhelmed—and after all that has happened, it is so very terrible for him."

Emmeline would not have said this, but Kate's straightforward sympathy suited some people better than her shy retreating "reticence."

"I knew it, I feared it. Poor fellow!" said Mr. Willoughby. "Yes, it is nonsense to talk of ourselves when we think of him. Where is he? Does he know that I am here?"

"I will ring and ask," said Kate. "I am very glad you are going to him; I do so long for someone to tell him dear

Frank's message that he was not to distress himself about what passed that day."

"Eh? what? Ah! I see you had rather not say. Poor Francis! Well, there must be good in it for him," said Mr. Willoughby, as if talking to himself; and at this moment the servant coming in, Kate asked if Sir Francis knew that Mr. Willoughby was come.

"I told him, Ma'am, but he did not seem to take much notice," said the servant hesitatingly.

"Is he in the study?" said Kate.

"No, Ma'am, he is in Mr. Frank's room." Kate looked sorrowfully and inquiringly at Mr. Willoughby.

"Your mother is with him, of course," said he. "Ah, I should have inquired for her before. This must be very trying for her."

"Oh, she is very well—pretty well, I mean," said Kate, "but she is not there—oh no—she will come down presently."

"I will go to him at once, then," said Mr. Willoughby. "Will you show me where the room is, my dear? Your mother will not wonder when she hears that I am gone to him."

"Oh, that I will," said Kate, leading the way, and feeling as if the house was already less dreary since Mr. Willoughby had come into it. And yet, as she led him up the stairs, she could hardly bear the thought that she was taking him to the room where he lay lifeless, who was, as Juliet had said, "the very light of his eyes."

"Oh, this is so sad for you!" said she, as she paused at the head of the stairs, to point to the right door; and her tearful eyes spoke the rest.

"My dear," said he, as he pressed her hand to thank her, "I ought to be too truly rejoiced for *his* sake, to grieve so much for my own. Don't waste your grief on an old man who has not many years before him. Yes;" and as Kate kept hold of his hand, and looked at him doubtfully, he added, "do you think I would not rather go and see my dear boy?"

"Oh, you are so good! Yes, it is so like Constance. Everybody can bear things better than I," cried Kate, hiding her face on her hands clasped on the bannisters, and bursting into tears.

"Constance! Surely Lord Herbert is not worse!"

"Herbert is very ill—dying!" said Kate, in a low voice of repressed sobbing.

"My poor dear girl! And we are bringing our troubles to grieve you too. Indeed I am very sorry," said the good old man. "But you must tell me all another time," he added; "I must go to poor Francis now. The second door to the right, you say."

Kate watched him as he went along, and then sighing deeply and wiping her tears, she went to tell her mother where he was.

That conversation had done her a great deal of good, it had relieved the fulness of her heart, and she felt that she had someone to depend on. There was great comfort in knowing that poor Sir Francis was attended to, for the thought of his lonely grief had hung painfully and accusingly upon her. But what amazed her most was, how Mr. Willoughby and Constance could bear their trouble. Kate had not yet been able to make up her mind to write to Constance, she knew her mother had done so, and she thought that must suffice; she could say nothing consoling, nothing that would not give her sister additional pain.

She found Emmeline awake and better, comfortable, and alive to what was going on. "You have been a long time gone, Kate," said she. "Whom did I hear you talking to on the stairs?"

Kate looked doubtfully and inquiringly at Miss Townsend, and answered, "To Uncle Willoughby."

Emmeline asked no more. Her senses and powers of observation were awake; she had recalled the danger they had passed, and she knew but too well what was meant by the silence. She had heard Edwin's voice, his name had been mentioned before her; but Frank's had never been spoken. It would be agony to think and know that he, their one bright spot, he on whom their thoughts had centred, he who was doubly loved for his oddness, his strange half-provoking ways, he who had taken so much care of them, should have been swallowed by those surging waves. She would not bring the conviction home while she could help it. So there she lay, occupying her still feeble thoughts on little things around, the pattern of the paper, the flowers on the chintz bed-curtains, the lights and shades from fire or sunshine; and if a word of grave or sad import was spoken near her, she would not hear it. Death had never come near the sisters before. Kate could not even recollect the being told of her father's death; and though Emmeline could just remember having seen Constance cry and cling to Mrs. Ellison, she had little personal feeling for the loss. One school-fellow had indeed died, but at her own home, at a distance, and beyond the moment's shock, it had made no impression. Now, for the first time, they knew what it was to miss one from their own circle, and know he would never return again; for the first time they felt the cold heavy weight of the knowledge that in one room close at hand there lay that same bodily frame that had lately eaten, drank, and talked with them, shared their pleasures and pursuits; but now how different! the same, and yet how far from the same!

Emmeline held her peace; it would have broken her heart to have heard it said in so many words that Frank was dead! There was a vague belief that he was happy in the other world, but she wanted him here; her home would be too dreary without him. Poor Emmeline! she was looking anywhere for peace but in the right place; and her spirits were ruffled, and she was fretful and complaining, with a heart too sad to be amused, and yet resolved to drive away care and thought, and therefore vexed and discontented with all around.

With Kate time passed less slowly, because she had much to do, and much to think of. She did not see much of Mr. Willoughby, for he was taken up with his brother, whom he had roused with some difficulty from a stupefaction of grief, alternating with violent bursts of anguish, for he was like one distracted, and Mr. Willoughby could scarcely quiet him: but with the day of the funeral, there came a change. Sir Francis's grief was more violent than ever in the morning: he could not attempt to attend it, and his brother scarcely knew how to leave him; but behold, when he came back, Sir Francis seemed to have driven away all thoughts of sorrow; he was walking about the house, giving orders in a shaking querulous voice, and Kate, when she came down, was startled to find him in the drawing-room, looking, indeed, ten years older, but reading the newspaper, and talking about Indian news, just as if nothing had happened. Her mamma looked quiet and composed, Edwin had been coaxed and petted into very high spirits, Janet's black dress seemed to make her look more cold, white, and moody; and up-stairs, even the sight of their mourning had not induced Emmeline to say one word. This absolute silence seemed to Kate more painful than any lamentation; it was truly his place knowing him no more; but there was no one to whom she could speak, for Emmeline, though beginning to recover, was still so weak that no one dared to press a painful subject on her. And then the daily fear of what the post might bring from Malta.

Kate resolved that she at any rate would not forget him, nor his last words about Confirmation and Communion; and that she would certainly read that book of sermons he had mentioned. At her first free moment, the next morning, with trembling steps she walked towards what had so lately been the chamber of death. There was an awe-struck feeling on her, almost a terror, which increased as she came nearer; and at last, but for very shame, she would have retreated. She threw open the door noiselessly, but hastily, and hurried forward.

"Oh! my dear!" How violent a start Kate gave, and then how crimson she blushed as Mr. Willoughby rose from the chair where he had been sitting. "I am very sorry," said he, in his kind, earnest, apologizing manner. "I have frightened you sadly. There, sit down, don't tremble so, I am very sorry indeed."

"Oh, it was very foolish," said Kate, half smiling at herself, as she really was obliged to sit down; "I am very sorry indeed to have interrupted you."

"Don't speak of it, pray don't," said Mr. Willoughby; "I am going."

"No, pray don't," said Kate. "I was only come to look for a book. It was a book of sermons. One of the last things that dear Frank told us, was to fetch it from here and read it. I will go directly."

"No, no, don't go," said Mr. Willoughby, "unless you are in a hurry to return to your sister. I have been wanting to see you all this time, to thank you for all your kindness to him."

"Oh, Uncle!" said Kate, her eyes filling with tears, "I did not know it. No one could help loving him, but—"

"You shall hear what he says himself," said Mr. Willoughby. "In all his letters, all through his troubles, poor fellow, he has always said how kind you two were; he did not know what he should have done without you and your sister."

"Oh, it is pleasant to hear!" said Kate; "but—but I wonder, for he never would talk to us about them. Oh, was it not beautiful of him, Mr. Willoughby? he told us we should either be double faced, or get into a scrape, and so he never said one word to us. Oh, Frank, Frank, dear Frank! how good he was, and how could anyone make him so unhappy? Oh, and there is his Euclid, with the parallel ruler sticking in it, just as he left it on Tuesday!" cried Kate, bursting into an ungovernable passion of tears.

"My dear, my dear, this should not be!" said Mr. Willoughby, laying his hand on her gently, and looking much distressed; "but it is my fault; her spirits are weak, and I have overset her," said he, talking to himself.

"Oh no," said Kate, "don't think so. It is everyone's forgetting him that I cannot bear; it makes him seem more gone."

"They cannot forget him," said Mr. Willoughby, "do not fear that, my dear. But if you really like to talk of him—"

"I had rather do that than anything."

"And if it is not too much for you—"

"No, it is the saying nothing that is dreadful."

"Well, then, it is the thing that I have been wishing most of all, that you would tell me about him; especially, if you can bear to think of it, of that last hour. But don't if you had rather not; don't if it would overcome you. Remember that, I beg, for it was a fearful thing for you."

"I should like to tell you all," said Kate.

"Very well, and thank you. I will not keep you from your sister now, but by-and-by, when, as I think they said, the others go out to drive, perhaps you could be spared to walk with me. I think you must want a walk; you look sadly pale."

"Thank you," said Kate; "I should like to come. I suppose I must go away now;" but still she lingered, and gazed round on all the familiar remembrances, the blotted books over which they had so lately laughed, a few half-finished contrivances for the amusement of the children, his watch lying on the table. "It seems hard to believe," said she; "but the worst is, that I cannot bear to think how unhappy he was all these last months. Oh, if anyone could have guessed—"

"Yes, that is what his poor father has been saying continually," said Mr. Willoughby. "He little knew what he asked."

"Frank's heart and soul were so set on you and Dumblethwayte," said Kate.

"Poor fellow! Yes, it was but natural, for he had never known any other home; but it was more than that. 'Twas a longing for no earthly work, no earthly home. He has it now. Shame on us that we cannot be glad!"

"He felt it very much when he gave it up," said Kate.

"He was more unhappy before he had made up his mind," said Mr. Willoughby, "when he could not tell which was the higher duty. It was sad work, but he has stood the trial nobly, my dear boy has; and, my dear, before you grieve at what he had to go through, think whether he would have missed it now."

Kate did not understand. "Missed all that great unhappiness!" said she.

"Thank God," said Mr. Willoughby, "dear Frank's life had always been so smooth and so happy—goodness seemed to come so naturally to him, as I may say, that where would have been the trial but for this?"

"Surely he would have been just as good," said Kate.

"You forget," said Mr. Willoughby. "You know even the Captain of our Salvation was made perfect through suffering; and even when he felt it most severely, I am sure Frank would not have done otherwise than bear his cross too. Oh no, perhaps we did not see it, but assuredly the dear boy needed the trial, to perfect him in some point that was wanting. Poor Francis, when he was trying to make his boy shine, as he thought, in the world, he did not know that he was working to make him the readier for Heaven."

Katherine looked up surprised, and knew not what to answer, and at the same moment she heard herself called. Her mother had sent Edwin to look for her, and was annoyed at her red eyes. "My dear, you must not go on in this way, you will make yourself ill, you will quite upset me, and you will distress poor Sir Francis just as he is beginning to recover his spirits again. Don't let me see you melancholy, and recurring to distressing subjects. It is over now; and you know he was not your brother after all." (How angry this always made Kate!) but she had no occasion to answer, for her mother had sent for her to consult about certain crape mantles that were to be ordered for her and Emmeline, and which were to be the object of Lady Willoughby's drive to-day.

Strangely did Mr. Willoughby's words recur to Kate. Her notion of life was, that people were to be as happy and as good as they could; they ought not to do wrong at any cost; there were a great many misfortunes in the world, and those were lucky people who got clear of them, though sometimes they both punished and cured bad people. Such was her practical view; intellectually she knew more; in books and sermons she heard of a Guiding Hand, of an unseen world, and of being led through affliction to the perfect day; but she was quite as little able to apply it to actual life as she would have been to command in a battle after reading a book on military tactics. She had thought more in the last few days than ever before; she was losing her childish shallowness. The being forced to stand alone, without Emmeline's guidance, was forming her; for hitherto she had never troubled herself to make an independent reflection, but had thought on in her sister's channels, catching the idea from look or eye, even when not spoken. For the first time her mind began to acquire a mould of its own. And now she was walking thoughtfully by Mr. Willoughby's side, along the path trodden but a week ago with Frank. She showed him the places where they had played with Edwin, and repeated even the things that had been said. Mr. Willoughby's wish was to go to the very spot where the accident had happened, and as it was now nearly low water, they walked down to the beach.

But Kate had not calculated on her own nerves. No sooner were they in the first of the little coves, than she started, and trembled at the sound of the dash of the waves, and though she knew they were retreating, instead of advancing, she could not help looking back every minute to measure the space between the water and the rocks behind, stammering and forgetting what she was saying. She did not express her fears, for she knew they were vain, and school-discipline had taught her to hide, and put down with a strong hand, all such secret terrors and dislikes; but Mr. Willoughby perceived them.

"We won't go on," said he, stopping; "I am sure you had rather not."

"Thank you, I do not mind," said Kate; "I can go on very well; there is nothing really to be afraid of. It is all nonsense."

"No, no, we had much better go back," said Mr. Willoughby. "It was thoughtless in me to bring you here."

"You are very kind," said Kate gratefully, "but it is al nonsense, and I should like to conquer it."

"That is right," said Mr. Willoughby; "only you know you have had a great shock, and you may not be fit to try these experiments on yourself just at present."

"How very kind you are!" said Kate; "but indeed I had rather. We shall never walk on these sands again with anyone able to take care of us, and Emmie will mind it the less if I had been there before."

"Then let us go on," said Mr. Willoughby approvingly, but keeping on the inner part of the beach, as much as possible away from the sound of the waves, and giving her time to collect herself. She wondered how such an old bachelor could have learnt so well how to treat a young lady's nerves : she had yet to learn how exquisite a tact is taught in the perfect rule of charity. She led him to the place where they had taken refuge ; so high and so steep did the ascent now look, that she could hardly persuade herself it was the same; she told him how carefully Frank had helped them, she repeated all his words, which came back on her in the very scene. Who could believe that the broad expanse of shining beach had been lately covered to such a depth, by those waves that now rolled themselves away with a feeble dull surge, far in the distance?

"I can hardly believe it now," said Kate. "How long ago it seems, and yet it is all just the same as when we went down that day I"

"You should bring little Edwin here," said Mr. Willoughby; "let him learn it by heart, and don't let him forget his brother ; he is so like him, so like what Frank was when I brought him home to Dumblethwayte, fourteen years ago. Yes, fourteen years, it seems no time at all I" he added musingly, "and yet it was almost all his life. You see, I must learn the place exactly, my dear," said he, half smiling, "for there will be old Grace, and Mrs. Dorey, and Lawrence, all wanting to hear all about it."

"And shall you have to tell them all?" said Kate.

"Yes, of course. You do not know how fond of him they were. There is Grace, who had the care of him ever since I had him first, she loves him like her own, I do believe. Poor Grace I I did not know how to tell her when your mother's letter came; but I do not know how it was—she saw something was amiss when she came in with the breakfast, and soon had it all. She was in such a state, poor thing, I was obliged to send for her niece to take care of her before I came away. Oh yes, they all loved him with their whole hearts ; and no wonder, for he was always doing something kind for them, something that no one else would have thought of. He walked all the way to Kenderton one day to get Lawrence a new pair of spectacles ; and if you could see the screen he made for old Betty Glover, to keep off the draught as she sat at the door ! Yes, Frank has left many a sore heart at Dumblethwayte, but they will like to know that he thought of them then. It is a thing to make some of them, at least, more thoughtful."

"Ah ! and Juliet, how fond she was of him !" said Kate. " I am trying to write to send his love, but I cannot bear to begin, it must be such grief to her."

" Yes, they were very fond of each other. Poor Juliet, it will be a great sorrow, for they used to be very happy together. And so he thought of us all, did he, dear fellow ?" said Mr. Willoughby, leaning against the rock, "his old uncle and all ! O Kate, you were a happy girl to hear it, I could almost grudge it to you."

" I would not have missed it for anything !" said Kate earnestly.

" And the early Communion on the Annunciation, and the last thing to put his little brother in safety, and say those words !" said Mr. Willoughby "O my boy, could I have sought anything better for you ! "

" The early Communion," said Kate ; "I did not know of that."

" It was Mr. Brent who told me—he never missed ; he was one of the few that morning, when little did they think it was to be his last here."

" He told us," said Kate eagerly, " he begged us so much to think of our Confirmation and Communion ! "

She was surprised at Mr. Willoughby's look of consternation.

" My dear, why, surely you have been confirmed ? "

" No," said Kate, more ashamed of the omission than she had ever been before, and frightened at seeing the old man very much shocked.

"Nor your sister?" said he; then laying his hand on her arm, he added, "Then indeed you have double cause to be thankful that you were spared!" and Kate was sure he was giving thanks, though she did not realize what he meant; and neither at the hour of peril, nor subsequently, had she considered the danger of her own death, and the life after it. The thought that those green waves might have closed over her also—that she and Emmeline might have been in the unknown world of spirits, where Frank was—yes, and that the good old kind man who stood by her side, whose rejoicing almost swallowed up his mourning for his nephew, would scarce have thought of her in the same manner. The horrible remembrance of the rising water and dashing spray came back again in all its vividness; the rock became to her imagination what it might have been in reality, the portal of two worlds, into one or other of which she must have entered. And which?

"O Uncle Willoughby!" cried she, and the thought almost took away her breath; and as if it was his part to pronounce her doom, she added, "Do you mean that all—that our being saved depended upon that?"

He looked at her very kindly and compassionately as he said, "It is not for us to judge of particular cases, but surely you know what the Catechism says."

"Generally necessary to salvation!" repeated Kate. "Oh, I never thought of all that! I did not know we were doing anything so dreadful! I know we were not nearly so good as Frank, not nearly so fit to die; I know we—I mean I—have numbers of sins, but I thought—Oh! I don't know what I thought. Mr. Willoughby," she added, trying to recover her voice, and speak coherently, "will you tell me all about it? for I believe I am all wrong and very bad indeed, and nobody has ever said a word to us about these things since Herbert went away." And she burst into tears.

"Compose yourself, my dear, compose yourself," said Mr. Willoughby, making her sit down upon a rock. "Indeed, I did not mean to distress you—I am sorry—no, I am not sorry,

if this is to be better for you. You shall tell me anything you
please, ask me anything; you know—" and he kindly put his
hand on her shoulder—" you are Frank's sister, so you must be
like my child."

Kate laid hold of his hand and held it tight. "How can
you be so kind, when you think me so very bad?"

"You are Frank's sister, you know," repeated the old man,
"if I had no other reason for caring for you. Besides, perhaps
I do not think you so very bad."

"Oh, you cannot think me worse than I am!" said Kate. "I
see how little I have cared really to do right, and that I have
thought hardly at all about holy things. Yes, I know I am very
bad, but I did not think that you would think I should—I should
not have been saved—if—if I had been drowned that evening."

"My dear, my dear, do not think I said any such thing!"

Kate looked at him, and went on—"I thought if I put my
trust in our Saviour's mercy—but perhaps I don't do that right.
I do not really understand it."

"Come with me now," said Mr. Willoughby; "let us walk
homewards, and I will try to answer you."

Kate rose; and though the tide had begun to come in again,
she did not think of it as she heard only his voice.

"My dear child, I did not say—Heaven forbid I should—
anything so dreadful as what you imagined; though it may
fairly, and with all truth, be said that each moment God spares
us, it is in His mercy, and because we need a longer time to fit
us to go. And it is not what I think, but what you are."

"I can't feel that I was good enough—no, that nobody ever
could be; but surely—Emmie, who thinks so much more, and
makes such good schemes—surely you don't think so of her!
Oh! you don't half know how good she is!" said Kate.

"Yes, yes, my dear, I believe it all; but it is of yourself
that you are talking."

"I can't think of myself without Emmie," said Kate; "but
then, she has so much more thoughtfulness, that it is all a
different thing; she does think about doing right, and I think

about I don't know what. But the Confirmation, that is the thing; how does that make such a great difference? I know it is a great solemn vow that brings all our Baptismal promises home to us in an awful way, and that is why we were afraid of it, it would be so much worse to break it."

"But Confirmation is not only the vow."

"Yes, the blessing, the giving of the Holy Spirit," said Kate: "but that we receive at our Baptism too. And so many little children die before they can be confirmed."

"Yes, but we know what the Church has decided in their case. Besides, they have not had so many years to sin away the grace received at Baptism."

"Then if I had been confirmed, that grace might have kept me more in earnest about doing right."

"Surely; but that is not all."

"I have thought of something," said Kate, looking down, and flushing deeply; "I know now why you were so shocked. That text about 'Except ye eat the Flesh of the Son of Man.'"

She saw that it was what he meant, and after a pause, she said, "They tell us to put our trust in our Saviour, and that that is all."

"It is the root of all, the life of all," said Mr. Willoughby earnestly; and there he stopped, but his silence was suggestive.

"But these are the means, the means of profiting by it," and she looked up at him. "I see better now."

"I was sure you would," said Mr. Willoughby.

"'The means whereby we receive the same, and a pledge to assure us thereof,'" said Kate. "Yes, it is very odd, I knew it all the time, but I never thought—Oh, I see, I see, I remember! was it in a book, or in a sermon of Herbert's, that it said, that love and trust in our Saviour is the stair up to Heaven, and that these things, these Church ordinances, are the steps? Oh yes; and you are so happy about Frank, because you know so well that he had firm hold of the steps."

"As far as it is given to man to see, thank God," said Mr. Willoughby fervently, "he did indeed hold fast to them

N

inwardly as well as outwardly; their grace was always round him, and he went on from strength to strength!"

"They had a book at Copseley," said Kate, "where there were emblematical pictures; and in one of them there was a great ray of light reaching down from Heaven, and good people were walking up it; like the path of glory, as Edwin called it, over the sea that evening. Was not Frank's life like that?"

The half smile, and the tear in the old man's eye, showed that she had given him great pleasure; and earnest as Kate had been on her own behalf a minute before, the thought of him, of Frank, of things present, were overpowering the more personal ones; and she was beginning to talk on about Frank, but Mr. Willoughby brought her back. "And let us try to make our lives as like it as may be, by God's grace."

"Oh, I wish I could, I wish I could try!" said Kate. "But no, I could never be good enough for glory. I don't want glory, I only want to be safe; and you see I have not got hold of even one of the steps, and what is worse, I am afraid it is our own fault."

"How, my dear?"

"We were to have been confirmed at school," said Kate, "but it was to have been just at the time that Mamma and Sir Francis came home, and we were shy about speaking to them about it, and I am afraid we did not think it important enough; besides, we were afraid of it, and of the Holy Communion, and so we missed it, though we had been prepared—I mean as far as examination could prepare us, and had even had our Confirmation tickets."

Mr. Willoughby thought that this might not be entirely Kate's own fault, so he would not dwell upon it, but asked if there was not soon to be another Confirmation. "Yes," said Kate, "and dear Frank has been trying to stir us up to it ever since he first heard of it. I am sure we would not miss it now for anything, but I do not know how to begin about it."

"Should I speak to Mr. Brent?" said Mr. Willoughby.

Kate caught at the proposal. "I am sure Emmie and I shall

both be very glad if you will be so kind. But I don't want to be ungrateful to Mr. Brent, and we do look up to him very much, but we are very much afraid of him; I wish you could teach us yourself."

"I will answer anything you like, I should like nothing better than to try to help you," said Mr. Willoughby; "but I shall not be here long, and Mr. Brent is your own clergyman."

"If you think it right?"

"Shy, shy," said Mr. Willoughby, "but that is soon got over. Hark! there is the bell. Do you wish to go home to your sister, or will you come to Church this evening?"

"Emmie will not expect me yet," said Kate. "I should like to go."

They crossed the fields which led towards the town, and entered the church. It was the first time Kate had been there since the morning before the accident, and there was something strange in finding it so unchanged. As she stood, knelt, and followed the Prayers and Psalms, her thoughts often roamed away; a desultory life like hers had been no training in devotion. She was in earnest now; her eyes had been opened to perceive that Frank had led a hidden life—that there was something going on within him, of which his outward acts were the tokens; and for the first time she saw that that hidden life was the real one—that she herself, while satisfied with the material world, was living in a dream, and that it was only they who look at the things that are not seen, whose life had any reality. There was the abiding consciousness that, except her Baptism, she had missed the taking hold of the pledges of salvation; and far and dark arose behind her the long array of actions, faulty in themselves; and how few, if any, performed because she stood in the presence of God!

She had looked forward to joining in the Thanksgiving with especial thoughts of her preservation from danger, but her attention had gone away, and she felt herself humiliated by having thus missed it. She came out more dissatisfied with herself, and yet hoping that this might be the starting point for doing better. They lingered a little, and Mr. Willoughby, looking across towards the east end of the Church, said, in a low voice, "There." Kate saw the new-made grave, but they could not go up to it. She could not separate Frank from the body that, as she shuddered to think, lay beneath the green turf. Herbert, too—might it not be even now the same with him? And Kate herself—she had escaped death once, but it must come some time or other—she was going on to the grave. If she could but be safe ! Mr. Willoughby walked slowly, and stopped several times, till presently Mr. Brent overtook them. He shook hands with Mr. Willoughby, and inquired with much interest after Miss Berners and the rest at home. " Here is a catechumen for you," Mr. Willoughby said, "who has only been prevented by a little shyness from applying to you before."

Kate had been far from expecting this, and crimsoned all over as Mr. Brent asked, rather as if pleased than otherwise, " You are not confirmed then ? "

" No," said she, looking down ; "nor my sister."

" I thought it must be so," said Mr. Brent, " and—"

" My brother's coming home took them from school, and their Confirmation was prevented, unfortunately, last year," said the much quicker Mr. Willoughby, "but they are very anxious for it now. Perhaps, when Miss Kate has seen her mamma and sister, and spoken about it, we may be able to make some arrangements about your seeing them."

" Certainly," said Mr. Brent. " I suppose it will be better for me to come to you ? "

" Oh, thank you, yes, pray—" said Kate hesitatingly, and rather frightened, " but my sister is not well enough yet, thank you."

" Yes, yes, we will make further arrangements," said Mr. Willoughby soothingly.

" I shall be very glad to do whatever will suit you best," said Mr. Brent, who knew he might safely trust his arrangements to Mr. Willoughby.

"Thank you, you are very kind—good morning;" and they went their different ways.

"Did I frighten you? did I hurry it on too much?" said Mr. Willoughby, apologetically.

"No; oh, no—thank you; I am very glad to have it done," said Kate, sighing; and then they walked fast till they came indoors. Kate ran eagerly up-stairs, and into the room where Emmeline sat wrapped up in shawls, in a great chair by the fire. Miss Townsend was by the table, reading aloud; but as soon as Kate entered, she rose and went away.

"Well, dear Emmie, how have you been? Have you wanted me?"

"No, not much; Mamma came up before she went out, and Nurse brought in Cecilia for a little while, and she was very pleasant and good. You must have had a long walk."

"To the beach with Mr. Willoughby," said Kate gravely.

"You have not? No, don't talk to me about it. Kate, I can't bear it!" and Emmeline shuddered.

"And we have been to Church," said Kate. "And I have had such a talk with Uncle Willoughby."

Emmeline turned her head away, she was afraid to hear about it.

"And, Emmie, he has spoken to Mr. Brent about our Confirmation."

"Has he, indeed?" said Emmeline, starting, and speaking half reproachfully; "O Kate!"

"I said you were not well enough for the examination," added Kate, "and you shall not be hurried; they were both very kind, and Mr. Brent will do everything to suit us."

"I am sure I must be very well indeed, before I can undergo another examination," said Emmeline.

"But you would not miss another opportunity on any account," said Kate. "Remember—"

"No, indeed," said Emmeline; "but I am not well enough to think yet. O Kate, this little sitting up has tired me very much."

CHAPTER XV.

Prune thou thy words, the thoughts control,
    That o'er thee swell and throng ;
They will condense within thy soul,
    And turn to purpose strong.
                    Lyra Apostolica.

IN the evening came another letter from Malta, very short, for Constance could spare little time from her husband, who still lived, though in sad suffering.

" Poor young fellow ! " said Sir Francis pettishly, as if angered at sorrow being brought before him again.

" My poor Constance ! " softly murmured his wife ; " it will be enough to break one's heart to see her come home a widow. Only nineteen, poor love ; I am sure I shall never bear it ! "

Sir Francis was still too much subdued to impeach the Daily Service as the origin of Lord Herbert's illness, but he did what was almost as unpleasant—speculating on what Lady Herbert's income would be. Kate turned her eyes on him, and wondered if he could be the man who, two evenings previously, had been so overwhelmed with grief. The furrows on his face were more deeply ploughed, his eyes were sunk, he looked more worn and old ; but the grief had been like a tornado, crushing, tearing, uprooting, and passing away without any fertilizing effect on the soil.

" Don't you think," said Kate, suddenly breaking into the midst, " that Emmie ought to hear this ? "

" Ah ! poor Emmie. My dear, you must be cautious. Remember, she is very weak."

" Yes, but the shock will be so much worse when it does come," said Kate.

" Quite right, I should think," said Mr. Willoughby, looking up.

Lady Willoughby thought that she ought not to be told till Mr. Edwards's sanction had been obtained ; and after both she and

Sir Francis had brought several instances to support their opinion, she desired Kate to ring for the bed-room candles.

Mr. Willoughby's look and pressure of the hand gave a soothing refreshing sensation of sympathy and affection to poor Kate; though she did not know how he was pitying her in his heart, and thinking how hard it was for her good impressions to take root in such an atmosphere.

All the way up-stairs, Lady Willoughby was bewailing this sad event, coming just as they might hope to be recovering their spirits; it was most untoward; and exactly when she was looking forward, too, to introducing Emmeline and Kate.

"I am sure it will be a long time before we feel gay enough to enjoy that! thank you, Mamma," said Kate sorrowfully; "and I had much rather be *safe* than gay."

"That is what I say," continued her mother, without much attending to the latter part of the speech—"your spirits are quite gone, and while this sad state of things continues, we can do nothing to raise them. And to be sure, the poor good old man likes it, and he is not going to stay long, and he is Sir Francis's brother, so that I would not have you do anything at all like neglect of him; but I think those long walks with him are very bad for you. You come in with your eyes as red! And what is the use of dwelling on the poor boy for ever?"

"Mamma," said Kate, aghast, "those walks are my greatest delight."

"Well, they will not last long," said Lady Willoughby. "It is very kind and attentive in you, and I certainly would not prevent it, for I believe his nephew is a great loss to him, poor old man."

"I wish I could be as good as he is," said Kate.

"You are quite good enough for me, my dearest," said Lady Willoughby. "I do not know what I should have done without you this sad time."

If there had not been much on Kate's spirits into which Emmeline did not choose to inquire, she would assuredly have seen the bad news in her face, for she was broad awake, and her sister was obliged to exert herself to talk and read her to sleep. But when she was at length asleep, and Kate knelt down and hid her face in her hands, she did feel comfort; for now, for the first time, she truly felt that her Baptism had made her a child of God, and that He was the living Father of Constance and of Herbert too, and could send comfort upon them all. And if the thought so relieved her, wandering, erring, and unthankful as she had hitherto been, what must it not be to them who, as she believed, had never gone astray?

She slept quietly; and her morning walk to Church with Mr. Willoughby, far from depressing her, as her mamma fancied, braced and cheered her. She had the sad pleasure of telling him all about Lord Herbert, his arrangements in his curacy, and how happy they had been together, and of seeing that he thought it all admirable. And the thorough reality of his faith in the unseen world, and his conviction that all was ordered for the best, raised her for the time to something of the same tone. Kate was very impressible; and now, for want of Emmeline's guiding influence, her mind was fast winding itself round him. Would this last when he was gone?

Mr. Edwards held that Miss Berners had better be told of Lord Herbert's danger, since it might be difficult to conceal the tidings of his death when they should actually arrive, and the shock would then come without preparation, and might have "a serious effect on her delicate frame."

Lady Willoughby would never do anything painful, and of course the communication was left to Kate, who, though generally ready to rush into saying anything at the first moment, had been frightened by all that had been said; and when at last she went up-stairs, she looked so desperate and resolved, that her face alarmed her sister into saying, "My dear Kate, what is the matter?"

"Do I look as if there was anything the matter?" said Kate, in a rigidly calm voice.

"You do, indeed," said Emmeline, growing frightened. "Come, tell me, Kate."

"There is a bad account of Herbert," said Kate, doling out her words as Miss Danby used to do.

"Say it at once, don't keep me in suspense," said Emmeline, "he is dead!"

"Oh no, no, *no!*" cried Kate, "do not think so."

"I am sure of it," said Emmeline, "and Mamma has ordered you not to tell. Come, Kate, say. O Constance!"

"No, Emmie, he is alive—indeed he is—at least it was so when Constance wrote. Here, read for yourself, the letter came last night."

Kate threw both letters into her lap, and watched her face eagerly. It was better than she expected, for even they were a relief. Kate did not know whether to be glad or sorry, when she saw the tears flowing fast down her sister's cheeks, as she drew a vivid picture of what might even now be passing at Malta.

"O Kate, never to see him again, and when we have been so happy together! and sweet dear Constance, drooping and saddened for life; she will not live long, Kate, I am sure she will not. She loves Herbert too much. Oh, is it not cruel?"

"Don't say such things, dear Emmie, it only makes us more unhappy, and you know we shall have to comfort her when she comes home."

"Don't talk of her coming home," cried Emmeline; "it will be only to see her droop and fade. I know what it will be like:—

"'Despair it was come, and she thought it was content,
She thought it was content, and yet her cheek grew pale,
And she drooped like a lily broke down by the hail.'"

"Yes," said Kate, crying bitterly; "but we must show how we love her."

"Our love—yes, we love her with all our hearts," said Emmeline, with an expressive gesture; "but what can we do? Don't you know, Kate, that the very utmost of sisters' love is nothing to what she is losing?"

"Losing! oh no, never losing," said Kate: "how often you

have said that love never dies. Mr. Willoughby does not feel as if he had lost Frank's love."

"It may be there," said Emmeline; "yes, I believe assuredly it is, but it is not warm about one's heart, as it is here. O Kate, Kate, how dreary the world will be now! Every bit of our happiness is gone away for ever."

"Not each other," said Kate; and she whispered, "not trying to be better!"

"But think—think," said Emmeline impatiently, "of day after day going on, trying to find something to care for, and a stupid walk every day, and hearing nothing but Mamma and Sir Francis all the evening. And he for whose sake there was some pleasure in exerting oneself, he who made all bright that he touched, he whom I loved like a brother—O Kate, Kate!" and again Emmeline hid her face, overpowered with weeping.

Kate would have taken this moment for telling her how affectionately Frank had mentioned them to his uncle, but Emmeline would only talk herself, of the notion that all her happiness was over; Frank had been their only comfort in their own house, Herbert and Constance their only hope beyond it; and she had not energy enough to catch at the thought of comforting her sister; the dread of meeting grief only oppressed her, as it did her mother.

Kate was called away, having caught all her sister's despondency, and conscious that she had not said anything that she ought. She did not get a walk with Mr. Willoughby; her mother made a point of taking her for a drive, and she was obliged to endure the Marine Promenade.

Weary, sad, heavy-hearted, her spring of hope in the desire of goodness fast failing her, she slowly walked up-stairs, leaning on the balusters. That consciousness of being the child of a loving Father, had left her—the thought of Frank's path of glory was away—she only saw that he was gone, that Herbert was going, that Emmeline was ill and miserable, Constance probably broken-hearted, the world all dreariness and sadness. She entered the room: Miss Townsend was reading aloud, and Emmeline was sitting upright, leaning forward, her hands clasped, her eyes glistening, her cheek touched with a "dawning bloom."

"O Kate, it is so beautiful!" exclaimed she; and Kate, taking off her bonnet, and sitting down, heard the concluding page of a sermon; after which Miss Townsend closed the book, and as Emmeline eagerly said, "Oh, thank you, is not it most beautiful?" answered in her demure voice, "Yes, it is very striking," then put some coals on the fire, and left the room.

"She has not one spark of enthusiasm in her," cried Emmeline impatiently. "Kate, I wish you would begin again, and read it over to me. I want to drink it in, and see if you do not delight in it."

It was in one of those volumes which Frank had desired them to read. Emmeline had begun by scarcely attending, but the beauty of the language gradually had attracted her, and she was now full of excitement. Kate willingly complied, for she was rejoiced for her sister's sake and glad for her own, to be brought back to the unseen realities of which she was beginning to lose her grasp. The sermon seemed to have been sent as an answer to their complaints of loneliness and dreariness. It spoke of the glorious company to which they belonged; of the Angels at their side; of the Saints made perfect, who were their brethren; of the whole Catholic Church praying with them and for them; of the Comforter within their hearts; of the Brother who is touched with a feeling of our infirmities; of the Father whose hand is ever over us. Dreary and dark the world around might be, but the path of the righteous would only be a shining light, shining more and more unto the perfect day.

It was beautiful, and how doubly beautiful because it was true, less than the truth instead of more! Peace returned to Kate's ruffled breast, as the invisible unfolded itself so refreshingly; joy glanced in Emmeline's eyes, as if it had been some new thing that she had heard. "It is a message from Heaven, sent us by our dear Frank," said she. "Oh yes, Kate; the gloomier the night around, the brighter shows the Christian's path."

"Indeed it does," said Kate; "we can see now the bright thread like those in 'The Dark River.' Don't you remember, Emmie?"

"Oh yes!" exclaimed Emmeline, "it is a different thing now, for we all bear a charm within; you and I, Kate, may live in a world of our own."

"The real world," said Kate.

"Yes, the only reality. Oh! where have our hearts been so long? That is the world, Kate, where we may truly meet dear Frank, and Herbert, and our own father—yes, more truly than those with whom we have outward intercourse."

"When we really do come near—to the Altar, I mean," said Kate; "O Emmie, don't you wish for the time?"

"With all my heart," said Emmeline; "then we shall be full Christians, united to the better world within and above, and independent of the earthly world below and around."

"Yes, I am very glad Uncle Willoughby has made a beginning, and spoken to Mr. Brent," said Kate; "I hope we shall soon be able to fix a day."

"Mr. Brent!" repeated Emmeline; "yes, he is a very good man, and I am sure we have every ground of strong gratitude, but I do not at all look forward to a meeting with him. His dry, cold, matter-of-fact manner, is what I could never bear on a subject like this; it would drive away all my feelings."

Kate sighed, and disliked the notion of the interviews more than she had done before. However, when she went down-stairs again, it was with a cheerful, trusting, hoping heart.

These thoughts did not lose their force; Emmeline found in them her only rest from her sorrows. Perhaps, indeed, she liked to make the worst of her home, for the sake of feeling herself and her sister still more of bright lights in a naughty world. Kate went along with and was guided by all she said, and was the happier for it. She still walked with Mr. Willoughby, while her mother and Sir Francis drove out together, often taking Edwin with them; Miss Townsend read to Emmeline, and Janet walked with Cecilia and the nurse.

Now Nurse liked nothing so well as to parade Cecilia up and down the Marine Promenade, or the terrace, where people often used to stop her to admire the pretty child, and where other nursemaids were to be met, to whom she could have the pleasure of telling the history of the accident, her master's grief, and her own exertions. Nurse, in her new mourning, and with the two little girls in black, felt herself a person of still more consequence, and paced along with great dignity. Now, to Janet, this stately orderly walk was no small punishment in itself; she was told to play with the children who were with the other nurses, but she was shy, and shrank from them; while the sweet-faced Cecilia laughed and looked delighted; or she hung back, and kept aloof from the talk of the maids, with a repugnance to hearing the history of her brother's death and her father's grief gossiped over. Then Nurse pointed her out, and told the other maids that there never was a more sullen jealous-tempered child; unlike the others—how very unlike dear little Miss Cecilia; and poor Janet saw the evil eyes of the nurses, and the wondering curious glances of those happy little children, whom her imagination pictured as calling her "that naughty little girl." Her belief in her own jealousy grew, and with it grew the temper itself, and bitterness against her brother and sister; for there was no concealment that Edwin was the pet and the hero; and he who had been hitherto her companion in comparative neglect, was now set above her everywhere but in the school-room. There, shall we say that Miss Townsend's strong feeling for her poor little neglected Janet did not bias her a little too much in her favour? or was it that Edwin was really "set up," and less well-behaved? Certain it is, that Edwin was often in disgrace, and Janet was never sorry for it. Frightened at her joy in his misfortunes, she hid it carefully from all eyes, and went on in moodiness and reserve.

Saturday morning came, and Mr. Willoughby must go back to the solitary home, from which the brightest earthly hope was gone for ever. Kate walked by him to Church that morning.

"Would it—would it be too great a favour," said Mr.

Willoughby, as they were going home, "to ask you to write to me sometimes?"

"Oh," cried Kate eagerly, "may I? Would you be so kind?"

"The kindness will be to me," said Mr. Willoughby, in his thoroughly-in-earnest manner.

"But to write silly young ladies' letters to you?" said Kate.

"Never mind," said Mr. Willoughby, "if it only is not taking up too much of your time. You see, my dear, I hope it is not selfish of me, but I shall miss my boy's letters, and I shall want to know about my brother, and your mother and the children, and of Lord Herbert and your sister."

"Oh, I do not want any persuading; it will be the greatest pleasure, the greatest comfort to me," said Kate.

"Thank you. I am afraid you will not find me a good correspondent in return," added Mr. Willoughby. "An old stupid country parson has not much to say out of his parish—humdrum letters, I am afraid."

"Oh no, you know I have heard so much about Dumblethwayte," said Kate. "I know almost all the people: Grace, and Lawrence, and Mrs. Dorey, and Betty; you will tell me all about them. And perhaps some day Sir Francis will bring us to see you; how I should like that!"

He smiled, well pleased. "Ay, ay," said he; "and you will tell me about your Confirmation, and how you get on with Mr. Brent."

"Oh yes; and may I ask you—will you answer me when we are in a difficulty? Oh, how kind you are! Now I have some hope of keeping up the remembrance of what we cannot see."

"May you never lose it, my dear," said he; and they went into the house.

An hour after, Kate stood at the door with the rest of the party, wishing Mr. Willoughby good-bye. She felt as if the "God bless you," with which he shook hands with her, was a holy charm.

Before he went, he had assisted in making an appointment

with Mr. Brent for the next week. Emmeline was much better, able to drive out, and to be down-stairs all the evening. She was, however, still weak, nervous, and excitable, sometimes rather feverish, and as Mr. Edwards and Lady Willoughby used to say to each other, her constitution had received a great shock, and the oppression on her spirits prevented her from rallying. The truth was, that she could talk to Kate, read, and work herself up into great excitement, and be happier than in any of her former visions, for there was more self-approval and certainty that it was not a dream : but this was only when they were alone together; when with the rest of the family, she was abstracted and melancholy, and the vacancy which Frank had left struck her more sensibly, as the others were becoming in some degree accustomed to it.

Both dreaded Mr. Brent, and looked forward to the interview with reluctance, not lessened by their shame at having such feelings towards their rescuer., His stiff dry manner disagreed with Emmeline's enthusiasm, and the remembrance of the old awkwardness with the London curate served as a bugbear; but it was inevitable, if they were to go through with the Confirmation, and they were thoroughly in earnest in meaning to do this, if it were only for the sake of fulfilling Frank's dying request.

The day had come; and in the morning Emmeline received a long letter from Juliet, describing her uncle's first Sunday at home, and the strong tokens of affection everywhere testified by his parishioners for him and for his nephew.

The letter made Emmeline cry, and she looked very languid when she came down to her mother's dressing-room. She was restless and nervous about Mr. Brent's coming, and was working herself up to a very unnecessary and exaggerated degree of dread. If Frank had been there to laugh at her, it would have been the best thing; but Kate was of the same mind, that it would be very formal and unpleasant. And Lady Willoughby thought it very awkward, very strange; indeed, when she was at school, people were confirmed without anything like such preparation.

It was all very right for poor people; but Mr. Brent could not doubt that they had been properly instructed. Moreover, she was sure Emmie was not fit to see him to-day.

"Oh yes, Mamma, I assure you I am; I would not put it off on any account," said Emmeline feebly.

"But there will be plenty of time, my dear, if you are so anxious about it. The Confirmation is not for a month."

"Hark, there he is!" said Kate, as there was a ring at the door-bell.

Emmeline started up, looked nervously about, and her colour went and came.

"Indeed, my dearest, you must not go down," said Lady Willoughby; "pray, my dear, you had much better not."

Emmeline knew it would not do her any harm, but the disinclination which she had been nursing was quite strong enough to make her ready to seize any excuse.

"See, she is quite in a flutter, poor child," said Lady Willoughby. "Come, lie down on the sofa, and think no more about it, my dear; it is very bad for you."

"Mr. Brent in the drawing-room," said a servant.

"Tell him we are very much obliged to him, but Miss Berners is not well enough this morning," said Lady Willoughby, looking doubtfully at Emmeline.

"Oh, stop, Mamma," said Kate, "I had better go down."

"You, Kate!" said Emmeline, "and alone? No, if you do, I must."

"It would be so odd, my dear," said her mother.

"No, I had rather speak to him, at all events for a moment," said Kate, her colour coming into her face as if it was a great effort. "I will come presently."

"Well, then, I suppose I must come," said Emmeline piteously.

"I do not see any occasion for that," said Kate, mustering resolution as she had done about the waves; "you had better stay quiet, dear Emmie."

"Yes, that she should, my dear," said Lady Willoughby;

" see how much overcome she is ; and it will do just as well
another time, and not be at all uncivil to Mr. Brent. I will
write a note and send to him down-stairs."

"That it will, Kate," said Emmeline; "what is the use of
your going? it will be only very disagreeable."

"I think I had better," said Kate. "It can't hurt *me;* and
I should like to feel I had done something."

"Very well, my dear," said Lady Willoughby, "perhaps it
will be more civil if you do make our excuses to him, but you
need not stay long."

It was nearly an hour before Kate came back, and she returned
with a bright though serious face.

"Well, Kate, what an enormous time he has kept you! How
did you get on?"

"Oh, pretty well," said Kate cheerfully; "he read with me
a little, and talked, and it was much better than might have been
expected. I do not think I shall be in the least shy next time,
when you are there. He was very kind, and he is to come
again this day week."

"Then you got on pretty well," said Emmeline, as if the last
part of the information was not the pleasantest.

"Yes, very well," said Kate. "I assure you we need not
mind it a bit next time. I am very glad it is over, for it takes
away all fears for the next meeting."

"And was he very dry and cold?" asked Emmeline.

"No—no, I do not think so ; he said many things I liked,
and seemed full of considerateness. And I will tell you what
he said, Emmie," said Kate, leaning over her, and speaking in a
low voice : "he said we felt strongly now, and no wonder, and
all this trial had stirred us up, but we must take care that the
impression does not go away."

"That it never can," said Emmeline. "So he calls all this
mere feeling. That is just like Mr. Brent."

"But, Emmie, I thought he was right. Uncle Willoughby
said something very like it. Mr. Brent said, new scenes, new
people, or employments, might put these things out of our

O

heads; but that we must try to have root in ourselves, stability of character, and that that was one great help in Church rites. Besides the grace, which is the great thing, the associations will always be revived."

On that evening, when the post came in, there was a letter for Emmeline.

"A letter for me?" said Emmeline anxiously.

"Yes, my dear!" said Sir Francis, "a foreign letter; but not your sister's writing."

A dead pause.

"It is a red seal!" said Kate, in a would-be hopeful voice, though she gasped for breath.

"Let us hear, let us know the worst!" said Sir Francis, getting up and walking about the room.

"Yes—ah! my poor Constance!" said Lady Willoughby; "my smelling-bottle, Kate dear."

"Open it, Kate; I can't," said Emmeline faintly.

Kate with trembling hands broke the seal, and scanned the beginning of the letter.

"Speak, speak!" sighed Emmeline.

"No better," began Kate—"a dreadful night—but—" she turned the page, and again became silent, looking fixedly at the letter.

"Don't, don't!" said Emmeline, grasping at the letter.

"I could not, because I was choked," said Kate. "O Emmie, he is better—they have hope," and she hid her face on her sister's shoulder and cried.

"Hope! hope, did you say? Let me hear! Oh, I can't read," said Emmeline.

Kate managed to clear her voice again. "It is this little bit," said she, "at the end. Constance breaks off suddenly, and the rest is from Lord Somerville:—

"'Constance cannot leave Herbert, and I must finish and send off her letter, with better tidings than I ever thought to have to send again. It seems that the late terrible suffering has been caused by abscess in the lungs, and we hope the worst may now be over. For the present, at least, he is much relieved, and they give us leave to hope, though he is so much exhausted that there is still great present danger : and of course it is impossible as yet to judge how it may be, or how far the original mischief is removed. For the time, however, the relief is infinite. Constance is very well; it is wonderful to see how she has borne up through the last few weeks."

"There !" said Kate, with a deep sigh.

"Dear Constance," said Lady Willoughby, "I only hope this may be a permanent improvement."

"I wish it may be so," said Sir Francis ; "but don't raise your hopes too much. It is a deceitful complaint." He spoke in the fretful manner that had, since the loss of his son, become almost customary with him.

"And Lord Somerville writes himself," said Lady Willoughby ; "how extremely kind ! How does he sign himself ?"

"He has not much room to sign himself at all, Mamma," said Kate ; "it is squeezed up in the corner, 'Yrs. sincerely, S.'"

"And had they received my letter ?" said Lady Willoughby.

"No," said Kate, looking over Constance's part of the letter, "they could not have done so."

"But here is a bit in the envelope," said Emmeline :—

"'A letter is just come for Constance, which I have not yet given her—from your mother, I think, and with a black seal. I hope nothing amiss. I mention it lest you should think it had gone astray.'"

In two days time came another letter, from Lady Herbert to her mother, and very short. No one could imagine, said she, the comfort of seeing him able to lie flat, and breathe freely. She wrote in much anxiety on Emmeline's account, and expressed strong sympathy with their grief for Frank, whom she said she knew well enough to see what a loss he must be, and what comfort there still was in his death. She had not ventured as yet to tell Herbert of the adventure, as he was to be carefully guarded from all excitement.

After this, Emmeline and Kate laid aside their fears, and talked themselves to sleep, with delightful anticipations of a home in the parsonage at Copseley, a peaceful life, "alms all round and hymns within," the moonlight walks to evening service, and the morning teaching in the pretty school, under the superintendence of Herbert's bright lively eye, and Constance's active sisterly affection.

CHAPTER XVI.

Those golden palaces, those gorgeous halls
  With furniture superfluously fair ;
Those stately courts, those sky-encountering walls,
  Evanish all like vapours in the air.
                              Tragedy of Darius.

WHEN Kate came down to breakfast the next morning, Edwin was acting charioteer at the top of a pile of chairs. "Kate, Kate," shouted he, "I am going to London ; we are all going to London."

"What, in your coach, Edwin?" said she, after paying her morning greetings, obediently offering to sit down wherever Edwin might choose to dispose of his passengers.

"No, in the train, in the real train," said Edwin, "and next week."

"Yes, Kate," said Sir Francis, laughing and looking as good-natured as he used to do ; "what do you think of our plan?"

"To go to London," repeated Kate, "to stay there?"

"Yes, to go to London for the season," said her mother; "it is time for you both to be introduced, and we shall soon have dear Emmie better, when her spirits are raised by the change."

"Nothing like society, nothing like society," repeated Sir Francis.

"And the hippopotamus!" roared Edwin. "I shall see the hippopotamus."

"But do you really mean next week?" said Kate.

"Yes," said Sir Francis, rubbing his hands together; "Thursday, the 20th. Rather short notice, perhaps, but I hate take-leave visits; two or three days will be enough to leave our p. p. c. cards and pack up."

Edwin roared them all down again with an announcement that he should take all his shells, and pack them up in the great box. Lady Willoughby put up her hand as if deafened, but Edwin was privileged, and there was not soon another lull. At last Lady Willoughby turned towards Kate, and said, "Why, my dear, you seem as if you would never recover from your surprise. Shall you not like it?"

"Trust her for that," said Sir Francis, laughing. "I suppose I ought not to say what a sensation two such young ladies will make."

"I was thinking of the Confirmation," said Kate.

"Oh, my dear," said Lady Willoughby, "you will soon have another opportunity. People will never know whether you are confirmed or not. It will not make any difference whether it is now or a little while hence."

"We should be very sorry to miss it," said Kate; "it is only three weeks hence!"

Kate had never made a shadow of objection to other people's plans before, and both Sir Francis and Lady Willoughby looked surprised.

"My dear, it is a pity, but it cannot be helped," said her mother.

"No, Mamma, of course I don't wish to interfere;" but she could not keep back a tear of disappointment.

"In three weeks, will it be?" said Sir Francis, touched by his favourite Kate's quiet resignation, and perhaps so far improved by his affliction and his brother's influence, as not to choose again to oppose what was felt a religious obligation.

"Yes," said Kate; "the day is the 30th of April."

"Well, I don't know, if you are so anxious about it, if it might not do better in this way: if I was to go on to Town and look at a house, and have all ready for you, and then come back to fetch you. Eh?"

Lady Willoughby did not look. "I am sure the girls are very much obliged to you," said she; "but they would not wish

by any means to interfere with your plans. And really I should
not like to put off the journey. I do not like you to go
alone, and not take care of yourself at an hotel, and we to be
left alone to have all the bustle of paying bills and packing
up. With dear Emmie so unequal to everything, too. Oh
no, we cannot do without Papa. I am sure Emmie and Kate
cannot wish it."

" I don't want them to be disappointed," said Sir Francis,
looking good-naturedly at Kate ; " it is the concern of you ladies,
and you may settle it as you will, only don't let it be said that I
stopped this Confirmation business, in the face of their wishes."
And Sir Francis with a sigh pushed his chair from the table,
called Edwin to come out with him, and left the room, while his
wife was saying, "I am sure you are very kind. We will see
what Emmeline says."

" And now, Katie, my dear," said Lady Willoughby, when
the door was closed, " let me beg of you not to make a point of
staying on here for this Confirmation."

" I would not, indeed I would not, dear Mamma," said Kate,
" if—if I did not feel that it was the only hope of being good,
and one of the very last things that dear Frank begged of us."

" You speak as if there was never to be another," said her
mother, with more pique than Kate had ever heard before in her
gentle tones.   " Are not they always going on in London ?"

" I don't know," said Kate ; " but now we are in the way of
being prepared, I am sure Emmie would be very sorry."

" Ah ! there is the very thing," said Lady Willoughby, lowering her voice confidentially ; ' poor dear Emmie ! she is the
principal reason I wish to leave this place. She will never
recover her spirits, nor Sir Francis either, among all these
melancholy associations ; and you see, Katie, her health depends
so much on her spirits."

" Yes," said Kate thoughtfully.

" Then you see there is that Mr. Brent. After what has
happened, you know, it would be too uncivil—quite impossible,
in fact—to object to his seeing her ; but then you see how

nervous she is at the very prospect, and the interview itself would be so bad for her. Mr. Edwards tells me that he quite dreads the sight of Mr. Brent going into a patient's house."

"O Mamma," said Kate, "I thought we had resolved never to believe any more of the stories against Mr. Brent."

"Kate, my love, I really cannot think what makes you so extraordinarily pertinacious this morning," said her mother, "when there are so many reasons for making us desirous to leave this place—when, after all that has occurred, we can never expect poor Sir Francis to recover his loss here. And you are looking pale too—change is quite necessary to us all."

"Indeed, Mamma," said Kate distressed, "I should be very sorry to interfere; and if I was quite sure about what is right—"

"Right, why that must be what is best for all," said Lady Willoughby; "and you must perceive yourself, my dear, how much better it would be for Emmeline and for all of us. I am sure I thought we were giving you pleasure."

"Mamma! oh yes, dear Mamma, we are very much obliged to you; don't think us ungrateful, but the *thing* is, we are so afraid to stay unconfirmed any longer."

"Afraid, my dear?"

"Yes, Mamma, if we should miss it again—and die."

"What are you thinking of, my dear? Indeed, it is true, as I always said, that nothing can be worse for your spirits, all of you, than remaining here. It makes us all so melancholy, that I really cannot tell what will be the effect of it; and now that the present anxiety about poor Lord Herbert is over, I am so desirous to bring out you and Emmeline, so as to cheer you up again, my dears."

"Thank you, Mamma," said Kate, rather ruefully.

Instead of going up to Emmeline, Kate walked out into the garden. She had grown more scrupulous about over-ruling her mother, who, as she perceived, was quite in the power of Emmeline and herself. She could not bear the thought of arraying themselves and their influence in opposition to her.

She did not know how far the remaining at Herringsby might be prejudicial to Emmeline's health; and it certainly would be much more agreeable not to "make a fuss," as well as to miss any more stiff conferences with Mr. Brent. On the other hand, it could not be right to delay the Confirmation—it was a safeguard for which she longed in the midst of the scenes which awaited her—it would be too dreadful to neglect that entreaty of Frank's; and how vexed Uncle Willoughby would be. Moreover, a little persuasion would, as Kate had little doubt, bring round her mamma to think they had much better not be in such haste. She would let Emmeline judge.

Therewith Kate ran up-stairs.

"Emmie! only think, they are talking of going to London, all of us, and we are to come out. They had proposed next Thursday, but—"

"Then we shall not have any more of Mr. Brent," said Emmeline.

"Yes, that is the *thing*," said Kate. "But Sir Francis has been so kind as to say they will wait for the Confirmation if we wish it." Kate looked at her sister's face, and saw that Emmeline did not know whether she wished it or not. "The worst of it is," said Kate, "that Mamma has set her heart upon going as soon as possible, just as if it was for the sake of escaping from the place, and she fancies all this preparation for the Confirmation is hurting you."

"Well then, Kate, we had better go if she is so anxious about it," said Emmeline.

"Another thing I was thinking," said Kate. "Don't you think it might be possible for us to stay behind, as it is only for a fortnight? Miss Townsend might remain with us here and follow them, or perhaps we might stay with the Miss Shaws."

Emmeline burst out laughing. "The Miss Shaws and Mr. Brent! No, no, Kate. And Mamma would never consent to the other plan. No, we must give it up, and it is not our fault, you know."

"I am afraid of its being our fault," said Kate, "since Sir Francis put it into our power."

"No, Kate, recollect we owe more duty to Mamma than to him."

"Yes," said Kate sorrowfully; "but isn't this our duty to God?"

"But, Kate, there will be another Confirmation," said Emmeline impatiently.

"Not to neglect it again, was what dear Frank said," replied Kate.

"Yes, but we are not neglecting it, we cannot help it; and I am sure dear Frank would not have had us set ourselves up, and make everything give way to us, and make Mamma perfectly miserable."

"No, I suppose it would not do," said Kate, with a deep sigh; "but shall not you be sorry to come away?"

"Sorry, to be sure I shall! There is much here that we can never forget. Oh yes, we shall love the place for ever; but it is quite impossible to persuade them to stay here now that they have got into this restless state, so we must submit."

Emmeline did not ask herself how much of her submission was occasioned by her wish to avoid Mr. Brent; and Kate, deserted by her ally, became almost ashamed of her strenuous opposition. So no more was said against an immediate departure, and the day was fixed for Thursday.

In the mean time, there was a great deal to be done, and it chiefly fell upon Kate, as Emmeline was not equal to exertion. It was wonderful to find how many things had accumulated in ten months, and how many recollections had bound themselves round the walls and in every corner.

"Look here," said Kate, as she knelt before a chiffoniere, and explored its dark recesses, from which she drew forth a bundle of half-made poor children's clothes.

"How long it is since we have touched them!" said Emmeline. "Dear me, Kate, what a strange world of recollections they do bring up! It seems as if our war with Mr. Denham and the poor Miss Shaws was a hundred years ago!"

"It does indeed," said Kate, thoughtfully.

"As if we were not the same people," said Emmeline. "As we are not, Kate; for the mind—the soul, I mean—has a more real and true genuine existence than the body. It is that which is the self, and I am sure that is changed in us."

"We ought to be daily renewed, as the Blessing says," was Kate's answer in rather a mournful tone.

Emmeline was always uneasy under any mention of the Confirmation, and she came hastily to examine the bundle. "I should like to finish them," said she, "if it is possible. I am ashamed to send them home unfinished."

"It would not be impossible if we worked hard," said Kate; "and perhaps we could get Miss Townsend and Janet to help us."

Emmeline fetched her work-box and began to look for the part where she should go on. There was the rusty needle coiled up in the thread, and stuck in the hem; how well she remembered her laying it down when Frank's merry voice summoned her to come and help to paper the tower; and then how occupation, amusement, and whim, had rapidly succeeded each other, and what had at first been neglect had become repugnance, and the misunderstanding with the Miss Shaws had arisen, and so the engagement had been unfulfilled.

"Well," said she suddenly, "I am glad we are going away. It is impossible to be really a Christian without doing something for the poor, and that is impossible here. I see we were wrong in going into Mr. Hunter's parish, but Mr. Brent will let us do nothing."

"Perhaps he would do so when he knew our Church principles, and saw us Communicants," said Kate, sighing. "But it is of no use to talk about that, only there were those children of the poor sick man."

"To be sure there were," cried Emmeline. "How could we forget them? O Kate! you must find out about them, and let them have all the money we can possibly give."

"I will. We will ask Mr. Brent about them," said Kate. "But what shall we do for the poor in London?"

"I don't know," said Emmeline; "but we shall not stay in London always. There will be Copseley again, Kate, perhaps before the summer is over, and we shall go about again in the little paths of chequered shade, under the oak trees, and talk to Herbert and Constance, as in the dear olden time."

"Beautiful Copseley," said Kate. "And we shall see the quiet little lawn, with its fuchsias and geraniums, and sit at the open window and read to Constance."

"But there is a hot restless world to come first," said Emmeline. "Fineries, and gaieties, and balls, and hot rooms, and Mamma talking of her daughter, Lady Herbert, and this world would be everything—"

"And oh, what shall we do that it may not be so to us?" said Kate.

"Pray, and fix our faith steadfastly," said Emmeline, glancing up. "These things are all pomps and vanities, and emptiness. We may be among them, but not of them; they cannot taint the charm within us."

"I should so hope more, if—"

"I know what you would say, Kate; but it is not our fault this time at least."

It was not Kate's, for she had done all she could.

Emmeline and Kate worked hard, and obtained the aid of Miss Townsend and Janet, the latter of whom was made very happy by being asked to do anything as a favour to her sisters. She worked till her little forefinger was quite sore with hemming, and her pale face flushed with joy when she was kissed, and told that she had done wonders.

Kate went to take leave of the two old ladies. They were very kind, and would scarcely let her make any apologies. They said they knew how it was; and as they nodded to each other as usual, Kate perceived that many a young lady had taken up a fit of school-keeping and laid it down again.

"Good-bye, my dear," said Miss Penelope, as Kate rose to go. "I am sure we shall never forget all your kindness."

"Kindness! I wish it had been so," said Kate.

And bearing the old ladies' love to the whole family, collectively and individually, she left the tall narrow house for the last time, then turning, looked back and sighed; wondered whether she should ever be equal to those two old ladies in earnest piety and self-devotion, and yet wondered what was amiss in them.

The next farewell was to Mr. Brent. Lady Willoughby had sent one of her politest notes, with all manner of thanks, and saying what, if the girls had seen it, they would scarcely have allowed her to send—that her daughter Emmeline regretted exceedingly that she was not allowed to thank him in person, but that her feelings were so acute, and her whole nervous system had received such a shock, that it was not thought advisable to expose her to any agitation.

Kate was vexed when she heard that Mr. Brent had been desired not to come again. She thought it was using him ill; and she had, besides, one or two things to say. She was glad that he was of that sort of age that she need not be afraid of putting herself in the way of speaking—not indeed quite as old as Lord Liddesdale, but much older than Lord Somerville. So on her last morning she waited for him to overtake her when she came out of church. When he was sorry he generally looked harsh, so that she scarcely knew how to begin.

"Are you going to-day?" said he.

"Yes, in a couple of hours," said Kate. "My sister is not strong enough to take the whole journey in one day."

"I hope the change will be beneficial," said Mr. Brent, in his dry voice.

"Thank you," said Kate. "We are very sorry to go. I wish we could have stayed."

"Yes, it is a great pity, for I hardly know when you will have another opportunity, now that the Easter Confirmations are over in London."

"It is our own fault," said Kate; "it was very wrong to miss the opportunity when we left school."

"It was greatly to be lamented," said Mr. Brent.

"And I wanted to ask you," said Kate, looking down—"Is there anything you would advise me to do now? I am afraid we shall be obliged to go a great deal into company, and what shall I do to keep from forgetting everything?"

His tone was kinder, as he said, "Remember always that you are in course of preparation for a great privilege; bring it back to your recollection on every occasion—at your prayers, at church, whenever you are preparing for any amusement."

"I will try," said Kate, sighing. "My sister will help me. And one thing more, Mr. Brent; here is a little money, if you could spend it for those poor children that—that my brother was interested about. I wish we had thought about them more."

"Thank you," said Mr. Brent. "It shall certainly be done. We are hoping to get the eldest girl into a place, and this will be a timely help."

"I wish—" said Kate, but there she stopped; and as they had now come to the spot where their road parted, she only held out her hand, and bade Mr. Brent good-bye. He replied with a warm shake of the hand, and a look of kind regret.

Kate lingered, and when she thought no one was looking, she turned, and stole back to the churchyard, and across the green turf, till for the first time she stood by the side of the new cold-looking white stone, with its strongly cut black letters. There was more upon it than Kate's taste approved. Besides the "Francis George Willoughby," which was all that was left of Frank upon earth, there was, "eldest son of Sir Francis Willoughby, Major General in the Honble. East India Company's Service, and Mary his wife. Born at Calcutta, April 12th, 1832. Drowned, March 25th, 1850. This stone was erected by his afflicted father."

"And this was all that Sir Francis could give him," said Kate to herself. "Dear Frank, do you know that I am come to wish you good-bye for myself and for Emmie, your own sisters. O Frank! we shall never forget you—never. Indeed, we will try to keep what I promised you, and I hope that you are praying in Heaven that we may. I wish I could tell you that we are happy about Herbert again, and that Uncle Willoughby is very kind to us.   Good-bye, dear Frank ! "

Kate gathered a daisy that grew on the new turf, and holding it fast and tenderly, turned away, drying her tears. As she came to the gate, she started at seeing another figure lingering in the churchyard, as if to wait till she was gone. In spite of his desire to shun observation, she saw that it was Sir Francis, but she did not venture to go near him, and hastened back to the house.

CHAPTER XVII.

With me the muse shall sit and think
How vain the ardour of the crowd,
How low, how little are the proud,
How indigent the great.

Gray.

BEFORE the end of another fortnight they were settled in a house in Belgravia. Kate had found a church with daily service, near enough for her to go every morning before breakfast, and Emmeline hoped to accompany her as soon as her strength was fully restored.

Moreover, the accounts of Lord Herbert continued to improve so fast, that the hopes of his return were no longer a day-dream ; and at last came a note from himself, written on the first impulse of having been told of the adventure at Herringsby.

My dear Sisters,
        Constance has only just told me of your danger, Emmeline's illness, and the loss which you must feel so deeply. It will not be long, I hope, before I see you again ; and Constance will scarcely allow me pen and ink, so that I must not say half that is in my mind, only how thankful I am that we are to meet here once more, and how great is the responsibility of being spared, as we have been. It is as if more were required.
                        Your affectionate Brother, H. S.

It was the first time that he had attempted to write, and they thought it a great honour ; but it made them more melancholy than rejoiced. "A pretty way for people to live, who have been brought back from the gates of the grave," said Emmeline, pointing to the cards of invitation which lay on the table. "How I hate it! What are you reading, Kate? Is that from Uncle Willoughby?"

"Yes," said Kate; "hear what he says in answer to all our dislikes and fears of gaiety : 'I shall like to hear all about your gay parties in London ; perhaps you will hardly believe how I enjoyed the ball forty years ago, when my dear sister Janet was the beauty of the evening, and the only young lady who had learnt to dance a French Cotillon, as we called them then, so she had to teach them all. It is just as well to be afraid of all this ; but remember what Frank said about things not being his own will ; don't think about yourself, and don't look out for admiration, and you will do very well.'"

The first time that Emmeline and Kate were really to be admitted into this formidable world of society was about a week after, when they were to dine at a grand party, given by some of the great East Indian people to a distinguished officer just returned home. There was great preparation ; Emmeline and Kate were to be as handsomely dressed as their mourning would permit, and they looked remarkably nice and lady-like—nay, even elegant, in their black gauzy dresses, which set off their very white well-turned necks and arms, and with their soft pretty light brown hair trained into some fanciful braids, exactly alike. Kate, with her pink colour, which had grown brighter under the influence of the Herringsby sea breezes, and her deep blue eyes, was positively pretty : and Emmeline, though still pale and thin, was, from her delicate fairness, not much less so. Their mother was very proud of them, and so was Sir Francis ; but Emmeline, with a mournful expression in her downcast eyes, leant back in the carriage, wishing that she was far away.

They were at the door—they were throwing off their shawls —they were walking up-stairs secretly holding each other's hands, behind their mother. A door was thrown open ; a blaze of lights, a buzz of talking, "Sir Francis and Lady Willoughby, and the

Misses Berners" proclaimed before them, and then the two sisters were anchored on the end of a sofa, not very far from their mother, and able to look up and around them.

They were not much edified; perhaps they were prepared to disdain most of the people they saw; however, people were not to be expected to be cut out after the Rowthorpe fashion. Where was the great man? Emmeline had been rather inclined to dread the sight of great generals after her disappointment with Sir Francis, but he suited her ideas a good deal better than she expected. And she thought better of Sir Francis when she saw him shaking hands cordially with him like an old friend; she was more willing to belong to him than before. But behold! who was that who was being introduced to the hero? Lord Liddesdale himself, with his red ribbon. She had not known him to be in London, and how very grand he did look; how superior to anyone else! Shaking hands with Sir Francis, too! Now Emmeline had a property in somebody of whom she might be proud.

Emmeline's neighbour at dinner seemed to enjoy the turbot particularly, and not be able to talk of anything else; Kate's, when he had asked her if she liked riding, had nothing more to say: the dinner was very long; there was an immense quantity of talking, and none of it could be heard distinctly enough to be entertaining, so that they were very glad when the ladies rose, and they found themselves in the drawing-room, able to sit together. They knew scarcely anybody, and looked forlorn, while Emmeline moralized upon the emptiness of the scene, and its complete want of attraction for people whose minds were fixed upon higher objects.

The gentlemen came up without making matters more brilliant, excepting that the girls had the interest of watching Lord Liddésdale. They saw him go and exchange a few words with their mother, and presently his eyes met theirs; he smiled, and they saw him making his way towards them. He was soon shaking hands with them, and asking them when they had heard from Constance. Lady Willoughby was serenely rejoiced when she saw her daughters making room for Lord Liddesdale

to sit down between them ; and Sir Francis heard it asked who
the two pretty girls were that Lord Liddesdale was talking to.
Quite unconscious of this reflected splendour, and only delighted
by his kind attentions, Emmeline and Kate were comparing their
latest intelligence from Malta with that of their friend, who, tired
of a stupid party, was very glad to find out these two nice little
girls, and to have someone with whom to talk of his son Herbert.

"They must not be in too great haste," said he. "We must
not look for them till May is over, at least. I would not have
him meet the cold wind of May on any account, but before June
I should think they might safely set off; allow a month for the
journey—yes, they may surely be here before the end of June."

"By the longest day," said Emmeline, "their wedding-day."

"Yes, I suppose it will be a hard matter to prevent Herbert
from setting off to Dearport forthwith."

"To Dearport?" said Emmeline.

"Yes—what, have you not heard? I thought Frances or
Constance would have told you, that a connexion of mine has
offered him the living of Dearport."

"Indeed, and will he take it?" said Kate, in consternation,
as she thought of Copseley.

"He has accepted it," said Lord Liddesdale, "on condition
that if his health should fail again, it shall be given to his friend
Mr. Redlands."

"And they will never go back to dear old Copseley!" said
Emmeline.

"Ah! that is giving up a great deal, is it not? You see,
Dearport—I don't know whether you know the place—"

"Oh no, not in the least. Only that it is on the south coast."

"Yes, so far it is in his favour; it is a good climate for him,
but it is a miserable place; one of the minor ports from which
the trade has gone away, and a great watering place has grown
up round it, one half mud and misery, and the other half finery.
It has been sadly neglected, and there is an immense quantity
to be done for it."

"And does Constance like such a horrid place?"

P

" There is a clergyman's wife for you ! Herbert had this offered
to him, and he had reason to think that it would not be satisfactorily disposed of if he did not take it; but he could not
bear to bring Constance to such a place, instead of their beloved
Copseley, so the decision was a good deal left to her."

" So she chose Dearport ! "

" Yes, she said nothing could make her so unhappy as to
think that consideration for her should hold him back from full
usefulness."

" Very like Constance," said Emmeline, " but still I cannot
think how she could bear to give up Copseley."

" And will it not be too much for Herbert ? " said Kate.

" That is the chief doubt," said Lord Liddesdale, " but he is
fitter to be the head than voice. With such a staff of curates
as he must have there, he will have less occasion for exerting his
voice, than if he had to depend on himself alone in a smaller
parish."

" Certainly," said Emmeline, " I do admire them very much,
but I cannot help being very sorry."

Lord Liddesdale smiled, and confessed that it was something
like his own case ; he was very sorry that they should leave their
pretty home at Copseley, in his own neighbourhood, " But considering how much they gave up, we need not pity ourselves,"
said he. " We may be glad enough to have them in old England,
on any terms."

" Indeed we may," said Kate earnestly.

Then came a brief pause, followed by an inquiry, on Lord
Liddesdale's part, where their house in London was. He said
his daughter Frances had been staying with some friends for the
last three weeks, but he was going the next day to fetch her ;
and he talked again of the merry meeting that he looked forward to with his two sons and Constance, saying he should insist
on Herbert and his wife coming to Rowthorpe in the autumn ;
and the two girls should meet them there, and he would get
Emmeline to read Shakespeare to him. Then he surveyed her
with almost fatherly kindness, said she was looking unwell,

asked Kate if she was really better, and told her to take care
she did not knock herself up with gaieties, for she must keep
herself quite well to meet Constance.

He talked to them till people were going away, and went
down-stairs with them, causing a considerable difference in their
opinion of great parties. They were eager to tell of Lord
Herbert's living, though they knew with how little sympathy it
was likely to be received ; and of course Sir Francis wondered
what it was worth, while Lady Willoughby rejoiced that her
poor Constance would now be in the way of meeting good
society.

Two days after, rather earlier than the usual time for morning
calls, as Emmeline and Kate were reading in the drawing-room,
they were interrupted by the arrival of company, " Mr., Mrs.,
and Miss Allen ; " and in came a little quick-looking well-dressed
elderly lady, and—Emmeline had time to see no more, for a
damsel darted up to her, caught hold of both hands, and kissed
her eagerly. " How do you do, dear Emmie ? " then turning to
Kate, " and Katie too," embracing her too. " Well, this is
delightful! Here, Mamma, this is Emmie—and here is dear Kate."

Mrs. Allen held out her hand with almost equal eagerness.
" You must let me be like an old friend," said she, " I have
heard so much of you from Susan. She has been quite wild
ever since she heard you were in London, since her brother mentioned that he had the pleasure of meeting the Miss Berners the
day before yesterday. You must let me introduce him—my son
Henry."

Emmeline recognized in Mr. Allen the gentleman who had
been next to her at dinner, but who had been so engrossed by a
lively conversation with his other neighbour, as to leave her
entirely to the attention of the admirer of the turbot. He was
good-looking, tall, and gentleman-like, and spoke pleasantly.
" I fell under Susan's grievous displeasure for not having found
you out before," said he ; " but in the evening, when I had
discovered that you were the ladies whose names I had heard so
often, you were better engaged."

"Oh, I was delighted to hear you were in London," said Susan, "and so provoked with Henry—"

Sir Francis and Lady Willoughby now came in, and all the civilities began again; Mrs. Allen representing that her daughter and the Miss Berners had been the closest friends in the world at school, and that Susan talked of no one else; and Lady Willoughby, who had reasons to think well of the fashionableness of Mrs. Allen, on her side, politely making the utmost of having, about twice, heard the name of Susan Allen.

Susan, in the mean time, sat between the two sisters, talking eagerly and caressingly. "Oh, I was so delighted when Henry told me; I could not rest till we had found out where to find you. And was it not tiresome of him? Oh, I did scold him so!"

"What, for finding us out?" said Emmeline, smiling.

It is not perhaps necessary to inquire how much of all this violent friendship would have existed, if Mr. Henry Allen had not reported that he had met those school acquaintances of hers, those daughters of Lady Willonghby's, pretty looking girls enough, and that old Lord Liddesdale had talked to them all the evening. Her affection was not entirely acting; she had liked no one at Miss Danby's better than Katherine Berners, and her kindly recollections grew into extreme fondness, when she thought of her as the sister of Lady Herbert Somerville, and intimate with Lord Liddesdale and Lady Frances, who were far above the Allens' own circle. Moreover, the history of the Miss Berners being half drowned had been in the newspaper, which gave them a new charm.

Of this, however, Emmeline and Kate knew nothing; they were surprised and pleased to find the black-eyed Susan so fond of them, and fully responded, glad to talk over old times, and inquire after old friends. The time for taking leave came only too soon. Mrs. Allen apologized for having made a visit of such unreasonable length, but said she did not know how to separate the friends sooner; and Mr. Allen said a few words, half jesting, half complimentary, about young ladies' friendships.

They soon met again : the Allens were at home when the call was returned; they were at a morning concert the next day, and had much pleasant talk about music, in which Mr. Allen seemed to excel as much as Susan had always done at school. Susan recommended her singing-master, and quantities of new music; and Emmeline began to take it up more in earnest than she had ever done before. Then came a dinner-party at Mrs. Allen's, whereat, in spite of the presence of Miss Winstone, Mr. Allen paid Miss Berners a great deal of attention, talked, laughed, and sang with her. She did not hate dinner-parties at all now; for, though she thought Henry Allen not a superior man, and certainly an idle pleasure-seeker, still it was not disagreeable to know that there would be one person, at least, with whom she could have plenty of pleasant small talk, and that she should not have to sit forlorn, as at first.

The first ball was now in expectation, but not with the flutter of ecstasy with which young ladies of the olden time used to look forward to a ball. Emmeline and Kate were immeasurably superior, in both the religious and intellectual tone of their minds, to any mere pleasure in dress, in dancing, or in display. Dancing was only connected in their ideas with dancing-masters and constraint; they were resolute against waltzes and polkas, they hated nonsensical talk, and thought the sight of a flirtation too shocking to be laughed at.

Kate tried to comfort herself with Mr. Willoughby's consolation—that as long as they did not like it, it could not be doing them harm; but Emmeline did not seem to wish for consolation, and with a sort of melancholy resignation, prepared, as she said, to be dragged along, bound to the chariot wheels of vanity.

Susan Allen laughed at them both, and told them that she did not promise that they would like their first ball, or their second, but she was sure they would soon be delighted, quite as fond of balls as herself. Emmeline thought this an insult, and could scarcely smile politely. Kate went on answering Susan's advice about their dress; but even she was soon reduced

to look down, to hide the pain it gave her, when Susan lamented
their mourning, and asked if they could not make it slighter; it
must be nearly six weeks since—

Susan had got on unsafe ground; there was a pause, a dead
pause; she had been misled by the quiet soft way in which
Lady Willoughby talked of "poor Frank."

"Indeed, I am very sorry," said she earnestly; "I had no
idea—you must have been very fond of him—indeed, I beg
your pardon; it must have been an immense shock to you—"
She stopped short, in hopes of a full account of the accident,
but both the sisters were incapable of giving it to *her*, and
Kate presently said calmly, "Then you think those white
wreaths will look well?"

Susan Allen could never be their *great* friend, that was felt
by both. They had afterwards to dine at Lord Liddesdale's,
and see Lady Frances for the first time. There was a large
party, and all the beginning of the evening they could have
scarcely anything of Lady Frances but the warm shake of her
hand on their arrival, and afterwards, the distant view of her.
calm quiet face and soft brown eyes, full of an ineffable smile
of happiness.

Later, however, in the midst of the sounds of music and
talking, she came to them to exchange a few happy questions
about Herbert and Constance. "How much I have to say to
you!" said she; "but it won't do now. I will come to you
some morning, and try to have it all out. Well, and how's all
wi' you, as the people at Rowthorpe say? How do you like
coming out?"

"It is not as bad as we expected," said Kate.

"But the worst is to come," said Emmeline; "a horrible
ball to-morrow."

Lady Frances laughed.

"You don't like balls, you never go to them," said Kate.

"Very seldom," said Lady Frances; "but you know I am
getting into years, and going in instead of coming out."

"O Lady Frances!" cried Emmeline, shocked; while Kate,

with more of the simplicity of two years ago, said, " Did you like balls, when—when you were young ? "

" No, I do not think I did ; but then I did not like dancing, nor late hours. I used to look at them with great indifference after the first. Yes, I only liked going for two years," and then her sweet soft grave look came over her face. " Dear Annie used to enjoy dancing very much."

" Did she ? " said Kate eagerly.

" Yes, very much, dancing for the sake of dancing ; and she used to look so like a fairy—you would hardly fancy this room one twilight evening, some seven years ago, when Herbert and Annie, slim things of eighteen and sixteen, were waltzing about it together, almost flying—and Somerville standing there, by the fire, in a state of virtuous contempt and indignation, with Papa laughing at him."

" Oh, the polka and waltz ! " said Emmeline. " Did you—did she dance them at balls ? "

" No," said Lady Frances ; " she used to say that it was a very good thing there were so many, to prevent balls from being too delightful and bewitching, by keeping her sitting down, with her feet longing to be moving."

Lady Frances had never said so much of her sister Anne before, but it seemed as if she could not be happy without thinking of Annie as happy too ; and besides, perhaps, she had a reason for it—she might not like to give positive advice, but this was a hint, in case they might not find balls quite as horrible as they expected.

The time came, and to the last minute Emmeline was disconsolate. Even while her white wreath was being settled upon her head, to the entire satisfaction of Clements, Nurse, Kate, and the upper-housemaid, she was, as well as the necessity of holding up her head would permit, scribbling, in pencil, a poem about the chariot wheels of vanity, and an aching heart. Their own chariot wheels did not put the verses out of her head, but two beautiful stanzas were composed to their accompaniment ; and even the sound of the music, and the brilliance of the crowded room, did not drive them out. Nay, the bright dresses, the graceful gliding figures, the animated smiling faces, only gave additional ideas to be wrought into them. There was little interruption; they had not yet many acquaintances, especially among the dancing part of the male community; they were pretty and elegant, but far from striking or distinguished enough to attract attention; and there they stood, side by side, near their mother—Emmeline lost in her poetry, and feeling herself immeasurably superior to the people who seemed to delight in this crowd of folly; Kate trying to find amusement in watching the dresses and dances, and wondering if those bright-faced young ladies enjoyed themselves in as wholesome a way as Lady Anne Somerville had done.

Sir Francis got into a fuss, and asked them if they did not want to dance; they were magnanimous and indifferent, until at last, just as a quadrille was beginning, the Allens found them out, and Henry asked Miss Berners to dance. Miss Berners danced well, and enjoyed it; she walked about with him afterwards, and was very merry. He brought her back to her mother, and asked Miss Katherine for the next dance; it was a polka, and Kate, colouring deeply, thanked him and refused. He stood a little longer laughing and talking with them, and then seeing some other acquaintance, quitted them.

This was nearly the whole history of the evening. Emmeline had one chance of a partner again, but it was for a waltz, and she refused. So ended their first ball.

CHAPTER XVIII.

I sighed for something—what, I could not say;
I fancied virtues which were never seen,
And died for heroes who have never been;
I sickened with disgust at sober sense,
And loathed the pleasures worth and truth dispense,
Contemned the manners of the world I saw—
My guide was fiction, and romance my law.

H. More.

It was not long before Emmeline and Kate again met Miss Allen, and she forthwith attacked them about their dancing. Not choose to dance the polka! It was absurd, it was ridiculous, it was like nobody else, it was prudish, it was censorious. Emmeline had a liking for the idea of being persecuted, but there was not the same kind of vigour about her now as formerly. She fought a tolerable battle; said she did not blame waltzers, only she had rather not herself; she knew many people who disliked it, &c. Susan Allen answered that many girls thought so at first, but Emmeline would find it would not do, and would soon be like other people.

"I don't want to be like other people," said Emmeline, as soon as Susan was gone, "I had rather be unlike this world."

"Unlike it when it does wrong," said Kate, "but not to be unlike for the sake of unlikeness."

"That is the point," said Emmeline. "I would never do anything for the sake of avoiding persecution; never bow my head to the god of this world, but—"

What that "but" meant must remain undecided.

An evening party, where there was dancing, followed on the next day. The Allens were there, and Henry, with a look of meaning, asked Emmeline to be his partner. His sister was near, and it seemed to her that a refusal to waltz would entail a bantering, from which all her feelings shrank. She had rather do the deed than hear it talked about, so she accepted, and was soon in the midst of the whirl.

"Well, Kate," said Susan, "I hope soon to see you follow your sister's good example."

Kate smiled, and Susan being at the same time asked to dance, she was left to her own thoughts. It was not wrong in Emmie—no; gentle Kate could never conceive such an idea; it looked very pleasant, much more so than standing in the hot crowd, close to Lady Willoughby's chair. The lady of the house introduced a gentleman, who asked her to join the waltzing, but, without thinking, habit made her at once refuse. She wondered the next moment whether she was sorry or not—she would have enjoyed it; it would have been doing like Emmie; but Kate recollected Mr. Willoughby, and the waltz seemed incongruous; and then she thought of Lady Anne Somerville, and thenceforward her mind was made up.

Now that Miss Berners had once begun, she could not leave off; she could not refuse other people when she danced with Mr. Allen, so she danced nearly all the evening. As they went home Kate was pitied for having no partners; and Lady Willoughby said, rather sleepily, that she hoped she was not going to make herself talked about by not waltzing.

Emmeline, as soon as they were in their own room, began talking. "I was obliged, you know, Kate, or Susan would have made such a rout, and that would have been dreadful. Besides— But don't you mean ever to do it?"

"Dear Emmie, you won't be vexed with me if I don't," said Kate imploringly.

"No, I can't be vexed with you at all, Katie darling. It is just as one feels."

There it dropped; but Kate's feeling was more and more that here was the one proof of sincerity, by which she might try herself, whether she was still anchored to the feelings with which the events of the spring had inspired her. It would be, as Lady Anne had said, a bit of self-denial to keep gaieties from being too delightful.

Susan Allen teazed her, but she got through it pretty well, by laughing and owning herself silly. As to her mother, her uneasiness on the matter was calmed by Mrs. Allen, who said, "It would all come right; such things would settle themselves in course of time; girls always said so, and changed their mind by the end of their first season." So, ball after ball, Kate stood contentedly by her mother, while Emmeline danced. Not a word more was heard about the chariot wheels of vanity.

The sisters were now in the full sweep of that vortex which whirls young ladies round during their first London season. From morning to night their time was engrossed. Masters, and the preparation for them, took up from breakfast till late in the afternoon; then came the daily drive, and the dressing for the evening's amusement, which generally lasted till half way through the night. There seemed to be no time to think, or to build castles; or, if Emmeline built any, Kate was not summoned to help her. Externally, the girls led almost the same life, excepting Kate's persistence in avoiding the polka, and in going to the early morning service. Of the latter, indeed, Emmeline was not capable; for her strength was not yet fully restored, and the additional hour of rest in the morning was absolutely necessary. Excitement seemed to keep her up, for whenever there was a vacant interval she grew extremely weary. If there was time between the drive and dinner, she lay on her bed and drank tea, reading some light book; and on Sunday she was sure to be very tired.

They saw very little of Lady Frances, who did not go out much, and whose line of society was not the same as theirs; and the Allens were the persons with whom they were most intimate. Susan Allen, by means of comporting herself as if she were Emmeline's greatest friend, was actually making her believe so, and establishing considerable influence over her; and besides, there was the brother.

Henry Allen was as far as possible from Emmeline's beau ideal of a hero with a poker in his back. He was nothing but a fashionable young man, who ought to have had something to do, and who could talk agreeably, but very shallowly. Emmeline knew this, and from a distance she would have heartily despised him—nay, she did so at present; but he was the first person who ever paid her that sort of attention which flatters a vanity of which she had not yet been sensible. He meant nothing by it, nor did Emmeline consider whether he did. If she had analyzed her state of mind, she would have been taken by surprise and shocked; for she would not have found a particle of attachment, but a great deal of gratified vanity.

It was a state of intoxication; music, amusement, dancing, admiration, had got hold of Emmeline's mind, and carried her along. It was all present, she had no space for past or future; if she had, her spirits flagged more than her bodily strength. Future visions had lost their zest; she was tired of them; a dreary grey had taken the place of the rainbow tints of former days. For the past, Emmeline could not look back to it; it only reminded her of that sad loss—of disappointments, and, worst of all, of what she scarcely dared to remember, of vanished impulses of good, of resolutions from which she had fallen. On every unemployed hour was written, "Vanity and vexation of spirit," and therefore Emmeline left none unoccupied. She read, studied, played, danced, and gave herself up more and more to the fascination of the Allens, chiefly because they served to banish thought.

So passed more than a month, when one Saturday the Allens and the Willoughby party went to the opera together. There was a great deal of talk about music, ending in a proposal from Susan that Emmeline and Kate should go with her on Sunday morning to hear the service at a Roman Catholic Chapel—the most beautiful music, as both she and her brother said, that could be imagined.

The sisters were shocked, but Susan seemed to think nothing of it; "Henry went almost always," she said, "and she and Mamma very often. Everyone did; there was no danger of their being taken for Roman Catholics, if that was what they were afraid of; and they could go to church in the afternoon."

"Impossible, I cannot think of it, dear Susan," was Emmeline's ultimatum on Saturday night; and no more passed at that time.

As the girls were going to bed, Emmeline added to Kate, that her whole mind revolted at the idea of making a spectacle of a religious service.

On Monday Henry Allen brought them a report of the beauty of the service; on Friday he showed them a programme of the music which was to be heard at High Mass on the next Sunday, and the name of a famous preacher who was in everyone's mouth. "Surely," he said, "you will not persist in your refusal."

Emmeline made no direct answer. Kate said, "I don't like to miss church;" but Kate was not the person chiefly sought, so her reply was not regarded.

On Saturday evening they again met Susan, who, with her saucy wilful air, said, "We mean to come for you to-morrow morning, mind, Emmie."

"Oh no, pray don't," said Emmeline.

"Indeed I shall; and mind you don't keep us waiting, or we shall never get seats. There is such a rush always when Dr. —— preaches. I would not miss hearing him for the world. You cannot guess what beautiful language it is—so powerful and metaphorical. It is perfect poetry, I assure you, and you were always fond of poetry—in that exquisite chapel too. Oh, you are just the person to be delighted. You will never forget it. Now then," as her mother was rising to go away, "it is a settled thing. We shall come in the carriage and call for you."

"Oh no, no, pray don't, Susan, I had much rather not," said Emmeline; but Susan shook hands with her with an arch look of meaning.

"I hope they will not come for us!" was Emmeline's heartfelt exclamation that night.

"I hope not, I am sure," echoed Kate; "it will be very disagreeable to have to refuse."

"And I should like it after all," said Emmeline, "for once in a way—it must be so gorgeous and impressive. It must be the realization of what one has read of."

"One would not know whether to join in it or not," said Kate; "it would not feel right to be merely looking on; and yet—oh, I should not like it, Uncle Willoughby would not like it."

"Uncle Willoughby has old-world notions," said Emmeline.

"O Emmie!"

"Well, I wish Susan would not be so pertinacious," said Emmeline; "I don't half like going, and yet I do want to see it, and to hear that music. It would be a thing to dwell on. But I have told her it must not be, I hope we shall hear no more of it."

"I hope so," replied Kate.

Morning came, and the family were at breakfast, when a carriage stopped at the door; there was a double knock, and Henry Allen was ushered into the breakfast-room.

"My mother and sister are in the carriage," he said; "they have deputed me to summon the Miss Berners to join us."

"Oh, Mrs. Allen told me last night," said Lady Willoughby; "she has been kind enough to offer to take them to hear the music at St. Bonaventura's this morning. We are much obliged to her;—it will be such an advantage to your music, my dears."

"I thought I told Susan—" faltered Emmeline hesitatingly.

"Susan and I have ventured to judge for you," said Henry. "You do not know what you would give up."

"There is nothing particular in going, I am told, my dear," said Lady Willoughby. "The most fashionable people do so."

"May I be allowed to hasten you," said Henry; "if we are not early, we shall not secure a good place."

"Then thank you, do pray go without us," said Emmeline, beginning a hurried explanation to her mother; but Mr. Allen made a demonstration of obstinacy, as if he would not move without her.

"Come, young ladies," said Sir Francis, "you are keeping Mrs. Allen waiting. You should have made up your minds sooner."

"Well, then, since—" said Emmeline, slowly rising, and leaving the room. Kate followed her.

Emmeline began hastily to put on her things, with a little

petulance. Kate helped her, saying, "Emmie dear, if you go, it will be civility enough to the Allens, without me."

"O Kate, won't you go? It will be no pleasure without you."

"I think I should be more comfortable if I did not. Don't be disappointed with me, dear Emmie. Somehow I can't make up my mind to it."

"Very well," said Emmeline, "I can't stop now. You are getting quite determined, Kate."

The first time she had ever been pettish with Kate; but there was no time to recall the expression, down she ran, and with a few words of explanation, was setting off.

That Emmeline was eager and curious, cannot be denied; but at the same time she would have preferred giving up the expedition. She knew it was wrong, though without entering into all the reasons against it; and she had not been used to act directly against her conscience, so that it would not let her be at peace.

The Allens were delighted, and greeted her eagerly, without much caring for Kate's absence, though it was a dart to Emmeline, unused as she was to do anything without her sister. There was something uncomfortable in their satisfaction at having captured her; it had so much of exultation, that it seemed like a triumph; and she, who had such ideas of the magnificence of resistance and firmness, could ill brook to feel that she had been persuaded against her better judgment.

Emmeline talk of firmness! What had her whole life been since she left school? Had it not been one course of fluctuating purpose, half-executed projects, vague dreams? Unstable! was the history of all she did; and wherefore? We read that a double-minded man is unstable in all his ways. Poor Emmeline, we cannot call her double-minded, in the sense of insincere; but she was not single-hearted, though she little knew it, and deceived no one but herself. She talked, she fancied great things, she had high designs of virtue, but little reality; she left untouched the practical duties that lay at once before her, and strained after high things of her own imagination, while utterly neglecting the means she had always been taught was the especial channel of grace.

As in the state of dissatisfaction above mentioned Emmeline sat by Mrs. Allen's side, she happened to glance from the window, and exclaimed at once, " I do believe it is Herbert ! "

Was it only a vision called up by conscience, imagining Lord Herbert in every clergyman walking forth to his Sunday-school?

The recognition, though it might be only a fancy, did not tend to compose her spirits; but she did not wish the Allens to think her alarmed at the thought of her brother-in-law, and therefore talked gaily in order to appear unconcerned. She had nearly succeeded by the time they arrived at the place of their destination.

It was a most beautiful edifice, built according to the rules of perfect architecture, and adorned within in exquisite taste, with great richness and splendour, and with attention to the emblematic signification of each ornament; one of the places in which Romanism is displayed with the greatest attractions to educated and imaginative minds, keeping back as much as possible all that is offensive to a truly Catholic principle, and putting foremost what is really true and beautiful, what it possesses as being a Church, and hiding much of what belongs to Romanism, *as such*.

Emmeline's admiration was won in a moment, the surprise and delight almost taking away her breath. She had feeling and taste enough to understand as well as admire; she saw the appropriateness, where the Allens simply wondered, and her mind was entranced.

It was the same with the service. She knew Latin enough to follow in some degree, and with the ordinary ignorance about the Roman Catholic services, she was very much taken by surprise at finding so little that was objectionable, and so much that was extremely beautiful. The music, the ceremonial, the appearance of reverential awe, so much greater than what she was used to see—all had their effect; everything she saw and heard combined to bring her into a state of enchantment such as she had never known, and which made her feel more devout—

or perhaps, more properly, excited in her devotion—than she had ever been before.

Not that she was inclined to become a Roman Catholic; she knew that there were too many reasons against that to be enumerated; but a deep impression had been made upon her. Had she a right to subject herself to such impressions, when it is certain that the *whole* of the system which conveys them is not the truth? Was it not running after temptation? Years after, Emmeline had reason to lament that visit to St. Bonaventura's.

She had intended to go to church in the afternoon, but they were late in returning to Mrs. Allen's, and she had to take luncheon there; this occupied a long time, and the bells were ringing before they had finished; then came callers, and the end of it was that she could not leave her friends till nearly dinner-time, when, with her ears full of the music, and her head of the vague dreamy thoughts of *exaltation* that the talk of the afternoon had confused, not. driven away, she went homewards, almost glad to have missed the afternoon service; it would have sounded, she thought, so cold and tame after what she had just heard.

When Emmeline was gone, Kate felt somewhat disconsolate. She did not like to be left behind, or to miss what Emmie was doing, and was afraid that her sister thought her particular and disagreeable. However, it could not be helped, so she returned to the breakfast-table. Her mother and Sir Francis, though surprised to see her, agreed that she had judged wisely in not crowding Mrs. Allen's carriage.

The breakfast-party had just settled down again, when there was another knock at the door; and the next moment, Kate could hardly believe her ears or eyes, for she heard the announcement of "Lord Herbert Somerville;" and there stood Constance's Herbert, tall and slight, dark-haired, bright-eyed, and red and white, just as he went away; and his hand was pressing fast her own, and his brotherly kiss on her forehead, as she had so little hoped would ever be again; and yet she could hardly rejoice, while Emmeline was missing.

Q

Lady Willoughby received him in her graceful way, Sir Francis with cordiality ; and then followed his anxious inquiry for Emmeline—was she well ?

"Yes, very well," said her mother. "She will be so sorry—it is very unfortunate, but her friend Miss Allen has taken possession of her for the day, and carried her off. How annoyed she will be !"

He soon proposed to Kate to walk back with him, and join Constance and the rest of his family at church, promising to bring her back after the afternoon service, when Constance could come with them. She was delighted to accede to his plan, and as it was getting late, he begged her to put on her bonnet quickly.

While she was doing so, a thrill of consternation came over her again : "What would Herbert and Constance think of Emmie's present occupation ?" "Oh," she answered herself, " they have been in Roman Catholic countries ; " and therewith she was satisfied, and only pitied Emmie for having lost this delightful meeting. When she came down, she found that Lord Herbert had promised to come to dinner that evening.

They were soon walking fast along the street arm-in-arm. She would have been completely happy, if Emmeline's loss had not been in her mind.

It was her first exclamation, " Why, Herbert, how well you are !"

He smiled. " Yes, that Italian spring seemed to be made of freshness and renovation. You can't think how beautiful it was."

" And do you never cough at all now ? Oh, there, Herbert—unless you did so on purpose."

" No, I did not—it is only what Somerville calls my unconstitutional cough."

" I am sorry—I thought you were really going to be thoroughly well."

"Why, lungs are not to be mended like tea-kettles, and mine are never to be expected to be very sound affairs, though they may be tinkered up for a time."

Then, as she looked up at him anxiously, he added gravely,
" We have seen how life and death are beyond our guesses.
Half a year ago, who would have foretold which of us—Frank
or myself, would be walking with you at this moment?"

" O Herbert!—that dear Frank—I am so glad you knew him
a little."

" It was very little, but enough to show that there was something very deep about him. There was a truth of character—I
hardly know how to describe it, except as the reverse of being
double-minded—and originality, too."

" Oh, you did understand him very well indeed!" said Kate,
holding tighter by her brother's arm, as if it was an additional
link ; " but there was so much more—I must tell you all about
it some day, all about his great trouble when Sir Francis would
not let him follow the wish of his heart and be a clergyman.
Dear Frank, he has the wish of his heart fulfilled now, as Uncle
Willoughby says."

" I remember how we thought him cut out for parish work.
He had such a particular pleasant way of speaking to the poor
people at Copseley. I was sure you would be fond of him in time."

" Fond! he was our one bright spot! But don't speak of
him to Emmie, please, Herbert, for she cannot bear the sound
of his name. It was different with me, for I was a good
deal with Uncle Willoughby just after—but poor Emmie was
very ill at first, and has never been able to begin talking
about him."

" Do you think her quite recovered?"

" Yes—no—she is not strong, poor dear, and gets so tired."

" I am very sorry to have missed her ; we reckoned on being
all together, as we were in those merry days at Rowthorpe.
Are you confirmed, Kate?" he added presently.

" No ; we were so sorry, but we left Herringsby just too soon.
Why?"

" Shall you mind walking to St. James's Place alone after
church?"

" Oh no, not at all."

"I think this first Sunday we must all be together there," said Herbert in a low voice, as if apologizing to her, as there was a tone of regret in her voice.

"Oh yes, I did not mean that—it is our own fault, I know, that we are shut out from—from you all and Frank." She whispered rather than spoke the last words, and tears were in her eyes.

Lord Herbert spoke very kindly: "I believe the Bishop intends to confirm at Dearport this autumn; we must try for you to come in for that."

"Then you will prepare us. Oh, it is what we always wished!" said Kate joyfully.

"And where is Emmie gone? Whom is she with?"

"The Allens; Susan was an old school friend."

"Is she staying with them?"

"Oh, no, only gone with them this morning." A reluctance to say where came over Kate, and she finished, "She will be so vexed to have missed you."

"Gone with them where?" said Lord Herbert, quite unsuspiciously.

"Why, they took her to go with them to hear the service at St. Bonaventura's; they say the music is so very fine, and Dr. —— was to preach."

"To a Roman Catholic chapel?" said Lord Herbert.

"Yes—the new one—it has been built since you went, and is so beautiful."

"Have you been there?"

"Never, nor Emmie till to-day. She did not like going, but they almost carried her off by force. Susan is so determined."

Lord Herbert made no answer; and turning the corner of the next street, just as the bells were beginning, they came in sight of the two pairs walking together, Constance on her father-in-law's arm, Lady Frances with her brother. They made all speed, and in another moment Lord Somerville had looked round, seen them, and they had met, with a whole world of glad greetings sounding round Kate, and an anxious inquiry from Constance

for Emmeline. "Well; but just gone out for the day when
Herbert came. Oh, such a pity!"

"And Mamma?" Constance joined company with her sister,
locking her arm into hers as they walked on.

"Oh yes, quite well, dear dear Constance!"

"Is not Herbert looking well?" said Constance triumphantly.

"Yes, indeed, how glad—"

"And let me just look at you, sweet Katie, that I may know
your own face again."

The sisters turned their faces to each other with a bright sunny
look of love; ending in the playful laugh with which of old they
used to play at trying which could look at the other longest
without smiling. Constance was scarcely altered, except that a
wifely ungirlish expression had come over her face. Kate was a
little ashamed of the difference between their dress; her own,
hardly to be called mourning, a lilac muslin, flounced and
trimmed to the height of the fashion, with a black lace polka
and bonnet, with lilac flowers and ribbons; while Constance
wore a plain black silk, and a straw bonnet trimmed with white.
Kate had the uncomfortable feeling of being *smart*, one which
is particularly disagreeable in the company of persons of higher
rank.

Only a few happy words had been exchanged before they were
at the church. Lord Liddesdale put Kate under the escort of a
servant, for her solitary walk after the service was over. She
had never felt it so wrong to be obliged to go away, nor wished
so much to remain. "And the door was shut," returned upon
her several times; and she felt as if Frank, as if everything good,
were there, and she herself shut out. She sat in Lady Frances's
little morning room, trying to distinguish in her own mind between the real desire for what she had missed, and the mere wish
to do like the others. She had more hope now that Herbert and
Constance were come; how pleasant it would be to tell Uncle
Willoughby, and how dear Frank would have rejoiced for her.
Emmeline—Kate's thoughts went to perplex themselves as to
whether Herbert was displeased with Emmeline, and there they

wearied themselves. Her happiness that day was by no means unalloyed.

Clouds rolled off, however, when the party returned ; how should they not among such happy people, so kind in their happiness, and making her so entirely one of themselves ! There was no sensation of being in the way, or only admitted for Constance's sake ; they all showed themselves glad to have her to share in their gladness, and old Lord Liddesdale was especially affectionate and fatherly in manner.   It would have been almost pleasure enough to watch his deep heartfelt happiness in having his sons back again ; the benevolence that seemed more than ever to beam about him, and his air of not being able to make enough of Herbert.

Constance and Kate were both silent in their gladness; but Lord Somerville was in very high spirits, and kept up a sort of boyish fun and bantering with sisters, brother, and father, that Kate thought both delightful and marvellous at his mature age.   And she saw that Constance, who used to be a little bewildered and frightened at his unexpected speeches, now treated him with perfect ease and familiarity, even calling him by his own nickname of " Jack," which had no connection with his Christian name, but was the remnant of days when the brothers and sisters used to act the adventure of James III. of Scotland, in " Tales of a Grandfather," and he had acquired the appellation of " Spears and Jacks," since become simply " Jack."

" Well," said Lord Somerville, as Kate stood waiting in the drawing-room for a moment while the others were getting ready for evening church, " I hope you think that Constance does credit to my care."

Kate laughed, and tried to find something to say, which resulted in " She is looking very well."

" I have learnt a great deal from Constance," said Lord Somerville ; and as Kate looked up eagerly, he added, " how to write a letter when there is nothing but brown mud in the ink-stand," speaking with the same gravity as he had begun the sentence, so that his jest or earnest was as doubtful to Kate as it used to be two years ago.

With a little blush and hesitation she said, "We ought to thank you for what you wrote to us. It was such—such a comfort."

" You owe me thanks," he said, smiling, " for I grudged very much the time I had to stay away from him, to write, either to you or to my father, with the fear that I was raising false hopes. We kept the letters to the last moment, that we might be able to say something decisive; but when I sent them, I little thought the next would be hopeful."

"He was so very ill then," said Kate, in a low voice.

" So much exhausted, that—in fact, I don't think he would ever have got through those two days—but for—" (he hesitated in his turn) " for Constance. There, I—think it is but right you should know what a sister you have ; and as you'll never hear it from themselves, for Herbert would think praising her praising himself, I may as well tell you that nothing—"

Unluckily, as Kate thought, Constance and her husband came in at the same moment, and Lord Somerville ended his speech —" I may as well tell you that nothing can excel, not to say equal, Constance's talents for making blinds draw up rightly."

"I was in hopes I should have heard of something less common-place," said Constance ; "some perfection better worth lecturing Kate upon."

"On your humility, for instance," said Lord Somerville ; "I shall begin lecturing on punctuality next, if Frances does not appear, unless she has become like the lady—was not she at Copseley, Herbert ?—who thought it was not genteel to come in time."

"No, I don't own to that lady," said Lord Herbert : "I believe she is mythical, and fastened on to everyone who has a parish."

" No, we must not have Copseley abused now," said Constance.

" We keep that for Dearport," said Lord Somerville.

Constance shook her head, and looked determined.

"Ah!" said Lord Somerville, "I know how it will be. Every letter will represent Dearport as an earthly paradise—"

"A maritime one," suggested his brother.

"Each letter will enhance its charms and beauties till I positively am taken in to believe in them, and come and see you—I shall find an atmosphere of mud and fish; have to pick my way on tip-toe through a pavement of hakes' heads and scates' tails, diversified with periwinkles and cockle-shells; find my Lord and Lady Herbert teaching eight sailors in a drawing-room twelve feet square, and go away persuaded by Constance's eloquence, contrary to every one of my own senses, to believe and pronounce it paradise complete."

Kate looked from one to the other in a puzzle, whether it was really likely to be so very disagreeable at Dearport, and whether Lord Somerville so very much disapproved of their going there; but they only laughed, and soon all set off to church.

After service, Lord Somerville and his sister walked with the others to the Willoughbys' door. There, Lord Herbert said he should go on with them to call upon his aunt, and return long before dinner. Constance and Kate entered together, Kate wondering if her sister felt as she did on the like introduction.

In a few seconds, Constance was receiving such an embrace and affectionate greeting as had met her sisters eighteen months ago. Sir Francis was a good deal more ceremonious with Lady Herbert; but Edwin, the only one of the children in the room, gave no space for talking. His sister's sweet face enchanted him, as he proved by thrusting his toys before her, and making them unmercifully perform their several varieties of squeak. Emmeline was not yet come home, and everyone repeated how disappointed she would be to have missed her sister.

After sitting for some little time, and exchanging many affectionate words with her mother, Constance begged to see the other children.

"I'll go and fetch Janet and Cecilia," said Kate.

"Do let me come too: I should like to visit little Janet in

her school-room; I want to see Miss Townsend too," said
Constance, springing up.

"Oh come, come, do; Cecilia is such a darling," said
Kate.

"Do you like to go, my dear?" said Lady Willoughby. "It
is up so many stairs, and we can send for the children; Janet
was here just now, but Edwin was making such a noise, that
we sent her away."

Constance was only the more bent on going; and with Edwin
holding her hand, she skipped lightly up before Kate, and was
presently in the school-room, where Janet sat by Miss Townsend
in a moody state.

"How do you do, Miss Townsend?" began Constance at once,
shaking her hand with the cordiality of a renewal of their old
acquaintance, which brought a glow into the little governess's
cheeks. "And Janet, little Janet!"—she put her arms around
her and kissed her—"what, have you not a word for sister
Constance?"

Janet was certainly gratified, but jealousy and the feeling of
injustice were upon her, and she stood, with drooping head, in
something between shyness and sullenness, by no means mended
by the triumphant exclamation—"Here is the dear little woman!
Here, come to sister Constance!" with which Kate proudly
brought the beautiful little Cecilia into the room, and held her
up for admiration.

Constance was delighted with her, kissed her, and fondled
her, but soon turned again to talk to Miss Townsend and Janet,
though without much success; for frank and free as Constance
was, there was no subduing the governess's shy frightened
manner, or making Janet look up. Kate began to be impatient
—"Come, Janet, are you cross? Why can't you do like the
others, when Constance is so kind to you? See, Edwin and
Cecilia are not so silly."

This was the very thing to make it worse, and Kate next
turned to Miss Townsend, saying, "Is she naughty?"

Miss Townsend looked hurt, and shook her head.

" We will not torment her any more," said Constance. "We will be better acquainted one day, Janet, woman."

Patting her on the head, Constance left them, and begged to come and take off her bonnet in her sisters' room. "It would be so natural," she said merrily.

"Oh! do, dear Constance;" then, as soon as they were out of the school-room, "I never saw such a child as that Janet! She is always sulky, and I do believe Miss Townsend encourages her!"

"I hope not," said Constance. "Poor child! Well, Cecilia is a beauty! What curls! So this is your room, Katie. Oh, how glad I am to see that dear old sandal-wood box again! It is so like old times! And all your old curiosities just the same. Now if Emmie would but come back, we should feel just like ourselves, when we three were alone in the world. Is not it strange to recollect that time, Katie?"

"I do wish Emmie would come!" was Kate's answer. "I cannot think what she can be doing."

"Do you see much of the Allens?" said Constance.

"More than of anyone else; Susan is so fond of Emmie."

"Is she? That was not so at school. Is Susan altered?"

"Not much," said Kate. "She seeks us out more than we seek her. It sometimes seems to me quite unnatural that Emmie should have a friend all to herself."

Constance glanced a little anxiously at Kate; but there was no time for more, for at that very moment the door was slowly opened, and there entered, with the languid step of one weary with an unsatisfactory day, Emmeline herself. One moment she stood transfixed, then, with a little cry, on each side, she and Constance were in each other's arms, Kate laughing, and saying she supposed Emmie had not been into the drawing-room to hear the news.

"No, indeed, I have not. Is Herbert there?"

"No, he is coming to dinner. He came to fetch me just as you were gone."

"Then it was he that I saw. I could not believe it. And is he well?"

"Quite, quite well," said Constance : "better than I ever knew him. Oh, now it is so *very* nice! We came last night —landed at eleven o'clock, and the first thing after breakfast he went to look for you all."

"To think of my being out of the way!" said Emmeline. "I could not get away sooner; we came home late, then there was luncheon, and people coming in; but if I had only known —Dear, dear Constance, how like yourself you look! Well, it was most beautiful! Oh, such a sermon! And that magnificent service—how you must have enjoyed it abroad, Constance!"

"I never was there through the service," said Constance.

"What!" exclaimed Emmeline: "Susan has been saying it is the one thing she envies you for being at Rome. Surely you did not think it wrong. So many good people do it."

"No, I would not say it was wrong," said Constance; "but we had a feeling against treating it as a sight. Besides, when I was able to leave Herbert for a little while, I could not have spared once missing our English service, when I could have it to join in."

"You were not often at places without an English congregation?" said Kate.

"No; Herbert could not bear that we should. But ought we to stay up any longer away from Mamma?"

"It is so comfortable!" said Kate.

But Emmeline was not so willing to stay. She had an uncomfortable abashed feeling, and a dread of what Constance might say next, which made her restlessly glad to get downstairs. While Constance was engaged with her mother, she drew Kate apart, and begged to know what Herbert had said, and how he had looked, on hearing where she was gone. "He seemed surprised," said Kate, "but he said nothing. But, Emmie dear, only think, there is to be a Confirmation at Dearport, and he will bring us in for it, and examine us himself after all."

"Oh!" said Emmeline, but without any tone of alacrity.

Lord Herbert arrived, and Emmeline met him with a shade

of constraint. If he was displeased he did not by any means intend to manifest it; yet, unconsciously perhaps, he talked less to her that evening than he did to Kate; and certainly she did not address him with the same ease and readiness, but this might be owing to her not having spent the day with him in the free atmosphere of Lord Liddesdale's house. Few persons ever were more agreeable than Lord Herbert. He had not the odd, sarcastic, unexpected ways of his brother, and did not cause his cleverness to be so much perceived; his manner was very simple, but had a stamp of high birth and breeding, which gave every act of attention and good-nature an air of refined courtesy.

Lady Willoughby was completely enchanted with her son-in-law; and when the ladies went up after dinner, she made Constance listen to her raptures, which Constance heard with very pretty gratified blushes, pleased, in her turn, to talk over his wonderful recovery, and to say again and again how very kind Lord Somerville had been.

The girls began to hope they should hear no more of "poor Constance." Next, Lady Willoughby gave Constance a long lecture on the necessity of his being prudent, avoiding cold, and not exerting his voice, to which she listened with ready acquiescence, saying they meant to be very careful.

But how was poor Lady Willoughby shocked, when it was disclosed that they meant to walk home! Sir Francis was for ringing the bell, and ordering the carriage, but Constance earnestly begged him not to think of it. "Lord Liddesdale would have sent for us, but we thought we should enjoy the walk: pray don't."

Up-stairs she ran, to fetch her bonnet, followed by her sisters; while her mother, in dismay, silently wondered where was all the care she talked of, and Sir Francis mentally despised Lord Liddesdale for not sending out his carriage on a Sunday. In a minute she came down, with a great worsted comforter, which she held up to her husband.

"This!" exclaimed he. "My dear Constance! Was there

ever a woman born out of India who would have the conscience to propose to an unfortunate man to muffle himself in such a thing in the heart of June? Why, how did you bring it here?"

"In my pocket," said Constance. "Now do, Herbert."

"That pocket of hers! Do you know it, Kate? Everything comes out of that pocket, and we suspect it of being uncanny. The last thing was a lucifer match-box, candle, and all. It was not lighted—I will say that for her."

"Why, your brother left it behind him on the table at Brussels, and I only saw it the last moment," said Constance. "So what else could I do with it? But what are you going to do with that poor thing, Herbert? I wish you would be a wise man, and put it on."

He rolled it up in a ball, and pretended to throw it away; he waved it high in the air above her reach; but at last, with various comical faces of resignation, he let her put it round his neck, and only rebelled so far as not to let her bury his chin in it; then arranging to meet early to-morrow, they wished good-night, and walked away, leaving Lady Willoughby persuaded that he was the most imprudent man in the world, and Emmeline thinking that there were more things in Lord and Lady Herbert Somerville than were dreamt of in her mother's philosophy. Kate was supremely happy, Emmeline trying to think herself so.

Lord Herbert and his wife walked on in the gas-light a little while without speaking. It had been the first sight of her family, and neither liked to own the impression, or to ask the other's. He was the first to begin.

"How Kate is grown and improved!"

"Oh, is not she?" responded Constance with delight.

"She has such a very sweet face—as she always had; but now it is something more."

"And Emmie?"

"I could not make Emmie out. I did not see nearly so much of her, but I thought she was not looking well."

" Yes, there was a fagged look, as if she was over-doing every-thing, and I fancied there was a constraint about her."

" That, I thought, was from anxiety as to what you might be thinking of her expedition this morning."

" Did you hear what she thought of it?" ·

" Not much—she was in haste to go down-stairs; but I am afraid her imagination has been a good deal impressed. She asked me whether I thought it wrong to have gone. I told her how we had felt on the matter, and that silenced her. It was no plan of her own devising, you know."

" Kate was careful to tell me that."

" I don't understand it," said Constance; " those two used to be so entirely one in everything, and I doubt whether it is quite the same now. I don't like to hear of the intimacy with the Allens. Susan was no favourite of mine at school, and her family did not seem to be quite what one would wish."

" Well, we will try to have them with us," said Lord Herbert; "and as to Kate, I am sure she is all right. I should guess that she had been making a stand against Emmie's expedition this morning."

" Kate make a stand against Emmie! Things must be changed indeed, for it to come to that. But you did not see the little ones, did you?"

" Only the boy! Sir Francis was playing with him when I came in. He is a fine fellow!"

" I wish you had seen Janet. I wanted to know what you would think of her."

CHAPTER XIX.

The hollowness of human things,
The wear of feverish thought,
Each to the heart a shadow brings
From tombs of mem'ry brought;
A broken cistern ev'rywhere
Proves nature's purest joy;
Though fresh the draught imagined there,
How soon we taste alloy!

R. Montgomery.

In the course of the next fortnight, the sisters saw the Somerville party every day, and Lady Willoughby was completely bewildered by the ways of her daughter and son-in-law.

They used to walk in almost every morning, and after a short stay, set off together on foot. And it would transpire that their business was seeing churches, orphan asylums, and schools, visiting model lodging-houses, &c. In the afternoon, Constance and Lady Frances would call to see if the girls would come with them in the carriage : and in the evening, it was generally contrived that the three sisters should meet.

Kate was less involved in her mother's engagements than Emmeline, and was able to be more with Constance. She thus knew all the arrangements about Dearport ; how it was said to have one pretty region, and one very wretched, and how the beautiful grounds of Bayhurst almost bordered on the town, and they had permission from the non-resident proprietor to use them as they pleased, which Lord Somerville said Constance would interpret into giving routs for school-children. The Parsonage was in the worst part of the town, where it was said that "nobody could live ;" however, Lord Herbert meant to judge for himself, for he was going to take possession of his living, and stay there about ten days, which time Constance was to spend with her mother.

Emmeline and Kate were enchanted; all must be well when they had Constance to themselves ; her, who had, from the time

the forlorn little girls were sent from their Indian home, been
at once motherly nurse, elder sister, play-fellow, and guide.
"Dearest Constance!" said Emmeline, "she has always been
more to us than the whole world besides. There is joy in her
very presence."

Constance arrived, but they were soon obliged to feel that she
was no longer their exclusive right. All the evening she was
taken up with Lady Willoughby's low sleepy murmurs, and
afterwards by the whole series of Sir Francis's Indian stories.
Emmeline could have no talk with her till bed-time, when she
invited the two to have a nice long coze in her room. They sat
hearing the history that they had but half entered into from
Constance's letters, the whole account of Lord Herbert's illness;
but Constance was still the careful "old mother" that she used
in former days to be called, and would not let Emmeline's pale
cheeks and heavy eye-lids remain long absent from the pillow,
especially when the eyes and cheeks both began to brighten with
the eagerness of talking; and in vain Emmeline declared that
the only time she never was tired was after midnight.

The hope of a morning over Constance's sketches made
Emmeline rise in good spirits; but here was fresh annoyance.
The breakfast became more interminable than ever, for Sir
Francis was so pleased with Lady Herbert's bright attention,
that he did not spare her one of his political comments over the
newspaper. Afterwards Emmeline was about to claim her sister,
when Constance recollected that she had not been to the school-
room, and it would be unkind not to visit poor Miss Townsend.

She found the little governess in an agitation of tears and
smiles, and as Lord Somerville used to say of her that no one
could be ten minutes with her without making her a confidant,
she soon discovered that Miss Townsend's sailor-brother was just
come home from a five years voyage, and that she was divided
between rejoicing at his safety, and despair at not being able to
go to see him.

Straightway Constance went to her mother, telling the news
so eagerly, and so much as if it concerned herself, that Lady

Willoughby lifted up her eye-lids in amazement, "Well, my dear!"

"It is such an excellent time," said Constance; "now that I am here, you can spare her so much better."

"Spare her, my dear? Sir Francis would not think of it; there are all the children!"

"Oh, we will take care of them, Mamma; we can manage very well; and it will be so pleasant to have them all to ourselves. It is just what I wanted, to get acquainted with Janet. And poor Miss Townsend is in such a state."

"Well, my dear, poor thing, I don't know what Sir Francis would think—but, my love, they will surely be too much for you."

"Nothing is too much for me, Mamma," said Constance laughingly. "Do, for a treat to me, let me have Janet and Edwin for this one week!"

"My dear, you are so energetic! But Sir Francis must decide—I can't tell."

"He is at home, I think," said Constance. "I'll run and see if he is in the drawing-room."

With consternation did Emmeline and Kate hear Constance propounding her scheme. They were too good-natured to start any objection, for they felt it would be shameful to prevent the poor little woman from going home to see her brother; but Emmeline could not help wishing that Sir Francis would say no; and when she heard him acceding, she mentally declared that peace was at an end, and it was folly to expect that anything would turn out well with her—a being doomed to disappointment.

Another moment, and Constance was in the school-room; the permission was so far beyond all Miss Townsend's most daring hopes, that she burst into tears of joy, and was unable to utter her usual "So very kind."

"I'm so glad," said Constance heartily. "Now, can we help you? Shall Janet finish her reading to me? it would be a pity for you to lose any time."

R

" Thank you—oh, thank you ! " and Miss Townsend, entirely
overcome, retreated, while Janet read straight on. Constance sat
considering, and presently sprung up, and knocked at Miss
Townsend's door, to say that she was going out with Lady
Frances, and to offer to set her down. The thanks were more
nervous and alarmed than ever, and it was hard to distinguish
whether she was more pleased or confused ; but the matter was
scttled, and Constance again sat down, while Janet went on
reading her small history in a monotonous voice ; until having
finished the chapter, she left off as if she had been a machine
come to the end of its winding up, and sat looking straight
before her in the same position.

" Well, Janet, what do you like to do next ? "

" I should like to go to Miss Townsend."

" Are you sure you would not interrupt her when she wants
to pack up ? "

Janet sat up rigidly, without changing countenance.

" You will miss her very much, sha'n't you, dear ? " said Constance kindly ; " but you know it will only be for a week, and
we will see what sister can do for you."

" A week is a very long time ! " said Janet.

When Kate came to bring notice that Lord Liddesdale was in
the drawing-room, she found Janet on Constance's knee, helping
her to write to brother Herbert, that they were trying to make
up to each other for his absence and Miss Townsend's.

Constance thought the expedition would be no loss to her
sisters, but Emmeline was annoyed at losing her for the afternoon,
after the whole morning had been engrossed by other people.
Lady Frances, when she came to take Constance up, was of
course glad to be of service to the governess, and saying there
was one place more, asked who would come with them.

" Suppose we take Janet," said Constance. " She would have
the pleasure of being with Miss Townsend to the last."

" My dear," Lady Willoughby interposed, "you will crowd
Lady Frances to death ! "

" No, thank you," said Lady Frances, laughing. " She knows

how I pine alone in that great carriage. Pray let us have the little one."

Edwin could hardly believe that sister was going to take Janet out without him, and Janet's tone of triumph over him was not agreeable ; but Constance held her opinion in suspense, especially when Miss Townsend took courage to say in reply to her inquiries as to the management of the children, " Pray do not think Janet sullen. I know the Miss Berners think so ; and to strangers, I believe, she is not an attractive child ; but she lives so much in her affections, poor little thing ! "

There was a brightening sympathy in Constance that enlivened all she approached, and she and Frances had made Janet so happy by the time they came to Miss Townsend's home, that the meek governess was almost hurt to find that her charge could part with her so easily, not knowing that the secret of this happiness was that she was to work a bag to surprise her with on her return, and was impatient to get rid of her that she might set about it.

" Constance is at the beck of everyone except ourselves, who belonged to her most," sighed Emmeline, as she saw the three children enjoying a game of genuine active play with her. And after dinner again, Emmeline felt as if she was injured, when Constance sat contentedly listening to her mother, who was trying to make her very anxious and unhappy at trusting dear Lord · Herbert to take care of his own health, repeating the assurance that he looked so very delicate, and talking of damp beds, and new houses, and open windows on summer evenings. But Constance would not be alarmed : she said she did not think Herbert was inclined to be imprudent ; it was very warm weather, and he was in no damp new house, but staying with the Curate of the new chapel in the upper part of the town.

Then came some dreadful discoveries on poor Lady Willoughby. They had decided on living in the old Parsonage, which she knew was in the vulgar part of the town, though Constance mercifully spared her the description in Herbert's letter. " The last occupants," he said, " must have lived upon nothing but

apples, to judge by the scent; the two parlours are not much
more than Jack's twelve foot square, and I can touch the ceiling.
Nevertheless, it is in the part of the parish where I should
most like to be, and I believe you will make it habitable, so
I have written to Mr. Forester to despatch our goods from
Copseley."

Next Lady Willoughby was shocked by finding that neither
carriage, horse, nor man, were in their list of necessaries, and she
was roused to commiseration. "Surely, my dear, I thought
you had a handsome income."

" Yes, Mamma, we are very well off."

" I should like, if it is not intruding, to know what you call
very well off, my dear?"

" Let me see!" said Constance. "Yes, I know. Herbert
told me it was about four thousand a year of our own."

"My dear!" Lady Willoughby opened her eyes. " Why, with
such a fortune you might live in the first style! you might do
anything! Something is due from you, Constance—indeed it is."

"Yes, indeed," said Constance; "it is such a sadly destitute
place, and wants so much to be done for it."

" I dare say, my dear," said Lady Willoughby. " I am sure
you will do a great deal of good, but you know your position
requires something."

"Indeed it does," said Constance, earnestly; "you can't
think how deeply Herbert feels it. That is the very thing."

" But, my dear, with your rank and fortune to live in the
way you propose! You might as well have married a curate!"

"Well, mamma, so I did," said Constance, playfully; "indeed,
you need not fear we are going to do anything odd or strange;
we only want to live quietly and do our work, and make our
means go as far as they will."

Lady Willoughby observed, while taking her other daughters
to a party that night, she was afraid dear Lord Herbert was very
odd and eccentric, and it was very sad for poor Constance,
though she bore it so sweetly. She hoped Lord Liddesdale
would interfere.

Constance, in spite of persuasions, had chosen to stay at home to write to Herbert, and was glad she had done so; for on going up-stairs she heard mournful sounds, and found poor little Janet in bed, in Miss Townsend's room, in an agony of terror at the loneliness and darkness. To gather her up in her arms, and carry her off to her own bed, was the work of a few moments; and the delight of sleeping in sister's room was almost too great, when in the morning Janet found her ready to wake at five, and tell her stories till it was time to get up.

Emmeline was shocked at this discovery, and more so when she encountered Janet's crib in progress into her sister's room, telling her she would never have any peace, and there was nothing so bad as losing her morning's sleep.

"You owlet!" said Constance; "awake at midnight, and now—

> "'It was about half after five,
> Her usual time for sleeping!'"

"But, Constance, have you considered? Telling that child stories from five to six would kill me for the whole day, and she will make you do it every morning."

"Oh, I am used to early waking—Herbert's cough always used to get worse in the morning, and now I can't sleep after four or five."

"Where are you going now?" said Emmeline, disconsolately.

"I left Janet writing her copy, and I must go and inspect it."

"We never speak to you in comfort!" sighed Emmeline.

"No, we are in such a household, there is very little time for our own talks; but I look forward to Dearport, as soon as we are settled there. We will make up for everything then. How charming it will be, quite as nice as Copseley!"

"Not as Copseley, without a garden."

"My garden!" said Constance; "that will be—

> "'Silver bells
> And cockle shells,
> And pretty girls all in a row;'"

and she went away singing.

The castle of having Constance with them being as much a failure as the rest, Emmeline continued in her habitual state, divided between languor and excitement. She did not guess how anxiously her sister was watching her, and revolving every mode of doing her good.

Constance much disliked the intimacy with the Allens. Of Susan they saw comparatively little, for she had never at school liked Constance Berners, one of the steady girls, who were almost authorities, and always discountenanced pertness and giggling; and now, after one visit that enabled her to entertain her friends with a description of Constance Somerville, (as she called her when out of her hearing,) she preferred keeping her distance. It was the brother who was most in her way. He haunted the drawing-room perpetually in the morning, and poor Constance was sick of his conceited *dilettante* talk; but she could not escape, for it was the time of day when her mother never appeared, and she could not leave her sisters unchaperoned. She made Janet and Edwin bring their books down-stairs, and sat trying to write her letter, and attend to them, though all his self-complacencies about "Raphaels, Corregios, and stuff," by no means consoled by the credit she was earning, when he whispered to Emmeline that Lady Herbert Somerville was such a charming, superior person, with so much taste for art.

Heartily glad was Constance when Lord Liddesdale or his eldest son came in, as they did almost every morning. Their coming generally occasioned Henry Allen's departure; nothing else effected it, till Lady Willoughby came down dressed for her drive.

One day Constance, while hearing who her sister's partners at a dance had been, could not help exclaiming, "Mr. Allen! there is no end of him!"

"I am sure I don't care about him," said Emmeline, petulantly; "I wish he would not be always coming here, I don't want him."

Thereupon Emmeline escaped, and craved no more confidential conversations with her sister; but Constance took her own measures, and succeeded in making Lady Willoughby take alarm: "It was very unlucky—Emmie might do so much better —it was so bad for a girl to get the name of flirtation—did Constance think there was really anything in it?"

"I don't know anything about such things," said Constance; "but I believe Emmeline is too superior to be really attracted by such a man. She would never think of him more if she was once out of sight of him."

"Very likely, my dear; and we shall soon be leaving town. I have known many things go off in that way. How fortunate that you are here, with nothing to do but to sit in the drawing-room and watch them. What a comfort it is to have a married daughter!"

Next morning Mr. Allen stood over the piano where Emmeline and Kate were practising; Sir Francis was imparting scraps of newspaper to all who would listen; Janet was inserting the white eyes of the pink stars on her bag; Edwin appealing to "sister" continually for assistance in the puzzle he was putting up; Janet always answering for sister that she must not be interrupted, and then applying to her on her own account the next moment. In the midst of this, Constance was writing as follows :—

If twelve foot square can be made practicable for four people, I should like to take Emmie and Kate home with us at once: I want to have Emmie in a calmer region than this, and out of the reach of the hero of the R. C. chapel. The girls would enjoy the fun of a scramble. I see how to manage, if you approve.

Two days after, she heard in answer—

By all means let us have the girls; I have hardly seen them yet. It will be great gain to have them to help you at the flitting. I had thought of asking if you could dispose of Redlands, if I told him to come to us the first night; but I had rather have the sisters.

Constance immediately made it her entreaty that her sisters might be spared to her; and the dread of Henry Allen caused her mother to consent. They were both pleased; Kate always happy to be with Constance, and anxious to feel herself actually commencing her course of preparation, and Emmeline kissing her sister in a transport, and saying now they should leave the hot restless glare of the world, and be happy together in peace, all in all to each other, with no one to interrupt.

When, a couple of days after, Lord Herbert came back, Emmeline found that they should not be absolutely alone, for Constance had undertaken to manage for the accommodation of Mr. Redlands, and he was to be at the parsonage till he could choose a lodging; but this she could very well endure, as there was no fear of his being much or long in the way.

For the three days of their further stay in London, Lord and Lady Herbert were at the Willoughbys'; their family coming, the last evening, to meet them there at dinner.

Lady Willoughby took the opportunity of entering a protest against the proceedings at Dearport. She asked Lord Liddesdale, in confidence, if he did not think these dear young people of theirs were inclined to be a little over-enthusiastic.

He looked amazed, and answered, "I think Constance may be trusted. She has a sensible head of her own."

"I can't tell, dear Constance is so sweet-tempered," said Lady Willoughby; "but surely you must agree with me, that it is a pity they should begin on the scale they purpose."

"There they must be left to their own devices," said Lord Liddesdale; "they have plenty of solid good sense, both of them, and as they think right, they must do. Constance will take care he does not knock himself up;" then, as Lady Willoughby still looked distressed, he added, "I shall soon go and see after them, and take order if they do anything foolish."

This was all the comfort she could obtain, though if she had known Lord Liddesdale's real feeling towards his son, she would have little trusted to him.

She did not prosper even so well with Frances, who tried to listen demurely to her fears, and not succeeding, laughed and said, "they were quite satisfied, Papa and all, that Herbert would never do anything extravagant." And yet poor Lady Willoughby overheard Lord Somerville warning Kate that some day he should find "twelve foot square" converted, one half into an asylum for orphan gypsies, the other for pauper lunatics.

That evening was a sad one for Janet, who had such a passionate attachment to sister Constance, that even Miss Townsend's return did not comfort her. Her only satisfaction was an invitation to come some day and stay at Dearport, given by brother Herbert himself, as she sat on his knee, undecided between liking him for his own sake, and hating him for being the lawful owner of sister Constance.

CHAPTER XX.

The crocus hails her time to come ;
For she is not the delicate
Who shrinks from aught may fit her state,
But wears a cheerful hardy brow—
Glad combatant of frost and snow ;
Yet prudent are her ways the while,
Both warmth and tempests to foresee.

S. R.

SELDOM was there a livelier party than that which started for Dearport ; and as they left the London atmosphere, and glided from among tall roofs and overgrown chimneys into the fresh dewy air of the country, fields sparkling under a silvery morning veil, and meadows newly cut, or fragrant with piles of hay, even Emmeline's weary spirit was exhilarated, and she joined with something of her former animation in the gaiety of her companions.

Yet Emmeline could not entirely comprehend that blitheness and light-heartedness that there was about the Somervilles—that capacity for laughing, and that playfulness, which never seemed to fail them, especially Lord Herbert, so serious, so reverent, and self-denying as they were—it seemed to her a contradiction that they should be so merry. She only knew gaiety as forgetfulness, a moment's confusing away of her cravings and discontent.

"Be silent, vain deluding mirth,"

was a line she could understand, but she did not see the force
of the next—

> "Till in thine altered voice be known
> Somewhat of resignation's tone,"

nor perceive that it was this very tone that made their hearts so
free and light, and their cheerfulness no vain delusion. Of
course, natural temperament has a good deal to do with such
things, and Emmeline was naturally grave, while Lord Herbert
was one of those whose buoyant animal spirits seem almost a
compensation for frail health; but it was the principle within
that had sustained that cheerfulness, and even gaiety of heart,
through long and severe suffering.

They were at Dearport station by twelve o'clock, and Lord
Herbert recommended their walking to their new abode.
"There," said he, "let me introduce you to the great maritime
paradise of Dearport, forming, you see, an amphitheatre above
the mouth of the navigable river."

"How beautiful!" was the exclamation, as they looked at
the bay beneath them, scattered with many a white-sailed vessel,
and inclosed on two sides by curving wooded banks, one of
which was thickly studded by numerous houses of the better
class, while the other showed only park-like glades of green
embosomed in trees.

"That is Bayhurst, I suppose," said Constance. "How very
pretty! And this is our domain?"

"Yes; there you see the genteel regions," said Lord Herbert,
"with all their desirable summer residences; and that is the
spire of their chapel."

"That lath-and-plaster affair!" said Constance; "but where's
our church?"

"You can't see it. It is behind that slated six-story monster
of a warehouse."

"But what a hill, Herbert! you did not prepare me for that,"
said Constance, dismayed at the sharpness of the descent, for
hills always betrayed the weakness of his chest.

"Better to have it at one's outset," he said, as he conducted them down a narrowing street, the pavement of grey shingly stone, the gutters plentifully bestrewn with remains of fish, and empty periwinkles and whelks; the shops small and poor-looking, with a nautical air about the goods, and a large proportion of slovenly women and idle men of seafaring aspect. Emmeline and Kate looked at each other in consternation, and repeated to themselves their mother's compassionate "Poor Constance!"

They were near the wharf, when Lord Herbert guided them into a side-street, narrow, but more quiet, as the great warehouse of sea-stores occupied one side, and a dead wall the other, and there was a wholesome odour of new ropes. Beyond they came on the little old church, its yard thick with grave-stones, little children climbing about them, and lines of clothes hung out to dry. Lord Herbert led the way round the posts that permitted an entrance for foot-passengers, and taking a paved path that traversed the church-yard diagonally, led them to a moderate-sized elderly-house, separated from it by a low wall and narrow flagged court. The girls, as they walked behind, saw him looking in his wife's face. They thought everything so wretched, that they could not bear to say a word; Constance must be so disappointed, and he so vexed for her.

"How very nice!" was Constance's exclamation. "You did not tell me what a respectable old place it is. How could you doubt about its being habitable?"

"I don't think I did about your making it so."

"It is capital to have the church-yard to look into instead of a street. The church is very pretty; that is a beautiful window."

"You must get rid of all those festoons of linen," said Emmeline.

"And the dirty children," said Kate. "What little grubs!"

"Yes, when they are ordered off it may do," said Emmeline.

"What a fine act of tyranny you want to begin with!" said Herbert.

"Tyranny!" said Kate.

" If you had one room, half a dozen children, and all the garments of the family to be washed and dried, and no open space but this—" said Constance.

" But is it not teaching them irreverence ? " said Emmeline.

"Another question," said Lord Herbert, " entirely different from the æsthetic one at the commencement."

"Then you do mean to get rid of them ? "

" The present point is whether we are to get into our house or not," said Lord Herbert, for they had all this time been waiting for the door to be opened. At last Constance tried the handle; it yielded, and they entered the narrowest of all vestibules, choked with packed furniture, while a voice was heard in the distance of some one in despair. " Bless us ! Come already ! I never thought they would ever come before dinner-time ; and there's not a place for them to sit down in, nor nothing for them to eat."

What would become of Constance ! thought the sisters ; but Constance laughed, and tripped on, guided by the voice, and her kind tones were heard reassuring the frightened maid, almost apologizing for taking her by surprise, and telling her she was sure they should be quite comfortable by the evening ; it was all so very clean. Coming back, as gay as ever, she took the lead in treating the general confusion as a joke, and the personal exertions they felt bound to make, a frolic. They would get it all set to rights before Mr. Redlands came ; and what fun it would be ! so much better than walking into a house in apple-pie order, with nothing to do. Her only care was lest Emmeline should be hungry or tired, and Lord Herbert undertook to go and cater for them.

Meantime Constance ran up and down, admiring and praising everything, and giving a helping and settling hand wherever she went, decided on her line of operations, and declared she was very glad to have come now, for she could settle things right, according to her own ideas from the first.

Emmeline was forbidden to tire herself, and the only chair that was forthcoming was applied to her use, in spite of all her

resistance; while, on Herbert's return, his provision of ginger-
bread and penny cakes was displayed on the dining-room table,
on which the party not only dined, but *sat*. They were all very
hungry, and the irregularity gave it the zest of a pic-nic. Lord
Herbert exclaimed, "Who would not be rector of a town where
they make such penny cakes!" and the merriment rose to its
height when Constance, insisting on Emmeline's having her
daily dose of wine, Lord Herbert cut the cords of the hamper;
and then, bringing out a black bottle, held it up, and shook his
head at it, and said, in a quiet matter-of-fact tone, "You've not
got a cork-screw in your pocket, Constance, my dear?"

To his surprise, as much as that of anyone, Constance at once
put her hand in her pocket, and brought out one.

They laughed till they were weary; Lord Herbert exclaiming
that he wished "Jack" was there, and Constance pretending to
see no cause for being derided, for she knew Emmeline must
have her wine, and she thought that in a new house there would
be sure to be no cork-screw. When at length Lord Herbert
had been reduced to leaning exhausted against the wall, saying
it was a shame of her to make them laugh so much that they
could not stand when there was nothing to sit upon, the wine
was administered to Emmeline in a tea-cup; and the rest, being
all decided water drinkers, were supplied from the pump. Then
to work in earnest, though Constance obliged Emmeline to sit
still, insultingly giving her her travelling-book to finish; and
she was really tired enough not to make much resistance. The
other three carried the furniture, and settled its places with
great alacrity, and so much merriment and laughing, that the
chief recollection that Kate preserved of the hard-working flitting
to Dearport was of a party of pleasure, unequalled, unless by
the Rowthorpe expedition to the ruined castle, or the tea-drinking in the tower at Herringsby. Constance was so glad to see her
Copseley possessions once more, as they emerged from their
cases, and there were so many recollections connected with
them, that they could hardly make progress for talking over
them; except Constance herself, whose briskness and readiness

could work effectively in the midst of any amount of diversion and confusion.

At last they were interrupted by a message that the clerk wanted to speak to his Lordship, and Herbert left them.

"I am glad he is gone," said Constance : "we shall get on all the faster now you and he are not hindering each other with talking nonsense, Miss Kate. I expected every moment he would make you laugh my fine buhl clock to death."

"I don't think you would have cried if he had," said Kate.

"I should not mind it so much if it would either go right or go away," said Constance; "but it will do no harm up there upon a bracket. Well really, 'twelve foot square' is beginning to look decent. I think we may begin upon the dining-room."

Lord Herbert came in to say that the clerk had told him of a sick man in need of being visited; and the ladies continued their arrangements without him, till by half-past five the two down-stairs rooms looked quite pleasant and comfortable. The apartments consisted of these two, besides a little dark den, the centre of the apple smell, a wall almost blocking the window. This Constance decided would do for putting books into, and speaking to people, and it was to be called the study; though as to Herbert sitting there, it was out of the question. At the back were some tolerable offices, and there were four rooms on the second floor; two looking into the church-yard, and two into a timber-yard with a high wall, far beyond which rose the green wooded slope of Bayhurst.

Constance, thanking Kate for all her help, and triumphing in their great deeds, shut her sisters into their room, one of the front ones, telling them to rest and dress, and they entreated her to do the same. She said, "Yes, it was almost time," and shut the door.

"How tired she must be!" said Emmeline. "Are not you, Kate?"

"Oh no, nothing to signify!" said Kate, "only with laughing."

"I wish she would have let me help," said Emmeline,

languidly ; " but it is all for nothing ; they never can stay here. I never saw such a horrid place in my life ! "

" It looks much better for what we did to-day," said Kate ; " and I am sure they don't seem to mind it."

" No, that is all Constance's sweetness ; but I am sure she must feel the change from Copseley."

" A change, indeed," said Kate, looking out at the slatternly women who had come to take in their clothes.

" Wretched ! " said Emmeline. " Poor Constance ! I was so sorry for her all the time, though she did carry it off so well."

" Ah ! there is Herbert coming home. And oh ! there she is with her bonnet on. She is meeting him, and now they are gone into the church together. I hope Mamma will never see this place ! "

" It can't last," said Emmeline, decidedly ; " they must go and live in the upper part of the parish. This house is not even second-rate ; it is perfectly miserable, and this dismal northern aspect."

They found Mr. Redlands, the new curate, in the drawing-room. He was one of those brown, sallow, shrivelled people, who look as if they never had been youthful, and hardly could be aged. Lord Herbert had been his pupil at Oxford, and had the greatest regard for him. There were to be two other curates, but one was not yet ordained, and the other could not come for a month ; and there was also Mr. Woodman, who belonged to the chapel in the new part of the town.

It was nearly eight when they left the dining-room ; the sun was not set, for they saw its light on the top of the church tower, but it could not penetrate to them, and the little northern drawing-room, literally rather more than " twelve foot square," was already beginning to darken. Constance seated Emmeline in the innermost recess of the sofa, put herself next, and Kate on her other side, and with her arm round one sister, and her hand playing with the fingers of the other, she exclaimed, " Now for a nice comfortable talk in the dark ! The gentlemen won't be in for an age : they have all their plans to settle. How snug we shall be !"

At that moment the knell began to ring a deep and solemn toll. Constance felt how Emmeline shuddered.

"That poor man !" said Constance. "Herbert thought it must soon be over. He left him quite insensible."

"It is very solemn," said Kate.

"And we shall have to see the burial !" said Emmeline. "O Constance, Constance, you can never bear to live here !"

"My poor Emmie," said Constance tenderly, "I have brought you here too soon. I am sorry you have had such a long tiring day."

"I am sure it is a bad omen," said Emmeline, hiding her face on her sister's shoulder, and speaking in a gasping whisper ; "I should not have told you so—O Constance !—but I could not help it."

"Emmie, love," said Constance, "you would not think so if you were not tired and out of spirits. It is a fancy, that will go off another time."

"Oh, but it is so dismal !" said Emmeline.

"Dismal ! No, I don't think so. Hark, how deep and musical ! there is something soothing as well as solemn in the sound."

"Do you like to live here, Constance ?" said Kate, presently. "You are not disappointed ?"

"Oh no : it is much better than Herbert led me to expect."

"What a description his must have been !" said Emmeline.

"But, Constance, do you really mean that you like this as well as Copseley ?" said Kate.

"My dear, how can you ask such a question ?" said Constance, laughing ; "Copseley was a delightful place to begin with, but too delightful to last."

"Yes, nothing pleasant does last," sighed Emmeline. "But I don't understand it, Constance. You can't really be pleased with this dismal place, though you make the best of it not to vex Herbert."

"No, no, Emmie, that is not it," said Constance. "I do honestly like being here; why should you think me acting a part?"

"Oh no, Constance, not that, but—"

"I'll tell you how it has been," said Constance: "when Herbert began to get well, he always had a feeling that he ought to do something more than just go on in an ordinary sort of way. And when the offer of this parish came, it seemed like a call. You know Copseley is safe under Mr. Forester, but his taking this place seemed its only chance; so we could only make up our minds to come and do our best, if his health will but hold out."

"Yes, yes; but why live in this den?"

"Why, Emmie, surely it is right for the parson to live in the parsonage; and if it has four walls, and is weather-tight, it would be a shame to be too fine for it. We seemed to be most wanted in this poor forsaken crowded part of the place, and I dare say we shall get on very well. See what lots of luxuries we have, that we can't get rid of. It is a very good house, if you would only think so."

"But Herbert—when one thinks what he has been used to!"

"O Emmie, that is not talking at all like your old self!" said Constance, rather indignantly; then adding, after a little thought, "I do believe Herbert, from having been brought up to grandeur, misses those kinds of things less. You know Copseley was a considerable come-down from Rowthorpe, and there's not so much difference in our style between this and Copseley. But that is not the point. We have come here to be servants to our parishioners, and all we have belongs to them; so all we have to look to is, what is best for them. I mean what is right as becoming our station, and what will help them most."

"And you like it!" said Emmeline.

"Can you ask, Emmie! Is it not a great thing to be allowed to have part with him? O Emmie—I can't talk about it—but there is something in it so very happy!"

s

Emmeline was struck. It was what she used to fancy her own turn of mind, and in Constance it was genuine and practical. But its being so practical was the very reason Emmeline was unable to enter into it. "I could understand it—if—if it was Madeline—if it was a missionary—but it is self-devotion, it is very beautiful—only this little poky house—"

"My dear," said Constance, laughing, "I believe the fact is, that with you it is like love in a cottage : you can believe in—such things—in a convent, or a sister-of-charity—only you don't understand it in a modern clergyman in a cloth coat, and a little common-place house. Is not that it? Indeed, you know we must take things as we find them, and not sit still and amuse ourselves, though we do happen to be born in the nineteenth century. Things were common-place to those old people that are romance to us, you may be sure."

Constance had spoken as she felt in her inmost heart, and as she seldom had expressed herself; and with a sort of reserve, she instantly changed the subject to some playful discussion of the labours of the morrow. Kate answered, Emmeline was silent, for even this free uninterrupted conversation, easy, open, and tender, was not satisfying to that constant aching craving for something more.

The place was forlorn and mean, and Constance was provoking for being satisfied with what was merely disagreeable, not striking. Emmeline wanted something to please her imagination, and as this was not accomplished, she missed the beauty of the unobtrusive self-sacrifice, and simply disliked its severity.

This dingy abode, it was too true, was Constance's home, but it could never be the goal of her day-dreams, and that active contentment of Constance herself, showed that now that she was a wife, she was only a reflection of her husband, and would no longer be what Emmeline had figured to herself.

All was a failure, and nothing was left but to sigh over the truth of

"Man never is, but always to be blest."

CHAPTER XXI.

How rarely boyhood loves to paint
In glowing tints his future bright !
A picture where no line is faint,
Whose very clouds are tipped with light,

And girlhood hails a world unknown,
And reads it in her own glad dreams ;
As lilies see themselves alone
Reflected in their azure streams.

C. F. A.

How busy Lord and Lady Herbert were, may be easily guessed, and how heartily Kate aided them. There was much that was disagreeable ; the church arrangements wretched ; the attendance on the daily service almost nothing ; the school such a stifling den, that till something could be done, Constance begged Lord Herbert to hear all his pupils in the dining-room ; the instruction at the lowest ebb, and the greater part of the parish sending their children to dissenting schools. Dissent was rampant, and at the first view, it appeared as if the town was divided between nonconformity and absolute irreligion—" heathenism," as Kate called it, till Mr. Redlands said it was worse, for it was Christianity forgotten. Poverty and all its accompanying evils of dirt, sickliness, and hard indifferent recklessness, met them at every turn. Nor was all satisfactory in the upper town ; and Constance perceived many difficulties awaiting her the first time she looked over the books used at school.

It was *àpropos* to this matter that Kate related the history of their own troubles at the school at Herringsby, very much to Lord Herbert's diversion, and as Kate candidly allowed, it was just what they deserved for acting against his warning.

" But, Herbert," said she, " I do wish you would explain to me the rights and wrongs."

" A serious undertaking, Kate."

" Emmie and I have talked it over, and we do not understand it—do we, Emmie ? "

"It is only a result of the uncomfortable disunion and party spirit of the time we live in," said Emmeline, as if she wanted to bring the matter to an end.

"Well, I know, so it is," said Kate; "but I want clearly to see what is to be done, and what we ought to have done. It was a great pity to be of no use."

"So thought Titus Manlius when he killed the champion," said Lord Herbert.

"But it was a great shame of old Manlius to execute him!" said Kate.

"We aren't going to execute you, Katie," said Constance, "but don't you see that it is not safe to break the rules of discipline for any good? Besides, do you think you were absolutely called on to begin teaching on your own authority?"

"No—perhaps not," said Kate; "and I know we were wrong in our notion of Mr. Brent; he would have made us useful in the right way if we had but put ourselves under him."

"But if he had been really bad—what should you have said then, Herbert?" said Emmeline.

"There would probably have been something to guide you— you would have been thrown in contact with some one in need of help. Besides, if he had been bad, as you call it, he would probably have been so indifferent to the state of his parish, that your teaching would not have been in opposition to him."

"Most likely," said Kate; "but suppose he held the same opinions as that Mr. Denham—what should we do then?"

"I don't much like answering such cases of conscience," said Herbert. "What do you say, Constance?"

"I don't know—I was thinking; but I believe what would strike me as the fairest thing, would be to tell the clergyman that if I taught at all, it would be according to the strict sense of the words of the Prayer Book, and then let him take his choice whether he would employ me or not."

"Yes, I think you have settled that question," said Herbert, "and I suspect it would end in your being allowed your own way."

"How I should hate the settling it!" said Kate; "I think it would end as it did at Herringsby."

"But those good little old Miss Shaws puzzle me much more," said Emmeline. "They were so thoroughly good, and kind, and self-denying, and humble, one could not help loving and honouring them with all one's heart, and yet—"

"I do believe that Mrs. and Miss Charlton are going to be just as bad," broke in Kate. "I saw one of the very worst of the tracts the Miss Shaws used to give, in Miss Charlton's basket, this very morning. Don't you remember, Emmie, it was one about a very religious man, who had nothing to eat, and he prayed, and presently he came to a pit with some bread and meat in it, wrapped up in a handkerchief." *

"The sawyer's dinner, probably," said Lord Herbert.

"And pray," said Constance, "may I ask whether you assisted in the distribution of this instruction in morality?"

"No—luckily not," said Kate, "for dear Frank found it out, and I thought he would never have ceased asking us 'what became of the handkerchief?'"

"But what do you think about the old ladies?" said Emmeline.

"They must be too really and deeply good for us to dare to censure them," said Herbert. "They probably have grown up without guidance from the Church, as to the right way of doing good; they have done their best, and if their doctrine is defective, and their practice irregular, it is not likely to be their fault."

"And that kindly visiting is not wrong, even in Mr. Brent's parish?"

"No; not when they don't leave tracts which they know he disapproves, and even then it is a case of knowing no better. The kind care of the bodily wants must be right."

"I do believe the old ladies themselves would never interfere or do anything you don't approve, if it was not for their friends,"

* It is a fact, that this tract was left in a Bible by some visitors to a new church.

said Emmeline; "they are all kindness and goodness them-selves."

"And simply believe what they are told by the persons whom they have been used to respect," said Herbert. "It is the spirit of obedience and teachableness that is in them, depend upon it, though it may not always be directed the right way. By-the-by, Constance, I think we had better ask Mrs. and Miss Charlton to tea some evening, and perhaps you may manage to come round them quietly about the tracts."

Emmeline and Kate were convinced that this was likely to succeed, for poor Mr. Brent's want of manner had always told against him, while Lord Herbert had every natural gift of pleasing, and his delicate appearance gave stronger interest in him, when gossips shook their heads, and said, "Ah! poor young man, he won't be here long."

All this certainly was in his favour, and much more was the general admiration of his sermons. He did not often preach, for he was obliged to spare his chest; but the chance of hearing him brought many to church who would otherwise have stayed away, and there was always some excitement at the upper town, if he was likely to come to the chapel on one part of the Sunday.

This was telling in some degree on the rich, and attracting such of the tradespeople as were half Dissenters, only because they had been neglected by their clergy; so that there was less opposition than had at first seemed probable, though there was a great deal of up-hill work, and the prospect of more un-pleasantness when the novelty should have worn off, and his plans became more developed. Among the poor, there began to be some hopeful signs; though for each of these, there was opened some fresh vista of want and sin.

Well might work thicken upon Lord Herbert and his wife, who were engaged almost from morning till night. Breakfast, the early dinner, and late tea-drinking, were the only times when they were sure to meet, though they were in and out of the house half the day. Lord Herbert was beginning to gather his Confirmation classes, and he asked his sisters if they did not wish to begin their preparation. Kate was ready and anxious, Emmeline quietly acquiesced; so he gave them books to read, and questions to answer on paper, but without at present seeking for conversations on the subject.

Emmeline continued dispirited, languid and reserved. She did not appear unwell, but she was reluctant to exert herself, and her best efforts at courtesy did not conceal that she found Dearport dreary and uncomfortable. The last of her visions, the return of Lord Herbert and Constance, seemed as great a failure as all the rest, for here was she in their house, as little contented as ever. Kate went hither and thither, worked as hard as Constance, had a class at school, knew numbers of the poor people, and was in continual activity and enjoyment. She caught no head-ache in the stifling school, or if she did, a sea-breeze blew it away; she did not mind the fishy smell of the streets, and had something else to think of than its disagreeableness when she entered a house. She was keeping too close to Constance to mind such things more than she did; but Emmeline saw nothing but the disagreeables, did nothing but what she was positively asked to do, always had a letter to write, or a book to read, some occupation when she might have come to be useful in the morning, though the results of her employment generally seemed to be nothing but dreaming, and pining at the dismality of their church-yard aspect; and in the afternoon, she would always, if possible, make Kate come with her to walk in the Bayhurst grounds, and expressed great disgust at the streets, with much of her mother's tone and manner.

They all were uneasy on her account. They thought she had never properly recovered either her illness or the shock of Frank's death; she had constantly been much more tired than was good for her, when in London, and continually excited, without having sufficient time for rest, either mental or bodily, and this was a reaction from the long excitement she had been under. They must wait, and let her be calmed and soothed, till her frame recovered its full health, and her mind its tone and vigour; so Constance was patient and tender, did not try to rouse her by exhortations, or force her confidence, but only gave her every proof of affection, and devised means of finding her beneficial occupation.

But weariness of spirit, and unformed longings of discontent, hung on her day after day. Devotional employment simply gave her pain, from which she took refuge in the dull coat of dreary formal indifference that was fast growing over her. It made her unhappy to think, so she did not try; she did not care to do anything, she was tired of everything; restless enough almost to wish the visit was over, though there was nothing but dreariness in the prospect of joining Sir Francis and Lady Willoughby at Cheltenham. Her mind would sometimes even recur to the chance of meeting the Allens there; they amused her, and filled up the vacancy of her mind, and she continued the correspondence which she had commenced with Susan, always looking the first thing for some sentence beginning "Henry desires me to tell you."

It was a Sunday evening. The day had been one of considerable toil; Constance, Kate, and Mr. Redlands, had been school-keeping whenever they were not at church; Emmeline had been teaching a class at home, and Lord Herbert, besides taking part in the early service, had been to the chapel in the morning, and had catechized in the afternoon. This evening his sermon was too often interrupted by the unwelcome sound of his old short cough. It was chilly and wet, a small cold rain drifting like a wall of mist from the sea, dense, grey, and oppressive; and when they came out of church, and saw the glaze of wet on the tomb-stones and roofs, which there was just light enough to distinguish, heard the plash from the dripping eaves, and felt the damp to their feet, while they breathed the unwholesome cold moist atmosphere, Emmeline shivered, saying that it was wretched; she felt it in all her bones.

Constance did not stay to hear her, but hastened across the flagged path into the house. The sisters followed, and went up at once to take off their bonnets, Emmeline sighing all the time at the forlorn place, and at Herbert's cough, while Kate tried to console her, by putting her in mind that before next Sunday the young deacon would be arrived. "Oh, but it is the place!" said Emmeline. "Just think what it will be a little later in the year. And this is only August!"

Emmeline was too disconsolate to put much alacrity in her movements, and Kate waited to help her, so that it was more than ten minutes before they came down-stairs, cold and forlorn, into "twelve foot square," which they expected to find more dingy than ever.

Behold, it was glowing with brightness, which streamed forth as they opened the door. It was not merely cold candle-light, but a fire was shining with the warm pleasant smile peculiar to unexpected fires on ungenial summer evenings, lighting up gaily the gilded bindings of the books, while the tea-things were reflecting the red light, each with its own polished glance, and Constance's blythe face and glossy hair beamed over them. Herbert leant back in the glistening chintz-covered arm-chair, in the luxury of repose, his eyes and smile showing he had just been saying something to cause the laugh that had not quite passed from Constance's face, nor from that of Mr. Redlands, who stood on the other side of the fire, very glad to be spending the evening in this pleasant room, instead of walking home to his small lodging over the stationer's shop, half way up the hill.

A chair on each side of Constance was ready for her sisters, and the substantial meal looked most inviting to people whose early dinner had been snatched in a hurry. Even Emmeline was obliged to exclaim with pleasure, and declare that the room looked delightful ; and then how comfortable and agreeable was the desultory talk that went round about the affairs of the day ; that parish talk most engrossing to those who have their hearts in such things.

An hour had passed away in this pleasant manner, when a message came in that a little boy had been taken very ill, "Mrs. Sims's little boy, up in North Hill Street." Mr. Redlands exclaimed instantly that he would go ; it was in his own especial part of the parish ; Lord Herbert must not think of going out in

this chilly damp night—all the way up the hill too—and it was
in his own way home. Herbert was extremely reluctant, but
was obliged to acquiesce when he had opened the front door, and
the damp had made him cough and shiver, and Mr. Redlands set
out at once, in great haste. In the mean time, Constance was
inquiring of the messenger about the child's illness, and presently coming back, she said, "I think I had better go and see
about him. I think I know how to manage the croup, and the
doctor is so far off in the upper town."

"Very well; it is too late to be out in the town by yourself,"
said Lord Herbert, "I had better go with you—it is all
nonsense."

"Nonsense, indeed, for you to think of going!" said Constance.
"Besides, I shall have Lucy Sims to walk there with, and Mr.
Redlands will see me back. Come—" answering his look—
"never mind, Herbert, don't you remember, we settled not to
mind such things?"

"If Redlands was not gone," said Lord Herbert.

"Oh, but do let me go with you!" cried Kate. "Do, pray,
Constance; I should so like to go and see that dear little boy."

"You, Kate! How would Mamma like it?" said Constance.

"Oh, never mind, you know we can't help that. Do let me
go. Make her take me, Herbert!"

"Well, if Katie goes with you, I don't so much mind." And
seizing this consent, the two sisters hurried off, and were next
seen for a moment muffled in cloaks.

Lord Herbert and Emmeline remained, sitting in the arm-
chairs on the opposite sides of the fire. He was apparently in
deep thought; Emmeline had taken a book, but was not reading.
It was her first *tête-à-tête* with him since his return, and she
dreaded what he might be going to say—a Confirmation lecture,
perhaps, searching into a state of mind which she shunned to
investigate. Each minute that he kept silence was a relief,
though he might be only preparing his speech.

The fall of a coal in the fire made her start; and Lord
Herbert, while he laughed, and arranged the fire, said, "I beg

your pardon, Emmie; I had fallen into a brown study. I was thinking of the wonderful castles Annie and I used to build."

"Did you ever build castles?" said Emmeline, looking up with eager interest.

"That we did! Sitting here, opposite to you, put me in mind of the days when Annie and I were not arrived at dining late —when we used to sit, while the old people were at dinner, one on each side of the fire, and such schemes as we used to make!" said he, smiling.

"Oh, I wish you would tell me what they were like!"

"One was about the Knights of St. John. Annie was reading Vertot, in the school-room, and used to tell me the history every evening, and we used to compose beautiful adventures. I was to be a Knight Hospitalier, and Annie was to revive the Sisters for her own benefit!"

"That was delightful!" said Emmeline, "and too unreal to be ever spoilt."

"I think it reigned a whole winter, at least till we set up another vision, a missionary one, for being Bishop of a desert island. I mean," he added, laughing, "not quite to teach the coral worms, but we were to have a picked race of amiable savages, and admirable settlers; besides which, Annie especially stipulated that there should be no volcano."

"There I quite agree with her."

"The Southern Iona, that was its name. We even drew a map of it, which Frances has still. It had all the zest of a desert island story added to the rest. Cocoa-nuts, and canoes, and coral reefs, and shipwrecked sailors. There were adventures enough to make a romance."

"Oh, I do enjoy that. But I never should have guessed that you had made castles."

"It was more dear Annie's doing than mine."

"Had you any more?"

"One, which came when we were rather older, and which was full in my mind this evening. I was to have a living in some very miserable town, where one would have to be almost a

missionary ; Annie, of course, was to live with me ; we were to
have no more comforts than the poor themselves, and to devote
everything to them, doing immense good, winning every one,
carrying out every perfect scheme, feeling and seeing our
success."

" So then you are really living in your own castle ? "

"And just at the moment the coal fell down, I was wondering
what Annie would think of seeing her brother dawdling by the
side of the fire, while other people are doing his work."

" Day-dreams had better not have any fulfilment at all ! "
exclaimed Emmeline.

" Well, Emmie, I don't at all agree with you there. I can't
think it grateful to lament that our wishes are accomplished."

" If they were," said Emmeline ; " but they only pretend to
be, that they may mock us with their insufficiency."

" You mean," said Lord Herbert, smiling, " that South Iona
would have had a volcano in it."

" Or something worse," said Emmeline. " It would have
failed or palled, or turned to the disappointment that everything
is ! "

" Indeed ? " said Lord Herbert inquiringly.

"Disappointment, yes, life is disappointment," sighed Emmeline, resting her forehead on her hand, speaking so low that he
could hardly hear, and murmuring to herself the last lines of
some verses she had lately been working up :—

> "Delusive pageantry, that masks
> The hollowness of mortals' tasks."

" Oh, if you are writing poetry about it, of course you are
bound to try to believe it," said Lord Herbert.

Emmeline thought herself taking a very grave and serious
line, suited to a clerical auditor, and by no means relished this
reception. " It is not fancy," she replied ; " I wish it was, but
I have lived long enough to feel its truth."

" Are you sure that it is the fault of life ? " said Herbert.

" What can I think, Herbert ? I have felt, I have seen,
I have known. Indeed, indeed I do not speak without sad

experience; all the dreams of my youth have been nothing but disappointment, and those that have been half fulfilled have been worse than the others."

"You have had vexations and griefs, I know," he said kindly, and Emmeline was irresistibly impelled, by the gentle interest of his manner, as well perhaps as by the desire to justify her dejection, to go on.

"Ever since I left childhood behind me, it has been disappointment. We were happy enough with you and Constance; then came your illness, to spoil everything."

"I am very sorry," said Herbert apologetically.

"Well, then there was that dearest vision of our hearts—Mamma's coming home; and O Herbert! you have seen enough of us to understand that our home is the disappointment above all. There was but one whom with our whole hearts "—the tears were gathering in her eyes—"we could love, and how we did love him! We never knew how much, while—" her words were mixed with weeping. "And he was made to suffer—he had to bear—was persecuted—his darling vision taken from him—he who was better than all! And because we loved him, he was—he was taken from us."

"Yes. You might well have a great affection for him," said Lord Herbert; "but, Emmie, you are scarcely looking on his life in the true way. Perhaps his trouble was the one trial he needed, and his death assuredly opened to him the fulfilment of his own scheme. It brought him into the fulness of that service which he sought; it spared him the secular life he shunned. I am sure, from what Kate has told me, that his last feelings were of this kind."

"Dearest, dearest Frank! I dare say Kate knows more of his last sayings than I do, for I was so chilled and frightened at the time, and so confused with illness afterwards; but I have never been able to bear to ask her."

"I am sure you would find great comfort in talking them over with her."

"I will, I will, when I can bear it, but I can't now. O

Herbert, you have always had a happy home! You little know what it is to lose the only bright spot. But don't you see, Herbert, I have tried everything, and it has failed me; it all turns out to have no permanent pleasure in it. Home, and caring for poor people, and learning, and occupation. Yes, I see what you are going to say—religion—but indeed and indeed, Herbert, I have tried that too, and in earnest; and I don't know how it may be with other people, but it does no more than the rest for me. I always thought it would be right, and I should be happy again if you and Constance were but at home; but here you are, and—oh dear! I don't feel a bit less like Mariana in the moated grange."

Herbert repeated the couplet about Mariana;

> "'Said she, I am aweary, weary;
> I would that I were dead.'

Is that what you mean, Emmie?"

Emmeline paused, and then spoke rather fretfully. "You will not understand me, Herbert: it is only poetically."

"Or, perhaps, you agree with the young lady in Dickens, who exclaims 'I hate everybody, and wish everybody was dead!'"

"Herbert, how can you?"

"My dear Emmie, I only want you to get rid of what is nonsense and put on for the sake of poetry, and then perhaps we may be able to see what is the matter. I know you are unhappy and out of spirits, but at the same time you think it a very fine thing to be weary of the world; and till we get to your real self, I don't know how to talk to you."

"You think all I have said affectation?" said Emmeline, a good deal hurt.

"No, by no means all, and quite unconsciously; but when we come to Mariana—"

"Perhaps that was too strong," said Emmeline; "but it is what is always coming into my head. I seem to have no hope, no purpose. I don't care where I am, or what I do; one place is only more tiresome than another. Now, Herbert, you shall believe at least that you have got to the bottom of me; for I'll tell you the very truth, shock you as it may. The only things this summer that have really made me alive, relieved this vacancy and weariness—I don't know how to express it—the only things I can care for are, dancing, and going to that Roman Catholic service. There! now despise me as you will, but be sure I have told you the truth."

"Yes, I see. Excitement," said Herbert quietly, without looking as horrified as she expected, which would perhaps have gratified her craving for this same excitement. "But, Emmeline," he added, turning from that branch of the subject, "should you dislike looking into each of these matters, where you say your hopes of happiness have failed you? You might find out why—"

"Very well," said Emmeline, adding within herself, "I know what you are going to say—that we were not religious enough."

"Well," said Herbert, "you began with—let me see—your first vexation was the not being able to come to Copseley that Christmas."

"Oh, no—no—don't put it in that way, Herbert: do you think we were such wretches of selfishness?"

"No, no, I was only thinking how far our excursion had been personally a cause of vexation to you. However, that could not be helped."

"And after all, we were much happier those holidays than we expected," said Emmeline. "We *had* visions then."

"So we need say nothing about that. Now for your home. You say that you had but one to love there. Why do you pass over all the children?"

"Poor children! we are fond of them, of course; but they are no companions. The boys are rude; Janet is fretful; Cecilia a mere baby."

"I suppose Anne and myself were no companions to Frances, when she used to watch us with such motherly care. I am sure the habits we gained then of looking to her for our pleasures, was of advantage to us ever after, and made us all the happier together when we were on an equality."

"I am sure you and Lady Anne must have been more agreeable children than ours. It would be so tiresome to be watching them all day."

"You seem to find other things tiresome," said Lord Herbert; "besides, you are rather adding to what I said."

"You think we neglect them?" said Emmeline. "Did Constance tell you so?"

"I spoke chiefly from your entire omission of them as sources of interest. What Constance did tell me was, that she regretted you did not take more notice of Janet, who, she thinks, has a very deep earnest character, likely to develop into something fine, but undemonstrative, and in danger of being soured for want of affection."

"Did Constance see so much in little Janet?" said Emmeline. "I know she was very fond of her."

"You had better talk to her about it," said Herbert. "I only meant to show you that you might be passing over one ingredient of happiness and interest at home, if we only look on it as a means of happiness."

"As a duty!" said Emmeline.

"True; and though I don't want you to answer me, I should like to put it into your head to ask yourself whether there are no more home duties than you have avoided, for fear of their being *tiresome?*"

"If things had been different, I should not have avoided those duties," faltered Emmeline.

"Perhaps not; but have you any right to complain of home being disappointing, while you neglect your part there?"

"I don't think it would be a bit better if we were what you call attentive daughters," said Emmeline sadly.

"Then you own that has not been the case?"

"If you knew—"

"I don't want to know; I have to do with *you*—not with Kate, nor your home, but individually with you. You own that you have not been an attentive daughter nor elder sister, because you found these duties irksome ?"

There was a reluctant assent in her movement.

"Then I can't wonder that home was a weariness, nor much at anything else. Next, what did you try ?"

"Poor people," said Emmeline; "but you will say that failed because we set about it in the wrong way."

"That was an error in judgment," said Lord Herbert; "and I don't think it was the whole cause of the failure."

"It was silly of us to give up teaching altogether for fear of Mr. Denham," said Emmeline.

"It was not on principle you gave up ?"

"No, but because we dreaded Mr. Denham; it would have been so disagreeable. Besides, the poor people were not what we liked."

"And you neglected them because you were tired of them. You sought them out—why ? "

"Because we thought it would be nice."

"There's the key again, Emmeline : it became no longer nice, and you gave it up. You had not begun because you felt it a duty, so it was only another castle. Next, you said learning."

"Yes, I wanted to know as much as Juliet Willoughby, and I had liked learning so much at school. It was very pleasant at first, but it grew stupid and unsatisfying."

"Because it had no object ?"

"Just so. It was not coming to anything. Yet one is told to learn and cultivate one's mind—or is that worldly nonsense ?"

"We are told to do so, because each faculty is one of our talents, and we must improve and brighten and multiply it, in case a call should come for us to put it out for our Master's use. Was this the reason you studied ?"

"I never thought of that. It seemed to me that Juliet was happy and satisfied—we admired her And then poetry fills up one's mind."

"For bad or for good," said Lord Herbert. "Well, learning failed you."

T

"And then it was dreariness. Your worst time came, and
Sir Francis tormented Frank. It was horrid every way, I
thought; it could be no worse, till—Well, I did feel then that
religion might be a comfort, and I knew what it had been to
Frank, so indeed I took it up. Yes, I did, Herbert; I read,
and I thought, and now and then I was quite lifted up out of
myself, and felt things in such a way! But then you got better,
and that very moment we were all obliged to pack up, and set
off for London; and when I got into the whirl, everything grew
disgusting together! I could not feel to care about religion—I
grew tired of all the good books and thoughts, and church-going.
Herbert, don't think me wicked for it, but church-going has such
a sameness—not always as you manage the service, but at that
church in London it did not make one a bit devout. Everything
is weariness together, and I shall feel so all my life!"

"Stop, stop, Emmeline! You have not let me ask you how
it was that religion failed as you say."

"Because I must be too bad for anything to do me any good,
I suppose," said Emmeline, despondently.

"Hush, Emmeline! None of the chosen people of God have
a right to speak in that way. But, tell me, what do you understand by religion?"

"Oh! thinking—caring about holy things; stirring up one's
spirit—feeling love to God—those kinds of things—liking holy
things—" hesitated Emmeline, somewhat puzzled.

"There is the main-spring; but that is but half the matter.
You had the beginning, but what came of it? How was it
evidenced? You tried to feel, what did you try to do?"

"I was not well—I could not do much," said Emmeline.

"But what did you try to do? Did you try to be more
attentive to the home duties in which you had fallen short?"

"I did not think that was it."

"Did you try to conquer your reluctance to letting Mr. Brent
enter into conversation with you?"

"Mamma did not wish it."

"Did you try, when you were taken to London, to keep from

following the foolish undesirable ways of other people of your own age, which you yourself thought wrong at first sight?"

"Do you mean the polka, Herbert?"

"Or did you, in the new scene, allow yourself to relax in the devotional exercises you had taken up? Don't answer me, but yourself."

"I can't think how you know everything, Herbert. But, you see, religion won't do for me."

"I don't see any such thing. You have had a fit of excitement of feeling, which has passed off, but you are not thinking that you have been without religion all the years of your life."

"Oh no; but that is not what one means. That is too shocking."

"You are a Christian. Each right action or feeling, each act of faith or prayer, through your whole life, have not they been fruits of your baptismal grace?"

"I suppose so; but there have been few enough of them."

"And do you think that is caused by any defect in the grace then given you?"

"Oh no, no."

"But they have been passing, fleeting, unstable, of late. You have had no rest in them, no comfort of mind, no true wisdom, nor strength, no firmness, no abiding sensation of love and fear of God?"

Emmeline gave a sort of groan, that showed that his words went home to her heart.

"And you say it is the fault of religion? Emmeline, our religion holds out to us a means of receiving the strength of the Holy Ghost, the Comforter, giving us the Spirit of wisdom and understanding, the Spirit of counsel and ghostly strength, the Spirit of knowledge and true godliness, and the Spirit of God's holy fear."

"Confirmation!" said Emmeline. "Oh, Herbert, would it do all that for me? I do believe it would be peace at last."

"Emmeline, I am sure it would. It is not I that tell you so; it is the promise of God through His Church."

"Yes; but it is on a condition! How am I ever to fulfil that condition? I may make the vow, and intend to keep it, and believe fully, but the feeling will go. I shall be unsteady again."

"If you were to stand in your own strength, not in the all-sufficient grace, you would; but besides prayer, will there not then be open to you the especial means of strengthening and refreshing our souls?"

"But how many there are no better for being confirmed!"

"How can we tell? They may be better, or if they fail, it may be that their hearts are not prepared. They wanted prayer, or they wanted faith, or they were not in earnest, or they fell away through some unresisted temptation, not from any defect in the Confirmation grace, which will yet restore many."

"Then you think if we had been confirmed we should have avoided our faults?"

"No, I say no such thing. I cannot tell how you would have kept your vow, but I know you would then have been obedient to that summons of the Church; the grace would have been given to you, and if you had used it rightly—"

"Ah! I do believe that it would have made a difference. I know I should have been afraid to stay away from the Holy Communion after your letter; and then I should have watched myself more, and perhaps been saved from these faults, though I never thought they were so bad before. I knew I was good for nothing, but I could not make out that I did anything very wrong. Oh, I am very glad we are to be confirmed now!"

The little gate was heard to open, and Lord Herbert hastened to undo the front-door. Glancing drops fell from the umbrella as it was closed, and bright were the faces that the lamp-light revealed.

"Better, much better," "We put him in a hot-bath," "The doctor thinks he will be much better to-morrow," "He was so good," "He is such a dear little fellow," were the exclamations, while Lord Herbert and Emmeline helped them off with their cloaks and shawls, and the muslin dresses were unfolded.

"You are sure you are not wet?"

"Oh no, not in the least. We splashed home so merrily. Mr. Redlands watched for us, and saw us to the churchyard gate."

"There, now, take a good warm, and dry yourselves thoroughly." And Herbert put his wife into one great chair, and Kate into the other, and turned them round full before the fire, till they cried out that he wanted to roast them.

Very early the next morning, Kate was waked by a sudden flare in the empty grate of her bed-room. Emmeline was kneeling beside it, and in reply to her exclamation of inquiry said, "Only burning some trumpery papers."

"Not your verses, Emmie?"

"Some of them."

Five poems, namely, besides rough copies, on the emptiness and "hollowness of mortal tasks." "Kate," she added, "Herbert has shown me all. I know now why everything was unsatisfactory and hollow. We worked without a foundation, we pleased ourselves, and shrank from duty, and so it came to vanity and vexation. And now our Confirmation time is coming, we will cease to be children, and reeds at the will of every wind, but learn to have some steadfastness of purpose."

"Yes, if we may only receive strength from Heaven," said Kate; "but we have erred so far, and neglected so much already, that I am afraid to think of it."

"And it was my fault," said Emmeline. "You would have done better alone. O Kate, I almost dread lest something should happen to prevent the Confirmation again!"

CHAPTER XXII.

But when our childhood's morn was ending,
And we, 'neath holy hands, were bending
Beside that altar's witness stone,
That prayer had caught an altered tone—
The cheek with shame and hope was burning
To a lost Father's house returning;
It seemed to chide and yet to cheer,
And to that blending hope and fear
It brought our endless birth-right near,
And from the rude world seemed to sever,
Binding us to that shrine for ever.

The Cathedral.

"HERE'S a mischance!" said Constance.

"What's the matter?"

"The girls have a summons from my mother to come back to London, to go to Paris with her and Sir Francis."

"To Paris! How soon?"

"In ten days time; as soon as Alfred's holidays are over. There is some business about my father's property to be settled with my Uncle Berners—some papers that he and Mamma must sign together. He has persuaded them to come and meet him at Paris on the 20th of September, and so they have written for the girls."

"Very unlucky indeed!" said Herbert, musingly. "Of all the places that could be devised for taking Emmeline to, with her excitable temperament, such as even in our quiet life we can hardly keep sober enough not to give great fear of reaction—and what a reaction it will be at Paris! and missing the Confirmation again! Constance, it is impossible! it must be put off. I'll write to your mother—I'll go to London."

"The girls are vehement against going before the Confirmation!" said Constance. "Poor Emmie was nearly frantic at first, saying she knew it would be so, and she had forfeited the chance of ever being Confirmed. The worst of it is, that I don't know how far we should be justified in detaining them, if my mother wishes for them; and there has been a degree of neglect of her that makes one afraid not to make her the first object. But I can't judge in the least what is right; you must, Herbert."

"I can't see what is to be done! If it was only Kate, and yet to make her give it up! But why should not we remonstrate? Why can't they put off the journey?"

"I should not think they could. You know Uncle Berners is not a very easy person to deal with, and it would not do to miss an appointment with him."

"The Confirmation day is the 1st of October! I see how it can be managed, Constance, if to Paris the girls must go: I would take them the next week—I could go there and back between two Sundays."

"And what a cold you would catch!"

"Oh, I would take care! It would be a holiday."

"If they would consent to that, it would be the very thing; and Kate is really steadied: I don't think London hurt her in the least; and as to Emmie, she is made to have ups-and-downs, and all the religious teaching we had at school encouraged feeling rather than action; but I do believe she is learning a calmer tone under your management. She would be on her guard, now she knows her danger, and has had more definite teaching."

"So you think that might answer?"

"It ought," said Constance; "yet—if they are necessary to Mamma for the journey—I don't know how to judge—I seem to have missed all experience of a daughter's duty."

"It is a very difficult question," said Herbert, "and one I don't like to decide. We might be teaching them that to sacrifice is better than to obey; we might, on our own responsibility, be bringing them to these higher privileges at the cost of a sin, and before they are fit for them."

They walked on in silence, till Lord Herbert exclaimed, "I'll tell you what we will do, Constance! Some of us can go to London for a day, and settle it with Lady Willoughby. We shall be able to perceive better how much she really wants them, and what will be right for them to do."

Emmeline was even more anxious about the Confirmation than Kate, and her distress was extreme. She expected that Lord Herbert would absolutely oppose their going, and intended to be very heroic in following his advice; and she was disappointed to find that his views were undecided between the two duties. She proceeded to fall into an agony about its being her fate to miss Confirmations; she had once, twice, thrown away her chance, and Kate's too, and now she had forfeited these privileges for ever, and there was no hope for her.

This was a strain Lord Herbert never allowed her to continue, and he silenced it, saying, "You threw the opportunity away then, but you do not know that you have lost it now."

"Oh, I am sure I have!"

"And if you really have, which is not certain, it will be not that you have forfeited it for ever, but that you require a further probation. It may be that more chastening of temper, more perseverance is required of you, before you are accepted, and that in order that you may the more esteem the privileges you once did not rate highly enough, you are kept from them for a time."

Emmeline burst into tears, and said it had been her fault, and she deserved to lose everything. Kate took far more than her share of the blame; and it was with some difficulty that Constance soothed them, when Herbert had left them to her, saying that he would not speak to them on the subject any more till they had brought themselves to a more temperate frame.

They did not meet him again till just before the service, when Kate contrived to walk with him across the churchyard. "One question, Herbert," said she, hesitating. "If we were ill, or *anything*, could we receive the Holy Communion as we are now?"

"Certainly, Kate," said he; "there never has been any doubt that those who are willing and desirous to be Confirmed may be admitted in case of emergency."

"That is a comfort," said Kate. "Only we are going to a

foreign country, and after the only death we have seen, I don't know how we can dare to reckon on time!"

It was settled that Lord Herbert should take Emmeline to Town on Monday morning, and return on Tuesday, after arranging with Lady Willoughby. He talked of taking both sisters, but they begged that one might be left with Constance as a hostage.

By that time Emmeline was in a more rational state, and liked the idea of being escorted to Paris by Herbert after the Confirmation. Going abroad was an old castle of hers; she was eager about the sights of Paris, and meant to show her sincerity there, and it would be a great deal pleasanter than Cheltenham. So with renewed spirits, she set off, bearing an offer from Constance to take charge of the children, if one was to be left behind, to keep it at the Parsonage; if more, to settle them in lodgings with Miss Townsend, and especially inviting Janet.

They arrived about noon, and found Lady Willoughby alone. Their plan was eagerly told, and her consent was more readily given than they expected; she was so very much obliged to Lord Herbert, and she only hoped that dear Constance would accompany them, and then perhaps they might all spend the winter together so agreeably at Paris, quite a little society among themselves. Herbert smiled, and went on to Constance's offer for the children. Lady Willoughby was pleased, and said she thought that Janet would be very troublesome on the journey, and dear Constance was very kind. It was very annoying; but here was that brother of Miss Townsend's going to sail again, and Janet and Alfred had actually come down to ask leave for her to go home and see him—very improper of her to let the children make such a request, when she must know it could not be granted.

Lady Willoughby was interrupted; for in rushed both the boys—Alfred in the last half-year having grown into a fine independent school-boy.

"I say, Emmie," said Alfred, pulling her into the window, "I am glad you are come, only it ought to be Kate. It has been

horrid without you—Edwin is such a bore, and will be till he
goes to school, Janet and I have no peace for him.—Get along,
Eddy; Emmie and I are speaking to each other; don't poke
your nose into everything—now, Emmie, you must stay and look
after the children, for Miss Townsend's sailor brother is going
to sea, and Papa and Mamma won't let her go home to see him,
and what's worse, they will say she put us up to ask leave,
though I told them it was all Janet's doing of her own head."

Emmeline looked towards Lord Herbert, and heard him proposing that Janet should go home with them, but this was left
to be determined till Sir Francis came back; and in the mean
time, Herbert set out on an expedition to order coppers and
boilers, for the wash-houses, that were to free the churchyard
from its white drapery.

When he was gone, it appeared that Lady Willoughby was
in an unusually complacent mood; she thought dear Lord
Herbert looking much better, and it was very kind in him and
dear Constance to wish to keep the girls longer, and to take
Janet. It would be a very comfortable arrangement; it was never
pleasant to travel with a large party, especially abroad—so
troublesome to find accommodation, so liable to interruption; it
would be much better to get settled first, before dear Emmie
and dear Kate joined them.

Presently Sir Francis came in, but it did not appear that the
proposal was equally agreeable to him. He was so restless and
fidgetty, that he could not bear to be tied down to remain in one
place; he said testily, that they should be leaving Paris by that
time most likely; they might have left it already; it was
nonsense to trouble Lord Herbert; only further nuisance and
expense. The girls might do as they pleased; but it must be
Paris at once, or not at all. Emmeline could not hesitate.

"Very well," Sir Francis said, "'tis your own loss. You
have had the offer, remember that, and don't be begging us to
wait for you after this Confirmation."

"Oh no, certainly not."

"I can't think what all the young people in these days are

after!" continued Sir Francis; "but, mind, you have your free choice."

"Yes, entirely, thank you."

"And don't be in too great a hurry, my dear," said Lady Willoughby. "Consult with Katie first."

"Kate's mind is made up, Mamma, as well as mine. Our only doubt was whether you wanted us."

"Thank you, my love," said Lady Willoughby, influenced perhaps by a recent discovery that Henry Allen was at Paris. "Of course I am always glad to have you with me, but then there must be great advantages in being at Lord Herbert's and meeting his connexions. I don't know whether that is not quite as well for you as being in more society; and indeed, I am always too much of an invalid to go about with you, as much as would be required of me at Paris."

"We should not care about going out."

"Oh! but, my love, it would look so strange if I did not take you out. Of course nothing else could be expected, and you know you must not let yourself be made religious and melancholy. I am only afraid they are that kind of people."

"It is the merriest house I ever was in, Mamma," said Emmeline, smiling.

"Well, it may be all right. I am glad you should be there, and you are both full young for Paris gaieties, so perhaps it will answer best.—Don't you think so, Sir Francis?"

"As you please, only don't let them say it is my doing."

Emmeline had not expected to be given up so easily, and was mortified at not being more wanted, but she began to speak of Janet. Free consent was given; they might take her home at once; and Miss Townsend, after staying till the departure of Alfred for school, should join her at Dearport, whilst Edwin and Cecilia were placed under the charge of a French *bonne*.

Janet was much pleased to go to sister Constance, and was even unselfish enough to spare Miss Townsend. Her chief care was for Florentina Matilda, her immense wax-doll, a birth-day present from her papa, and whom Janet regarded in the light of a protégé persecuted by both the brothers, and coveted by Cecilia, so as to be exposed to so many perils, that Janet's tender care for her welfare would only allow her to enjoy her society in her refuge, Miss Townsend's room. Emmeline's promise that Florentina should be welcome, was the only thing wanting to make Janet's satisfaction complete. It was not till very late that Lord Herbert came in, but Emmeline contrived to speak to him, to tell him that she and Kate were to stay at home altogether.

"Well, Emmie, I am very sorry for your disappointment."

"Sir Francis will not wait for us. He says now or not at all; I suppose it is a punishment for our delaying the Confirmation, for I should have liked it very much."

"And you are sure your mother does not want you?"

"I am sure she does not care," said Emmeline sadly. "That is my fault too, I suppose."

"I am sorry," said Lord Herbert again, "that you should miss the pleasure; but perhaps it might have unsettled you again, and I am glad you should have the opportunity of testing your sincerity."

"Then I have none, Herbert; for when I found they did not want me particularly, and heard how pleasant their plans sounded, if it had not been for very shame, I should have asked to go! How can I be in earnest?"

"Don't torment yourself with motive picking. It is rightly settled, and that is enough. What about Janet? Does she come with us? Ah! there she is. Come here, little woman; are you coming to pay sister Constance a visit to-morrow?"

"May I take Florentina Matilda in the railroad with me? for she won't go into a box. I should like to come very much, if she may."

The Allens dined with them, and in the evening Susan came to her. "My dear Emmie, what is the meaning of this? You don't mean that you are not coming to Paris!"

"Indeed I do."

"What, are you afraid of Revolutions?"

" Oh no, that is not it."

" Come, you won't be so silly as to stay at home. How stupid you will think yourself all your life for having missed such a chance ! "

" I can't help it," said Emmeline, as Susan began a glowing description of the galleries of Versailles.

" And we should have such a winter there ! Did not you know that we are all coming ? Henry is there, finding apartments for us. Mamma would take you to everything. Come, Emmeline, I assure you it is very silly of you."

"Mamma thinks us too young."

" Too young ! You are going on for nineteen, are not you ? Besides, Emmie, let me give you a little bit of counsel. Don't you," she whispered archly, "don't you let yourself be thrust into the background because Lady Willoughby does not care to show two such tall daughters."

" I am not kept back," returned Emmeline gravely ; " we were quite at liberty to act as we pleased, and it is our choice to stay with Constance."

"Henry will be so vexed," said Susan. " He was reckoning so much on going over the Louvre with you."

Emmeline was secretly vexed ; but since she had been more occupied, Henry Allen's name had begun to lose its attraction, and her vanity was only slightly tickled.

" I declare," proceeded Susan, " Henry will be quite mortified ; he will so question me about you ! I say, Emmie, I am sure Lord Herbert has got a handsome curate."

Emmeline was so disgusted at the vulgarity of the question, that she hardly deigned to answer, and wondered how she could ever have made a friend of Miss Allen. Susan took her reluctance for confusion, and persecuted her all the evening. She had at first been flattered, but soon grew provoked, and sensible what she had brought on herself by having allowed this pert vulgar-minded girl to assume so much power over her. Worse than all was the being asked whether Lord Herbert was afraid to trust her in a " Catholic country ; " and the last words, as she bade her good-night, were a declaration that the Dearport curates had better keep out of Henry's way.

Susan little knew that she had for ever disgusted Emmeline with the very name of her brother, shocked her with the idea of having given an opening for such impertinent speeches, caused her to regard her incipient flirtation with little short of loathing, and entirely consoled her for not going to Paris, by the reflection that she should have to meet him there.

The next morning was spent by Lord Herbert in conference with an architect, about the first of his proposed churches; by Emmeline, in collecting everything she ever wished to see again from the house in London; and by Janet, in a very affectionate leave-taking of Alfred, who had patronized her, and made her his companion in such a way as to compensate for his boyish tyranny.

Emmeline felt that she had much to atone for when she perceived her entire uselessness in the family, and knew that she would be missed by no one. When she met them again, she would try to make herself loved; in the mean time, there could be only repentance.

After luncheon they departed, with many kisses from Lady Willoughby, and messages of love to dear Constance and dear Kate, and a repetition from Sir Francis that it was all Emmeline's own doing.

Kate was honestly much disappointed. On no consideration would she have missed the Confirmation; but she would have much enjoyed the tour, and had fully reckoned on going in October. However, she soon consoled herself by thinking that they would have so much the more time with Constance, and should not miss the visit to Rowthorpe in the autumn, which Lord Liddesdale and Lady Frances took care should not be forgotten.

Kate had better consolation in a letter from Mr. Willoughby —such a letter as made her eyes overflow with the soft bright tears of gratification, humility, and tender affection.

Constance must share the letter; for the three sisters were again as united in sympathy as they used to be.

And Constance, when she had coaxed Kate into permission to show it to Herbert, told him that she was convinced that the secret desire of Katie's heart was to have Uncle Willoughby present at her Confirmation.

"I should like to ask him here very much indeed," said Lord Herbert; "but, my dear Constance, have you reflected that 'twelve foot square' is not made of Indian-rubber, or do you happen to have a few portable bed-rooms in your pocket?"

"Oh, I can manage!"

"After these magical words, I have no more to say."

"Nothing need be done but putting up a bed in the study; and as to 'twelve foot,' we shall never have everyone in it at the same time."

"Very well, I don't want to be persuaded, for my own sake almost as much as Kate's. Ever since Frank's visit I have a great desire to know his uncle, and the good ways that have come down unbroken through so many years."

Kate knew nothing of the invitation till Lord Herbert put into her hand the answer, the beginning and end so formal and old-fashioned, and the middle so like Uncle Willoughby himself, full of simplicity and warmth of heart, showing how entirely the old and the young clergymen understood each other.

If ever Kate was happy in her life, it was when she sat at work with her sisters, listening to him and her brother-in-law talking over their parish work and Herbert's plans, in the full confidence and sympathy of like-minded men, "in fervent old age, and youth serene." She perceived that her brother and sister's kindness to her had been the means of procuring for Herbert such a friend and counsellor as he most valued and esteemed, and of her placing her dear old uncle in the way of a new friendship and interest, to lighten up the latter years of his secluded and now bereaved life.

Uncle Willoughby told her that it was such a refreshment, as she would understand when she had come to his age, to meet such a young man as Lord Herbert; and on the other hand, Constance told her that she had never seen her husband more

pleased with anyone, and that Mr. Willoughby had cheered him
greatly respecting his own discouragements and the prospects of
the Church.

That Uncle Willoughby much disliked his brother's journey
to Paris was evident, and he had a still greater aversion to
Edwin's being under a French *bonne;* but he was much rejoiced
to find Janet in such good quarters; and indeed the sunshine
of the Parsonage at Dearport seemed to have gained such an
influence over the little maiden, as to make her almost an
engaging child. She was of such a disposition as to be more at
ease when with grown companions than with children; and in
this atmosphere of wise and tender kindness her better qualities
expanded, her affections unfolded, and her spirits mounted, till
she hardly seemed the same child. The only play-fellow she
required when her sisters could not attend to her was Florentina
Matilda, though apparently that important charge gave her much
anxiety, judging by her numerous lectures, in the finest words
at command, respecting her behaviour to Mr. Redlands and Mr.
West, who had taken so much notice of her, that, in the words
Kate once overheard, " it has completely overbalanced your dis-
cretion, and worked a revolution in your intellectual organs."
And when Kate looked at the grave sallow face and earnest
shake of the head of the little monitor, and the composed waxen
countenance and fixed staring blue eyes of the pupil, she could
not help laughing to such an extent, that she was obliged to run
away. And it was to be feared that the disorder of Florentina's
intellectual organs would be completed by Uncle Willoughby!

A present of Juliet's last new work was sent to Emmeline by
Mr. Willoughby, who said she had turned her attention more
than previously to the poor people at Dumblethwayte, and often
gave up a great deal of time, and walked long distances to teach
at the school, or to attend to Frank's friends in the village.

Kate had almost finished knitting Uncle Willoughby's Grace
a warm grey-worsted shawl for the winter, and only waited to
know whether the border must be black, or might be scarlet.
No one will doubt that Uncle Willoughby's look of delight and

gratitude repaid Kate for having continued it steadily, when the double wool was a great deal too hot to be pleasant. Janet was so stimulated by it, as to forsake the knitted polka for Florentina, in which no one's patience but Constance's would have endured helping her so far, and to set about a pair of scarlet muffatees for Grace, that there was a reasonable hope of her completing in time, as she was a very skilful little work-woman for her time of life.

The 1st of October had come, and the cards bearing the words "Examined and approved, Herbert Somerville," were given and received. How differently were they looked upon from the tickets that Emmeline and Kate had kept in their desks for the last twenty months!

"Examined and approved!" How many reflections must pass through the mind of each thoughtful catechumen as those words are presented! Approved by him who watches for their souls; approved—true; but he can know but the outward appearance, and there is One who looketh at the heart! And oh! is that heart so sincere, so faithful, and so humble, that it may indeed trust that it may come near to the Hand stretched out to bless?

Repentance, trust, steadfast purpose, and loving hope, these are all that we can bring, in the full consciousness of our own weakness, and of the all-sufficient grace.

Such dependence was, as Lord Herbert trusted, in his sisters; and he was glad that Emmeline, though evidently feeling deeply, showed no undue excitement. There were many others to whom his attention must be given; and the house was necessarily the scene of much coming and going, and of considerable preparation for the reception of the Bishop; and it was well that the sisters could be placed under the charge of Mr. Willoughby.

He took them to walk in the Bayhurst grounds, among trees yet unstripped by the wind, but their foliage glowing with autumnal tints, the sun shining on them with clear though sober brightness, and the sea gleaming through their boughs.

U

The stillness of the green lawns was more noticeable after leaving
the busy town. There they walked, and spoke of Frank;
dwelling on him with peaceful tenderness, as Emmeline had
never hitherto been able to do ; going through his happy self-
ruling course, a pure bright stream through the school-boy life
that had been his world, of the trial so well used, and the joy
and peace that had been his to the end, even among the surging
waves, that were the means of his entering into the haven where
he would be.

In quietness they talked, with voices hushed and without
tears ; for the two sisters, as well as the old man, felt that they
must speak with reverence of that repose where he now was ;
and in their present frame, close to one of the moments when the
things of the hidden world have a perceptible effect on the outer
life, there was not room for one selfish longing for his presence.
The whole scene was gravely still in autumn beauty, the sea
scarcely heaved, and the "path of glory" was shed along its
surface by the sun ; and solemn peaceful awe rested on the
hearts of the sisters, a frame of thought—

> "soft—for He drew nigh
> Who moveth all things quietly ;
> Yet grave and deep—for to His sight
> Heaven's secrets are undazzling light :
> Content—for He on healing wings
> The promise of the Father brings :
> And Comfort in His name : yet so
> That in His promptings here below
> A wistful uncomplaining sadness still
> Must deeply blend with joy's adoring thrill."

In such silence they went home. The sisters went to their
own room, and still in silence knelt together. Constance came
in, and herself arranged their white veils, kissing each of them.
With her and their uncle they walked to church, and were
placed among the many maidens, with white-covered heads, and
grave modest faces.

And now the time is come. The demand is made, to be
answered once and for ever, whether they renew the vow of
their Baptism, and take on themselves the promise they never

can unsay, engaging in their own persons to fulfil the *perfect* Law.

" I do."

Multitudes of clear young trembling voices make answer in one note. " I do." Wavering unstable Emmeline, unreflecting easily-led Katherine, now can you dare to bind yourselves to such an awful covenant with Him who is Justice itself?

Hear the answer :—

" Our help is in the Name of the Lord ;
Who hath made heaven and earth."

And now their brother in his white robe stands at the entrance of the chancel, and signs to them, and his face seems, in one look of love and earnest hope, to sum up all that he has striven so long to infuse into them.

They kneel on that Altar step where they never have before approached, and the Apostolic hand is on their heads; the blessing is spoken ; that unspeakable Gift imparted, that, unless they fall away, will increase daily more and more, till they come to the everlasting kingdom.

Sunday is come, and again Emmeline and Katherine kneel on that step, and now it is beside their sister, while their brother and uncle admit them to the partaking of that Meat and Drink indeed, which can preserve their souls to everlasting life.

Here, then, in the safest and holiest place on earth, let us leave them, trusting that the grace now given and ever renewed, may never be cast away by their own sin ; that it may stablish, strengthen, and settle them, guard them, and be with them, wherever their future lot may be cast. So might earthly visions rest in the sure homes and peaceable habitations, which are but the portals to the mansions above.

THE END.